Spectrum City

ALFRED KHOLI

To Richard and John Gilmore.
Thanks for being there when I was growing up.

PART 1
SANCTUARY

1   THE LINE

FOR THE PRIVILEGE OF ENTERING SANCTUARY, ONE MUST STAND in line. That is what we have done for nearly two weeks. We were joined by thousands of wanderers hoping to make it inside the great metropolis. Now we were finally nearing the end. It is said that Gotham will allow only two hundred refugees inside to be processed daily. Every day, about two hours after sunrise, the line moves at a few paces. Then it stops, and we wait for tomorrow. What happens to us once inside is anybody's guess. Down the line, we heard many rumors. Ultimately, what will happen when we get in doesn't matter; we are now waiting for our turn. We had no choice but to wait. And wait. Every morning, I made a point to look behind, and each time the line had grown.

What made it bearable is that I'm here with Gabrielle. She somehow manages to take anything in stride. To keep our place in line, we agreed with our neighbors to watch each other's places if someone needed private time. When we came across a body of water, a few of us would fill all our canteens and return to the line. We shared our food, making our supplies last longer. At night, we take turns standing guard because people will try to move in front of us, steal our supplies, or worse, just kill us as we sleep. A few don't care if they get in at all. Some groups manage to make a living selling supplies to people standing in line. However, there are worse groups. Like scavengers roaming the depths of the Wastelands, these people will prey on the others in line, taking whatever they wish. They can do it with impunity because Gotham doesn't care. They made that reality very clear. Three days before, I saw a patrol of guards walking by as a family was attacked. A group of six men manages to take everything from the family to the amusement of the Watchman. They are worse than Enforcers from Cibola. That means we must protect ourselves.

To make it clear, I did intervene. Taking out my pistol and stinger, I walked twenty meters behind us. There, I saw the thugs had taken all the women away but one. A man and a boy are dead, their bodies mutilated. Picking up my pace, I rushed to help a young woman no more than twenty, being held by two men. They were waiting for their friends to return for her. I looked for a moment to see if one Watchman had any inclination of conscience to come and help. They didn't. So that left me alone. My only hope is that they are too busy with her to notice me.

Not feeling charitable, I place the stinger on half strength. These creatures didn't deserve a quick death. Before I struck, I looked over and made sure their friends were still at their transportation, securing their captives. Neither was too concerned about somebody coming to her aid. This wasn't their first time. They were so confident that they proceeded to force her to the ground. One thug held her arms, his friend was preparing to have his pleasure. Wanting to join their fun, one of their friends joined them, securing her legs. All the time, she was screaming for someone to help her. Fighting the three thugs as best she could.

With my pistol, I struck all three of them. Stunned, they all staggered away, freeing the girl. I stepped forward, placing myself between them and the girl. With a blade twice as long as my dagger, the one on my right lunged at my ribs. I blocked the blow with my stinger, hitting his forearm. His hand going numb, he dropped the knife. Unarmed, he tried to run, and I struck the back of his head. He wasn't going to get up any time soon. Then the girl screamed.

And I looked to my left. Another man returned to his feet, about to pounce. I had no other choice, I fired my pistol, the discharge hit him in the stomach. He is dead as well. The remaining thug was about to get some help.

His friends heard the shot. Not taking chances, I fired my gun at the closest. About twenty meters away, he fell dead. Now there are three remaining. Fortunately for me, they decided to take what they had stolen and run. The man who had faced us ran to join them. They drove off.

The girl ran after them, but I caught her, struggling to free herself. She screamed, "We have to go after them."

That is out of the question. Their machine didn't look impressive, but it was fast enough to escape us. Besides, these gangs are part of a larger group. One important thing to know is that predators are not fools, and revenge isn't in their line. I said firmly, "Listen to me. "She did, "What's your name?"

Quietly, like she had to remember it, "Paloma."

In a softer tone, I said, "Paloma, they are gone."

Turning towards the horizon where the gang drove off, she cried, "But my sisters… Elena."

I turned her towards me with both hands. I held her, looking at her frantic brown eyes, I said, "Look, if you truly love them, then survive. That is all you can do. And if possible, they will do the same." Anything is possible. Releasing her a bit, I asked, "Do you understand?"

She nodded, so I let her go. I continued, "So get what you need. I'll look over our dead friends."

She did as I had told her, while I searched the packets the thugs had left. Taking anything that I considered we could use. It is the law of the Wastelands. Those whom I had killed, what is theirs is now mine. I was lucky they still had their rations, and their canteens were full of water. I found a fourth canteen that had some alcohol in it. I took a sip of it. I made a point and gathered my new knife. I looked over and found more problems brewing. Paloma has taken exception to other people in line ransacking the corpses of her father and brother. Sentimentality isn't something a person can afford out here. Maybe inside the city, it is possible. With my new dagger out, I went to help her again.

I managed to pull her out from the middle of a crowd that engulfed her. That is when the contingent of Watchmen finally decided to do something. Moving between us, the leader immediately inquired, "What is going on here?"

In all seven Watchmen had placed themselves around us. I felt it was best not to make trouble. But Paloma beat me to it: "My father and brother are lying there, and these vultures are going over their bodies."

The Watchman leader made a further inquiry, "Is that true?" Nobody confessed to the surprise of no reasonable person standing in the line, but the Watchman who had asked the question. Before he could say another thing, Paloma made it clear she wasn't going to let it go.

"That flashlight belongs to my brother. That flask belongs to my father, that pouch is Elena's." She was pointing as she went. The people she had accused tried to hide them. The Watchman was satisfied.

"Place them all here." He ordered. Reluctantly, the people obeyed, making a small pile of what they had stolen. The watchman turned to Paloma, "Now take what you want. I don't want to have any more trouble with you."

Paloma was not finished, "Where were you twenty minutes ago when my family was?" I covered her mouth with my right hand and with my left. I turned her so I could speak to our benefactor, "She was still a little upset. She would like to thank you for your help."

"Who does she belong to?"

Still struggling, I tried to hold her and replied, "She is with me. My group is about twenty paces up ahead."

"I suggest you head right up there."

"I will, sir."

The Watchmen left us, heading back to their city. I waited until they were well out of range before I dared to let Paloma go. Pulling out my gun with my left hand, I pointed it at our friends to convince them not to try to take their stuff back. Finally, I released her. To thank me for all I had done for her, she proceeded to slap me across my face, hard.

"I guess I had that coming. Now get your stuff and let's go."

She knew I was right. Quietly, she did as I said. Together, we headed towards our place in line. She was terrified of meeting the others in her new group. I just glanced at her once or twice. I didn't want to force things on her before she was ready.

2   FRIENDS

WE REJOINED GABRIELLE AND THE OTHERS. GABRIELLE IMMEDI-ately went to help Paloma. Introducing her to our other friends. First, she walked up to our youngest member, Olivia. She was about nineteen, with short golden blonde hair and dark blue eyes. Her cream-colored skin shows some red from the sun. Like Paloma, Olivia is the last of her family, as each member sacrificed to get here. Next to her was her companion Cassandra, who had arrived together in taking their place in the line, a year younger than Gabrielle, with dark brown hair and amber eyes. She never said much about her past. Next was our second couple: Natalie and Mitchel. Natalie was a young woman with straight blonde hair in her late twenties, her husband Mitchel stood about my height with short dark hair with patches of grey. He is trying to pass himself off as a much younger man. I wasn't sure of them. They seemed to have a business arrangement rather than any love between them.

Two days ago, we gathered water together, and he wanted to cool off since it was a hot day. Taking his shirt off, he promptly dived into the water to relieve the heat. I stayed on the shore filling the last canteen. Swimming for a few minutes, I told him I was finished and heading back. He returned to the shore and grabbed his shirt.

That is when I saw his mark above his right nipple. I remembered seeing that marking once before. I encountered it when I was living in the northwestern part of the country. The marking belonged to an army of marauders called the Krieg. Far more dangerous than the Prophet. Enforcers from Cibola defeated them in a battle. For once, they did something constructive. But their benevolence didn't last long. When I saw that, I looked away, hoping he didn't see me. Just in case I armed my pistol. We walked back together. Since that day, I haven't trusted him.

Finally, we were joined by an older couple. Deb and Henry. Both are in their late fifties; Deb is a short woman with platinum hair, and her husband was my height and had sandy brown hair that was balding. They made a great pair. Deb told us they are planning to re-enter Gotham. They were citizens of Gotham who had foolishly outlasted their visas. Now they are forced to be processed like the rest of us. Deb immediately took Paloma in her arms, comforting the child as she had lost everything. The rest of us just returned to our place in line as we waited another day to go in.

That night, it was my turn for guard duty. Sitting alone with almost everybody else sleeping in the endless line. Looking at the skyline, the lights from Gotham became even stronger, making it harder to see the stars in the sky. A new moon was forming as we stood in this damn line. Fortunately for us, what we salvaged from the thugs and Paloma's family, we had enough food for five more days. We can only hope that a roving group of vendors will arrive with provisions to sell. But for now, we won't starve. We are getting closer.

Paloma woke up during the night. She had a nightmare. Trying not to wake the others, she joined me as I was still on guard duty. We were looking at the few stars that were out. Placing her head on my shoulder, I tried to comfort her. Taking out the old knife that my friend Walker gave me as a gift before we left, I handed it to Paloma with its sheath.

"Take it," I told her, not sure, I put it in her hand, "Keep it close to you. It can be your best friend."

Taking the blade out of its sheath, she showed me her blade

with no blemishes on it. Hopefully, for her, it will stay like that. But it is very unlikely. Returning the blade to its sheath, she carefully placed it on her belt. Locking up, she confessed, "I don't know how to use it."

"I'll teach you if you want," I assured her. She nodded her yes. "Good lessons start tomorrow. You better get to sleep."

With a timid smile, she went back to her knapsack. I replaced my old dagger with a new one that I found next to a dead man earlier today. Inspecting it for a moment, I noticed it had not been cleaned. I decided to place it where I could get to it quickly with either hand. I placed it next to my stinger on my left side.

For the rest of the night, I thankfully sat there by myself.

For the next three days, I kept my promise to Paloma. I taught her how to use her new dagger. Right at dawn, the city gates opened, and we moved forward. If we were not ready, there was a great danger, we could be trampled to death by people behind us. After twenty minutes of moving forward, we stopped. When the gates closed. We sat down at our new campsite and had breakfast. After that, Paloma and I stepped aside, and I began to teach her how to use the dagger.

That first day, I wanted to teach her the most important thing: how not to get stabbed. I taught her a deadly dance of life and death. As I moved forward with my right foot, she stepped back with her left, then when I moved with my left, she countered by stepping back with her right. There, we followed the simple steps until she did it without thinking. Then it was her turn to strike. There we danced, moving forward and backward, learning how to keep our balance with a silent killer that will be in our hands. Always make sure you keep eye contact with your opponent.

On the second day, we continued our training. Without warning, I tried to remind her of the seriousness of what she was learning. There are no rules in fighting and no room for error. Make a mistake and you will die. She understood.

By the third day, I taught her the nine targets: how to strike and how to deflect your opponent's strike. She learned quickly. With what she has gone through, she has developed a strong determination to survive, which makes her determined to learn. Austen had taught me when I was only a few years older than her so long ago. At the end of each session, I told her to never forget this deadly dance. Like, I never forgot it.

After her third day of learning, Paloma gave me a rare smile. It didn't last that long, but it was there. She will never forget what happened to her family, but maybe she can learn to live with it. It is a hard lesson.

When we finished, Paloma joined Cassandra and Olivia. Gabrielle walked to me with a very serious expression. I think I am in trouble again.

"Should I be jealous?" she asked me, "You never taught me how to fight."

I replied, truthfully, "I've seen you fight." Seeing that didn't convince her, I added, "You can teach me some moves."

I was forgiven, I think. Three times she had vanquished several armed men with great ease. With a lot more skill than I have. Just in case I changed the subject, "It should be a couple more days now."

We both looked towards the city. It became far more defined in the clear blue sky. From the west, storm clouds are coming. We had to prepare.

3   THE GAME

THIS MORNING, AS WE HAD FOR THE PREVIOUS SIXTEEN MORN-
ings, we rose at dawn and started to move forward, carefully
trying not to crowd each other. When the line stopped, we sat down
and had our breakfast. Henry estimated we had two full days of
rations left. But today was different. For the first time, we saw the
gate. We are almost there. Together, we decided to cut our rations
in half as a precaution. All around us, morale was up.

For Paloma, it was different. She had a mission, revenge, not
with those who wronged her but with anyone like them. Her grief
had turned into hate, and I fear that I'm leading her on that path.
This was not my intent. I wanted her to become confident and not
rely on anybody.

Last night, just before she went to sleep, she mimed the strikes
I had taught her. With her last move, she lunged underneath her
imagined opponent, plunging her dagger into the target's heart.
With deadly intent, she held it in place with a desire to watch her
enemy die slowly. Pulling her blade back, she calmly returned her
knife to its sheath. With a smile full of hate, she looked at me and
said softly, "I will kill all of them."

I didn't respond. I just let her go to sleep. As for myself, I just sat up and pondered what I should do. Hate is a powerful ally, but it can destroy you and your enemies. In the end, I found it wasn't worth it. This morning, I would have to teach her something new, and I had no idea how to do it.

After our morning duties were over. She eagerly came looking for me for her next lesson. I figured out what I was going to teach her.

"Keep your knife. We are going to try something new."

I turned towards Gabrielle and asked her for a favor, "Gabby, I need your help."

Gabrielle came over, and I said, "Gabby here is going to teach you some tricks." Both women looked at me in surprise, so I said proudly, "Gabby here can throw a full-grown man across the room."

"Really."

All attention was on Gabrielle now. She glanced at me, and immediately she knew I had my reasons, so she went along with it. "Well, it is possible. I'll need my assistant, Duncan, to help me."

I knew I wouldn't like this part, but I agreed.

Together, the three of us found an open space. Between Gabrielle and Paloma, I found myself on the ground forty times. I knew that because I kept counting. Each time, I had to pick myself up and do it again. Both women seem to enjoy themselves at my expense. Maybe this is my punishment for taking an interest in Paloma. But I just wanted to help. I had counted seven ways to get myself on my back. First, Gabrielle demonstrated the move, followed by Paloma repeating what she had learned and repeating it until Gabrielle was satisfied, she had the move down. I patiently did my part in the lessons.

We became quite a spectacle as others in the lines started to watch us. For Gabrielle, her technique proved to be a simple one. She used leverage and my weight against me to do what she wished. One thing I noticed about Paloma is that she was a quick learner. Four days is a very short time to teach someone how to defend themselves. In the afternoon, after my fortieth fall, Gabrielle looked over at me as I lay on my back. She decided that Paloma was getting tired. She ended her training session with applause from the crowd. They enjoyed our little entertainment.

As for myself, I was too tired to take a bow. I just found a place to sleep and did just that. I had missed dinner, choosing to sleep instead. Finally, Gabrielle felt guilty and brought me some water. I was thirsty, so I drank what was left in the canteen. She sat down and placed my head on her lap. Looking up at her sad green eyes, I suddenly felt better.

"Does it still hurt?" she asked me.

"Yes," I replied, wincing in pain. "I hope you enjoyed that?"

Gabrielle admitted, "I think I took it too far."

It was clear she was jealous of my attention toward Paloma. She wanted to teach me a lesson. And she did. I made it clear that she had nothing to fear from Paloma. I'm not sure if that satisfied her. We walked back and rejoined the group.

That night I slept. After three shifts of overnight guard duty, I was glad to have the night off. At dawn, I awoke first. Gabrielle had night duty and was there greeting me. We awoke the others to prepare for the gates' opening. Together, our small group marched closer to the gate. Tomorrow we will finally be on the walls. As we sat down for breakfast, we made our plans. Deb surmised we had enough food for two more meals. After a brief discussion, we agreed to eat three meals today. As for tomorrow, that will take care of itself. Next, Olivia, Paloma, and Cassandra will refill our canteens. Half an hour later, they returned, handing out the canteens to each of us. Paloma asked if we could do more training, and I said no. We are about to have more serious problems coming our way. I promptly gave Gabrielle our pistol after it was fully charged. I told her, "Keep everything close to you. In case anything happens."

"What's going on?" she was concerned.

I tried to assure her, "Maybe nothing."

"I don't like the silence either," she added, I can't hide anything from her. She felt it too.

A contingent of a dozen Watchmen walked by us. Each one was armed with their powersticks. I found it to be a strange weapon for such an advanced society. No more than five feet, it appeared to be made of some type of metal. But that was it. Each Watchman is wearing heavy gloves. It looked like a weapon that a scavenger might have. Tapping me on the shoulder, I looked at Gabrielle, and with a concerned look, she pointed to the other side. Looking to my left, I saw a second patrol of Watchmen that numbered about a dozen, each armed with powersticks. I noticed its leader was the same man who intervened five days ago.

"Look at the gate," Cassandra exclaimed as she looked ahead of us. As a group, we looked ahead of us and saw a score of Watchman standing in formation in front of the gate. They sensed it too.

Smiling Mitchel revealed a machete and a dagger in his belt. Disgusted, I looked at him. He could have helped me when Paloma was attacked. He knew what I was thinking because he stated, "You didn't need my help."

Ever since Gabrielle and I joined this line, we have heard murmurs of discontent. People were dissatisfied with being in this line for so long. Once we get through the gate, there is no guarantee that we will be allowed to stay. Gradually, the murmurs became whispers. As we stood longer in line, we began to hear talk of doing something rash. That didn't concern me with people who constantly complain and rarely do anything about it. They are content to hear themselves talk about doing something important. What concerns me now is their silence.

Now it will take just one rash action by an angry fool to start it. It will be futile because the Watchmen have handled this problem before. And are more than happy to crush it. As the sun moved higher in the sky, the field became hotter. At about midafternoon, the two contingents return to join their comrades up front. That had triggered something.

I don't know why, but I looked over at Mitchel, and he was signaling other people along the line. It was some kind of signal. Something was going on. When I started to walk over to Mitchel to challenge him, Natalie stopped me. She said nothing, just shook her head. That had convinced me that something was being planned.

It started about a mile behind us. Crowds of people had left their places in line and rushed forward. About a hundred Watchmen joined their comrades and formed a line. The hordes of people stopped a few meters from the line. Many were screaming for food and water to help them endure the humidity and lack of shelter. Those demands fell on deaf ears as the Watchmen taunted the mob to attack.

Those behind us began to move forward, crushing people in front of them. Like it or not, we are in the middle of a riot. Olivia lost her footing and nearly got pulled under a wave of humanity to be trampled to death. Henry and Cassandra pull themselves and two young children to their feet. Working my way over to him, I suggested, "Take them to safety," shielding them with my body as I tried to keep them from being crushed, "I'll stay here."

Deb replied, "You're right. Let's go."

Henry looked at me for a second an ounce of respect came over him, "What about Natalie and Mitchel?"

Looking into the melee I saw they were in the middle of it all, disgusted I said, "Fuck them." Henry looked ahead and saw what I had seen. He understood. He grabbed Gabrielle and left the line. She didn't go willingly. Somebody had to stay behind and protect our spot in the line, or we would have to go back to the beginning.

She turned back, "Why aren't you going?"

"We will lose everything."

I quickly lost sight of them. Around me, other rioters had moved to join the ones ahead of us. My attention turned in front of me, as Mitchel stood in the forefront, leading the mob forward. With him were other agitators convincing those around them to rush the gates. That is when I witnessed the secret behind the Watchman staff. They gave out an electoral charge that, luckily for Mitchel, wasn't fatal. It just stunned him. He fell to the ground; I helped Natalie pull him to safety. He was lucky this time. I'm sure that thing can kill if they wish it.

Undeterred, the crowd still rushed forward. When reinforcements came in from the city. Each member was armed with shields and stingers they placed themselves in front of the Watchman with their staffs. Creating a shield wall. Now behind them, the watchman leveled their staffs, holding them out like spears. This battle formation is something I have never seen before. It would prove

to be effective. Seeing the formation caused the unruly crowd inti-
mated retreat a few paces.

Keeping their tight formation the Watchman advanced. Again,
forcing the rioters back. In defiance, the mob regained their courage
and pushed back. Hurling themselves upon the shield wall. Hoping their force of numbers will trump this well-armed formation. I
stayed out of this. Refusing to pull out my weapons.

At first, the rioters held their ground and stood firm. Gradually,
their numbers began to dwindle as the Watchman managed to use
their weapons to thin the rioters' numbers. Many fallen people were
trampled to death. As the Shield wall began to retake momentum
and pushed back the rioters.

Undeterred, a handful of rioters decided that if they couldn't
go through the watchman. They will go around. To my surprise,
the Watchman let them climb the walls of Gotham. I then saw why
the Watchman didn't stop them. They didn't need to. A force field
is more powerful than anything Cibola had activated. Made sure
they couldn't scale those walls. Almost immediately, the poor souls'
flesh burned away from their bones as their hands remained in a
death grip on the wall. Some lucky ones who somehow managed
to let go fell to their deaths. I looked away as I tried not to see any
more of the carnage, but I couldn't avoid their cries of agony. Nor
their smell.

Finally, it was all over. The force field was deactivated, and those
still alive fell to the ground. The survivors, still in agony, cried out
for help. Cautiously, help came to do what they could for the scared
survivors. As for the riot, it had ended. Discourage the mob finally
dispersed. Leaving behind their casualties. Satisfied, the Watchman
returned to the city as the gate closed behind them.

Sullenly, the people returned to their places in line. Walking by
the remains of the dead, still clutching the wall that surrounds the
city. A grim reminder for us of all that happens to all who challenge
their authority. I managed to keep our place in the line. With me
is Natalie, treating Mitchel's wounds. He had a couple of burns on
his chest. To cool his skin, she poured cold water on a bandage she
had made from her blouse, soaked it, and placed it on the burn. He

felt nothing, but he was still unconscious. I just sat there. Trying to understand what had just happened.

The only difference is that the line is smaller now. Many people decided to go home. Getting into Gotham is not worth it. I had no other place to go. I stayed here waiting my turn. Natalie looked up at me, "Thank you for saving him."

I made no reply. Mitchel was one of the leaders of this fiasco. I saved him because we agreed to look out for each other if we are in this damn line. She understood, ashamed of her part in the riot.

Gabrielle returned first, and she hugged me. With my right arm, I returned the embrace, too tired to look at her. The girls had joined her, and Deb and Harry joined us in line, bringing our supplies. There we sat down and waited for tomorrow. There was nothing else for us to do.

———————

At dawn, we rose to our feet. But the gates didn't open. For three hours we just stood there hoping they would finally let us in. Finally, they made the announcement, "All entries are to be suspended until further notice."

The line just sat down again and made their camp. Contended to their fate. We had no desire to protest. If discontent dared to return all it had to do was look at the rotting poor souls still clutching the wall in death.

To pass the time I continued Paloma's training. This time I made it more intense. She had to know this was no game. Gabrielle decided to teach the other girls how to defend themselves. None of us knew what it was really like inside those walls. For the first time, I felt a foreboding about sanctuary.

By the next morning, Mitchel seemed to have fully recovered from his injuries. But the gates remained closed. We continued waiting in line until they decided to open the gates and let us in.

———————

They came from the north. In the afternoon. This was our second day of waiting for the gates to reopen. With our rations gone,

Deb and Henry managed to scrounge for extra rations. Not saying how they manage to barter for it. I didn't care that much about food. Enough for two more days.

Paloma and I had just finished our morning exercise. In time to see Mitchel going out to meet with eight men, in strange clothes. Behind them, the remains of the dead still fused upon the wall. From where I was standing, the men seemed unmoved by the sight. Making me believe they have seen this before. At this time, we were all watching Mitchel. With Natalie in front of us. Curious I stepped ahead and joined her and asked, "Friends of yours?"

"Associates, "she answered, looking at me with a concerned smile, she added, "We may have an alternate way in."

Not impressed, I replied, "What do we have to do?"

"Just pay the fee."

"With what?"

The men disbanded, going to certain parts of the line. Mitchel returned to us. Natalie went up to greet him. Together they walked towards us. Mitchel was smiling. With an excitement I have never seen before he proclaimed, "I found a way in."

Everybody was interested. I just listened. He continued, "Those are friends of mine. They know a way up north for us to get in."

Henry inquired, "What do they want?"

"Just a few credits," he answered, he added, "Less than what we have to pay to wait here."

"We must act fast. They can only bring a handful of people" said Natalie supporting her partner.

"I'll pass," I said, not interested. Gabrielle pulled me aside; she wanted to go with them.

"Do you like staying in line?"

"Think about it," I replied, trying to use reason, "If this alternate way exists, why are all of us in this line? It is a trick." I learned a long time ago to beware of Greeks bearing gifts. I don't know what exactly a Greek is, but I learned that there is no such thing as generosity in the Wasteland.

"It is a secret way in" Natalie interrupted, "it is controlled by our friends."

"I still say no."

Gabrielle looked at me. Although it was clear she wanted to go, she wouldn't leave me. I was glad she didn't call my bluff, for that it was: because, if she had joined them, I would have joined her. Knowing it was a trap of some kind. She looked over at Natalie, disappointed she whispered, "I have to say no too."

"Have fun sitting in the rain," Natalie said, we looked over to the western horizon and saw the storm clouds gathering. She walked away, joining the others. All I can say is I know I'm right in not trusting that couple. Keeping our distance, we saw more people interested in this new way.

Mitchel moved away from the line to keep the word from spreading. Finally, his group dispersed happy to wait for the call. Paloma came up to us first. For the first time, she had a smile.

"By tomorrow we will be inside."

"I hope so" I replied happy to see her with joy.

Surprised by my response she inquired, "You're not coming with us."

"Duncan thinks it's too dangerous" Gabrielle stated firmly. Looking at me with disdain.

I ignored her and stated to Paloma, "Think about it, if it is so easy to go that way. Why are most of us standing in this line for days?"

Without hesitating she answered confidently, "Because they keep it a secret by letting a few people in at a time."

"I see it is a secret," I wasn't finished, I looked over to see if either Natalie or Mitchel had come too close. Fortunately, they were with one of their friends who had returned. So, I continued with my point, "That means it's illegal. Once with them, they can do what they wish to do with them. If they get you inside."

Gabrielle understood my point. That was good. But Paloma, though concerned, came over her face but she had made her decision. Right or wrong she will see it through. "I'll take that chance."

In the end, it was her decision. Not that I blame her I haven't anything to offer her that is better. Eventually, we will be allowed in if we stay here. But that is at best maybe too optimistic. I have never been one. I am more of a realist myself. From behind her Cassandra and Olivia join us. I changed the subject and added, "So just remember stay together. Three is safer than one."

Surprised Olivia inquired, "You're not coming?"

Like she ignored what I had mentioned Paloma answered for us, "No they think it's too dangerous. They are reaming here."

"We better get ready; we will be leaving in an hour" Cassandra added.

Cassandra and Paloma left to gather their gear. Olivia hesitated for a moment she whispered, "Don't worry I'll keep an eye on them." She then hugged me, then she hugged Gabrielle. Before she could step away Gabrielle stopped her.

Taking our small pistol out of her pocket she discreetly placed it in Olivia's hand. "Here take this. Just keep it out of sight." Olivia did as she was told by placing it under a vest. She smiled and joined her friends.

Together we joined Deb and Henry who were busy gathering their supplies. Harris saw us and stopped what he was doing. Deb realized wear here and joined her husband.

"We're sorry you're not coming with us," Henry stated calmly. Deb went and gave Gabby some extra rations. Henry then added, "We must travel light. Just the essentials."

Gabrielle said, "I wish you could stay with us."

"I know. But we can't take another day like this. Mitchel assures us we will be all right. Besides, there is no guarantee we will be let in." Deb answered.

"I don't trust them," I replied earnestly. Hoping to convince them to stay with us.

Deb didn't want to hear anything else about it, so she changed the subject, "When you get in look us up. Here is our family's home." She handed us a little piece of paper that had a few names and numbers much like the one that Caitlyn had given us over six weeks ago. So now all that was left was to say goodbye. Looking at them I wondered if there were some other reasons why they would take such a risk. I wish to know what their reasons were. But I had no right to inquire further.

Deb hugged both of us. Stepping away she allowed Henry to have his turn. We shook hands and Gabrielle jumped into his arms. Quietly weeping on his shoulder. We didn't know them for long, but the couple proved to be a calming influence on our group. Mediating disputes between us and making sure everybody had an equal share. They enjoyed being with us. Henry mentioned each day we had rejuvenated them. Being around young people made them appreciate life. They taught us patience. Both Gabby and I lost our parents when we were young. For a while, we had some new ones.

The hour was up. A group of fifty people gathered to join Mitchel and his dozen friends. I let Gabby make her goodbyes first. I wanted to talk to Mitchel first alone. Natalie had walked over to talk to join the crowd, while Mitchel waited for our friends. Together he smiled at me and held out his hand to say goodbye.

"Thanks for what you did during the riot."

"You can thank me by taking care of the others."

"I'll do my best."

"I'm hoping you can do better. I've grown attached to them and would hate to see anything bad happen to them. You can say I will take it personally"

"I'll keep that in mine."

He walked away. If there were any doubts about him, they were gone now. At least he knew where I stood. Gabby escorted the others to say one last farewell to me. Cassandra hugged me first. She never mentioned anything from her past. When she let go, she nodded her head and gave me a sad smile. Silently she walked away with her belongings. Olivia was second. She reached up and kissed me on the cheek. Then placed her arms around my neck. I whispered in her ear, "Remember you made it."

Letting go she smiled and walked away with her small bag. She still had the pistol hidden in her blouse. Henry followed, again and we shook hands. Deb said goodbye with a gentle hug. When she finished, she pulled away and stated, "Remember you're more than welcome to visit us."

"Gabby has a friend living there."

They left to join Mitchel, leaving Gabrielle and Paloma. Paloma stood in front of me motionless looking into my eyes. Tears were forming in her eyes. In one motion she jumped and kissed me on the lips. Holding on with her arms around my waist, like she didn't want to let go. Olivia called for her and she knew it was time to leave. Letting go she looked down trying to say something, "Thank you for helping me."

Gently, I placed my hands on her shoulders. I looked at her and tried to give her some advice, "Remember that knife, it is your only friend."

"I'll remember."

"If you can't run then use it. And don't forget what he had taught you." I replied trying to give her one last bit of advice.

She reassured me, "I'll be fine."

Holing me one last time she gathered her belongings and raced to the others. Together they walked away back from the north. Gabrielle and I watched them as they headed out of our sight. We then returned to our place and waited for tomorrow.

One thing Natalie wasn't lying about, it did rain the next two days. And both days were still locked out. There we sat each day huddling under a wool blanket that Olivia had left behind. I should say Gabrielle was huddled under the blanket. She wasn't speaking to me at that time. For the first time, she had thought I had chosen wrong. I wanted to tell her I hoped that I was wrong about Mitchel and his quick way. They were my friends too. I'm not so petty to have them come to harm just to prove I'm right. I didn't say anything thinking it would do no good. I just sat there in the rain hoping that Gabby would take pity on me.

The rain did manage to cool the air around us a bit. At first, it felt refreshing from the two weeks of endless heat. Besides the constant downpours, we proved to be lucky with the lightning remaining along the horizon. It made an exciting show for us to watch. Still, I don't think Gabby will be impressed. As we sat in the mud. For a moment I began to second-guess myself. Maybe we should have gone with the others. Anything is better than having Gabby mad at me right now. But I knew I wasn't wrong. That gave me very little comfort right now.

At the end of the second day, the rain finally ended. With the return of the sun, the humidity came back. By morning we dried off. At dawn, the line rose to their feet in anticipation. This time there is no announcement. A cheer came over us for what happened next: the gates had opened.

We moved closer as Gabrielle anxiously took my hand for luck. Gradually we kept moving getting closer to the inside. Then we made it. We had entered the city. We are now being processed. About twenty people after we made it in with us. Behind us, the gates closed. Relief came to Gabby and me. After almost a year we made it to Sanctuary.

4   PROCESSING

WE FOUND OURSELVES CRAMMED IN A LARGE SQUARE WHITE room with a high roof. Forced to stay still while seven attendants came through, physically counting each person whom they had just let in. The attendants were emotionless as they did their job. Ignoring us completely. The room proved to be stuffy. That made the waiting worse for us. After what seemed to be an eternity, the attendants finally finished counting. Returning to their supervisor, they shared their findings. Three hundred twenty-five total, one hundred twenty-six women, one hundred twenty-six men, sixty-eight children, and five children under the age of four. From my perspective, it should be more.

The four supervisors then directed their attendants to divide us into three lines. The men will enter a door on the left. Women will enter the door on the right. Children will enter a door in the middle. The five toddlers were allowed to accompany their mothers for processing.

Right up to the last minute, Gabrielle held my hand, she didn't want to let go. Finally, a tall, muscular attendant came to get us in our respective lines. He was in no mood to be diplomatic, so I let her hand go. She went and took her place in line. As I did. Watching her, I was hoping to glance over at me one last time. She did, and I said, "I'll see you soon." She smiled and headed into the next room. As I did.

In the next room in two lines, we're an attendant at a desk, ten in each line, they were confiscating all our possessions. Three of the attendants who had just counted us in the previous room followed us in. They were there to make sure we followed directions. Fortunately, it didn't take long. I was sent to table 6 in the first room.

Sitting down on something other than the ground made me feel a state of bliss, a strange feeling sitting on a chair. Familiar with my reaction, a woman wearing glasses, waited until I was finished enjoying myself before she requested all my belongings. She handed me a small bag. Grabbing it, I looked at it curiously. "This is too small."

With a slight amusement, she replied with a crooked smile, "It gets bigger."

I gathered all my belongings and followed directions. Each time I placed something in my bag. I glanced up to see if she had any reaction. The grey-haired woman, just under sixty, really didn't care what I had on me. Almost finished, I had to ask her, "Will I get this back?"

"It will be secured."

I promptly placed my pieces of metal that we could use for currency and the line of credit Caitlyn had given me.

"Is that it?"

"Not yet."

I pulled out my new dagger and its sheath and placed it in the bag, followed by my stinger and its charger. Finished, I closed the bag. Damn, she was right it did get larger as I needed.

"Place it on the table."

I did what I was told. A piece of paper came out of a machine. Taking it, she handed it to me, and it was a list of all my stuff.

"Is that everything?" she asked when I looked at her.

"Yes," I said.

"Place it in the bag, please," she stated, reopening the bag. I did what she requested. She sealed the bag tightly. Then proceeded to place some strange device over the opening. Then she ordered, "Right thumb, please."

I put my thumb on a black opening that was the center of the security device. The black turned red. "There it is now secured. What is your name?"

"Duncan."

She glanced over at her screen for a quick moment. She then looked over at me and inquired," Last name?"

I paused for a moment. Not sure what to answer. Annoyed, she stated, "You can use Smith."

I didn't like that. Instead, I answered, "Walker."

"Very well, Duncan Walker, this will be ready when you are finished. Please head to the next room."

I did what she had requested. In the next room, there was a line of showers. I immediately felt the steam as a few who had gone before me were already in there. Despite its size, it is relatively clean. An attendant ordered me to strip. I'm becoming naked. Standing in line waiting for my return to take a shower. Once it was my turn, I was given some shampoo and soap. With some instructions on how to use the shampoo. I felt silly.

Each of us had twenty minutes to shower. They kept perfect time. In front of me was a screen with twenty minutes on it, so I watched it as I cleaned myself. When the timer ran to zero, a red light flashed, and I was finished. I must admit I did feel better after the shower.

As I left the shower, a different attendant handed me a white towel, and I entered a grey room. I quickly learned this room was for medical examinations. Impossible to hide anything, I was told to lose my towel and to walk to table twelve. In front of me was a woman in her mid-twenties, with short, dark brown hair and blue eyes. Her outfit was a grey one-piece body suit, much like the Overseers used to wear. She didn't act like she enjoyed this job much because she rarely smiled. She gave me instructions that I should follow.

At first, her instructions were nothing hard. Raising my arms to see if I had any scars. I had a few that she asked me about each one. She then asked me to stand on each foot to see if I had good balance. I did.

She followed that up by checking my lungs and heart. Followed by my blood pressure. Much like I did when I needed to see a doctor in the Wastelands. I was disappointed, I had thought she would use something far more modern. She then followed that up with something more evasive. Satisfied, she cleared me up for everything but a DNA sample. She asked me to hold out a finger. Pricking it with a needle, she allowed drops of blood onto a glass slab. She had placed it in a machine, and after ten minutes the machine flashed a green light. She then asked me for a urine sample, which I provided.

That had ended my physical. She then asked me some questions. Feeling awkward, sitting naked in front of her, I answered her questions as best I could. Some I had no idea on. After the twentieth question, she smiled and told me to go to the next room. I guess I passed.

Not all passed the exam. Twenty-three men were sent to another room. Their fate is a mystery to the rest of us. We who had passed received new clothes. An ugly grey one-piece outfit that didn't fit well. Our old clothes were destroyed. To cover our feat, we had a heavy cloth shoe that felt snug at first, but quickly became more comfortable as I had taken a few steps.

Next was a shave and a haircut. That didn't take long. Finally, our ordeal was almost over. When my name was called: Duncan Walker, I walked over to a desk that had the same woman who processed me earlier. Handing me my package. She stated, "Sign here."

Holding a metal screen in front of me, she gave me a plastic device, and I wrote Duncan Walker. Taking it back, she looked at it. Satisfied, she put it down next to her. She then returned to the computer.

Curious, she asked, "What was it out there?"

"Never needed one," I answered her. If I did have one, I wasn't told. Living out there in the Wasteland, there wasn't enough to need one.

Satisfied, she entered the name and continued with the next question, "Trade?"

Now that is a problem. I never learned a trade, not really. As a child, I was raised on a farm. But I don't think that she will be impressed. Collaborator in helping Overseers find their quarry, I don't think it will go over well. Finally, attacking Cibola will not be impressive. Austen did teach me how to survive in the wilderness, but there is no wilderness here.

Annoyed, the attendant asked me, "How did you get all this money?"

I hesitated for a moment about what I should tell her. I have done a lot of things I'm not proud of. Again, using people isn't a trade to be proud of. Glancing at my stinger and dagger, she looked at me and asked, "Have you done security?"

"Security?"

Raising her voice an octave, she stated, "Can you fight?"

"Yes."

"Good," she said, relieved, "I'll put you in for security." She typed that on her computer. Later, she explained that many prominent people hire people to watch over themselves and their property and family. Many times, in that order. After a few more questions, we were finished. I am now ready to enter Gotham. Made special by her cold greetings. Taking my belongings, I returned each one to my belt. When I finished, she had one more piece of advice for me: "Be sure to get employment in two weeks."

"I will," I replied, but I wanted some answers of my own. I asked, "What happens to those in room 3?"

With a sad expression, she looked over at the room where the other men were sent off. Meekly, she answered, "They are cast out." I looked over at the room, what did she mean about being rejected she added, "They are sent back to the Wasteland." Now I understood why the line was so long. Many people out there have tried a countless number of times to gain entrance. Only to be disappointed.

She said nothing more. Looking down at her screen, she was ready for the next one. So, I left. Heading out into the city.

In contrast to the bleakness of the grey-walled processing center, my first sight of Gotham gave me a full spectrum of colors.

Immediately, I walked to the edge of the patio overlooking the city. It was enormous, ten times larger than Cibola. What made it more humbling is that this area is one-tenth of the entire city. It was much cooler than outside, as a cool breeze came over from a large river that separated both sides of the city. I just stood there for a moment to savor it. For almost eleven years, most of them alone, I had tried to find Sanctuary. Now I have made it. I must find out what to do now.

Around me, fellow immigrants tried to reconnect with their loved ones. I chose to stay where I am. Thinking it is better to stay away from the crowd. With everybody wearing the same ugly grey uniform, it is easy for me to blend in. That will not be true for Gabrielle.

I found her. Her long red hair and cream skin made her stand out in a crowd, and her grey uniform flattered her. She looked over at me, with the background of an evolving cityscape, and smiled. Immediately, she ran over to me, stopping in front of me.

Smiling, she introduced herself, "Gabrielle Blue."

"Duncan Walker," I replied formally.

Kissing me on the cheek, she approved my choice of last name. I mentioned I liked hers, too. Walking hand in hand, she left the patio and headed down to the city itself. For a moment, I thought about the number of people who were rejected and their companions who would be disappointed to be without them.

This seemed to me to be a little unfair. But I was a newcomer here. Why should I tell them how to run their city?

First, we had to exchange our valuables for currency. A video of an older woman talking about something called a bank, recommending First Federal for all our money needs. We decided that it was a good place to start.

We found the First Federal two blocks from the Processing center where we entered. The bank made up a small corner of a very large building. This bank had large windows that allowed us to see inside. With Gabby leading the way, we entered the bank. Inside we we're greeted by a young woman a few years older than Gabrielle. Her name was Elena, and she had short, dark hair that she tied behind her. Her brown jacket blended with her slightly tan skin. Her pants were the same texture as her jacket. She spoke pleasantly as she asked what we needed.

"We need to exchange currency," stated Gabrielle, handing her a pouch of are metals. I handed her my pouch. Her eyes lit up when she saw what we had in there. That proved to be reassuring. Gabby then handed her Caitlyn's card authorizing a line of credit for us, "We also have this."

Elena looked at the card. She looked at us for a moment. Quietly, she stated, "This way, please." She directed us to her office. It has a desk, two chairs, and a computer. Not much else. On her desk was a small sign that said Elaina Castro. Silently, she made a few inquiries on her computer. I could tell she was suspicious because she became cold to her. That warm, friendly smile of hers had disappeared. This made me nervous. I didn't trust Caitlyn, thinking she had an agenda for the two of us, but I couldn't quite figure it out. But I don't think having us imprisoned was part of her plan. We waited.

Satisfied, she turned to face us. Her friendly smile returned, "So everything had checked out. With all your valuables, I will give you an account of two hundred thousand credits." She handed us two cards: "This will allow you to access your account."

"Can we do it right now?" I asked, examining the green card she had just given me.

"Yes," she answered. She then followed with a question, "Is there anything else I can help you with?"

"We need a place to stay." Gabby stated, then she added, "And some new clothes."

Elaina knew how to answer this. She leaned in and showed us a small map. "Right now, you're in Yellow level. This is where the merchants apply their business. Below us is Brown level, which is for workers. To sleep, I suggest Blue level, which is above us." Pointing at a map, she added, "Right here is the best Motel in the city. You can get there by taking lift 8, and it will take you directly to Blue Level. You want to head for Blue Section 8 Block 2. It is called the Southland Plaza. They can help you with anything you need."

"Thank you," Gabrielle said as we rose to our feet. Shaking hands, she escorted us out of the bank. Offering assistance for any future problems.

Following our new friend's direction, we easily found Southland Plaza. We walked inside, and around us, we were given a cold shoulder by everybody that we passed, and when we made it to the main desk, it didn't get much better. Behind the desk stood a middle-aged man haft my height. He acted like he owned this hotel, but obviously he didn't, because if he did, he wouldn't be here; he would be hiding somewhere out back. I knew this much. Annoyed, I cleared my throat and announced, "Excuse me. We would like a room."

"I see." The man looked up. He had a rat face and a silly paper-thin mustache that made me want to giggle. Gabby gently shoved her elbow into my kidney to stay focused and not laugh. "Do you have money?"

I handed him my bank card. He placed it in his computer. Once he discovered how much money we had. His demeanor changed for the better. A desperate smile came over his face. "Yes, Mister Walker, I have a suite for you and..."

He must have felt that he was on dangerous ground. Not wanting to alienate us further, he allowed me to name our relationship. "My partner," I replied. Gabby looked at me, amused.

"How long will you be staying?"

"A week from now."

He stated, "Glad to hear it." He placed the information in his computer, where he continued, "I have a suite for you for eight nights for a thousand total. It comes with all the gifts."

"That will be fine," I replied, looking at our clothes. I added, "Can you recommend a site where we can get some decent clothes?"

"If you like, Mister Walker, I can have my staff bring up some pieces for you to look at. He said eagerly. "They can be up there in twenty minutes."

Gabby tugged at my shoulder. "That will be fine."

The person called over a young man younger than Gabrielle. He was a polite kid with dark hair and a clean face. His uniform looked very uncomfortable. The man behind the desk gave him his instructions. Politely, the young man led us to our room. I placed my card in my pocket.

Our suite was seven stories above the lobby. Our guide opened the door for us and showed us everything in the room. There are five rooms in all: a bathroom that is so clean I was reluctant to use it, a bedroom with a bed larger than some rooms I had stayed in, a living room that had two chairs and a couch, and finally a dressing room with what is called closets that connected to the bathroom. A large window that gave us a clear view of the city. Gabrielle rushed to get a look at the bountiful blue skies. I turned to our guide and thanked him.

"If you need anything," added the young man, "We have two view screens that you can access anything you wish. Either entertainment, educational, or general information. There is one in your bedroom and a second in the living room. He pointed out both."

"I'm sure we will be very happy. Thank you." I gave him some credits that I had in my pocket. He bowed and left us, handing me two keys.

Shutting the door behind him. I turned and joined Gabrielle. With a puzzled look on her face, she asked me with all seriousness, "What is that blue that goes on forever?"

"That's the ocean. There is one bordering Cibola in the west." I replied, amused. She had spent her life far away from the ocean. I just assumed that she noticed it while she was in the western city of Cibola.

Annoyed, she said, "I was a prisoner. They weren't going to give me a tour of the city."

She was right. I didn't need to say anything more. I just looked out over the horizon.

"It's beautiful," she stated as we looked at the horizon together.

As promised, the person at the front desk sent up two teams of people with clothes for each of us. Each team had four people, as they had carts full of gowns and dresses for Gabrielle and both formal and casual clothes for me. Gabby entered our dressing room with her team. I joined my team in the bedroom. Inside, they laid out my choices on the bed, I already had an idea of what I wanted. I picked a standard blue canvas pair of pants to wear every day and a grey henley shirt that was loose around my shoulders. I had two casual outfits for business and a formal jacket that fit me almost perfectly. That was all for day wear. I chose a light pair of black and brown striped pants for sleeping. For shoes, I have versatile, black shoes that I can wear for all occasions. Finally, socks and underwear. With alterations, it didn't take us half an hour. As for Gabby, it took her nearly two hours. I sent my team home after they waited for an additional twenty minutes. I had my formal outfit ready for any occasion. I thanked them for their hard work and paid my bill, not knowing how long Gabby would be. To keep myself busy, I hung up my clothes in a small closet. Then I waited.

Finally, after exactly two hours and forty-five minutes, she had finished. Her team came out first to present their hard work to me. They earned their job. More importantly, when I saw Gabby, it proved to be worth the wait. She was even more bountiful. Her hair was set in a crown that was neatly placed up, exposing her cream-colored neck. Her dress was long and slender, which hugged her body. The lime-colored green managed to match both her red hair and green eyes. Gracefully, she turned around and showed me that her back was bare to just above the base of her back. She placed sleeveless arms on her hips and looked over her shoulder to give me a playful wink. Stunning.

She had bought three casual dresses, plus accessories, and one everyday outfit. She wanted to show me her nightgown. Placing it over her body flirting with me. I stood up, allowing her to give me a full inspection. She approved. We paid her bill. Thanking her team for doing such a good job.

Once alone, I suggested that we should go out for dinner. She agreed, knowing why I wanted to go out. Earlier, when we first came into the hotel, the crowd looked at us like dirt. We wanted to show them the dangers of prejudging people. She put on some shoes that made her taller. Taking her arm, we headed out. Locking the door behind us. Taking the same elevator that we came up in, we headed straight to the lobby. When the shaft stopped, I looked at her. She smiled.

"Are you ready?"

I nodded. The door opened and we walked out. Our plan had worked. Outside, the crowd of people stopped and watched us walk through. Heading for the front desk, I had a question to ask. Our friend was still there, seeing us, and he had his polite smile on.

"Mister Walker, nice to see you so soon, how can I help you?" he asked with sincerity.

"Gabrielle Blue and I wish to go out and celebrate our arrival in Gotham. Where do you recommend?" I asked him. I wanted to put out Gabrielle, especially.

"There is a restaurant down the block called Oldtown. It is very good." He answered quickly. I believed him.

"Thank you."

We followed his directions and made it there in ten minutes. We were seated quickly. Our friend made a reservation for us. He wanted to earn his money. Sitting down, we ordered red wine from somewhere up north. Then we ordered our dinners. I had a steak with all the trimmings. Gabby ordered a chicken dish with red sauce and cheese. We didn't know how hungry we were. After nearly three weeks of rationing food. This became our first real dinner since we left Shenandoah. Having a dessert that we shared between us. We finished and paid our bill. Heading home, the sun started its descent below the horizon. We made it to our suite a few minutes later.

Inside, Gabby headed to the window and saw the lights of the city that were so bright they drowned out the stars above. I turned on the lights and joined her. In a silhouette of the endless black on the horizon, she turned to me and stated, "My hair is driving me crazy!" She started to take out the clips that held her hair in place. I stepped towards her, gently pulling her hands down to her side, and put my hands at the back of her head. There I freed her hair. It was curly now. I proceeded to kiss her. She did the same.

We continued kissing. More patiently with each moment.

Maneuvering to the bed, we fell on it, not bothering to pull the sheets. With our heads on the pillows, I pulled back to take a breath. When my attention turned to her, I noticed she was asleep. I kissed her on the cheek. And joined her. That is how we spent our first night together in Sanctuary.

PART 2
SOUTHPOINT

1 TIDEWATER

OUR FIRST WEEK HAD PASSED BY QUICKLY IN THE CITY. WE FOUND ourselves adjusting to city life quite easily. On the last day of our reservation, our friend at the desk asked to see us after our week was up. He wanted to know if we were interested in extending our stay. He used a strange word, vacation. Vacation? Neither of us had ever heard of that term before. He explained to us that it is a time of relaxation. That is something we were never able to do.

We looked at each other and agreed that one more week of our vacation would give us time to find a more permanent solution for ourselves. Gladly, the manager put it in his records. Gabrielle thanked him, and we left for an ocean tour. Neither of us has ever been on the water before, so it will be an adventure for both of us.

Heading down to Grey Section, we entered a pod that would take us across the river to the harbor in barely a minute. We followed an escalator to Grey Pier One. An agent stopped us, asking for our tickets. We showed the young woman our proof of our tickets. Satisfied, she let us on. Before we left, we were both advised at the hotel that it is about ten degrees colder on the ocean, so bring a jacket. We did just that, placing two jackets in a pouch we brought. We don't need them now with the strong summer sun hanging high over our heads.

A little bridge connected the harbor to the machine that was going to take us on our three-hour tour. The zephyr is called a ship, and it floats on top of the water. From front to back, it is about a hundred meters long, not as long as the Zephyrs of the Train People, but still impressive. This ship is wider than a Zephyr as it can fit two single cars side by side and still have enough space to walk by. Inside the structure were ten rows of seats that could hold about fifty passengers comfortably. A small room in front of us served as a galley. That is what a restaurant is called on a ship for those of you who don't know that. Not hungry, we chose to sit up on the open deck above the cabin.

With Gabrielle ahead of me, we climbed the stairs up to the high deck. Behind us is what that purser describes as the bridge. She politely directed us a an area we could sit down.

Once full, the captain bellowed orders from her perch upon the bridge to her crew. Four men freed the ship from the steel harbor, and we were off. Moving slowly, we headed down a small channel to the ocean itself. Gradually picking up speed, our captain waited to be cleared of the harbor entrance. Once she was satisfied it was safe to do so, she ordered her ship to make the best speed.

This is when it became interesting. Immediately, we felt a strange sensation of rising a few feet. Gabrielle grabbed my hand out of concern as the ship moved more fluidly through the water. Curiously, I looked over the nearest edge, and I saw why we felt a sensation of rising over the water, because we did. Checking the other side, I saw the main hull of the ship being supported by four large stilts with long flat surfaces. Coming from the bottom, a constant humming came from under the ship.

With a sudden jerk of my belt from behind, I returned to my seat. I looked, and it was Gabby; she was getting scared that I would fall over. For now, my curiosity is satisfied. I just sat next to her, and again she held my hand. From the bridge, the captain spoke clearly, "Welcome aboard the News four. I am your Captain Miranda Vargas. My crew and I will guide you on this journey on the old lady we call the Atlantic Ocean."

"The ship had a name, how strange."

Captain Vargas continued, "We are now making forty knots. Our sonic jets will if the old lady allows us to move up to sixty knots." On our left, we can see a greater extent of Gotham. As the gigantic extent of the cityscape. The captain veered to the right, heading northeast, choosing to move away from land. Waves began to get larger as each one crashed against the front of the boat. An endless breeze went through us as we chose to wear our jackets to keep us warm. One thing I noticed about the wind out upon the Atlantic over the Wastelands is that it comes unhindered.

Gabby called over the Pursier, she was about the same age as Gabby, a little shorter with jet black hair. She is used to being out here on News 4, as she had just a long-sleeved shirt on. "Can we walk around?"

"Just be careful. Walking on a boat is a little different" she answered in the same demeanor as we first entered, "Where do you like to go?"

"To the front of the boat," Gabby stated.

The Pursuer corrected her, "You mean the bow."

We headed to the bow. You learn something new every day. The young woman wasn't kidding about watching our step. The constant surf, briefly lifting the ship and allowing it to crash down, made it difficult to keep our balance. Well, for myself, Gabrielle moved gracefully across the deck. Her only struggle is to keep her long red hair from blowing in her face. Looking back periodically to make sure I was still with you. Her pretty smile never left her. She was happy out here on the ocean. I never saw her feeling so free.

We stood together at the bow. Looking at the empty ocean. At a distance, the sky and water shared a grey-blue color. The sun above us keeps us comfortable in the late summer months. Looking down, we see the waves keeping their height. We witness the strength of the waves lifting the boat firsthand. Then I made the mistake of looking behind me and watching the captain and her two crewmen pilot News 4. By my count, there were ten crewmen, including the captain. Then I needed to sit down. I didn't feel so good. I stepped back and took a seat. Watching Gabby standing alone with her curly red hair blowing behind her.

It took a while before she noticed I wasn't beside her. She looked behind her and saw me standing a few feet behind her.

"What are you doing there?"

"I needed to sit down."

She stepped back to join me. Sitting on my lap, she placed her arms around my neck. I held her waist. She looked into my eyes. Her face became serious for a moment as she lowered her mouth and kissed me.

Damn ship, changing course forced her to stop, as she lost her balance for a moment, breaking away to regain her balance. Looking around, the ship was heading south for home. Turning her head towards me, she was disappointed with the realization that it would be over soon. Now it is my turn to kiss her. As she pulled away, I stated, "We can go again."

She smiled and lowered her head on my shoulder. We stayed like that until the ship returned to the harbor. Over time, the waves became less violent. The captain lowered the stilts, and the ship slowed down. When we docked, the captain thanked us for coming aboard, and we left with the other passengers. She gave us a souvenir photo of our trip. We looked at it, and it was Gabby and I at the front of the ship. Gabby asked for a second picture, and Captain Sanchez gave us a copy. We thanked them.

We held hands all the way back to the hotel. Once on land, the queasiness that overcame me briefly left me as well. Having her with me made me forget about it on the way back. She is magical.

That night, we ordered room service and ate in. We both ordered roast beef with all the trimmings. The manager offered a bottle of red wine to go with our meal. I ate slowly as my stomach settled. But we finished well after sunset. A waiter came for the dishes. We thanked them when he left. Giving him a nice tip for the trouble.

Now alone, we had business to talk about. We needed to find jobs for ourselves and permanent residents. A week ago, after we were processed, our agents gave us each a disc that had recommendations. We placed them both in a view screen, my employment recommendations came out with courier, security, and several others that didn't enter me. For Gabrielle, it is one thing: a singer. That wasn't hard. She had a beautiful voice. So, we both agreed the next day we would go out and look for employment. We copied our qualifications onto a small disc so we can give them to our recruiters. Sleeping that night to prepare for an early start.

––––––––––

That morning, after breakfast, we prepared ourselves for this new task. The following recommendations are on our disc on how to prepare for our new careers. The most important recommendation of the discs is a presentation, to show the best representation of ourselves. Gabrielle chose to wear a new dress she had bought the day before yesterday; a bright green dress that wasn't as elegant as the dress she had worn on our first night out, but still brought out her intoxicating green eyes. She chose to straighten out her lovely red hair, allowing it to drop freely to the base of her back. She wanted to portray professional elegance, whatever that meant. For myself, I chose a button-down blue shirt and black vest that matched black pants. We left together.

Fortunately for us, Gabrielle found her job in less than an hour. An agent heard her sing for a minute and offered her two thousand credits a week. I responded, "Is that a lot?" When they immediately doubled their offer. She signed a contract for four months. Her first night will feature a singer this coming Friday. A relic of an old world we had to get used to. Naming days and putting them together in a week to measure time. Outside, we just measured time by the seasons.

As for myself, it proved to be longer. What she was earning allowed us to get a furnished apartment in Yellow section. It proved to be a little larger than our suite. But it was permanent. When I wasn't looking for a job, I was escorting her from her nightclub to her home. Most of the time, she proved to be too tired to do anything but sleep. For two additional weeks, I looked for a job with no luck. Gabrielle was slowly growing impatient with my lack of success. Finally, she demanded I expand my options, and I reluctantly agreed. Working as a common laborer is better than nothing.

First, I had an interview for a courier. The company had an office in Yellow North Section 8, about ten miles from where we lived. Dressing In my best clothes I am determined to impress this company. For a second time, I crossed the river, taking a lift two levels above, I followed the signs to Hampton Security. Glancing in the window I decided I was ready to enter.

Once inside, I was directed to an elderly gentleman sitting at a desk. At his left is a control center that keeps him in touch with his workers. Silently, he held out his hand, for some reason, I figured out what he wanted, handing him my disc, silently, he connected it to his device. Looking up, he studied my history. With his hand supporting his white bearded chin, he studied it closely. I just stood there waiting for him to acknowledge me. Thinking to myself, this isn't going well at all.

Finally, he finished, turning towards me, he was surprised I was still standing. His bushy white eyebrows lifted, "Why are you standing there?"

"I didn't have permission to sit."

His white hair made him look like the stories I was told as a kid about gods living high above us, mere mortals. Rarely did anybody ever live as long as he had, if he had been living out in the Wastelands. Even my mentor, Austen, was a few years past fifty, to a twenty-three-year-old, which was ancient. In a softer tone, he allowed me to sit down. I immediately did.

"You survived ten years in the wastelands."

"I did."

"How?"

"I had good teachers."

He looked at my character report made out by the immigration agent. "You have your own weapons, I see. How did you get a stinger?"

I simply replied, "From a dead Enforcer." He wasn't impressed.

He simply returned to looking at my report. When he finally finished, he turned his head and looked me in my eyes. " Do you know what we are asking of you?"

"I am to carry information that can't be transmitted on your screens," I told him. I am sure there is more to it, but that is a fair answer.

The man continued calmly, "Some of these materials are very sensitive. Some people will be willing to kill to get them. I need to know I can trust you."

My previous answer had satisfied him. How am I to answer this question? I decided to just speak the truth, "I will not surrender any material to anyone but your clients. And I'll die before allowing it to be taken from me."

He looked at me and smiled. "You have the job. You start tomorrow at 600 credits." I decided it would be better not to haggle and agreed. We rose together and shook hands. He said, "Be here at 700 hours."

"Yes, sir." I walked out of his office feeling I had finally accomplished something in Gotham.

At home, Gabrielle relaxed on our couch. I sat down near her feet. She looked at me and smiled. Somehow, she knew I had good news.

"I have the job. I start tomorrow at 7 hundred hours."

"How much?"

"Not as much as you, 600 credits a week."

She sat up and placed her arm around my neck, "That doesn't matter. "She kissed me on the lips. We had a few hours to kill before she had to leave for work. We put it to good use.

Living with this new habit of measuring time taught me one thing: never be late. I made sure I made it on my first day ten minutes early. After giving some information to a woman at a desk. I found that I would be trained by another courier, Carlos Neva. I introduced myself as Duncan Walker, and he was amused that I hesitated to use my new last name.

"That is a clear tell you came from out there," he told me. He then said in a friendly tone, "Call me Carlos."

I returned his kindness and replied, "Call me Duncan."

Carlos had for most of his adult life worked as a courier, so he knew his job. He explained he started this job when he was thirty-three after serving as a watchman. Now, twenty years later, he boasted he had never lost a quarry or failed in making a delivery. So, I listened to what he had to teach. The man didn't look fifty, his hair was still jet black, and he had no wrinkles on his face. Standing barely six feet, he had a stocky build to him and a small belly. He showed no signs of slowing down.

In further detail, he explained what our jobs are, "Our network is convenient but not secure. Sometimes an individual doesn't want some things known publicly. Neither do they want a record of their transactions. So that is where we come in. We must be discreet in our missions."

"Do we carry money?" I asked.

"Not always" he answered but felt I needed more understanding, "But sometimes we possess some sensitive materials." He calmly took our assignment, reading the card of a thin package, he continued, "People sometimes are willing to kill for it." Seeing I was concerned, he reassured me, "Don't worry, this isn't one of those."

Silently, I showed him my stinger and knife. He showed me his pistol. "We're ready."

Over the next month, he showed me how to maneuver the streets and levels of the city. Making sure I understand one thing, without a pass and proper identification, I can find myself in terrible trouble. The watchmen allow us certain privileges because of our job. To maintain that entitlement, we are meeting a few requirements. Where are we going? How long will the assignment take? Do you have other responsibilities in your assignment? These are three questions an officer will ask a courier. They will make inquiries about my answers. Satisfied, a pass will either be issued or rejected. If it is the latter, it could mean my job. If I have multiple assignments, the project will be repeated, earning me some time to eat on another level. Carlos assured me that eventually, I could earn a permanent pass, giving me complete access to the entire city.

During our time together, he made sure I knew as much about the city as possible. He told me that Gotham had a strict class system to separate its citizens. Unlike Cibola, which is determined by genetics, whatever that is, Gotham divides it by location. Each color represented what part its inhabitants had to perform in society.

Carlos told me that Grey Section is all things government. That is why Gabrielle, and I were processed by representatives of Grey Section who handle all contact with the outside world. Over a dozen garrisons are stationed for the security and defense of the city. Making sure the processing of everything that is coming in and out of the city is running smoothly. I have firsthand knowledge of how well they handle that.

Green Section is responsible for providing food, water, and energy for the city. It covers large parts of the city through farming and manufacturing. To protect the vital recourses, it has its contingent of Watchmen.

Red Section is the smallest in area but has the largest in population. That is where the workers are forced to live, only leaving their modest spaces to work wherever they can find it. Crime is rampant in the area, but their problems are largely ignored by the other sections.

Slightly better off is Yellow Section. That is where merchants and traders live in work. Gabrielle noticed that motels and restaurants frequent this section, allowing people to move through the levels and enjoy the perks of the city. I told him I was familiar with Yellow section. He smiled like he knew some kind of secret that he wanted me to find out for myself.

Then there is Brown Section, which represents the industry. Those who are allowed to live there must have a job. Many times, Carlos explained, people who lost their jobs could find themselves cast down to Red level or worse. Carlos spoke no more about that.

Next is Blue Section, where Carlos raised his right hand and pointed. I looked over and saw beautiful buildings that were built on top of red and yellow sections. They made up the elite of the city. Living comfortably in their little world, far from the rest of us. That is where I must be careful. Any person caught up there without a proper pass will be immediately arrested and, if lucky, faced with expulsion.

"What happens if the person is unlucky?" I asked him not to take him as seriously as I should.

With a foreboding look, he replied, "You don't want to know."

He then proceeded to explain Purple section. They live higher than the Blues. Simply, Purple is made up of the ruling class. We will probably never be allowed up there. Very few are ever summoned there. They are called Highlanders.

In all seriousness, he continued, just remember this: if you look for them, you'll go blind. I you listen to them, you will become deaf. And if you manage to climb up there, they will cast you down to the Black.

"Black?" I asked curiously about this color. He just continued in the same monotone he had started.

That is what we call the Underground. Underneath the city is a second city in darkness. Its inhabitants are forced to live down there until they die or are allowed to leave. There are several reasons for being sent there: if you have no place to live, if you have no job, or if you are convicted of a crime. If you trespass and commit treason will send you down there. Most important to remember, if you become a problem, you will be sent down there. So just remember to keep your head down and do your work, and you'll stay out of there.

Skeptical I had to state, "How is that the worst?" It did seem strange that Carlos believes that is worse them expulsion to the Wastelands or execution.

Believing that showing is better than telling, with a look of him reliving the pain in his eyes, he silently lifted his shirt and revealed a large scar along his side. He then confessed, "To get out of there. I gave up a kidney. With the money I made from it. I was allowed to buy my way out, get a job, and find a place to live." His story didn't end with tucking in his shirt, he added, "That was two years ago, and I'm still trying to get my family out of there." With that, he was finished. For the rest of the day, he only spoke to show me how to get a pass and how their security systems work. When we fished, we went our separate ways.

2 A COURIER

MY FIRST ASSIGNMENT ALONE CAME THE NEXT DAY. I ENTERED our office, where I waited for my assignment. Being the new courier, I was last. As I sat down, I watched as each man had their name called and walked up to get a letter and an address. Each courier walked by me. Too busy to make eye contact with a young man who might be gone in a week. I heard them snicker as they talked to each other.

I quickly learned that there is no real order for each assignment. When Carlos was the seventh man called, he had more experience than the other six. The bearded Smith handed him his package, and the address needed to be delivered. As he walked by me, he looked at me, smiled, and winked at me. It was for luck.

Finally, after the twelfth courier had his assignment and left our office, it was my turn. In a gruff voice, Smith bellowed, "Walker!" Rising to my feet, I immediately walked to his desk. Not looking up, he handed me an envelope and stated, "Tidewater, Yellow Level 5, Section 16, Square 1. Do you know where that is?"

"I do."

"Go and be quick about it."

I just did what I was told. Tidewater is a District of Gotham, much like South Point. It sits across the river as it borders the ocean. I navigated myself through the busy streets. Heading for a tube that crossed the river. Once across. I asked for directions from an open screen. The lady's voice came up and showed me how to get there. Carlos showed me how to use these things. After that, it didn't take me long to finish the assignment. Handing it over to a nondescript woman at a bank. Being a low-security transfer, I didn't have to undergo any security procedures. Just a fingerprint. Reluctantly, the woman complied after I reminded her that the procedure is to return it to the sender. Satisfied, I left her with her dispatch.

During the return home, I looked around. To get to know each part of Gotham a little better. Carlos had warned me about the dangers of idling through Gotham. But old habits die hard. One thing I learned when I lived in the Wastelands is to know my surroundings as well as a person who has lived there all their life. It is how I manage to stay one step ahead of the Overseers, through the years. Carlos warned me about the security within the Spectrum. One thing I learned in dealing with the Overseers, no security system is infallible, and Gotham is no different. If I can find the gaps, I can do my job better.

By lunch time I had returned to the office. Fortunately, for me, I was the only courier available, and Smith had a priority delivery to go out. It was in Red Level. I didn't need any special permission to go down there. Quietly, he handed it to me and said, "Red level 2, Section 7, Block 12." He promised me that I would be free for lunch when I was done. I left on my second mission.

Red level. Carlos didn't give it any justice in his brief description. I suppose nobody could describe it. It is far worse than what I will tell you. The bulk of the population is crammed in the smallest area of Gotham. It is dirty with no privacy anywhere. People have made their makeshift homes along the streets. I tried not to look at the wretched souls along the street. The people who are unfortunate enough to live here are forced to stay here. It is where they will be born, live, work, and finally die. While the people above them have all the comforts the city has to offer.

Trying not to step on anybody, I made it to my delivery, handing it to a young woman who looked about sixteen. Her hair was mangled to the point where I couldn't tell what color it was. All I can say is it was long. Her face had two smudges of grease on it, one over her left eye and the other just under her mouth. Pleasant, she thanked me and eagerly gave me her thumbprint. Thanking her, I left and made it to the lift that I came down in.

An old Watchman whom I knew saw me come down from Yellow level and stopped me. Placing his dormant stinger on my chest. He stood a good five inches shorter than I, with a hefty build. With forty extra pounds on him, he didn't wear it very well.

"Where are you going?" he asked me, still taping his stinger on my chest.

Remaining calm I replied, "Heading home" It wasn't easy, I wanted to take this Watchman's stinger away from him, but I knew it would make things worse, so I handed him my work order. His assistant read it and nodded to his sergeant. With a disappointed look on him, he lowered his weapon and stepped aside. I smiled and thanked him. I stepped into the lift and headed to Yellow Level.

After lunch, I headed back to the office. Smith gave me another assignment. This time it was in Hampton District. That didn't take long. When I returned, I was finished, and I headed home to meet Gabrielle.

Tonight, we promised each other a night out. About this time, we first met. She had bought a sapphire blue dress for the occasion that fit her tightly. She chose to have her long red hair down. It fell freely to the middle of her back. I wore the suit from our first night at the hotel. Walking over to her from behind her, I kissed her gently on her cheek. She turned her head to me and smiled. Stretching out her hand. With my left hand, I gently held it and led her outside our flat.

It proved to be easy for us to pick a restaurant. The same one we ate on the first night we had arrived at South Point. This time we made reservations, and we reserved a window seat looking over the vast foliage of trees turning multi-colors as far as we could see. The setting sun, made an unforgettable picture of natural beauty.

Moved by the site, Gabrielle looked over at me and stated, "It's beautiful."

Looking at her, I responded, "Nothing compared to what I am seeing."

She smiled.

We ordered. Twenty minutes later, our food arrived. Strange were not as hungry as that first night. Not that the food wasn't good. We just didn't gorge ourselves like that night. Living in the city has changed us. After paying the bill we left for a nightclub to enjoy the rest of the night out.

Outside the restaurant, Gabby took my hand, it was her turn to lead me. I followed as she knew where she wanted to go. Taking lift seven, we headed up to the highest level of Blue Section. The contract she made with her club allowed her some privileges I didn't have yet. So, I became her guest. This wasn't the first time I was ever allowed up to Blue Section on a visa. For a month, I escorted her home when her club closed for the night. Many times, I just stayed up there and listened to her do her sets, becoming a fixture with the servers and the manager. Not that I minded, Gabby had a lovely voice, and her bandmates were very talented. Unfortunately, when I found this job, I couldn't escort her home as much as I liked. We barely saw each other for the past week. That made tonight so important. A night out with just the two of us.

Still leading me, we made it to our destination. A nightclub called the Dancing Stars. Once inside, I quickly understood why it is called that. On the roof over our heads are images of a star-filled night dancing to the beat of the music played below. At floor level in the center of the establishment, scores of people dance to a deafening sound of music. With excitement I hadn't seen in a while, Gabrielle grabbed my hand and dragged me to the floor.

Taking our place, she started dancing like the others around her. I tried my best to do the same, but at first, I just enjoyed watching her dance so freely. Right now, she is a young woman. Nobody is chasing her. Then I was reminded that it was my fault that she was being hunted. Then I remembered it was my fault that she was placed in danger. The guilt I had felt began to drain my energy. As I stopped dancing.

She noticed I was slowing down as my thoughts of what I did overwhelmed me. In one motion, she put her hand around me and turned me around in a circle. At a level so I could hear her, she exclaimed, "Duncan, come on, have some fun."

"I'm not very good at this," I confessed.

"Just take my hands."

I did and followed her lead. It didn't bother me any longer; she was happy with me here with her, and that is fine with me. When the music ended, she brought me close and kissed me. After the brief break, the music started again, and so did we. Funny, I am surprised that she wanted to come here, after working at a nightclub herself. Then I realized she wanted to attend a place where she worked without having to sing.

A loud bong marking the new day sounded across the nightclub, followed by a loud cheer. To my surprise, we had been dancing for over two hours without a break. The time just went by in what seemed to be a few minutes. We decided to take a break. It wasn't our choice; the musicians needed a short break. Walking upstairs from the dance floor, we headed for a bar for a drink.

Sitting together at the bar a handsome man about the same age as Gabby asked for our orders. Without asking me she ordered, "Two cosmopolitans." The short, brown-haired bartender nodded and walked off. I was glad to see him go. She turned to me and explained, "I've wanted to try it for a month."

"This is your night," I responded, looking into her pretty green eyes.

The bartender arrived with the drinks. I promptly paid him. He walked away, amused. Gabby said, "Jealous."

"Guilty."

We took a sip. It was refreshing, so good that we had three more each. At four in the morning, we headed home. It was fortunate that neither of us needed to get up in the morning.

3   CAPITAL

WHEN I FINALLY RECEIVED MY CREDENTIALS, I BECAME MORE active. I found myself earning more important assignments very quickly. Outside the city, summer becomes autumn, I take the time to just look and witness the changing seasons. Inside, you would never have known it was fall. Nothing changes inside Gotham. Sometimes I wish I could feel a cool autumn breeze. The air can be very stale.

It was in this setting that I walked into work. Once inside, I immediately took my seat. There I waited for my assignment with the twelve other couriers. After an hour, ten couriers received their assignments and immediately left. Leaving three of us behind. Smith, the gruff old man, left us without saying a word. Besides myself, Carlos sat waiting with me. His demeanor made me believe something was going on that included me. The third man was Silas Young, a man almost in his forties. A little taller than me, he still had a muscular frame despite his age. To make himself look vigorous, he had chosen to shave his head. I had to admit it worked.

Smith returned. He sat at his desk and shouted, "Gather around." Carlos and Silas immediately joined him. I hesitated for just a moment, thinking I wasn't involved. Smith looked up looking through me he proclaimed, "damn it man, what do you want a personal invitation!"

I thought better of answering him. I promptly joined him to get my assignment.

"Now we are all here, we can begin."

"Your mission is to deliver a package to Capital. It is about three hours up and three hours back, with lunch and other problems, we will allow you seven hours. Naturally, we will offer you hazard pay." I didn't like that part, what he was not telling us, but I dared not ask too many questions. I figured it would be more beneficial for me to let him tell us at his own pace. "Duncan, you will be the escort. Silas and Carlos will be in support. Now be on guard. He must make it on time."

He? This assignment is becoming a stranger every moment. What is our mission? Without a word, Smith brought in the package. A man about forty came in with him. Funny he didn't have anything with him. I looked over at Silas and Carlos, both men seemed to comprehend their assignment.

"You need to get him inside Government Square in time for afternoon sessions. Understand?"

With a cold professional, Silas asked, "Who is after him?"

Smith looked at the well-dressed man before he answered, "Don't know. It could be Disrupters or any other group of damn malcontents. Hell, it could be one of his rivals in the Forum."

Now I understand. Over the past four months, three factions have been fighting for control of Gotham. By taking this job, we are now in the middle of this power struggle. As for myself, I never really cared much for politics. But the money was good, so I didn't care about the danger.

Our package added, "There is a large bonus for all three of you."

Before we had a chance to ask, Smith exclaimed, "So get going, time is money."

I stepped forward and led our charge out of the office.

Smith called for me, "Duncan."

"Yes."

"Do you have a pistol?"

"No."

From below his desk, he placed a new pistol on top of it. With a passable grin, he said, "Take this one, it is fully charged."

I placed the holster on my belt and left with the others. Carlos met me and stated proudly, "He's beginning to like you."

Puzzled, I didn't say anything.

We headed to the closest Express Tube. Our client, honoring his contract, paid our fare to Capital. He managed to reserve a private car that was waiting for us. We entered our car and sat down. A minute later, the shuttle moved smoothly within the Tube. Since this is an express, we expected to be in Capital in two hours.

I sat there watching the world move in a blur of green. Silas said mockingly, "Homesick?"

Turning my head towards Silas, I replied, "Never thought about it."

"What is your name?" asked our charge, before I had a chance to answer he introduced himself, "I am John Fletcher."

"Duncan Walker."

"I am pleased to meet you, Duncan Walker."

I smiled at the man. It was a kind gesture from a man I would never see again after today. Glancing at Silas, I knew he was not done with me. With disdain, he stated, "You're unique. Most people from the Wastelands are ignorant savages. You have a rare intelligence."

Carlos came to my defense, "Leave him alone, Silas. I don't think you could last a day out there."

"Very true, Carlos."

Fletcher inquired, "How did you survive?"

"I lived in a small village along the ocean. When Cibola attacked us. I escaped north." I answered him. He seemed genuinely captivated by my story, I continued, "Later, I met a man named Austen, and he taught me how to survive." I felt it was better not to go into further detail about my other adventures, but I never got the chance.

A thud on the roof of our car ended all our casual conversation.

Silas immediately checked the security camera, he exclaimed," We have company!" He transferred what he had seen to the car's view screen. There we saw three dark figures standing on the roof. A fourth figure joined his comrades. That figure had the equipment the others needed to accomplish their mission. Kneeling, the figure began using his specialized weapon. Fletcher noticed a small trace of light moving through the roof. Pulling out our weapons, we stood ready for them. Placing ourselves between Fletcher and our uninvited guests.

We were in a perfect place for an ambush. Whoever is behind this attempt on Fletcher had to have known we were in this car.

Silas called out to Carlos, "How far are we to the next station?"

Carlos checked the schedule. "We're ten minutes out."

"We're not going to make it," proclaimed Silas as he looked up at the roof.

"We have to delay them," I stated.

Carlos quickly took something from his belt. It was a small tube that he placed carefully on the compromised roof. Stepping back, he advised the rest of us, "Get back quickly and block your eyes."

We did as he said. A silent burst of energy paralyzed the attackers on the roof. I saw one of them fall to his death. The remaining three were paralyzed for a moment. Giving us our diversion. Now we had to take advantage.

Carlos stepped closer to the hole and fired wildly at the assailants. This allowed him to take a position on the opposite side, enabling a crossfire to keep our friends on the roof. One assailant had the same as Carlos earlier. Discharging one of their shock grenades in the car neutralized us. Silas manages to stop him from firing his pistol, killing him instantly. I moved closer to help them. Carlos saw me.

He ordered, "Stay with him."

The two remaining attackers needed another way in. From our viewscreen, we saw them back off from the hole they had created. Silas and Carlos managed to maintain the standoff until the shuttle stopped at the next stop. Once inside the station, we realized our situation didn't improve.

A second unit of four assassins was lying there waiting for us. That was their plan all along: forcing us to stop here so they could make us do something desperate. As for myself, I had that desperate plan, but I needed a diversion from the others. Carlos managed to shoot an assailant who was still waiting patiently on the shuttle's roof, leaving one assailant. He jumped down and joined his friends surrounding us.

Believing this was our best chance. Silas signaled to the conductor to continue to Capital. That hope died quickly when we witnessed all the shuttles before us continue their journey, leaving us behind. We are stranded.

The five attackers opened fire. Blasting at our shuttle wildly. For now, the metal of our shuttle is strong enough to withstand several laser blasts. But that will not last forever. Worst, we can't fire back at the assassins. We were running out of options.

I told them my plan.

Neither of them liked it. To be honest, I didn't like it much either, it is at best a desperate gamble. If we are going to do it, we must do it now, before our friends outside get reinforcements.

"This isn't the work of Disrupters," stated Fletcher.

I had never heard of them before. I knew this wasn't the time to inquire. Fletcher mentioned they were not behind this attack. That made these Disruptors not important right now. He confessed, "Our friends outside are operatives."

Silas and Carlos knew what he meant. Seeing the expressions on their faces, I didn't want to know. All I needed to know was that at this moment, we're in trouble.

Carlos added, "This shuttle will not take much more."

Silas looked at me and smiled, but I didn't know why at that time. "Does anybody have any other ideas?" Nobody answered, he then made his decision, "We have one chance for this. When Carlos opens the door. We will rush them. Hopefully, they will not be expecting it. When we secure the bay, that will be your time to move. We will stay behind to create a diversion." Carlos rushed to the door control. Placing his gun in his left hand and his right on the emergency knob, he nodded to us, he was ready. Silas turned to me and said, "You better be as good as you think."

I didn't say anything. I was too busy trying to keep my nerves in check. Fletcher placed himself on his stomach on the floor of the car. Silas gave Carlos a signal. Carlos quickly turned the knob, and the door opened.

Silas led our counterattack. He fired his pistol, killing one assassin outright. Still caught by surprise, the remaining assassins were slow to respond. I was next to choosing my mark on our left. I managed to pin him down behind some cover. On my right, Silas did the same with the other assassin. Carlos, from his position in the shuttle, had a clear shot of the assassin on the left. With no hesitation, he fired the fatal shot, and the man slumped to the ground. I turned to cover the other two on the other side of the platform. Silas and Carlos turned their attention to the assassin on the right. We had to finish him quickly before his friends joined the fight. I didn't know who managed to get him as my attention was on another problem. When the firing had stopped, I knew we had killed the last one. It had been barely a minute, but now we outnumber the assassins, but we can't let them leave.

From their positions, they moved forward using the shuttle as a temporary cover. They had no intention of running. I saw a look of admiration from Silas, like him, they were professionals. They would either win or die.

Now I had to move closer to the pod. After we were all dead, the assassins would be free to deal with Fletcher. For now, he is safe, allowing me to get to him. As I ran towards Fletcher, the assassin on my right noticed me, before I could get under cover and stop him from shooting me, Carlos managed to kill him. I looked over at the last assassin on my left. I don't believe he was aware that he was all that was left of the seven who attacked us twenty minutes earlier. Not that it matters. I had a shot, and I took it. The fight was finally over. We gathered at the remains of the shuttle. Fletcher returned to his feet. My plan had worked,

Without a word, Silas hit the emergency button. He then turned to me and stated, "Now go."

Seeing I was confused, Carlos added," This line has been com-promised. So, take him to your backup line."

"We don't have much time," Silas said decisively, "We will stay here as a decoy." I had no time to respond, I just nodded and led Fletcher from the station, when I heard him exclaim, "Kid, you better be right!"

He said that to me before. Quietly, I responded, "I will."

With Fletcher in tow, we ran through Green Section, which made up most of Dominion, along with a Grey Section. A small area of Yellow Section allows the residents some comfort like their neigh-bors. Dominion has one of the largest in-area districts of Gotham, but has one of the smallest in population. Its function is primarily to provide energy and food for Gotham.

For the past week, I have made six deliveries into Dominion, so I knew the area well enough to move through the district without being detected. That is what we did, as we twisted through alley-ways and side streets, heading up and down flights of stairs, all to keep us one step ahead of any other contingents of assassins lying in wait.

Finally, after an hour, we made it to our destination. An old shuttle system that mainly brought supplies from Capital to South-point. It still had room for commuters, but it wasn't as fast as the newer lines, so Fletcher's enemies would never have thought to place it under observation.

I led him to an open, unsecured shuttle door, inside we found that it was full of produce. Fletcher hesitated. He found it undig-nified. With no time to spare, I had to find a way to convince him.

"Sir, this is the only way."

"There has to be another way."

"I bet my life on it." Then I had another foolish idea. I took out my pistol and I handed it to him. Puzzled, he looked at me, "If I'm wrong. You can shoot me."

That convinced him. He joined me in the freight car. In the dark, we felt the shuttle head north, at half the speed of our private shuttle.

It seemed longer inside the freight car. What was no more than a forty-five-minute trip, felt like two hours. Sitting in darkness didn't help us. Neither was sitting on the dirty floor. One unexpected benefit we discovered was free food. For now, we are safe. We just sat back and relaxed, knowing that we would have only one stop. That is when we will be on the move again.

Our shuttle arrived in Capital on time. We both felt the shuttle land back on the ground. With my stinger in hand, I stepped out. Fletcher remained undercover with my pistol at the ready. Still being cautious, I stuck my head out and looked around at the station as workers unloaded each car. This gave us a diversion from unfriendly eyes. Satisfied, I signaled to Fletcher to come out. Moving out to the open, he felt an immediate relief of being safe. He smiled and gave me back my pistol.

I couldn't afford to be so confident. So, we carefully walked up to a lift to Yellow Section. There we took a shuttle to Capital Green. Traveling through Red Section would be too dangerous. Being under constant surveillance of mercenary eyes. We would be too easily spotted because, looking at us, it is clear to anyone living there that we don't belong. Yellow Section is more secure.

At the end of the line, I saw a strange sight: Capital Green.

It was an oasis of the natural world. A large white building surrounded by a sea of green grass. With islands of flowers dotting the landscape. Two lines of trees with white flowers created a boundary line between the vast mountains of iron and concrete that were made by man. At the center of this is a large white building with an impressive dome of blue glass. That is the namesake of this entire district, that is the Capital of Gotham. With all that I saw, what I found most interesting was a wall of glass given to all the citizens living near the oasis of the Old World. An act of cruelty to the people of Red and Yellow levels has no way to access Capital Green. Forcing them only to look but not experience their park. So much for the people's park. As for the Blue and Purple levels, they are allowed this special privilege of access to the park. As giant lifts bring people up and down from the city.

Now, back to my current problem. Stationed all over Capital Green, at least a dozen assassins were waiting for us. How can we get there? That is a question I kept asking myself. Finally, I saw the solution.

'Can you get us to Purple Section?" I quickly asked Fletcher.

"Yes," he answered, understanding what I was thinking.

We headed for the lift. Taking it directly to Purple Sector. Once there, we were stopped by three Watchmen. It was their duty to detain people who entered Purple Level who didn't belong. That was me. A sergeant placed his dormant stinger on my chest. Before he said something, Fletcher intervened by giving the sergeant his papers; he didn't want to read them, believing they were beneath him, so he passed them to his second, who read them. With the color going out of his face, the officer desperately tried to get his sergeant's attention. Annoyed, the sergeant turned to him. His second immediately shoved the paper in his hand. Dropping his baton, he read and turned back to us. Unknown to him, his two associates stood at attention. His contemptible smirk was wiped off his face, replaced with sheer panic.

"What is your name, Sergeant?" Fletcher asked with his privilege being placed in full display.

"Jones, sir."

Fletcher ordered, "This man is escorting me to the Capital. He will have full access while doing his assignment."

"Yes, sir."

Fletcher continued, "I wish this not to be shared with anybody, do you understand, Sergeant Jones?"

"Yes, sir."

"Carry on, Sergeant."

Not waiting for a reply, we walked off, entering Purple Sector. I had to admit I did enjoy that. Passing a score of people, all well-dressed and clean. Barely acknowledged our presence when we walked by them. Because we weren't either of those things. I didn't care about that. My attention was directed at the view around me. We were so high above the city that it was like walking on air. I couldn't stop thinking that this must be what birds saw as they soared above us. Now I felt like the birds' equals.

Fletcher looked at me, amused at my sense of wonder. Envy

came over him as he no longer shared that sense of wonder—the cost of living among the clouds. We entered the direct shaft to the capital and headed down inside the building. I guessed right. The Assassins would not dare to place their officers inside the building. More importantly, they will not be able to station anybody up here in the clouds.

Without any more incidents, we walked to the chambers. He turned to me and told me, "Well done, Duncan Walker. I will remember you."

I thanked him and headed to the rotunda. To my surprise, in front of us stood Silas and Carlos, waiting for me. They had received confirmation that Fletcher had been delivered to the Capital floor. We received a congratulatory message for our job.

Silas was the first to greet me. "Well done," he said with a hint of admiration.

Carlos joined us, "Let's get something to eat on the company."

We had a late lunch. Well-earned feast on our company's expense account. It was the least they could do. Finished we headed home to report to Smith. After our journey back to headquarters and giving our boss a full report, we were free to go home.

It was well after dark when I made it home. Gabrielle was there waiting for me, she wasn't happy. Her arms were crossed over a light blue blouse. I knew she was off tonight, so it didn't surprise she had on black capri pants. She stood there quietly, trying to decide something about me.

"I heard of an attack between terrorists and agents from a security firm. Somehow, I knew it was you. But did you tell me that you were all right, nothing?"

"I didn't have time."

"Bastard!" she screamed. Now I knew what it was, she was both relieved and upset, she rushed at me and pounded on my shoulders. "You could have sent word after you had finished."

Her pounding on my shoulders hurt more than she intended. I managed to grab her wrist and said, "I didn't think." She calmed down, and I added, "I will always come home to you. I promised."

Tears came down her eyes, "You'd better."

She placed her arms around my neck. She kissed me passionately on the lips. I was forgiving this time. Stroking her hair, we stood there kissing. In the end, I knew she was right. I should have let her know I was all right. During lunch or on the way back, I had many opportunities to do just that. I had no excuse. All I can do is make it up to her somehow. For now, she is satisfied with me stroking her hair and kissing her. That was enough for me as well.

4   CAGERS

I WALKED INTO THE OFFICE AT THE USUAL TIME. INSIDE OUR HOLDing area, I found a room full of my coworkers. Because of our competing schedules, I had never met many of them. Besides myself, I counted fourteen couriers. Silas and Carlos were already present, sitting down and waiting for their assignments. When Silas saw me, he immediately stood up and smiled. Carlos followed his lead.

"There he is, our hero, Duncan Walker," Silas proclaimed proudly.

Before I knew what was happening, I was swarmed by the others. Each one wanted to personally congratulate me for yesterday. A far different reaction than what Gabrielle had given me last night. I still have the bruises where she struck me. As for my partners, they seem to enjoy this display of admiration.

"We'd better be careful; our friend here will be striking out on his own. We will be working for him." Carlos proudly proclaimed.

"That's not today! Sit down!" Exclaimed Smith. He had come in quietly, watching this little act of congratulations. All of us sat down. Smith remained silent for a moment after he sat down. The room was silent as we waited for each of our assignments. One by one, he called out each name, and they received their assignment.

Finally, there were the three of us left. Carlos, Silas, and I waited for Smith to call us.

Silas was first. He smiled as he passed me. Nervously, I looked over at Smith, who was looking down at his screen. His demeanor was the same as it had been since I had started. Not that I was expecting any kind of special consideration for what happened yesterday. It would have been nice. With the reaction of my fellow curious, I had expected more. When he called Carlos and sent him on his way, I was alone.

Three minutes later, he called, "Walker." I walked up to get my assignment. Raising his eyes, he looked right through me and said, "Walker, are you aware of our policy about making a report of each assignment?"

"We came home late. Silas told me we can do it today."

"That is good," he replied, "Both Silas and Carlos came early and did their own. Before I can send you out, I need you to fill one out. I'm it will be quite interesting."

"Yes, sir."

"You can go in there," he said, looking at a side office.

I did what he requested. Luckily it was voice-activated and I sat down and answered questions it had given me. When it asked for a statement, I gave a detailed description that I was able to recollect. Two hours later, I was finished. I returned to Smith and gave him the reference code. He just handed me my assignment. It was to be delivered at the River, Blue Level 9, Unit 3. I had been there before.

That day I had two additional assignments. The last one had taken me to Hampton. That made me return to the office at nineteen hundred hours. Walking into the office I was surprised to see Carlos and Silas there waiting for me. Smith was at his desk.

As usual, he didn't acknowledge that I came in. he asked, "Did you take lunch yesterday?"

"There wasn't time," I replied.

With a slight movement from his lips that I could only speculate was a smile, "These will make up for that." He handed each of us an envelope.

I opened it. Looking inside, I took out a flat plastic square that was larger than my palm. I glanced over at Carlos and Silas, who were both visibly excited. I read the markings on it. It was a semi-final match between Capital and Southpoint. A Cagers' match, the others had told me. We had special seating.

Since entering Gotham, I have seen the strange obsession people had with this sport called Cagers. It wasn't a unique experience. Clans of Train People will often play a game with each other for bragging rights. Sometimes, the rival chiefs place wagers for supplies. While traveling with some clans, I played in one of these matches.

The game was on Friday. Gabby will be working. That meant the three of us would have the evening together. It was clear that this was Smith's way of thanking us. I politely thanked him.

———————

Friday night, we agreed to meet at the office an hour before the gate opens. Arriving at the stadium, I quickly realized that this was far different than anything that happened out there. The stadium easily fits forty thousand people. After we were seated in a private suite that fit twenty people, a young woman walked up to us and offered us drinks. She explained when she scanned our tickets that all food and drink were complimentary. Smith must be really happy with us. Drinking a cold glass of draft beer, Silas and Carlos gave me a quick introduction to the game. Its relevance to the history of the sport. Southpoint hadn't won the championship in twenty years. Carlos had made a point that Southpoint hadn't made the playoffs in six years.

"Then you already won," I said, watching the pregame festivities on the field.

Both men turned to me with a look of disdain. That shocked me. Carlos then proclaims, "We want a championship."

I let that go. I asked them, "How many games have you been to?"

Carlos answered, "3."

Silas replied, "7."

Looking around, I asked them, "In here?"

They looked at me with disappointment. Silas stated, "No down there." He pointed down below us.

I looked down upon the mass of people crowded in the stands below. Many were standing with anticipation for the game. Watching all of this, I couldn't help but think of a warning Austen gave me years ago: beware of bread and circus. I didn't know what he meant back then. Watching Carlos and Silas, along with over forty thousand fellow spectators, I began to understand. Cagers are a distraction. Each person here has problems at home. Carlos is separated from his family. But for a few hours, he can forget that and focus on Southpoint winning a game. And if they win the championship, although the players did the work, they will all be champions.

When the players walked onto the field, the crowd became silent. Capital whore their away gold jerseys and red pants. Southpoint wore their home grey jerseys and gold pants. Carlos immediately corrected me that the grey uniforms were actually silver not grey. I decided not to argue. Southpoint immediately took up their positions on the western goal, and Capital will defend the east. The home team has this choice. They then switch after the first half.

Twelve players are on each team. Each individual has their assignments. The point of the game is to carry an oblong ball across a goal line; with the defending team doing everything it can to either stop them or gain possession of the ball. A team on defense can score points as well, forcing the offense to proceed with caution.

A neutral person invited a representative from each team. They will decide how the game starts. According to tradition, the official tosses a round piece of metal into the air, the visiting representative calls heads or tails. He called tails, but it came up heads. The winning captain will now have three choices: take the ball, defer to the second half, or challenge. The captain of Southpoint, as he did every time, had won the toss and chose a challenge. He had the approval of the crowd.

The two captains promptly took their positions on opposite sides of the circle. Holding the ball, the official entered the circle and placed it directly in the center. He then left it there and left the circle. He held up his hand, his signal that the game would start.

Carlos told me the two captains would battle for the ball. The one who has possession of the ball and can take it out of the circle will have control of the ball. This was how Southpoint chose to play this game to establish a physicality that they were lacking in previous seasons.

The official's hand came down, and the game started. The two captains, as Silas called them, rushed for the ball as the crowd became silent in anticipation. The two men struggled for the ball, with the capital player taking possession. Before he could leave the circle, the Southpoint player tackled him as he tried to take the ball out of his opponent's hands. He failed, and the Capital player made it out of the circle. The crowd showed their disappointment with jeers. But there was no time for a reaction as Southpoint had to go on the defensive. Capital then proceeded to score the first goal and take an early lead. Southpoint immediately answered and scored themselves. At the end of the first quarter, they were tied.

I had to admit, at first, the game was confusing. Added to Austen's warning, I looked at it all with disdain. As the game wore on, I began to understand it. I became enthralled with its tactics and physical spectacle. By the end of the half, Capital had a one-point lead. Sitting in my seat, I anxiously waited for the second half to start.

Capital had possession to begin the second half. Like they did to start the game, they promptly scored, adding to their lead. Southpoint wouldn't be denied, scoring twice and taking the lead—something they never relinquished. When the game ended, Southpoint had won 34 to 27. And I cheered as hard as the others in the crowd. Celebrating a victory that I hadn't earned but was sharing with the players down on the field. Forgetting all about bread and circus, I was hooked like the others. For the moment, nothing else mattered. I was hooked.

After the game, the three of us gathered for a victory drink. An hour and four large pints later, I staggered home, hoping that Gabrielle was asleep. When I entered the flat, I discovered she wasn't. Sitting on the couch, she looked at me, I knew I was in trouble. Carefully, I sat next to her.

"Did you have fun?" she asked me.

"I did," I replied, "I think you would like it."

"That's what some of the players tell me," She stated, trying to make me jealous. This was my punishment for staying out so late. That gave me some relief, she added, "Some of them come into the club."

I kissed her on her lips. "Can they do that?"

She smiled. "Maybe, but I don't want to find out." She placed her arms around my neck and kissed me. I was forgiven.

———————

When our payment cycle had ended. Smith revealed the owner's appreciation for my services. A full bonus that was equal to six months of work. After looking at my newfound wealth, I tried to thank Smith. Unamused, he just looked at me and grunted. That was his way of saying, " You're welcome. "

Outside, I met Carlos. He had a bonus of their own. Carlos was excited; he almost had enough money to get his family home.

"How much do you need?" I asked him.

"Don't worry, I'll get it." He replied, not wanting to share his problems with me.

Handing him my check, I asked him, "Would this help?"

His eyes widened as he looked at the amount. He was moved by my generosity, but he couldn't shake his cynicism about my gesture. "Why?"

"You helped me."

"That was my job, nothing more."

"Then take it for other people who had helped me," I told him.

He placed the check in his wallet. "Thank you."

"You're welcome," I replied and headed home.

All my life, I was a taker. Whether it was a roof over my head or food in my belly. All I did was find a way to get what I needed and leave when they hadn't more to offer. I would take information about a skill from someone and not think twice about it. Just once, I wanted to see what it felt like to give.

When I made it home. I told Gabrielle what I had done. She just gave me a quick embrace.

A week later, we had dinner with his family. His wife Maria was a short, petite woman about the same age as her husband. She was very appreciative of our help. Her three children were immediately taken to Gabrielle. By the end of our dinner together, they had called her Aunty Gabrielle. She eagerly volunteered to watch the three young girls while their parents could get themselves settled in their new life together in Southpoint. Each time Gabrielle had the children over, she had changed a little. She never directly came out and said it, but she hinted about having children. That was something I had never considered before. Watching her with Carlos and Maria's children, I did not doubt that she would be a good mother. And sharing it all with her, I wouldn't be opposed to it.

When the championship game was settled. Smith gave me his final appreciation for my work with Fletcher. Two tickets in the same suite. I chose to take Gabrielle with me. We arrived twenty minutes before the game started. Gabby was visibly excited about what she would be witnessing. I just sat there watching her. Like the previous game, it was all complementary, so we just sat back.

Like the previous game, it started with a challenge. This time, it was the visiting team from York that chose it. They wore their navy blue jerseys and pants, while Southpoint wore their home silver and gold pants. Gabby agreed with me that their jerseys did look grey. At the start of the game, Gabrielle cheered on Southpoint along with the others in attendance. She had an amazing understanding of the game. Picking it up faster than I did. When the game ended, Southpoint had won its first championship in twenty years. The score was 17-9. Gabrielle turned to me and held me, screaming into my ear. When she settled down, she noticed I was holding my ear in pain. She immediately kissed it to make it better.

We chose not to celebrate with the rest of the people of South-point. Instead, we walked along the river. I had found a quiet spot where we could be alone. It was a glass rotunda that overlooked the entire city. Outside, it was winter, and you would never know it living in the city. We sat together on a small bench, watching a blizzard that was raging outside. She placed her head on my shoulder, and we sat content with the world. For the first time, I had thoughts about her being my wife. Not that I could ever deserve her. But it was a nice thought.

PART 3
GOTHAM

1 CAITLYN

THERE IS SOMETHING I HAVE LEARNED SINCE LIVING IN SOUTH-point for almost a year: that a bad day in Gotham is far different than in the Wastelands. A bad day is enduring several mundane setbacks like being late for work, failing your assignment, or missing your ride. All three had happened to me today, I will confess. A bad day living in the Wastelands means it was your last if you're lucky.

Right now, I just want to go home and see Gabby before she leaves for work. My assignment sent me to Oldtown District for the first time. I discovered that Oldtown, like Dominion, covers a large area and is scarcely populated. That made a sparser schedule for the tube than in other districts. I found that out the hard way. Missing several possible shuttles. Oldtown had large sections of Green and small pockets of Yellow Levels. To make things worse, our client was located at the farthest point. Arriving an hour after my expected delivery time. After making my apologies. I had to listen to the manager's lecture on responsibility. I wanted to tell him what I thought about Oldtown, but thinking better of it, I just left. Certainly, I will get the same lecture from Smith tomorrow morning when I report for work.

I made it home to Southpoint at 1700 hours. A few minutes before dusk. To calm down, I just sat down and looked over to the western horizon, waiting for the final shuttle home. Outside the city, signs of spring had begun to make an appearance. Funny, we never noticed winter living in Southpoint.

Ten minutes later, I was home. In time to see Gabrielle. Before opening the door, I didn't think the day could get any worse. Walking into our living room, it just did. Sitting comfortably in a chair across from Gabrielle was Caitlyn Wylde. It has been a year since she left Shenandoah and returned home to Gotham. Living here suits her better than being out there, she told us. Her long blonde hair was neatly trimmed and hung beneath her shoulder blades. She wore a tight silver dress that went down just below her knees. Looking up at me, she smiled a little too friendly.

She is beautiful. For many reasons, I had hoped we would never see her again. But here she is in our home for an unknown amount of time, talking to Gabrielle alone. They are both Blues. Caitlyn has her own plans for Gabrielle, and she has made it clear that I am not involved in them. For that reason, I don't trust her.

"Caitlyn, what brings you here?" I politely inquired while sitting down next to Gabrielle. I reached over to grab her hand gently.

Gabrielle answered for her, "She is coming to see my show." I looked over at Gabby. Surprised by her response, I didn't think she liked her. But things changed.

"I was hurt you two didn't take my offer."

I said, "We are happy here."

"Caitlyn has been telling me about Gotham Prime. She makes it sound so exciting," Gabby contradicted me. She then stood up and added, "We'd better get going."

Rising to her feet, Caitlyn looked down at me and asked, "Are you coming?"

"Not after work," Gabby had answered for me.

Now it was my turn to contradict her, "I think I will come." Getting up to my feet, I added, "Just give me five minutes to change."

I left and headed for our room. I managed to change into a fresh set of clothes in four minutes. I didn't want to keep them waiting.

When I walked into my apartment, I was exhausted and ready to spend an evening just relaxing. Right now, I have my second wind. Seeing Caitlyn do that much for me, at least.

At the club, Caitlyn and I sat down at a table to the right of the stage. A young woman came and took our orders. She came back with our order. I thanked her, and she smiled and headed to her other tables. Gabrielle was in her dressing room getting ready for her three sets tonight.

Promptly at nineteen hundred hours, the manager walked on the stage to introduce Gabrielle Blue. She walked in and kissed the older manager on the cheek. The manager had left the stage, leaving Gabrielle alone with her band. Standing downstage, that was what Gabrielle described to me, her band was upstage of her, I guess it made sense. Gabrielle modestly introduced herself and signaled to her bandmates to begin playing.

As she started to sing, I was quickly reminded of how stunning Gabrielle looked. Her long red hair was set neatly, exposing her bare shoulders, minus a modest piece of her hair resting on her right shoulder. Her dress was new. Provided by the club's management. They often provided her with gowns to perform in or when she was doing a private show. Her customer outdid herself in choosing this dress. It is lavender that complements her body. Her shoulders were bare, and her dress opened in a V covering her breast, but not her arms. I thought that was strange, but not important. Then she began singing, and nothing else mattered. I just sat there wondering what the hell she saw in me.

Caitlyn leaned over to me and said, "She is an angel." It is the first thing we agreed on. Gabrielle is an angel.

After she finished her ninth song, she thanked the audience, bowing her head slightly to acknowledge the applause. She walked over and joined us. I stood up and held her seat out for her to sit down. She smiled at me, and I returned to my seat. Our waitress returned and offered to get her something. Gabrielle just asked for a glass of orange juice.

With a fresh set of drinks. Caitlyn began to make her. "Gotham Prime is the center of our little world. And you will be its queen."

"They have been good to me here."

"How much are you making now?"

"Three thousand."

With full confidence, Caitlyn stated, "I can get you ten thousand a week."

The club manager must have heard that. He was close enough. Without permission, he sat between Caitlyn and Gabrielle. Caitlyn was annoyed by him.

"We are old friends," Caitlyn stated in an insincere tone.

"I understand," he replied, looking at Gabrielle. When Gabrielle finished her glass of juice, he advised her, "I think you should get ready for your next set."

Without missing a beat, Caitlyn added, "That will give us a chance to talk."

Gabrielle rose to her feet; in her usual grace, she excused herself and headed backstage. With just the three of us, Caitlyn looked at me with a confident smile and proudly proclaimed, "Duncan, please excuse us. We have some business to discuss."

She didn't wait for my permission. Looking at the manager, she stood up and waited for him. I watched him do the same, he looked like a lamb heading for slaughter. At that moment, I knew we were leaving South Point. It would be a matter of time. She had wanted Gabrielle, and she was going to get her. Soon, it will be my turn. I would have to be ready.

By the end of Gabrielle's second show, Caitlyn returned with a sense of accomplishment. Gabrielle joined us again. Caitlyn told her, "How soon can you come to Gotham?"

Gabrielle was surprised. I had expected it. During that winter we spent together, I learned that when Caitlyn had a plan, she didn't waste any time in carrying it out; all you can do to counter her actions is to figure it out. I could only hope to find out her plan before it was too late. I had an idea of how to counter her.

"How is your friend, Jacob?"

With a cold stare that she managed to hide from Gabby replied, "He is alive, I think." She changed her expression, turned to Gabby, and repeated her question, "Well, when can you leave?"

She said, "I'll need to give my boss some notice."

'I can help you with that.'

Gabby reached over and gently squeezed my hand. Gabrielle made it clear we were a couple. Her response eased that reality a bit, "I would like to see what Gotham."

Caitlyn had to accept that for now, "It will take me a few weeks to set everything up for you two. I'll keep you posted. Gabrielle, I think you should get ready for your last set."

Gabby replied, "I guess so."

She headed back behind the stage. We were alone together. I had another concern about Caitlyn. And she knew it. If I had never met Gabrielle and Caitlyn and my paths would have crossed. I would have pursued her. Using her like I did other women over the years. Although I'm not sure how it would have ended, I'm probably lucky to escape with my life. That tension between us gives her an advantage. Right now, I have figured out what her plans are against me. She needs to alienate Gabrielle and me. This time, at least, I will be ready for her. As Gabby came out for her final set, we left our table and sat at the bar. We stayed there for all her songs. Whatever she had said to the manager, who I would never call timid, kept his distance, while the bartender was there to make sure she was happy. I tried to avoid her, choosing to focus on Gabrielle. It isn't that hard. Gabrielle is intoxicating. Sometimes, I looked over to see what Caitlyn was thinking. Finally, Gabrielle finished her set. Bowing slightly, she thanked the audience and headed backstage, under thunderous applause from her audience. Something we joined with the others. Quietly, the manager walked onto the stage, and the audience quieted down.

"I'm glad you enjoyed Gabrielle Blue. I was informed tonight that she will be heading up to Gotham. We are going to miss her. Gabrielle, can you come out here?"

Gabrielle returned to the stage as the audience rose to their feet to show their appreciation. Shyly, she thanked her audience for their show of support. You could see in her expression that she was truly moved. Finally, the crowd returned to their seats and calmed down, hoping Gabrielle would address them.

"Thank you, everybody," she started, making it feel like she was addressing each audience member personally. You made it so easy for me to perform for you. This past year had just flown by. Each of you made me feel so welcome. I will miss all of you."

Taking a step closer, the manager asked, "When will you be leaving us?"

Without any hesitation, she stated, "At the end of the month."

"I can honestly say that Gabrielle, we will miss you. And wish you all the luck in the world."

"Thank you." She said quickly, and then she returned backstage.

Curious, I looked at Caitlyn. As I had expected, she wasn't happy with her. It was clear that it had been longer than she had wanted. She had no choice but to honor what Gabrielle had just said. I ordered another round of drinks. Believing this was a good time, I decided to inquire about Jake: "Does he still work for you?"

"Who?"

"Your friend, Jake, you spent the winter with at Shenandoah."

Gradually, a sense of recollection came over her. "No," a cold expression came over her. "I didn't need him anymore, so I sent him away." It was clear that she no longer needed anybody; she would get rid of them. Then, when she returned to Gotham, she didn't need him anymore and sent him away. "What will it take for you to stay here?"

She has made it clear that she doesn't want me to go, but she will find it a lot harder to get rid of me. "You don't have enough money." I didn't allow her to respond; I just added, "I'll just stick around to make sure you don't hurt her."

"We want the same thing." After saying that, she moved closer to me. "You know, we don't have to be enemies." I stood there motionless as I felt her body on me. "I don't have to tell you we are alike." She moved in to kiss me. That is when I felt this was a trap. Gabrielle is right behind me or close by. I gently pushed her away. A look of admiration was revealed to me by her smile. She conceded that I would win this battle.

Placing her arm around my waist, Gabby joined us. "Missed me."

"Always," I replied. She kissed me on the cheek. She had straightened out her long red hair. Wearing the same street clothes, she came in with. She believed that people would not notice her. I'm not sure if it works. "Can I get you a drink?"

"Please."

I signaled the bartender, who immediately knew what to serve Gabby, bringing over a glass of white wine. Gabby smiled at the bartender; she thanked her.

"To Gotham." I held out my glass. Both Caitlyn and Gabrielle followed and repeated, "To Gotham."

Together, we drank. Caitlyn finished her glass of wine. Placing her glass on the bar, she turned to us and stated, "Well, I must go. I must be back home tomorrow morning." She took the turn and tried to give us both a sincere hug before she finished, "Tonight is on me, so feel free to stay here for a while."

"Can't you stay?"

"No, I have a lot of work to do."

Caitlyn exited the nightclub. She left her tab open. I turned to Gabby and proposed, "Let's buy a round for the entire club."

"Duncan!"

I understood that as a no. But I remembered I hadn't had dinner tonight. Gabrielle admitted, "Neither did I." So, we ordered two sandwiches and ate them when they arrived. When we finished, we headed for home. I still must go to work tomorrow.

With six hours of sleep, I managed to make it to work on time. Sitting down, I waited for my turn for my assignment. As I waited, I found myself being ignored by my fellow couriers. Neither Silas nor Carlos stopped to talk to me. When I greeted them, they remained silent. Be this is part of the punishment for yesterday in Oldtown. I kept it all in stride. It is possible, but I have never failed before. For an hour, I waited until I was called by Smith.

This is my official reprimand for failure. He led me to his private office. Closing the door behind us, he offered me a seat. Not wanting to look at me, he asked, "Do you like working here?"

"Yes, I do."

He turned to me and said, "Then when were you going to tell me you are leaving?"

Caitlyn must have made a stop here; she is thorough; I'll give her that. "I didn't know until last night."

"Do you want to leave?"

"Not really." To be honest, I am happy here. I don't want to leave." My girlfriend wishes to move to Gotham."

"I can understand that. I have seen her perform. If she were mine, I would follow her anywhere." That was the first time he complimented me. "How do you know, Caitlyn Wylde?"

"She was hiding out in a village we were living in."

Stepping closer to me, he stated, "Be careful of her."

"I don't trust her."

Taking a large envelope, with a rare smile, he handed it to me." This is just across town. After yesterday, I think you earned it."

"Thank you, sir," I said, surprised. We are not going to move until the end of the month."

"Then I expect you to be on time, until then."

"I will."

I left the office. After reading the address, I found it in the Blue Section, Level 9, Section 5. It was easy. I've been there before.

———

Friday night, Silas, Carlos, and I headed for a Cagers game. Our local team, Southpoint, is hoping to repeat its championship. With a new season, anything is possible. We bought tickets a month ago. They weren't as fancy as a sweet; they were down below the crowd in the stands. It was far different, but I think I liked it better. I must admit that this game is addictive. As I looked around, I saw that the gathering of fans was crowded with us. All residents of Southpoint were fully represented in the stands. But like outside the stadium, there is a class system. However, that didn't matter, as Southpoint was facing its longtime rival, Tidewater, to begin the season.

Before the game started, a banner for last season was revealed, embellishing their championship for the ages. Now, ready, the two teams have already come out on the field. Southpoint wore their home uniforms while Tidewater wore light blue jerseys and white pants. All through the game, both Carlos and Silas were distant. I knew they were aware of me leaving. It didn't matter when Southpoint defeated Tidewater 24 to 12. A good start for the season.

Caitlyn sent us the information as promised, a week before the end of the month, so we started to pack. We haven't lived here long enough to gather many belongings. Carlos and Silas volunteered to help us bring it down to the station. After we had carried out our things and placed them on a cargo line, to be shipped north to Gotham. After we cleaned the apartment, we did a walk-through with our building manager. Satisfied, she released us from our contract after paying a penalty fee. We shook hands, and now we are free to begin our new venture. Before we parted, I had one more question. "We had some friends who entered the city near Gotham. Is it possible to find them?"

Silas inquired, wanting more information. "They didn't enter with you two?"

"No, one of our members had friends promising a faster route. So, the other members of our party chose to go with them. Only Gabby and I went through Southpoint."

The look on both their faces told me I didn't want to hear their answer. Finally, Carlos told me about my friends' possible dire fate: "If they're lucky, they made it. If not, it depends on what they have to offer."

I thought momentarily about Paloma, Olivia, and Cassandra, three young, pretty girls. What fate have they faced? I didn't want to think about it. Henry and Deborah had money, enough to buy all five of their lives. I couldn't guess. Natalie and Mitchel were part of the gang; I was sure of it. For once, I wished I were wrong.

"Maybe they made it in. There are some honest smugglers." Silas tried to reassure me. But he didn't know Mitchel. He was a Krieg.

"I hope so."

On that day, we parted. I joined Gabrielle. We shipped our stuff ahead of us, we had two small bags with us. As we entered the shuttle. Sitting down, we waited for it. I glanced over to my friends Silas and Carlos, who sat there waving goodbye. But my thoughts kept returning to my friends we had separated from on the fringe of the Wastelands. We barely knew each other. But we had made a promise to watch over each other. And I can't shake the feeling that I had failed them. I tried to warn them. I should have told them what Mitchel was. Maybe that would make things worse. I don't know. I'll never know.

Gabrielle noticed I was depressed and wondered what was wrong. I chose not to share my concerns with her until, I was sure. I gave her some other excuse. She smiled and reassured me it would be all right. Just like that, we are off. Heading north on foot.

Two hours later, we went into Gotham Prime. To be clear, Gotham is an island surrounded by several smaller islands. It is the smallest district of Gotham in area, but in population, it is the largest district. The people of Gotham built upwards with buildings as high as mountains. People living in Southpoint all told me that Gotham Prime is the center of the universe, and now I understand what they meant.

Moving slowly onto a bridge, we made it to the station. Gabrielle led the way out of the shuttle, and I followed her to the address Caitlyn had given her a couple of days ago. It said: Blue Level 29, Section 9 Unit R. Twenty minutes later, we made it. A doorman stopped us, asking for identification. Gabrielle handed him hers. He read it and checked his list. Satisfied, I then handed him mine. Doing the same as before, he smiled and handed us our passes. Eagerly explain the security system of the building along with its rules. He ended with a hearty, "Welcome to the building."

Taking the lift, we took it to the fifth floor. We entered our new flat; it was amazing. All our property was neatly put away. Caitlyn is efficient; I'll give her that. On the dining room table was a bucket with a glass bottle—a welcoming gift from Caitlyn—a bottle of Chardonnay from an area I knew well, Napa.

I looked for two glasses as Gabrielle opened the bottle. After finding the glasses, I brought two over and placed them on a table. Finished, she returned the bottle to the bucket. I proceeded to pick up the two glasses and handed them to her. We walked together over to the window that overlooked the city. There we drank our wine. Finished, I walked over with the two glasses and poured each a second glass. Returning to Gabrielle, I handed her hers, and she looked at the cityscape.

"Beautiful," she stated with a contented smile.

Looking at her, I replied, "Yes, she is."

She sipped her wine slowly, looking at me shyly. She knew what I meant. I glanced out of the window overlooking the city. Gabrielle was right; it was beautiful, but next to her, it still paled in comparison. We finished the bottle and had dinner that Caitlyn had prepared for us. We then went to bed. It was a good first day.

2   MENAGERIE

FOR THE NEXT WEEK, CAITLYN MANAGED TO KEEP US BUSY. Promptly at eighteen hundred hours, she would arrive at our flat with a new assignment. She would bring a new dress and shoes for Gabrielle to wear. That will complement the event we are required to attend. I had to wear the same outfit each day. I wasn't important enough for the same treatment. Not that I had minded. Each night when Gabby revealed herself to Caitlyn and me, it was more than worth getting us up early the following morning to get my suit cleaned. By nineteen hundred hours, we left our flat to go to whatever venue we were asked to go to.

It all turned out to be somebody's residence—a private party for someone important. Once we arrive, Caitlyn introduces Gabrielle and me to our host and spouse, along with their guests. Then, we are offered some food for our trouble. Finally, at twenty-one hundred hours, Gabrielle sings for the hosts and their guests, usually with a three-piece band hired by Caitlyn. Her first event was the only time she didn't have one.

At one hundred hours, she will finish her set and mingle with her host, and her band will join me in some dark corner. At two hundred hours, we are done. After helping the musicians pack up, we headed for home, thankfully without Caitlyn. By three hundred hours, we are ready to sleep. Gabby goes to sleep first. For myself, I brought my suit to a cleaner for service. When that is done, I join Gabrielle.

Caitlyn had wanted us to understand the history of Gotham. How they flourished while being surrounded by the fall of humanity. Those are her words, not mine. Fortunately, we were spared Caitlyn's company for this event. She had left the address with Gabrielle. It was in Quadrant 4, Yellow Level 9, Section 13. If you haven't figured it out already, Gotham Prime had its system to get around in. Once we figured out that Gotham Prime is divided into twelve quadrants, the rest was easy. Still, it took us nearly half an hour to make it to where they were showing this documentary. Something called a Palace.

A woman in her seventies gave us the tickets that Caitlyn had reserved for us. Looking at my ticket it had no clear marking on it, just a black oblong thing the size of my thumb, with a little slit on one end. We took turns giving out tickets to a man younger than Gabrielle. While glaring at Gabby, he told us where our seats were. Flattered, she smiled at the young man. Trying to hide my jealousy, I led her inside the theater and to our seats.

Our seats were in the middle of the set of seats. In front of us is a giant screen about the size of a fully grown tree and as wide as our flat. It had nothing on it right now. But what truly impressed me the most was the ceiling. A giant painting depicts a strange act with thirteen men holding different banners surrounding one half-naked woman holding a banner that is larger than all the men's. I guess she is somehow their ruler. Each man had a distinct look about them. Above this gathering, sitting on its perch is a large eagle with a white head and black body. I had seen them occasionally in the Wastelands, doing their best to create a life for themselves. On the bottom of the gathering stood two other men with a young woman in modest clothes, pointing to the left. Whoever painted this must have worked for years on it. More importantly, he wasn't afraid of heights.

Promptly at 1400 hours, this documentary of Gotham began.

In a mundane tone, a male narrator announces every borough of Gotham.

It listed: Gotham Prime, York, Brunswick, Richmond, Northpoint, Queens, Newtown, Eastpoint, Dukes, Islander, Atlantic, Jersey, Midland, Tidewater, Hampton, Southpoint, Westpoint, Central, Union, Dominion, Keystone, Farpoint, Columbia, Oldtown, Capital, Lancaster, and Princeton.

It mentions that forty million people live comfortably and contentedly within Gotham City limits. This narrator never visited Red Level, I guess. His praises didn't end there. With pride, he proclaimed that Gotham, through constant vigilance and tenacity through technology, saved civilization.

Then he told us how. Giving us the history of Gotham. It started in 1629. When colonists come from a country across the sea, that is long dead. The following four hundred years witnessed wars, triumphs, and tragedies. Finally came the Four Horsemen. Desolation moved across the land in the center of a vast country. Forcing a mass Exodus to regions that still had fertile lands. As their government fell under the strain of this terrible disaster. Instead of welcoming the refugees coming to their lands and helping those who had lost everything. People on both coasts attacked the refugees. Expanding the Wastelands.

Back home, when I was in school. We were taught to be ashamed of our response to the refugees. Here in Gotham, they are proud of their defense of civilization. That is what the narrator called it, not me. As Gotham expanded, it built giant walls to keep outsiders out. That is when they discovered they needed migrants to replenish their workforce, for reasons known to the leadership living in Purple Levels. That is why they generously let us in. Somehow, I don't find myself very grateful. One thing I didn't know was that the Four Horsemen were entirely created by humans. That is something they are determined not to repeat. I hope they are committed to that promise, at least. One last thing I learned: the year is 2362 CE. I'm not sure what CE is, but I'm sure it is very important.

When the house lights came up, I checked my watch and saw we had been there for nearly five hours. Standing up, I looked over at Gabrielle. Holding out my hand, I helped her up, for a moment, because she was sitting for so long, her legs gave out for a moment, but she used me to steady herself. When she was ready, we left the Palace and headed for home.

We were outside our flat when I remembered my suit was ready. I told her I had to go out for a while. She offered to go with me, but I assured her that it wasn't necessary. Kissing her on her cheek, I left her there.

Twenty minutes later, I made it home. Walking into our living room, I called Gabby. There was no answer. Placing my clean suit on the sofa, I started to look for her. Looking in the kitchen, it was clear she wasn't there. Calling out again for her, I waited for an answer. There was no response. Growing concerned, I looked for her in a study, and she wasn't there. What made me concerned was that she was never there. Finally, I rushed over to our bedroom, it was my last hope. The door was closed, and I opened the door. Lying on her back, in her underwear, Gabrielle was crying. I had never seen her cry before. Nothing seemed to faze her in the two years I had known her. Dropping my suit at the cleaners, I sat beside her. She looked over at me, she tried to control her tears.

"Gabby what's wrong?"

She sat up and hugged me firmly around my neck. It felt as if she let go, she was afraid of losing me. Gently, I placed my arms around her waist. To reassure her, I wasn't going anywhere. She finally answered, "Caitlyn was here waiting for us. She was angry. She told me never to disobey her again."

"How did we disobey her?"

"She had selected a dress for me to wear for the event. Not to look like a common slut." Placing her head on my chest, she continued, "She said if I disobey her again. There are dark places in the city where she can put us." Raising her head, she looked into my eyes. I saw her sad green eyes surrounded by red from her tears. She added, "She will make it so that we will never see each other again."

"That won't happen today. I'll go talk to her."

"Please don't."

"Find. I'll wait tomorrow."

I laid her down gently so she could sleep. Kissing her forehead, she smiled at me. Trying not to disturb her, I lay down beside her and watched her fall asleep. Turning off the light. I decided to sleep on the couch. I couldn't help but think about Caitlyn and her threats. What is her plan for Gabrielle? Tomorrow, we will find out.

At nine hundred hours in the morning. We had doctor's appointments. The clinic that Caitlyn had chosen for us was along Grey Section in Quadrant 3, level 2. To keep the peace with Caitlyn, I asked her what she would wear. She replied, "Just be there on time." That we did.

Inside the clinic, we found Caitlyn waiting for us. Standing next to her was her executive assistant, Sonja Beaumont. I found her to be a good ten years older than Caitlyn. Her blond hair showed signs of gray and was curly. Other than that, there wasn't much to distinguish the two women.

Sonja stepped forward to rush me to my examination, leaving Caitlyn to attend to Gabby. Without saying a word, she rushed me to a room and told me to wait. And so I did. When the doctor came in, he asked me some questions. I answered it as best I could. Satisfied, he left, and my examination was over. I headed back to the reception room and sat down.

Looking around, I found I was alone. As I checked my watch, I found my appointment lasted twelve minutes exactly. Immediately, I found out that Gabby's examination was going to take longer. Not that I minded. She had been fatigued since we arrived in Gotham.

After half an hour had passed, Sonja entered the room. I guess the dress code that Gabrielle was under didn't apply to her executive assistant. She wore black slacks and a white blouse. Not very stylish if you ask me. Sitting next to me, she said, "Gabrielle will be out in a few minutes."

"Anything wrong with her?" I asked her.

"No. The doctor is giving her a potion for her fatigue. She will be like herself in a couple of hours." I couldn't help but think she was hiding something from me. I don't know what it was.

Looking around, I decided to change the subject. "Where is everybody?"

Amused, she replied, "This is a private clinic."

For some reason, that satisfied me. I just sat back and waited for Gabby. Twenty minutes later, she came out with Caitlyn. She was pale and sleepy. I immediately got up and tried to see if she was okay. Caitlyn reassured us that she needed to rest for a little while. She is in perfect health. Again, I had no reason to challenge her. Gabby reassured me before I found a reason. Thinking of her, I quietly took her home.

———————

At noon, a deliveryman arrived at the door. He had a new dress for Gabrielle that he placed on a table. Then he pulled some instructions from his pocket and handed them to me. I tipped him and escorted him out. When I returned, Gabby was already trying on the dress. It was a long green dress that hugged her body perfectly. Below the knees, a slit loosens up around her legs so she can walk around. It had a low neckline that covered her shoulders but was cut in a long V that was between her breasts. Her arms were bare. Turning around, she revealed her back to be bare. It was good seeing her smile again.

She handed me the letter that came with her dress. I read it quickly. It is a formal invitation to a formal presentation to society. I looked at Gabby for an explanation. She didn't know either. So, we will find out together. We are expected to be there at seven, and a hairdresser and makeup artist will arrive at four. Caitlyn said not to be late.

By six, Gabrielle was ready. Her hair was long and curly, which made her elegant. Taking her by the arm, we headed to the address. It is at Purple levels. An escort led us to the ballroom that held twenty-five well-dressed young men. Caitlyn stood next to the door, waiting for us. She immediately saw us. Rushing over to greet us. She wore a modest black dress. Still attractive, she didn't want to compete with Gabrielle. Immediately, she escorted a host of young women, all younger than Gabrielle but just as beautiful.

Caitlyn began to introduce the other woman she planned to present. The first is Savannah Tower, twenty-two, the oldest of the group. Shaking my hand, I noticed she was quite pretty, with short auburn hair and a round face. She wore a long red dress that covered her thin figure. Exchanging greetings, I turned to the next young woman.

Caitlyn introduced her as Kayla Rivers. She was a short woman with very long blond hair neatly placed over her right shoulder, which covered her low-cut dress. Her dark purple dress was held up by thin straps over her shoulders, which succeeded in showcasing her perfect figure. Barely twenty, she gave me a sense of her being manufactured.

It was the same with the next young woman, Naomi Smith, age nineteen. Taller than Kayla, with her beautiful black hair that she had in place, which hid its actual length. Her red dress fell on her thin body. Shaking her hand, I looked into her cold grey-blue eyes, which had given her a sense of mystery, and with a smile from her red lips, I found myself being invited to try to solve. Stepping over my foot to get away, I slid over to the next one.

The next woman was Isabella Navarre, I found her to have the body of a woman and the face of a little girl. Her black dress covered much of her olive skin. Her dark brown hair was treated, revealing her amber eyes. When she mentioned that she was twenty-two, I didn't believe her.

Caitlyn next introduced Selene Long. She was a stunning sight. Twenty-one years old, she had cinnamon skin, dark brown eyes, and an even darker mane of jet-black hair that covered her shoulders. Her navy blue dress fitted tightly on her body. She was neither tall nor short, but she was stunning.

Finally, Caitlyn introduced Elizabeth Hall. She was almost as tall as Gabrielle, with long, straight, strawberry-blonde hair that almost fell to her feet. Her dress matched her perfect blue eyes. Her skin had a rusty complexion. She was twenty-one years old.

Now finished with the introductions, Caitlyn had Gabrielle join her line of seven beauties. Proudly, she turned to her collection of young women and stated, "Now go on and mingle." The women obeyed. Gabrielle hesitated for a moment but obeyed. After they left, Caitlyn turned to me and asked, "What do you think of my menagerie, Duncan?"

"Stunning," I replied. I don't know what menagerie meant, but I wasn't going to tell her that.

"Yes, they are. I'm sorry, but you must stay here and watch the door," she said, pointing at a chair for me to sit. That is what I did.

Cast aside, I sat down and watched Caitlyn join the party. While I remained alone, I watched as crowds of men gathered around each of the girls. For the next two hours, it became clear to me that most of the men gravitated over to Gabby. Not that I blamed them. But I still felt a little jealous.

Two hours later, the party was still going strong. Twenty young men had to share eight young women. I knew this because I counted each one. I had nothing else to do. All I could think of was that I wished I had eaten something before I came here because I was starving, and I didn't dare ask for some food. So, I sat there waiting to go home.

Frequently, Gabby looked over my way, giving me a sympathetic smile. I just gave her a return smile. Sometimes, she tried to come over to accompany me. But every time, she was intercepted. So, I just sat and looked at the door.

My eyes then glanced over at Savanah as she was talking to Caitlyn. They were too far away for me to hear them. But with Savannah glancing over at me, I had a feeling it was about me. Once Caitlyn finished, Savannah nervously walked over to me and sat down next to me. Making herself comfortable, she looked at me and smiled.

"Caitlyn told me to come over and try to seduce you."

"I see," I stated, taken aback by her honesty. "Did she say why?"

"Not really. But I think she considers you a threat to her plans."

"What are her plans?"

Looking away, she confessed, "She has plans for each of us." Glancing over at her six sisters, she said, "Caitlyn believes that we should be Gotham's rulers."

"How does she plan to do that?"

She answered, "I'm not sure." She slowly turned to me and shyly added, "We are all pawns in her game."

Her strange honesty was refreshing. She lowered her eyes like she was afraid of something. She is strangely shy. So, I had to ask, "Do you want to seduce me?"

Raising her head, she turned to me and smiled, "I must admit it would be a pleasurable thought. You are handsome. But I find this action distasteful."

I was flattered. I smiled at her to thank her for her kind compliments. Rising to her feet, she looked at me and gave me a closing warning, "Well, that is enough tonight. Just to let you know, Caitlyn told all six of us about you and her desire to remove you. So, all six of us will try to tempt. So be careful."

"What will she do when you all fail?"

"I don't know."

In saying that, she walked away. She passed Gabrielle, giving her a slight acknowledgment. She looked over at me. Emotionless, she walked over to a table that held their buffet. I watched her take a plate and fill it with a generous amount of food. Once satisfied, she walked over to me and sat down where Savannah had sat. She handed me the plate and a fork. I thanked her.

"Should I be jealous?" she asked while I started to eat.

I wasn't surprised, as you may have expected, I replied, "Since she came over to try to seduce me."

Amused, she replied, "Was she that obvious?"

"Not really, she told me," I added calmly. Gabrielle had a sense of relief, so I added, "She is very honest. I do like her." She gave me a dirty look, so I confessed, "She warned me to be careful with Caitlyn."

She looked over at Caitlyn. She didn't look surprised. "She is parading us around for something."

Caitlyn glanced over at us. She is annoyed with her. But she couldn't come and confront us at this moment. Gabrielle had to return to the party. I smiled at her as she rose from her seat. As she walked away, I watched her. For the first time, I wondered if I could lose her. She stayed with me all around her and was the cream of Gotham society. Capable of giving her everything she deserved. Things I can't give her. I decided to wait for this evening to end.

An hour had passed when Caitlyn joined me. Sitting down in the seat of her charges, she just smiled. But this is no social call. "I need you to chaperone the girls on their dates. Monday, we have been invited to watch the Gotham cagers in their match with York."

"I'll be ready when you need me," I said calmly.

"I'll make the arrangements."

After saying that, she was off, back to her party. I believe she is like me. Right now, this is the closest we will ever get to this world of the ruling class. Although she is closer than I am. I am sure she has that as a small consolation.

At 200 hours in the morning. Our night had finally finished. Catlyn gathered his charges and brought them over to me. I was to escort each woman home. Luckily, all six lived close by to Gabby and me. Making it a little bit easier for me. It still took us an hour to get home.

Inside our home, neither of us could do anything else but go to bed.

The next day, we woke up at 1130, and our lunch awaited us. We ate in the same clothes we wore last night. Neither of us wanted to get out of them, so we slept in our fine clothes. I'm sure Caitlyn will have something to say about that. But this time, she will not know about it.

After we had eaten, we started to get dressed. Gabby took the first shower while I waited in the living room. I chose to watch something on the view screen. Nothing was happening in the outside world of note. A radiant older woman in a monotone voice went through a list of mundane events in a monotone voice. As I watched her, I couldn't help thinking she wasn't real. Something called a hologram. As I traveled through the city for the past year, I saw examples of this hologram doing several minor assignments.

For now, it doesn't matter. Gabrielle had left the bathroom. Now it was my turn. She had her hair wrapped in a towel so it could dry faster. She looked relaxed in her flowered printed robe. Not wanting to waste any time, I just grabbed some clothes and a towel and headed right in. Twenty minutes later, I exited the shower and proceeded to get dressed.

I had just finished dressing when the doorbell rang. Opening the door, I saw a small young man about nineteen standing in front of me.

"Clothes," he inquired.

"Yes, just a minute," I stated, gathering Gabby's dress from last night and my suit. Promptly, I returned to the young man, "Here you go. Nothing special. I'll pick it up when it is ready."

"Understood." After that, he left.

I shut the door and headed for the kitchen to get something to eat. Gabby joined me a few minutes later. I cooked some eggs and bacon. Nothing fancy, but it hit the spot.

At thirteen hundred hours, we had the expected delivery. Again, it was a different courier that Caitlyn had sent. He was a short, anxious young man who remained silent as he placed Gabby's new dress and a letter with our new event. Before he could manage to place it on the table, Gabby held out her hand.

"I'll take that."

Fear came over his face as he looked at her. Like he just glanced at something forbidden that will cost him his life for daring to glance at Gabrielle Blue. He tried to speak, as he tried to form words, finally, he gave up and placed it gently in her hand. Amused, Gabby smiled and thanked him. He just ran out, and I shut the door behind him.

Gabrielle opened the package; with a puzzled look, she pulled it out and held it up. It was a pretty dress, less formal than other dresses Caitlyn had provided.

"Try it on. I'll open the letter."

She handed me the envelope. Stepping into her dressing room, I opened it quickly, I immediately smiled; we had two passes for a Cager's game tonight. York will visit Gotham at nineteen hundred hours. Gabrielle came back into the room wearing the dress. She adjusted her dress a little bit.

"It fits all right. How does it look?"

She gave her dress to me. Her dress fitted her tightly right up to just above her knees, with patches of red and blue. So, I answered her, "It is perfect for where we are going."

"Where are we going tonight?"

"We have a private suite," I said. "Gotham will be facing York."

"Why are they doing that?"

"It is a Cagers game."

A look of disappointment came over her. After a dozen lavish parties where she was the center of attention. Now the attention will be on twenty-four guys on the field, not on her. But she did enjoy the game.

"I think this is for you."

"I strongly doubt that."

We arrived at our suite twenty minutes before the challenge. Caitlyn and the others were already there, seated. When she saw us, Caitlyn came over and greeted us. Without hesitation, she led over to a small table with a group of three men. She managed to get their attention. Immediately, they turned to greet their new honored guest.

"Gentlemen, may I present Gabrielle Blue and Duncan Walker?" she said. "Gabrielle, this is George Burger, the owner of the Gotham cagers." He immediately shook her hand. Caitlyn had two more young men to introduce. "This is his son William and Eric."

They eagerly shook her hand.

"Tell me, Gabrielle, are you a fan?"

"I haven't decided," she stated. Looking at me, she added, "Duncan is the expert."

He turned to me with his eyes lit up. "So, Mister Walker, are you a fan?"

All three looked at me eagerly, waiting for my response. "I am," I said, "a Southpoint fan."

Eric, the youngest, was curious, "Why?"

"We lived in Southpoint for almost a year. That is the team I was introduced to."

My explanation satisfied them. The elder Burger stated politely, "I hope you enjoy the game. It should be exciting."

In saying that, they headed for their seats. I did the same and sat next to Gabrielle. Sitting at the end of a row. I leaned over to greet the other girls in her little group. I looked over to see where Caitlyn was sitting. I wasn't surprised where I found her, sitting beside William Burger, whispering in his ear. Relieved, I sat back in my seat, making myself comfortable.

As the game started, both teams came out to their respective sides. York wore their visiting white jerseys and grey pants and stood on the far sideline. Standing on the opposite sideline with their backs to us stood Gotham in their home blue jerseys and red pants. That reminded me of something. Amused, I looked over at all six of the girls. They all wore clothes with the same color scheme, red and blue. Leaning over to Gabrielle, I shared my discovery. She looked over at me and frowned, she already knew how silly they looked. I don't know about looking silly, but they did look like they belonged.

At the center of the field, the lead official called over the opposing captains. Two members of each team answered the call. York, as the visitors, won the toss and wanted a challenge; it seems that it is the newest trend.

Following the official's direction, the starting seven take their positions on the field. Holding the ball, the lead official stood at the center of the field as he awaited the opposing players surrounding the circle. The players stood on opposite sides of the circle. The lead official was a small man who looked like a former player himself. Satisfied, he placed the ball at the center of the circle. To avoid the coming mayhem, he cleared out. As the players crouch in anticipation for the game to start. Taking his position, the official decided to milk this moment. All around the stadium, a silence came over the spectators. Gabrielle looked at me, puzzled about what was going on. I just told her to be patient.

The lead official blew his whistle. In one move, the two captains collided over the ball. Somehow, the York player managed to gain possession of the ball, escaping the circle. He passed the ball behind him to a teammate. The two players then charged down the field and scored the first goal. Allowing them to maintain possession.

One thing is abundantly clear: York and Gotham are long-time rivals, and their play certainly showed that. After the first half, York held a slim lead over Gotham at 10-9. Caitlyn returned to us right after the whistle sounded. She wanted her girls to join the Burgers and their guests. One by one, they stood up and obeyed her request. When it was Gabrielle's turn, she looked over to me and said, "Are you coming?"

Looking over at Caitlyn, she silently made it clear that I was not welcome, so I replied, "I'm all right for now."

Gabrielle stood up and went on ahead of Caitlyn. I glanced over and watched Caitlyn force the women to mingle with Burger and his guest. One thing is clear: his two sons are not interested in the score of the game. While their father was on a call. From his chaotic gestures, I could easily tell it was for business. Not that anyone was noticing his distress; Gabrielle and her friends made sure of that. I just watched it, making sure that Gabrielle and the others were safe.

The time between hafts is exactly twenty minutes. I know because the scoreboard counted down the twenty minutes. With amazing punctuality, the small party behind me had broken up and returned to their seats. Gabrielle returned to her seat. She reached over and squeezed my hand. There it stayed as we watched the second half. Gotham started for the next forty-five minutes and made a frantic attempt to take the lead. With a brilliant drive, they scored, earning the right to maintain their possession. But York rallied and retook possession. With two quick scores, York placed themselves firmly in the lead. Somehow, they held it for the remainder of the game. York won 24-20.

This made the majority of the sixty thousand fans very unhappy. I looked around and saw that many in our sweatshirts held the same disappointment. Satisfied, I leaned over to Gabrielle and whispered in her ear, "I don't think they are in the mood to socialize. Let's go home." Turning her head over to me, she smiled and nodded her approval. We left for home.

———————

At home, we relaxed in our living room. Gabrielle had poured some wine on herself before she sat down. I just had a glass of water. Not wanting to be disturbed, we made sure that the notification system was shut off. Just in case Caitlyn wanted to know where we had gone after the game.

"So, this is what you kept from me with your friends."

"I didn't think you would like it."

Finishing her wine. She joined me on the sofa. She responded, "I'm beginning to see why you like it."

"Good. Because I have an idea you will be attending A few games this season." I told her.

"Jealous."

"Yes, I am.'

Gabrielle moved closer to me. Placing her arms around my neck. Moving her mouth to my ear, she whispered, "Good." Saying that she kissed me on my lips. I placed my arms around her waist. She leaned forward, forcing me to lie on my back.

Pulling away, she smiled and unfastened my shirt. She then lowered her mouth and began to kiss my chest. Thinking this is quite odd. I lifted my hands to the top of the dress and unzipped it. She pulled herself away and slipped out of her dress. Naked, she kissed me on my lips. Her hands proceeded to pull down my pants. Standing up, she held out her hand. I took it and lifted myself to my feet. Holding her hands, I leaned in on her and kissed her. Pulling away, she smiled and turned towards our bedroom. She led me into the room and shut the door behind us.

3   THE SEARCH

THAT MORNING, WE CHOSE TO HAVE BREAKFAST AT A LOCAL diner. We both dress in casual clothes. Today, we didn't care if we violated any rules set down by Caitlyn. As I sat there looking at Gabrielle, she never looked more beautiful. It reminded me of the first time I had met her two years ago on a summer day. She had no makeup on and wore nothing exotic. Just a simple cotton dress and her hair not touched by outside hands.

The restaurant had a patio, so we felt the sun as we ate. After a little more than a year of recycled air, it was pleasing to feel a cool breeze again. It is funny when you realize how much you miss something simple like a cool summer breeze. What made this morning stand out was that we were allowed to sit and enjoy a tranquil day like this. Outside of Gotham, it was a constant struggle to survive. Two hours later, we were still eating, not wanting to leave. Finally, our server was forced by her manager to give us a gentle push-along.

We paid our bill and walked out into the city. After taking a lift down to three levels, we walked home. Opening the door, I was surprised not to find Caitlyn sitting in one of our chairs waiting for us. Ready to scold us for violating our contract. But she wasn't there. Gabby sighed in relief. She decided to get dressed. I sat down on the couch, placing my feet up, and taking a book off the shelf, I began to read it.

An hour later, the doorbell rang. I immediately got up and answered the door. Standing in front of me was the same young man who had brought over Gabrielle's package and instructions. Today, he had only instructions in an envelope. Neither did he want to come in. He just stood at the door holding out the envelope for me to take. Afraid that he might again have a forbidden glance at the goddess Gabrielle. Those are my thoughts, not his.

Amused, I just smiled and took the envelope. I thanked him, he gave me a nervous smile and ran to the lift. I just shut the door. I return to the living room where Gabrielle is waiting for me.

"Who was it?" she asked. She chose black pants and a red sleeveless shirt.

Holding out the envelope, I just replied, "Your admirer brought you this."

Taking the envelope out of my hands, she opened it and read it. Looking up at me, she stated, "It seems you're in luck. You have the next few days off." Her demeanor changed with a look of disappointment. "I have three seminars for the next three days."

"When does it start?"

"Fifteen hundred hours. It is for four hours."

"Does it say what it's about?"

"I'll find out when I get there," she said. "What are you going to do?"

I thought for a moment about what to do. I had an afternoon off. I then remembered a promise we made a long time ago. I had wanted to go with Gabrielle, but Caitlyn had made that impossible. I just added, "I think it is time to visit Harry and Deborah."

"I wish I could go."

"Do you have a message for me to give?"

"Invite them to come over with their family. It's time we had guests over."

I agreed.

I left an hour before Gabby had to leave. She looked at me, still disappointed that she couldn't go with me. I just gave her a quick kiss goodbye and headed out.

I still had the card our friends had given us. It is the address of her daughter, her husband, and their children. I read the address: Central District, Blue level 10 Sector 9, section A.'

Checking the local view screen after giving it some information, it showed me exactly where their apartment was. It didn't take me long to find their flat. It overlooked a vast green space about half the size of Capital Green. Taking a moment to look down at the trees that were dwarfed by manmade mountains that surrounded them. Curiosity came over me to find out if the masses were not allowed to visit this green oasis like in Capital. I couldn't tell. Thinking it wasn't important, I walked over to the door. I pushed a button to let the occupants know I was at the door. A few minutes later, a young woman answered.

"Can I help you?" she stated, not sure what to make of me. Looking at her, I was amazed that she was a younger version of Deborah.

"My name is Duncan Walker," I said. "I am a friend of Deborah and Henry."

Excited, she opened the door, revealing her red shirt and pants. "Mom and Dad, "her husband from another room inquired who was at the door, she repeated what I had told her. Remembering I was still outside, she invited me in.

Walking in her husband, an athletic, dark-skinned man a few inches shorter than I, joined us. He walked over to me and shook my hand. Inviting me to sit down, the couple sat across from me.

"I'm sorry for taking so long to call. My friend and I have been settled in Southpoint for the past year. They looked at each other with skepticism, like they didn't believe my story. I decided to give them some proof. "Your name is. Ester. And you are Jordan. They talked about you and their three grandchildren, Mary, Edmund, and Chandler, almost every day."

Ester added, "We have another child, Anne, she is three now."

"Congratulations"

She smiled. But her husband wasn't completely convinced. "Where did you know them?"

"Outside Southpoint," I replied, "We spent over two weeks together in line."

I went on to explain about the masses of people who are trying to get into Gotham. How we join forces with other people to share our food and water. More importantly, we keep our place in line while we defend our place against those who would want to cut in front of us. Then some have their sole purpose is to preying on the people who are waiting to enter the city. I finished by revealing that there were nine of us in our group.

Ester then revealed, "They were contracted to find a site for a possible new settlement that will connect the four junctions with one of our own. They decided to stay later, to help the inhabitants. My mother wrote to me saying their pass had expired."

"They did mention that." Looking around, I became curious. "Where are Deborah and Henry?"

Jordan interrupted forcefully, "Don't you know? You said we're all in line together. It was a year ago." Ester tried to calm him down.

"We became separated," I stated, I did understand what they had been going through for the past few years. Not knowing what had happened to them. I am becoming concerned about their fate myself. "A group of men came to offer a quicker way into Gotham. One of our group, a man called Mitchel assured everybody it was safer. Your parents and the others went with them. Only my friend Gabrielle and I stayed in line."

"Why didn't you go?" inquired Jordon, regaining his calm.

"I didn't trust them. I told the others, but they didn't believe me."

Judging others is an important trait for survival in the Wastelands. You must learn it quickly, and you can never be wrong. I hoped they didn't want me to go deeper into how I knew they were dangerous. I didn't want to confess that I was one of those sinister wanderers ready to kill for whatever stolen goods I could use to last another day. Thankfully, they didn't require me to explain further.

Ester revealed, "They never came home." She lowered her head in sorrow as she began to cry. Her husband tried to comfort her.

"What do you do, Duncan Walker?" Jordan asked firmly.

"Security and Courier, mostly," I simply replied.

"We would like to hire you to find out what happened to our parents. You can set your price."

"I will be delighted. But I'll do it for free," I said. I reached over with my hand, and he grabbed it. His eyes betrayed his sorrow. Softly, I stated, "I'll see myself out." Standing up, I walked to the door. Before I opened it, I felt compelled to say one more thing: "I'll keep you posted."

Heading out to the walkway, I headed home. Gabrielle would want to hear about this.

––––––––––

I made it home an hour before Gabrielle was due home. Immediately, I went to work to get supper ready for her. Neither of us liked to cook since we arrived in the city. Not out of laziness after all we did cook our food out in the Wastelands. We just became spoiled living in Gotham, the food is just better than what we can do.

Using the view screen, I ordered two dishes of parmesan, one chicken, and one eggplant with mushrooms. It is from a little restaurant two blocks from us. During the short time we have been living here, we have made that place our official go-to place for a quiet bite to eat. After paying for the food, I requested it to be delivered at 1930. Finish, I went into the kitchen to see if we had some wine. I checked the storage closet and found a bottle of merlot. I placed it on the shelf. Walking away, I started to clean a bit. Lastly, I set the table, placing the wine next to where Gabrielle will be sitting.

Right on time she came home. As I expected she was tired. She sat down. Silently I just opened the bottle and poured two glasses of wine. Walking back to the living room I handed her a glass of wine. She looked up and smiled, I sat down, taking a drink. I waited for her to do the same. When she finally took a sip, I thought it was safe to ask.

Not wanting to start with some bad news, I asked, "How was your seminar?"

"Boring."

Amused, I continued with my inquiry, "Was it for all of you?"

"That made it bearable," she said, "we have to do the same thing all day tomorrow" Taking a drink from her glass she is clearly frustrated, "I really don't know what Caitlyn has in mind for us."

I tried to hide my smile. I thought it was clear what Caitlyn was planning. I don't like it very much, but for now, I must endure her plans for Gabrielle.

Wanting to hear happier news, she asked, "How are Deb and Henry?"

I paused for a moment. I didn't want to ruin her day further. But she deserves the right to know about the fate of our friends. "They didn't make it in."

"Mitchel assured us all that it will be easy." Looking right at me, she sadly added, "How did you know?"

"I saw markings on his body. He was branded by the Krieg." I answered.

"Who are the Krieg?"

"Murderous band of thugs," I added, "they hide behind some military façade. They are at war with the world."

"Why didn't you tell us?"

I couldn't answer that truthfully. Natalie was the reason why I never challenged him. But there is another reason, I had a chance to reform. Why should I take that chance from another person? I just said, "I'm going to look for them."

Dinner arrives on time. I placed the food on the table. We sat down and ate silently. Drinking the entire bottle. After dinner, Gabrielle looked up at me and stated, "I know you're determined to go out and find out what had happened. I just want you to be safe."

"I will."

We just sat there staring at each other. For once, we are heading into different paths.

Early the next morning I prepared myself for the day's task. I gathered my stinger and pistol; I concealed them under my jacket.

Authorities have a strange attitude with their citizens walking around with weapons. Gabrielle was still asleep. When I was ready to leave, I headed over to her to say goodbye.

Sadly, she looked up at me and said in a whisper, "You're going?"

"Yes."

"Just come back, please," she said, concerned.

"I will." I kissed her on the lips. She smiled, feeling reassured.

There I left, heading to Grey section. I needed to talk with a member of the administration. To ask them hypothetical questions hoping for me to get an answer that can give me somewhere to start.

Strangely, Gotham has a small Grey sector. It made sense considering it is surrounded by other districts. It serves as the central administration for the entire city-state. Walking inside, I surrendered my weapons and checked them in. Austen told me discretion is the better part of valor. I knew their screening devices could easily detect my weapons. Placing him in a lock box, I signed for them and showed the guard I had a license to carry the weapons. Satisfied, he let me through.

Taking the main lift to level nine, I walked into a small office. The young woman who sat behind the desk couldn't have been older than Gabrielle. Her hair is cut shorter than mine as she busied herself with what task lay in front of her on her view screen as she states her commands. Her skin is pale, from being trapped in this office for ten hours a day, I surmised. As I stood there patiently, I waited for the moment when she was ready to deal with me. I discovered she has shy beauty in her modest features.

Finishing her work, she looked up at me and said politely, "Please, sit down." I did as she asked, after apologizing for keeping me waiting, she asked, "May I have your name?"

"Duncan Walker" she entered my name, followed up with my other information that I was giving while I was being processed over a year ago. When the information came up, she smiled and turned to me.

"How can I help you, Mister Walker?"

"As your system had shown you, I was allowed in Southpoint."

She nodded, so I continued, "There were originally nine of us who wanted to come in. My friend Gabrielle and I entered the city. The other seven decided to find a quicker way north."

A look of concern came over her face. "And they didn't make it in."

"Two of them didn't. I don't know about the others."

She moved closer to me; I expected that she wanted to tell me something that was both unpleasant and private. "We have only one other entrance area along the western districts, and that is at Westpoint. And that is much like Southpoint.

"If you wanted to smuggle people in, where can that be?"

Quietly she turned back to her viewscreen. After giving it a few directions, it gave her the answer she wanted, turning her chair to me and she showed me a map of Gotham and the surrounding districts. "Right here."

I looked over the map she had shown me. I saw what she had met immediately. A small, narrow river that separates Gotham Prime from Jersey. Its source begins outside the territory of the city. Some very opportunistic people can ferry a boatload of people inside the walls of Gotham and be let off safely in the heart of the city. Where they are allowed to disappear in the crowd. Now I know how they did. Next, I must find where they drop off their human cargo.

"Where would they land?"

Promptly, she again placed new information into her viewscreen. A second later, it gave her its findings. She then pointed at the possible spot. "Right here. The wharves are still intact but are not in use."

Now I know where to go next. But I had to have some other information. I stated, "It will take them a week to get to the little port and a day to travel by boat. But why didn't they make it in?"

"Did any of your friends have any money?" she asked as her tone had changed in her voice.

"Not much on him," I answered, "two of them had money in the bank." She remained quiet not expecting that answer, "They had lived here for most of their lives here. The only reason why they had left was to create a new district. Their mistake was they decided to stay out past their visa."

"Why," I asked her, if they are citizens, they should be allowed in, visa or none.

"Junction District is controversial," she explained, knowing she had to go further, "It is planned to allow the Clans direct access to enter into the city for trade."

Train People? Why would letting them enter the city for trade be a bad thing? It all seemed strange to me. "I don't understand."

She sat back in the chair. Her demeanor became more honest with her answer, "Gotham resources are limited. They are afraid that they will give an easy way into the city. We will be flooded by people they don't want." She shook her head in frustration. "Damn bureaucrats!" I tried to pretend to know what that word meant. Her mannerism changed again. She gave me a cynical look, "And you are charging a fair price from their daughter."

"I'm not charging them anything. Just keeping a promise."

That surprised her. Her demeanor changed to one of indecision. She wanted to believe me, but I guess living here had made her cold. But she had thought I earned this. "You may want to have them check their financial records. It will explain a lot."

"I will," I assured her.

"Why are you doing this?" she asked me bluntly.

"Have you ever had a good night's sleep?" I asked her.

Surprised by my choice to answer with a question, she replied, "Yes."

"That is a rare thing living in the Wastelands," I replied to her. I then added, "For two weeks we slept peacefully." She somehow understood my response. How can you explain something that never lived out there? Each of us living out there in the line kept the others safe. Even Mitchel, when he had guard duty, kept us safe. That is why the others trusted him. Alone, I had to sleep lightly with a weapon close by in case intruders might come across us.

With nothing more to say, I thanked her. She left her desk and shook my hand. She had a request: "I would like to inform the Watchmen."

"Please."

She smiled as I left after I thanked her for her help. At the security point, I retrieved my weapons and my license.

Once outside, I immediately called Ester. After reminding her who I was, I asked her, "Can you check your parents' accounts?"

She stated, "It will take some time."

I told her where she could get hold of me. And I went off.

Fortunately, the two wharves are not that far away from Grey Headquarters. I made it at 1410. It was abandoned. Looking around, I tried to find any signs of a boat. I felt a strong wind being funneled between the large buildings, making a stronger breeze. It succeeded in making the air a few degrees cooler than inside Gotham. On the river, the water became active because of the wind. Looking closer at the first wharf, I looked closely at the closest point of the water and the wharf. I noticed that the four locking points have been active recently. Next, I went to the second dock. Heading down to the second wharf, I again noticed the locking disc had been used recently.

Something told me I was not alone. I carefully reached for my gun. When I heard, "Dishonest men don't usually work during the day."

I turned around keeping my gun in its place. There I saw a tall robust man about fifty, well dressed and clean shaving. Not sure who he was, I kept my distance. I wanted him to make the next move. He stated, "City living has dulled your senses. I was watching you for nearly half an hour."

Taking my hand away from my pistol. Allowed him to step down and move closer to where I'm standing with a lecturing tone he continued, "I've seen it before with children of the Wastelands. Give them a taste of easy living and they start to lose all their survival skills."

"I didn't think I needed them anymore."

Amused, he just looked over at the water next to him. "You may find that Gotham can be more dangerous than the darkest realms of your homeland."

"I wasn't born in the Wasteland."

Ignoring my statement, he looked at me and stated, "Your training came in handy keeping Commissioner Fletcher safe. Well done."

Surprised, I asked, "How do you know about that?"

"When I'm dealing with somebody new. I like to know whom I'm dealing with" he added, "Inspector Xander Wells." He held out is hand, I immediately took it, and he stated, "Duncan Walker."

Moving away from me, he stepped closer to the water. Looking north, he inquired, "What is your interest in this case?"

Joining him, I answered, "They were friends."

"How much is their family paying you?"

"Nothing," I answered, "when you spent sixteen days standing in line with a mass of humanity. You become close. We had promised to get together when we made it in. But life happens."

A look of admiration showed through his smile, "We have several gangs transporting people into Gotham without being processed. The majority bring them in for a fee upfront. Once inside, they disappear into the population. But they must continue to pay for the rest of their lives."

"What happens to the minority of gangs?" I asked, already expecting the answer.

He confirmed my worst fears, "They will take all they own and kill the lucky ones." Before I could ask about the unlucky ones, "There are other terrors in the city."

"What's next?"

"We need to identify the gang first. Do you mind coming tomorrow and looking through some suspects?"

"I'll be there."

"I say 1000."

"I'll be there."

He gave me his address. We then shook hands and parted ways.

An hour later I made it home. Gabrielle wasn't home. I found a message waiting for me. As I played the message it was Ester. She confirmed what I had feared. Her parents' accounts have been emptied. I sent a reply thanking her for her help. I didn't want to tell her about my fears in case I was wrong.

Gabrielle came home a few minutes later. Fatigued, she just

wanted to go to bed. I couldn't help but wonder what Caitlyn had put her through. I never saw Gabrielle this tired. That doctor must have done something to her. What I learned today can wait until tomorrow. I followed her to bed after I ate dinner.

Tomorrow morning, we will wake up together. I told her everything I had learned over breakfast. Concerned, she asked if she could help. I told her to I'll hold you to that. Yesterday, Caitlyn told her to be on time. Not wanting to disappoint her, she left right after breakfast. Dodging my inquiries about what she had been doing the past three days. She just gave me her gentle smile instead of an answer. That is something I will have to find out when the time is right.

I made it on time for my appointment. Inspector Wells greeted me. Not one to waste any time, he immediately sat me down and started to look over pictures of gang members. They wear thousands of them. I separated possible suspects who might have been the strangers who came to visit us that day. I had told him I had only seen them briefly, over a year ago. But Gabrielle would recognize them. Finally, after two hours, I saw Natalie. Wells was pleased, now he could put a person to my recollections. With a new vigor, I looked for Mitchel. An hour later, his picture came up.

Wells put their history on a monitor. "Mitchel Kreig and Natalie Summer," he stated, "exiled four times for various crimes. They manage to find a way through our security by providing unsuspecting victims to a band of pirates."

"Pirates?"

Amused Wells stated, "Criminals who work primarily on water." I had never come across that kind of person before. Getting back to business, "Your two friends had no intention of going through processing. They would be easily discovered and sent back to exile or cast down to the underground."

I had heard of the Underground before. That is where Carlos forfeited his kidney to escape. It lies beneath Red Level. It is where

Gotham sent its citizens that it wanted to forget. It reminded me of the Wastelands.

"They were always planning to be smuggled in, using our friends to pay their way?' I asked him.

Wells replied coldly and simply, "Yes."

That made me more determined to finish looking over the remainder of their suspects. It had taken me two more hours, but I managed to finish the list. Unfortunately, I could not be positive about Natalie and Mitchel. Disappointed, I suggested my friend Gabrielle could do a better job. She has a talent for remembering faces. He handed me his file. As I stood up, I told him about what Ester had told me yesterday. Wells wasn't surprised. Saying our goodbyes, I promised to come back with what Gabrielle could remember.

An hour later, I made it home. To my surprise, I found Gabby waiting for me. Relaxing on our couch. I walked up to her and kissed her on her neck. Looking over her shoulder, she smiled.

"Surprise?"

"Was Caitlyn sick today?

"Not quite," she said as I sat down next to her, "We have a change of plan. You are escorting Niomi and me to another Cager's match, Gotham is hosting Islanders."

"Do you know why?"

"Not sure." She noticed the disc in my hand, "What's that?"

"This is a record of all the criminals who are active in the city." I handed her the disc and added, "Natalie and Mitchel are both on it." I proceeded to tell her about what I had learned so far. And what had happened to our friends? Gabrielle looked down for a moment as she wiped away her tears.

In a sullen tone, she murmured, "You wear right not to trust them."

"I wish I were wrong," I replied sadly, "You said you wanted to help. I was wondering if you could look them over."

Lifting her head, with a look of determination, she took the disc out of my hand. "Give me a moment."

She walked to the study. I just sat down on the couch watching the viewscreen and waited. Two hours later she left the study and handed me the disc. Eagerly. She gave me her full report. "I could only identify five of the seven of Mitchel's friends. I marked them down. I'm not sure about the other two."

I was amazed. Not only what had taken me a little over six hours. She did it in less than two hours. Not to mention, she had identified five members. But she acted like she had let me down. I thanked her by taking her out for dinner. It was the first time in a long while.

The next morning, I left for headquarters. I knew I was expecting to take Gabby and Naomi at sixteen hundred hours. Not wasting time, showed Wells about the five men she had identified. I assured him that Gabrielle didn't make mistakes. Impressed, he immediately checked on the identifications of the five men. When it came through the system. It confirmed Gabrielle's recollection. All five had been smuggling people, among other things, into the city for the past five years.

"What is our next step? I asked, now we know about the gang, we can do something about it to end this gang. To my surprise, Wells showed some reluctance. I wondered why he was so apprehensive.

"Sit down, Walker." I did as he requested, and now he was free to give me the bad news: "My superiors are not interested in heading outside Gotham. They believe what happens outside the city walls doesn't concern them."

I quickly reminded him, "My two friends were citizens of Gotham. And murdered trying to get back home."

"We don't know that."

"There is no other possibility," I stated, "what about if we catch them smuggling people into the city?"

"Then we can act," he stated, "but to do that we will have to have somebody reliable to work with us."

I smiled, figuring out the path he was maneuvering me to take, "I'll volunteer." Not wanting to waste any more time.

"I'll set up with my superiors. I'll get back to you within a week."

We shook hands. As I left his office to go home. I thought about what I had just volunteered for. I remember a rule that I based my life on for nearly ten years. Never stick your neck out for anyone. But times change, and so your rules must change. Cassandra, Paloma, Olivia, Deborah, and Henry are my friends. What had been their fate is a mystery I must solve. If Mitchel and Natalie had betrayed them, I would have to find out and make them pay for their treachery.

I escorted Naomi and Gabrielle to our seats. During this game, we had different luxury boxes than we did in the previous game. Caitlyn had told me about our itinerary for tonight. It was typical of Caitlyn. She wanted me to make sure that Gabrielle was to entertain Jayden Vaughn, a star player for Gotham. Naomi is to entertain the star keeper for the Islanders. Gotham wanted to entice him to join their team. Naomi could do just that. Before she left, I mentioned that Gabby was getting worse. She assured me that she would investigate it with the doctor.

Immediately after the game started, it became apparent why they wanted the Islander Keeper, Bryce Allen. He is amazing. Single-handedly, he stopped three quick scoring drives by Gotham. His obvious success enhanced Gotham's need for a new Keeper, as the poor fellow allowed three quick scores, giving the Islanders an eleven-point lead. For those who think I'm being unfair, he wasn't that impressed at the previous match. Gotham salvaged the opinion period with three points. During the second period, Gotham managed to work their way back into the game, scoring ten points. At halftime, the Islanders held a three-point lead, 16-13.

Gabrielle leaned towards me. She had quickly developed an understanding of the game. Her only problem was that she quickly became a Gotham fan as well. There is no accounting for taste. In contrast, Niomi was indifferent to the game. Not that it was a problem, but I just found it odd that Caitlyn chose her to entice a rival player to switch teams, believing her agent should at least have a basic interest in the game.

While Naomi was away, Gabrielle asked me, "What do you think?"

"I hope Naomi is up to her task," I replied.

Puzzled, Gabrielle wanted clarification. "What do you mean?"

"Gotham needs a Keeper," I replied.

With competitive outrage, she proclaims, "But we are only three points down."

"You still have the second half to play," I told her confidently. While I agree with her that Gotham has a brilliant team around them. Their keeper, who is the foundation of their defense, is terrible, to put it bluntly.

During the second half, Bryce Allen proved my assessment of Gotham's limitations. He only allowed four points against him. In contrast, Islander scored seventeen. The final score was Islanders 33 and Gotham 17. Gotham fans, including Gabrielle, were not in a good mood as they left the suite. She wanted to leave now, but I still had one more job tonight: deliver Naomi to her escort. I was glad that Gabrielle had her plans canceled.

As for Niomi, she was still indifferent until she saw Bryce Allen's likeness on the view screen. The young man was handsome; I'll give him that. About twenty-seven with light brown hair and blue eyes. Gabby agreed to wait for me, and I will walk her home.

Together, we walked down to the visiting team's dressing room. Naomi was a couple of steps ahead of me. I finally realized the young woman's dress was the same color as the Islanders' uniforms, turquoise, I think it's called. It was a silly idea of Caitlyn's to have her girls dress in these costumes, it would make no difference to the players. Maybe the owners are that full of themselves. But I do have to say it flattered the young woman's cream skin. Her long, black hair fell over her shoulders and covered her breasts. She is stunning.

A security guard stopped us before we could enter. Naomi presented herself and then added me as her escort. With her sleeveless arms, she presented the stern-looking middle-aged man with her official invite. After reading it, he smiled and let her in. With my job done. I quickly headed back to Gabby, and we went home.

Two days later, we were invited to another cager match. All the girls were expected to attend. This time, we will be heading to Queens District. They are facing their long-time rivals, Dukes. We will be the guests of Commissioner James Koch. None of the girls wanted to go, but Caitlyn insisted. And so, we went. Thankfully, the women were not wearing the teams' colors this time.

We made it twenty minutes before the match started. I remained close to Gabby when we entered the suite, which visibly annoyed Caitlyn. Not that I cared. But we stood in a reception line to be presented. I was last in line. But I still stood next to Gabby.

Commissioner James Koch, being a courteous host, allowed his special friends to meet his special guest first. A noble gesture. I watched him as if it were his turn to walk down the line. When it was Gabrielle's turn, I felt a surge of jealousy go through me.

He had to be at least thirty-six. There is no possible way he was younger than me. When he came to me and we shook hands, I tried my best to remain one inch taller than him. His tailored space made him look thinner than I did in my old clothes. To be honest, to no fault of his own, I didn't like him very much.

"This is Duncan Walker. "Caitlyn introduced him to me. "This is your host, Commissioner James Koch."

"Please to meet you, Duncan." he held out his hand, and not wanting to be rude, I took it. Then a sign of recollection came over him, "Do you know Commissioner Fletcher, by any chance?"

"I do."

His recollection quickly turned towards admiration. "He talks about you daily. Would you be interested in working with me?"

"I'm sure we can work something out."

He smiled, and we started to head for our seats. Gabrielle turned to me with a look of concern. "Is there something about that day you haven't told me?"

"I'm sure the Commissioner likes to embellish."

That didn't help her that much. But she had another question to ask. "What do you think of our host?"

"He seems pleasant enough if you like that kind of person," I stated, trying to hide my jealousy from her.

She glanced over his way as she sat down, with a look I hadn't seen before. "I think he is kind of nice."

I sat down quietly. What else could I feel? James Koch was rich, handsome, and educated, everything I wasn't. He deserved her more than I could ever hope to. If I do love her, I should be happy she found somebody who could give her a happy life. But I can't. What is worse is that the man seems to be a decent person. That meant I couldn't enjoy hating him.

I just turned to watch the two teams as they gathered on the field. The visiting team, Duke, wore their blue jerseys and white pants, and they defended against the north goal. The home team, Queens, wore their green jerseys and white pants and defended the southern goal.

After the challenge, Dukes won possession and began to move down the field and scored in a brilliant move. This gave Dukes an early lead that they held through the first period. In the second period, Queens had woken up taking a sixteen-ten lead at half.

During half-time, Gabrielle just left me alone in my seat. I watched her join Koch and a few of his friends. She quickly became the center of their attention. Not wanting to see anymore, I turned away. Leaning back into my chair, I tried to make myself comfortable. I shouldn't have been so surprised. Deep down, I knew this was what Caitlyn had planned for her. I had to be a fool not to realize her plan. I just fooled myself that somehow, I could measure up with my rivals.

Naomi had noticed my isolation. Sitting down next to me, she quickly made herself comfortable in Gabrielle's seat. Looking over at her, she smiled back at me.

"How was your date?" I asked her.

Her cream cheeks turned a slight shade red when she answered, "He was nice." In looking at her, I could see she was smitten by the athlete. She glanced over at Caitlyn to see if she was distracted by other matters. Caitlyn was busy introducing Savanah to two other prospective suitors. "We are planning to see each other on Wednesday night."

"I won't tell anybody."

"I know," she leaned over and quickly kissed me on the cheek, "thank you."

She left some remains of her red lipstick on my cheek. Taking a handkerchief, she immediately tried to rub it off. She had just finished when Gabrielle returned. Naomi quickly returned to her seat. Gabrielle returned to her seat. She said sternly, "What was that about?"

"It's a secret," I replied, amused. I suppose I should have told her more. But I thought it was her turn to be jealous. We didn't speak for the rest of the night. When Queens defeated Duke 35 -20, neither of us felt like celebrating. We just said our goodbyes and left for home.

The next morning, Gabrielle received a new dress. She immediately tried it on. By the end of breakfast, we had made peace with each other about what had happened the previous night with Niomi and Koch. Both of us understood that we had overreacted. With reconciliation, things became normal. Happy, she hurried to her room to change. Sitting down in a chair, I anxiously waited for her to come. It was worth the wait.

The dress covered her form from around her neck down to her ankles, leaving her shoulders and arms free to breathe. As she turned around, she revealed that her back was exposed to the small of her back. It is clear she loved this dress.

"What do you think?"

"I love it."

Without a word, she walked up to me and squeezed me with all my might. I couldn't breathe, but that didn't matter. I finally had to ask about our instructions." Letting go, she headed back to the package. Taking out an envelope, she opened it and read it.

"I am to have my hair and makeup done at seventeen hundred hours." Her face changed as she read on.

Finally, I asked, "What is it?"

Reluctantly, she stated, "We have a party at a penthouse at Star Casino."

"That doesn't sound so bad," I had stated.

"We are to be the guests of Rudy Klein."

"Doesn't sound that bad."

She was hiding something when she replied, "Your friends Henry Fletcher and James Koch will be there."

"Is Naomi going to be there?"

Gabrielle smiled, "Yes."

"Well, there you have it."

She smiled, knowing that I understood what was expected of her. She just turned around and headed to her changing room. I returned to my seat.

———————

Rudy Klein is a large mass of gluttony. That was the first thing I thought when I saw him. Well, in his mid-seventies, he was determined to fight a losing war against time. As he tried to maintain an illusion of a man in his forties. He failed. His second strategy is having a wife forty years his junior, he plans to make sure. Tall and thin, she is a pleasant contrast to her husband, for that part of his strategy had worked.

We were expected promptly at eight, with a warning not to be late. Not that Caitlyn needed any enticement to be on time. Being punctual has proven to be her lone virtue. She led us through the casino up to the penthouse chambers, where Klein was hosting his party. She entered the room first, followed by Gabrielle, who had her hair up, giving her an elegance that matched her soul. As for me, I was the last in line. That allowed me to watch the show ahead of me.

As I said before, Rudy Klein was a strange mess resembling a ball with legs. The pale skin with bleached white hair didn't look like it belonged on his head. Watching closely as Caitlyn greeted our host, he put his left hand on her bottom. Caitlyn showed no emotion and just continued down the line. That made me look very closely when Gabrielle came up to introduce herself. Thankfully, he didn't do anything to her. Naomi was next, and nothing happened. Down the line, I noticed he preferred blonde women. Kayla received the same greeting. Startled, she stepped back for a moment and just went down the line. Selene was next. I wasn't sure what she would do. I hoped that she would slap him on his fat face if he tried that with her. In the short time I had known her, I found that she had an independent spirit. But nothing happened. I was disappointed.

Savannah was next, followed by Elizabeth, and finally, it was my turn. Savannah introduced herself and moved on down the line. I saw she was nervous. Like Gabby, she had her strawberry blonde hair elegantly fashioned, exposing her neck. To make her feel at ease, I took a step closer. I had an idea.

True to form, after she had introduced herself and shook hands, he proceeded to strike her with his left hand. I quickly stepped in close enough to intercept the strike. Before he could react, I took his right hand and said smugly, "I'm Duncan Walker." Looking into my eyes, he immediately realized what had happened. he just responded with a grunt. I just smiled and happily went to his wife. Elizabeth looked behind and smiled, mouthing the word thank you. I just returned the smile.

As I said earlier, Katrina Klein was an amazingly beautiful woman. Despite being crowded by her husband. He couldn't eclipse her. Exchanging introductions, I just stood there and gave myself a clear memory of her. A tall, thin woman, she wore a white dress that complemented her curves. Her long, curly blonde hair fell on her shoulders. She smiled, and as she looked into my eyes, I could see her soft grey eyes doing the same to me. Unfortunately for both of us, we discovered that we were holding up the line. I just excused myself and moved on. As I glanced over to her husband, I found him oblivious to what Katrina and I had done.

Both of his sons were next to their stepmother. Both were older than her, making for awkward family get-togethers, I surmise. As I exchanged introductions with the brothers, I continually looked over at their father, I presumed that they favored their mother. Which isn't a bad thing. Gregory is the eldest and tallest of the two. He believes that at forty-five, he doesn't have to shave. Jeffrey, his brother, is six years younger. Shorter than his brother, he tries to copy his brother. Unable to find anything in common, I just moved on.

At the end of the line is Grace Klein, Rudy's only daughter and youngest child. She was lovely. With long straight blonde hair and blue eyes, she couldn't be older than twenty-one. She looked like her father, which made me realize that her father, when he was younger, must have been handsome. Like her stepmother, I found myself wanting to get to know her as well. Luckily for me, she didn't return the interest, so I was joined by an attendant.

Savanah had waited for me while her friends began to mingle. She had a one-piece black dress that covered her body from her neck to her ankles. Unlike Gabby, I don't think she liked the dress.

"Elizabeth told us what you had done."

"All in the service," I said. "I'm sorry I couldn't have helped Kayla out."

"She deserved it."

That surprised me. There is something she wasn't telling me. Savannah smiled. "She can take care of herself."

"Duncan Walker!" We looked around to see who could know me enough to shout my name. I quickly saw who it was. Henry Fletcher, as big as life, came toward Savannah and me with three other men. Before I could return the greeting, he just told his friends, "This is the man I had told you about. He is one of three security agents who saved my life. I heard you were in Gotham."

"How do you find Gotham?" asked an older, dignified gentleman.

"It is certainly different than Southpoint," I replied, embarrassed by this attention. Realizing that Savannah was standing next to me patiently, I said, "This is my friend, Savannah."

"Henry Fletcher."

"You must tell me about this adventure you had."

"It is all over the highlands." A large man, younger than Fletcher, had stated, "I'm Sam Bergeron."

Now it was the distinguished older gentleman, "John Gordon."

Finally, the third man introduced himself," Victor Gallo."

"Please to meet all of you. Now, I have a favor to ask. Please tell me, what are the Highlands?" Savannah asked them. She had asked that for my benefit, not wanting me to look foolish. The four men and she began to laugh at the apparent joke.

Gordon decided to answer, "That is what we call ourselves in Purple Levels."

Gallo asked her, "Who are you, Savanah?"

"I am one of Caitlyn's wards."

Gallo coarsely stated, "Her wards are improving."

Savannah replied, "I'll take that as a compliment."

Frazier and the other men were impressed with Savannah's tact. But Gallo was not having any of it." Has your friend, Caitlyn, found you any prospects?"

Before Savannah could respond. Gabrielle joined our circle with Kayla; they must have heard Gallo's demeaning tone with Savannah and wanted to change the subject. "Councilor Fletcher, you can do me the greatest favor."

"Name it, miss?"

"Gabrielle Blue," she answered, "Duncan has never told me what happened that day."

I interrupted, "I didn't want to worry her."

"And you two are?" he asked.

"We are lovers," she boldly replied.

"I see. Well, you would be very proud of Duncan here." He then proceeded to tell the story one more time. That was my time to leave the group. I didn't need to hear the story.

Taking a glass of something called champagne, I walked over and stood near the ledge of the window. There, I began to look around the large room. It was almost full of statues of the great man that Kleist believed he was. Everybody seemed to be having a good time. Except for Caitlyn. As she tried to mingle, the other guests treated her with disdain. I had not watched Caitlyn at the reception before. This group, called Highlanders, wanted to remind her of her place. As for Caitlyn, she knew enough not to press her position too far. If it were possible, I found myself pitying her. Not able to take it anymore, I decided to look outside and watch the setting sun going down in the western sky, drinking my champagne, which I had found to be surprisingly sweet but without a kick. But I liked it enough to give it another shot, placing my empty glass on a tray and replacing it with a full glass. I returned to my private show, the sun setting along the western sky.

I had just finished my drink, and the night sky was overcoming the landscape when I felt a hand on my right shoulder. I turned, and it was Gabby standing next to me. Without saying a word, she proceeded to drag me to an excluded area of the room. Away from prying eyes. I barely had time to put my glass down. When she thought we were alone, she pushed me against the wall.

She proceeded to kiss me hard on my lips. When she was finished, she pulled away and stated very tenderly, "That is for what you did." She then slapped me across my face, "And that is for what you did."

That is why I didn't tell her. I kept that to myself. She then kissed me again, and we stayed there until Caitlyn came to join us. Annoyed.

Gabrielle told her defiantly, "We were having an argument and made up."

She went back to the party with Catlyn. I stayed there alone for a moment and then returned to the party myself.

An hour later, I was working on my third glass of champagne. When Katrina joined me with one of her own. She gently tapped my glass with hers and took a sip slowly. "You intrigue me, mister Walker."

"How so?" I replied, "And it's Duncan."

She smiled. "Katrina." She glanced around the large room, and she stated, "You're not afraid of my husband."

"Should I be?" Ignorance can make a person very brave. But I wasn't impressed with the man.

Katrina looked over at Caitlyn. She turned to me and confessed, "My husband supported your friend Caitlyn in a power struggle in exchange for a favor. Eliminating a potential threat here."

"It explains many things," I stated calmly. She just clarified many things; I had often wondered why Caitlyn spent that winter in Shenandoah with her friend. Her friend had conveniently disappeared. I decided to change the subject. "How long have you been married?"

"Seven years," she replied, "I am his third wife."

I didn't say anything. I thought that if she wanted to confide in me further, she would do so, and it would be impolite to force it out of her. We just stood there drinking our champagne. I began feeling the effects of this drink.

A sudden loud crash brought us out of our quiet moment. Concerned, we looked around to see where it was coming from. There were two men and a woman struggling with Klein's security. Two other assailants, a man and a woman, were still running around screaming something I couldn't understand. With his sons, Klien went after them. As I looked around, I saw what they had done. Several of the artworks that were displayed on the walls had been damaged. Security guards finally managed to corner the final two intruders. Klein instructed his son to take the rope from the curtains. He had his men tie up the five intruders.

Seeing where Gabrielle and the others are. I immediately bought them with Kaitlyn.

"Disrupters," Caitlyn explained.

I had heard of them. Some kind of activist. But whoever they were or had done, they didn't deserve what came next. A security guard held each one. Their arms are securely tied. Klein walked towards each one to gloat. Walking up to the leader. He proceeded to punch each man in the stomach, followed by a slap across the face. Going down the line, he did the same for each one, sparing nobody. Finally, Koch had had enough and placed himself between Klein and the Disrupters.

"In the name of sanity, call the Watchman," he replied.

Klein calmed down. Quietly, he directed his men to take them to a joining room. I am beginning to like Koch. Sanity returned to Klein as he turned away from his prisoners. He directed his sons to lead his prisoners through a side door. Katrina joined him and had a private conversation. I don't know what they had discussed, but they agreed. Contrite Klein accompanied his wife to join his guest.

He stated, "My friends, I am sorry this happened. I have called the authorities. In the meantime, I invite you to head to my casino. Naturally, I instructed downstairs to offer you five hundred credits to use.

Most of the people seemed to be satisfied with that generous offer. Caitlyn didn't share the others' sentiments. "He will make it all back and more."

We all headed down to the main floor. Gabrielle, Savanah,

Niomi, and I went down the elevator. When the door opened, we were immediately subjected to a menagerie of lights and sounds. Leaving the elevator, we were joined by Caitlyn and the others. Caitlyn immediately handed out our credit chips.

She immediately instructed each of us, "If they offer you any credit, say no."

Entering the casino, I quickly learned why. The bright lights and loud sounds distracted the people from losing their money. Caitlyn had the girls join the other guests, keeping them company as they gambled. Gabrielle joined Koch and Frazier at a table called roulette. Not that I minded; it gave me time to explore the entire casino.

As I walked around the casino, I was amazed. It was an incredible piece of engineering. The casino stood nearly three stories tall. Each section was surrounded by a small, well-kept garden. As I headed up to the second floor, I wanted to get a good idea of the casino. The ground floor was designed in a cross. Each section had its own collection of games. Built as a circle are our two additional levels of games. I made it my mission to explore each one. But first, I used a few credits for a very large cup of coffee. To counter the effects of that sneaky champagne.

While I was drinking coffee, I walked around and looked over every aspect of the casino. I watched the crowds of people spend their hard-earned money to try to win a fortune. Gambling is all about dumb luck. Sure, a few random people are winning large amounts of money. What they do is put their winning on the board in the hope of winning larger amounts of money, only to lose it all. But people are having fun. If you play for fun, you will be all right. But to get rich, you can fall into a deadly spiral of self-destruction. I decided to stay away from the games.

Buying a second large cup of coffee, I headed outside the casino. There, I discovered that Rudy Klein had more ways to relieve his visitors' money. Surrounding the casino are four levels of stores, restaurants, bars, and shops. Where you could find anything if you wanted to pay for it. I'll just stay with my coffee.

Sitting down, I looked up at the night sky. Above me was a glass dome. I could see no stars in the black sky. Just the lonely crescent moon giving off light. The five towers surrounded the casino. I give Klein some credit for this impressive structure.

Finishing my coffee, I sat there wondering if I wanted to get another cup of coffee. When I saw a glimpse of something. It couldn't be. I immediately followed that glimpse from my past. It couldn't be that easy, I told myself. I managed to regain sight of that ghost. She walked into a small store that sold jewelry. From the window, I glanced inside. It was her. Cassandra. Without any hesitation, I walked into the small shop. As quickly as I could, I walked up to her, only to be thwarted by her escort. Without saying a word, he led her outside the shop and back to the casino. Undeterred, I immediately followed her inside the casino. Somehow, I managed to keep an eye on her as the big brute guided her to a poker table. Her friend allowed her to sit down by a man old enough to be his grandfather. She was one of three beautiful young women who accompanied Grandpa. I tried to join them, but Grandpa's bodyguards made sure I could not get close enough to my friend. That is when I decided to join the game.

There were six of us facing Grandpa's. A dealer who worked for the casino handled the cards. We were playing five-card stud. I didn't pay much attention to the other card players; my focus was totally on Cassandra. As I studied her, she looked dead inside. With no emotion, she just stared into space, trying to endure this private hell of hers. She never looked up to see an old friend. This made me more determined to talk to her.

I played my hand cautiously at first, winning some small hands and hoping to have a bank large enough to take on Grandpa. I looked over at Cassandra each time I spoke to see if she had heard me. She didn't. When the dealer dealt the opening cards, I carefully looked at mine, they were a King hiding and the seven showing. Grandpa opened with fifty credits, trying to bully us. It didn't work; none of us folded. A second showing card was dealt; it was the king of hearts.

An older woman on my left opened the bidding with fifty credits. Two others followed her lead. Grandpa, true to form, raised it to a hundred credits. Three dropped out immediately, leaving the older woman, Grandpa, and me. The dealer gave me another king. The woman dropped out with a pair of sevens. That left me to open with a hundred credits. Grandpa doubled my bet. This time, I just matched his bet. With the pot right, the dealer gave me my fourth king. I checked to Grandpa, he threw in three hundred credits. I tripled his bet. Thinking this was a good time to see what he was holding, glancing over at what he was showing, I noticed he had a possible full house. I'm willing to bet he had it.

Grandpa looked up at me. With one eye, he looked me over, trying to decide if I was bluffing. In a base voice, he inquired, "Do you have it?" I said nothing, not wanting to give my hand away. I wanted him to raise me. He finally asked, "How much money do you have?"

I quickly counted my stack. I looked at him and said, "Six hundred."

This time she heard me. A look of recollection came over her. Life had returned to her eyes when she looked at me. But she did not dare smile. Grandpa was too busy debating whether to raise me, and then he noticed two old friends reconnecting. He then made his decision and forced me to throw everything I had. Taking out some extra money, I raised him an extra hundred credits. That angered him. He raised me two hundred credits. I just matched his bet. We showed our hidden cards. A look of rage came over Grandpa. Cassandra cheered as I pulled out my money. Enraged, he was about to strike her.

I distracted him. "This has been fun." Standing up, I tipped the dealer.

Outraged, Grandpa exclaimed, "Where are you going?"

"I'm hungry," I replied. Looking right at Cassandra, I asked, "Would you like to come?"

Cassandra hesitated for a moment when she looked over at Grandpa. Then, with a look of defiance, she said, "Yes."

She got up to join me. A bodyguard tried to stop her, but Wynn stopped him with a gesture. She hugged me. Wynn said, "Who are you?"

"Duncan Walker."

"I'm Jacob Wynn. You do your best to remember that."

"Good, I was tired of calling you Grandpa."

Cassandra giggled as we walked away. Together, we heard a commotion of his men trying to restrain him. I didn't care; Cassandra was happy, just for a moment. Cassandra looked around, wondering what we were doing. She asked, "Where are we going?"

"We have to get Gabrielle."

Gabrielle is still with Koch and Fletcher. She sat between them as they played a game called roulette. They were still having fun. Savanah and Elizabeth were with them. We joined them. Cassandra stood on my left while Gabrielle remained in her place on my right. Noticing me, Gabrielle glanced over and said, "Where were you?"

I replied proudly, "I found an old friend." Stepping back, I revealed Cassandra. An expression of pure joy came over them both. They immediately embraced each other. It had been over a year since we saw one of our friends. I just stood there and watched them. Many of the players had noticed the two friends. Nobody wanted to break them. I decided to try my luck with this wheel. I placed fifty on black and won. I then placed a hundred on 7 red for a bet, and that won. That managed to get Cassandra and Gabrielle's attention. I proclaimed, "I'm beginning to like this gambling." I was finished, so I pulled my money off the board. "Let's get some dinner, my treat." I gave the young woman a couple of chips.

Both women agreed, and Cassandra led the way to the best restaurant. Cassandra knew where to go. We sat down and waited for a server to come. We ordered their best steaks and some wine.

"How did you learn to play poker?" Cassandra asked me.

"I had a friend, Austen," I replied. He taught me that the game is easy. The trick is reading people and remembering that there is always another hand.

While we ate steaks and drank some red wine. We told her about our adventures. Gabby started from the moment we had separated to the present day. I watched Cassandra as she listened to Gabby. Color began to appear on Cassandra's face as she was amused at my little quips of humor. But there was a cloud hovering over us. She had wanted to tell what had happened to the others and herself. And we wanted to know. But we silently agreed that this wasn't the time. We just wanted to enjoy our dinner in Gotham. We all struggle through the Wastelands for a chance at a new life. It was clear that she had suffered here.

With dessert and coffee, we asked for the check. Insisting this was my treat, I paid the bill. It was five hundred and twenty-one credits. I still had plenty of money.

"Now I know how Wynn made his money," I stated sarcastically.

Cassandra became silent again. Wynn must have done something to Cassandra. Making him less likable to me. Gabrielle then became silent herself. I looked over, and she looked tired, placing her hands over her face.

"Are you all right?"

Taking her hands from her face, she sat up. "I am just tired."

"I'll take you home."

Cassandra looked disappointed. She didn't want us to leave her behind. Immediately, Gabrielle tried to reassure her, "You can come with us."

Her eyes lit up for a moment. She wanted to come with us, but she had endured for the past year. "I can't," she stated, "I have only this dress to wear."

Gabrielle interjected, "You can borrow some of my clothes while we send for your clothes."

She confessed, "But I have obligations that I don't want you to get involved with."

It was my turn to interject, "We can handle it."

Gabrielle added, "We made a promise."

Not to be outdone, I joked, "Besides, Grandpa Wynn isn't that impressive."

Cassandra broke out in laughter. She shared my contempt for the man. Although she knew him far better than me. She agreed. Getting up, we made our way to the exit. Gabby still looked pale as we walked out. That didn't stop her from being practical. "We'd better tell Caitlyn."

She was right, of course. I simply replied, "I'll tell her. So go ahead, and I will catch up."

We didn't get the chance. Wynn and his three associates came to intercept us.

Scared, Cassandra cowered behind Gabrielle, hoping Wynn wouldn't see her. To protect her, Gabby and I stepped forward to shield her. Not impressed, Wynn stepped closer to me. Trying to intimidate us with his powerful personality. I wasn't impressed. Neither was Gabby. With my right hand, I simply activated my stinger. In case I needed it. I hoped that I didn't have to draw my pistol.

"I hoped you enjoyed your time with her, Mister Walker. But it's time to give her back."

"I don't think she wants to go back with you."

He spat out, "I don't care what you think!"

"I do."

Gabrielle stepped forward and made her opinion known: "She is our friend." Her anger brought color back to her face.

Wynn stepped back a couple of paces, allowing his three thugs to do their work. Gabrielle steps forward to intercept one of the thugs. She gently pushed Cassandra out of the thug's reach, who was assigned to seize her. Standing firmly, I reached behind me and had my stinger at the ready, just in case Wynn called my bluff. Before anything had started, Selene interrupted, "Caitlyn is looking for you."

Looking at Wynn, I stated calmly, "Just tell Caitlyn we will be along in a while."

Selene looked concerned. She didn't share my confidence in the situation. But she was going to get to Caitlyn. That is what I had wanted. Not sure what side she will be on, but I had to gamble that she will protect one of her assets. Wynn had heard of Caitlyn. With a concerned look, he ordered his men to stand down. Reluctantly, they obeyed their boss.

Two minutes later, Selene returned, leading Caitlyn to our little disturbance. Caitlyn stepped forward as the manager of the restaurant pulled his people out of harm's way. Like a showman taking the stage, she walked up confidently to Wynn. Giving him a sinister smile that drained all the courage from Grandpa's face. Now I knew he had heard of her.

She finally stated, "Now, what is the problem?"

Joining me, Gabrielle immediately let her know what had been going on, "Our friend Cassandra wishes to go home with us."

"And Grandpa here doesn't like that idea," I added. Cassandra snickered.

That brought Caitlyn's attention to her. Stepping towards her, she looked at the young woman with an intense examination. Not saying a word to her, she looked up to Gabby and stated confidently, "Leave it to me."

Her attention turned back to Wynn. Who made it clear that he is dreading what is to come. He meekly pleaded his case, "She is bought by me."

His meek objection fell on deaf ears. Looking at him, she clearly instructed us, "You three go home with the others. I'll take care of things here."

As we're leaving. Wynn tried to protest. But looking around made him think better of it. For the first time, I noticed what Wynn had seen. Surrounding us stood a dozen men, all of whom belonged to Caitlyn. Not wanting to watch what would happen to Grandpa, we joined Selene and headed home.

We had to gather the others. It didn't take that long. Caitlyn had managed to gather them in front of the main entrance. Selene had led us there. I silently made a head count and found two were missing. Kayla had left with one of the suitors. I didn't meet the man, but I was assured by Savannah that Caitlyn had cleared it. That was fine by me. Niomi was the second missing. Nobody could account for where she had gone. I had my ideas, so I decided to cover for her. Satisfied, we headed home.

It was well past three hundred hours before the three of us made it home. Sitting in the living room, Cassandra began to tell us everything that had happened to her during the time they had left South-point until tonight. By her best recollection, she had told us the fate of each of our friends.

She started with, "Almost immediately, Mitchel and Natalie sold us out. Once out of sight of you and the rest of the people in line. They quickly allowed their friends to chain us together, creating a long line of prisoners. About a hundred of us. They made us walk for days. I don't know how many. We stopped only to rest, with nothing to eat or drink unless we had something to barter with. And they managed to take everything from us. No matter how small. Soon, all of us had just the clothes on our back. But very quickly, our clothes became no better than rags. After that, the luckiest of us still had something to trade. A few moments alone in a private spot."

Stopping there for a moment. She lowered her head in personal shame. Beginning to weep, Gabrielle came over to comfort her. She feels self-loathing about what she had to do to survive; nobody has the right to judge her. Nobody. I had wanted to join her and comfort myself. Somehow, I didn't think I had that right.

When she regained her composure, she continued with Gabby remaining at her side, "When we finally made it to our destination. There were three boats lined up to leave for Gotham. None of them looked fit to make that trip. Mitchel and his friends headed down to talk with the captains of the boats. Natalie stayed behind, keeping her distance from the rest of us. Maybe she was pitying us. I don't know. Not that I had cared about that bitch. After a while, one of the captains and Mitchell exchanged money. He returned to us, and with a grin like the devil, he and his men lined us up. He explained how we were going to get on the boat. Anybody who couldn't pay for the passage was murdered where they had stood. Harry stepped forward and offered to pay for all of us. But after we made it to Gotham. Four other citizens of Gotham did the same. So, we were herded on this old boat."

A pot of coffee whistled in the kitchen; the sudden noise had startled Cassandra. I left to get us some coffee. When I returned with three cups, handing her cup to her, Cassandra proceeded to take a huge sip of her coffee, then she began again, "Somehow, we made it into the city. We had to leave at dusk. As we are smuggled in. When the boat docked, three men escorted Deb and Henry with the other citizens. We waited for what seemed to be hours. After the first light of dawn, they had finally returned. The boats had already left us behind. That gave us a sense of relief. Whatever happens next, we at least made it. Maybe they will let us go. Our belief in delivery was dashed very quickly. Not wasting time, Mitchel and his men began to tie the legs of the eight citizens with chains. At the end of the chain, there was some weight. Natalie and the other guards made sure we could see what happened next. With a sinister smile, Mitchel took out his knife and proceeded to cut each one's throat. When he finished, he threw them into the sea. All this time, the poor souls were crying, begging for their lives or their loved ones. That had fallen on deaf ears. But I sometimes hear their cries in my dreams when I sleep; that is why I don't sleep that much. I glanced at Natalie; a look of shock came over her as she watched the execution. Deb and Harry were the last. Mitchel personally enjoyed putting his dagger into their back, then sending their lifeless bodies into the river, where their bodies were quickly claimed by the water. None of us knew what was going to happen to us next."

She stopped and finished her coffee. I gave her some more, and she took a smaller sip. She didn't care that the coffee was hot. It was something she needed to tell her story. Now we knew what had happened to Deb and Harry. Gabrielle hugged Cassandra for a moment, and I remained alone, watching them comfort each other. Her story wasn't finished yet. When she was ready, she finished it. "Some transports arrived soon after. Separated into smaller groups. We were all gathered in the car. Olivia, Paloma, and I made sure we stayed together. We are all that is left now. Our transport rose into the sky and headed to Star Island. There, the remaining ninety were herded out of our transport. As I looked over, I noticed a second means of transport had joined us on Star Island. Most of us here are all young women from seventeen to twenty-five, reasonably healthy and attractive. A few young men in that same age range were also there. We waited for four distinguished men to arrive with their escort. Wynn was one of the men. Klein was the second. The other two men were called Delgado and Kim, I don't know much about them. The four men proceeded to bid on each of us. Olivia was the first. Mitchel had wanted her, and she went with him and Natalie. When Paloma was brought to the stage, she resisted. Somehow, she had managed to keep the knife you had given her hidden. Waiting for the time is right to strike. She quickly took it out and slashed at one of the bastards who held her. Before he had time to react, she sliced the man across the face, blinding him with his blood. The second bastard who held her was killed when Paloma plunged her knife into his heart. Now free, she dashed towards us so we could escape, but Natalie, armed now, stood between us. I told her to run. It was okay. She looked at me with tears going down her cheeks and made a run for it. I like to believe she made it. When Mitchel and his men restored order, the auctions continued. Taking no chances, each of us had our hands tied in front of us. Then it was my turn, and Wynn won me."

The color drained out of her again as she was about to finish her story. "From that moment to when you found me. I was his companion and inflated his small presence in his class. I am one of six women in his entourage. He made it clear that my position was temporary. He will discard me like an old piece of furniture whenever he wants."

She was finished. A tremendous sense of relief came over her. Like she managed to let go of a terrible weight she had been carrying for the past year.

Gabrielle reassured her, "You are safe now. It's all over."

I dropped to my knees ahead of her. Looking into her eyes, I added, "I'll find Paloma and Olivia. I promise you." She looked up and smiled; she believed me." I will make the others pay for what they have done to you and the others. I promise."

She smiled and replied in a whisper, "I know." She hugged me.

We all went to bed. Gabrielle had given her a nightgown to change into. Together, they went to the bedroom while I was on the couch. I turned off the light, and we all fell asleep.

4 REGINA

THE NEXT DAY, I ESCORTED CASSANDRA TO SEE INSPECTOR WELLS. She had borrowed a blue jumpsuit from Gabrielle, she hadn't worn it since we moved to Gotham. Caitlyn made it clear she didn't want her to wear anything from our days in Southpoint. Something about making the right appearance with her clients. As for me, she didn't care too much; on my own time, I could wear what I wanted if I dressed well during her events, which she made clear to me. I chose to wear blue canvas pants and a black shirt with sleeves that covered my elbows.

Gabrielle was still in bed. She wasn't feeling well. Her face was pale, and she felt nauseous. With no energy, she decided to sleep it off, assuring me it was the effects of last night. I didn't want to leave her. But she assured me that this is more important.

We walked into his office. Wells was annoyed to see me. Before he announced his protest of me being there, I stated, "I have a witness. Cassandra, this is Inspector Wells. She was with my other friend, who had disappeared."

Intrigued, Wells let her sit down. He returned to his seat. Turning on a recording device. I stayed in the background and observed. Cassandra proceeded to tell her story again. It was amazing, exactly like the story he had told us last night, with no diversions. She can't forget what happened to her and the others, no matter how much she wishes. She only hesitated to tell her story when Wells asked her a question to go further into a particular detail. She answered each question thoroughly. If she couldn't, she just said, "I don't know." Then she continued telling him her story exactly where she had left off at the interruption. Finally, when she had finished, she lowered her head for a moment to regain her composure. Wells came over to give her some comfort. She looked up and whispered her appreciation.

"You are a brave young woman," he assured her.

Looking up, she whispered, "I should have done more."

"You're doing it now."

Turning his attention to me, he gave me a strange smile and said, "Now we are in business." Immediately, I knew what that meant. His superiors didn't care much about the hypothetical murders. That is what I had gathered from earlier inquiries with Wells. Justifying his earlier annoyance. "Cassandra, can you identify anybody involved?"

"Yes."

He believed her story.

"We're going to need both of your help," he stated. "We have contacts in the area. We need you to arrive where the boats are docked. Get a passage and let us know when and where they are coming. Are you willing?"

We both volunteered.

"Good. Give us another week, and we will set it up. Do you remember the place?"

"I can," answered Cassandra.

"Then we'll be in touch."

We headed home.

As we entered our apartment, we were surprised to find Caitlyn sitting in a chair in the living room. Beside her, in a neat pile, were four crates. Seeing us, she stood up and walked over to greet us.

"How did your interview go?"

"Good. We will be helping them sometime next week."

"Well, I'm always happy to help the Watchmen," she stated happily, "I just wanted to check on Gabby and bring you all your property. They should be there."

Cassandra replied, "Thank you."

"If something is missing, please let me know, and I'll take care of it. But I don't think so, Wynn can be a dear when properly motivated."

Caitlyn was strangely cordial, which made me trust her less, so I changed the subject: "How is Gabby?"

"She is fine," she stated, "just needs to sleep it off." A look of concern came over her face. "But if this continues, I want her to see a doctor."

"I'll take her."

"That will not be necessary." With that, she gave me some news, "You will have some extra work in the coming months. Frazier and Koch personally requested you." Her attention returned to Cassandra. "Gabrielle will instruct you on what I expect from my menagerie. That outfit is expected for today. But I prefer to portray a particular image."

"Understood."

"Good. I had some of my associates prepare your bedroom. It is the second door on your right."

"Thank you."

"I'll see you tomorrow." She was about to leave when she turned around and added, "I need you to take Niomi for an assignment. Nineteen hundred hours."

"I'll be ready."

She left. I helped her bring her stuff into her room. Inside her room, I was surprised to see how it was prepared. Caitlyn doesn't waste any time. Satisfied, she said goodbye and left us. Leaving Cassandra and me standing there, perplexed. It is hard to figure out Caitlyn, she has an agenda that she will never share with anybody. You must just keep up with her. Cassandra went to her room; I headed to our room to visit Gabrielle. She was still resting. I decided to head to one of the spare rooms I had left. To rest before my assignment.

Right at nineteen hundred hours, I headed to pick up Naomi. Opening the door, she looked at me and smiled. She requested, "Just a minute."

She closed her door and left me waiting at the door. Exactly a minute later, she opened the door again. Closing it behind her, she looked at me and stated, "Let's go."

Taking her arm, I simply obeyed. We walked to the tube. Having the car to ourselves, we sat down and watched the city go by us. Naomi had on a sleeveless white dress that covered her knees, she had crossed her legs, showing off her white high-heeled shoes. Her black hair had been set up, exposing her bare neck. She had colored her cheeks red, which gave her pale skin tone some cover, and her lips matched her cheeks. She gave me a brief flirtatious wink of her eye, just to see what my response would be. When I looked away, she was disappointed.

"How was your time with the Keeper?" I asked her.

With a mischievous smile, she replied proudly, "We had fun."

"I covered for you with Caitlyn, "I told her, not expecting any gratitude. "Just be careful. Caitlyn wouldn't approve."

Keeping her mischievous expression, she muttered, "I know Duncan. I will. But she wants me to see him tonight."

I didn't say anything. Didn't need too much. Naomi is the most independent of the girls. She understood very well what she was doing, seeing Austin on her own. But she didn't care, she liked the young Cager. To her, it was worth the risk. I hope she will never suffer any consequences.

Changing the mood a bit, she confessed, "If you weren't so old, I might have tried to snare you from Gabby."

"Old." I stated, "Gabby is only four years older than you."

"She had lived out there."

She was right. You do grow up in Wasteland. The shuttle made it to its destination. We walked out to head for her rendezvous. As we made it outside the door, I stopped her. Turning her to me, I placed my hands on her shoulders. I stated firmly, "I'll be back at 2300 hours, no arguments."

With that same damn mischievous smile, she simply stated, "Yes sir."

She walked in. I just stood there for a moment. I'm not sure why I was offended back in the tube. I wasn't interested in her. I am in love with Gabby. But she had bruised my ego a bit. I walked off to get something to eat.

I returned to pick up Niomi at the appropriate time. Coming out alone, she was visually excited. Placing her arms around my neck, she gave me a quick kiss. Surprised, I pulled away. She was too excited to notice.

"You look like you had a good time."

"Gotham is getting a new Keeper," she replied, "and something more." She proudly displayed her left hand. Glaring for all to see is a ring with a large diamond. And it had a particular symbolic promise to it, from the old world. Naomi exclaimed happily." We are engaged!"

I didn't say anything. I just took her arm, and we started for home. It wasn't that I was not happy for her. I was. But Caitlyn has a clear plan for each of her girls. I don't fit in Caitlyn's plan with Gabrielle, she has loftier expectations for Naomi than a Cager. Playing for Gotham or not. She and Allen may be playing with fire.

Sitting alone in a private shuttle, we headed home. Inside, she started making plans for their life together. "We will live in a penthouse overlooking the park, living like royalty."

After that, I just sat and listened to her spell out all her dreams for their life together, she had everything planned for the next ten years. As for me, I tried to smile and share her excitement, but I couldn't. Suddenly, she noticed my reservations; her expression changed, and she inquired, "Duncan, you're not happy with me."

Sitting there, I hesitated for a moment, trying to think of something to say. Finally, I decided to give her some advice, "I am happy. But what about Caitlyn? She won't be very happy."

"I can handle her," she stated indignantly, that I brought up Caitlyn.

"I don't think you can." Looking at her ring, I added, "Just hide that ring. Maybe you can ease her into it."

She leaned back for a moment, for the first time, she was concerned for how Caitlyn would respond to her engagement. She finally muttered, "I hate her."

Like a fool, I stated, "When you tell her, I can put in a good word for you."

"I appreciate that, Duncan."

We remained silent for a moment. Looking outside at the night sky. Finally, I decided to ask her something I wanted to know: "What are Caitlyn's plans for you and the others?"

That gave her a sad smile as she answered my inquiry, "We are soldiers in her war to conquer Gotham."

That was a strange response. I needed her to go further. "How are you doing that?"

She gave me a surprised look, that somehow, I should have been told before now, in a casual tone, she explained, "Well, not with violence, silly. Gotham has over twenty times more people than we do. We plan to take over by marriage. For the past few years, we have been marrying off women like me to young men of the Highlanders. In a generation or two, we will be in control of the entire city."

It was an obvious answer. I had expected it. But there are flaws in Caitlyn's plans. So I asked her, "What about the men?"

"Men in our society are a problem," she answered, amused, "They were made with a terrible flaw; they are overly aggressive. You could say insanely violent." She looked over at the window with regret, thinking of somebody close to her. She confessed sadly, "Many of them were cast out. They organized themselves into bands of marauders. Only recently have we fixed their design flaw. But some men are cast out like my brother."

"I 'm sorry," I whispered. She smiled again in gratitude. I then stated with contempt, "Krieg." I always thought they were mutants. They were far more vicious than normal savages that roamed the Wastelands. But the fact that Mitchel is the same as Gabrielle or Naomi made me look at them all with disdain.

Niomi added, "But when we mate naturally, we found that we had more luck in developing normal humans."

What she just said made me pause for a moment. It was a strange thing to say. For right now, I don't want to inquire any deeper, for fear of what I may find out about Gabrielle. That somehow, I wouldn't like what I will eventually discover.

The train pulled up at Naomi's stop. Holding out my arm. She smiled and took it. We walked down the hallway together, side by side. Stopping only at her door. She turned to face me. Giving me a quick embrace. She then kissed me gently on my lips. As she pulled away, she stated sincerely, "Thank you for being my friend."

"All part of the service, Naomi," I replied calmly. Now, being a friend, I had to make one last request: "Can you do me a favor? Take off the ring, just for a while."

She sadly looked down at the ring. Knowing that I was right, she silently took off the ring and put it in her little bag. Without a goodbye, she turned towards her door and opened it. Entering her flat, she turned to close the door, she looked at me. Leaving me just standing there alone. I walked home.

At home, Cassandra and Gabrielle were both asleep. Before I went to bed, I jumped in and took a quick shower. Then I headed to my temporary bed and went right to sleep.

After about eight hundred hours, Caitlyn managed to wake us all up. She wanted to see how Gabrielle was feeling. Hearing Catlyn in the living room, Gabrielle left her room and greeted her. Gabby still didn't look well. Still having bits of nausea, she dared not leave her room. Her face was still pale as she tried to keep her composure. Caitlyn looked at her, concerned.

In an authoritative tone, she said, "That's it. You're seeing a doctor tomorrow. I'll make the appointment."

Concerned, I replied, "I'll see that she will go."

With a rare smile, she turned to me and stated, "I'm afraid that will be not possible. Your friend Fletcher wants you to escort him and Koch to a meeting at Union District. You should be back in three days."

"When do I leave?"

"At 1730," she said, "it will be good money for you."

I looked over at Gabrielle. She tried to reassure me and stated, "I'll be all right."

Caitlyn interjected, "Cassandra can take her."

"I will be glad to," Cassandra added.

Caitlyn turned to Cassandra and proclaimed, "You better get ready, you're going for orientation in an hour." She hands her a package. "The instructions are in the box. Don't be late." She gave her a gesture to get dressed. Cassandra left for her room. That allowed Caitlyn to turn her attention to Gabby, "Now go to bed." She did as she was told. That left me and Caitlyn, "You better get ready. The instructions will be here in an hour."

"Thank you."

"I'll keep an eye on both. Goodbye."

She left me alone in the living room. Heading into the kitchen, I proceeded to start breakfast.

———————

To be clear, I didn't want to leave Gabby feeling so ill, but this is an important opportunity for me. I made it on time and met Koch and Frazier in front of a private shuttle, with a third member of the entourage, a fifty-year-old woman named Lihn. A well-kept woman who wore a professional grey suit and peppered hair.

When the shuttle stopped, I walked in to make sure it was safe. Once satisfied, I allowed the three commissioners into the shuttle. I followed them, putting my stuff away in the compartment above and sitting down on the seats at the opposite end of the car. My clients began to discuss their business without noticing as the car began to move.

I remained silent during the entire trip south. My thoughts were back home with Gabrielle, and what would happen with the doctor tomorrow. This was the first time she had been sick since I had met her. She just never did. Constance and I had our bouts with a cold, like anybody else. But Gabby was the exception. I can't help but fear it is serious. I never wanted to come on this trip. But here I am, and I hope I won't regret it.

As they talked, I listened. After an hour and a half, I developed a better understanding of Gotham politics. It seems my Benefactor Fletcher and his friends are members of a reform party. For the first time in the history of Gotham, a third party is a serious challenge for leadership over the two ruling parties: Labor and Unity. A fourth party called the Nationals is determined to destroy the reformers by any means possible. Now I know who to look out for. If there is another attack.

We had gathered in a hotel located in Green Level. Located next to the water, it was a rustic spot. The hotel had all the amenities of the lavish Star casino, without the casino, thankfully, but in the middle of a forest oasis. A pleasant change for all who visit this place. I was thinking how much I wish Gabby were here with me. She would enjoy the tranquil setting.

For now, I have a job to do. The three of us were escorted by two employees who carried the luggage of my three clients. As for me, I had to carry my own, not that I minded. Once we made it to the room, I walked in first to make sure it was safe. Satisfied, I allowed the others to enter. Each one chose their respective room. I was happy, I had my own room.

I through my bag on the bed and walked out to give the two young men their gratuity. They both smiled and walked out. Their job was finished, and they quietly left us alone to relax. Half an hour later our dinner was delivered to us. With a device provided by Caitlyn before I left, I made sure there was no poison in the food. When it checked out, I gave them a nod of my head and we sat down and ate.

After dinner, we returned to our rooms for the night. Early the next morning, at about 815 hours, we were awakened by the delivery of our breakfast. Two porters had brought it up again, and I had to give them their gratuity, and they thanked me and left. Like I did last night, I made sure our food wasn't tampered with. Frazier didn't want to take any chances. Not that I blame him, since our last mission together was so interesting. I like this one to be as boring as possible. Not wanting Gabrielle to worry about me. When the food was reported safe, I headed into my clients' rooms and told them breakfast was ready. Each one came out fully dressed and sat down. I was still in my sleepwear. Deciding to eat breakfast first and then change, I joined them myself. As I ate, I listened to them talking shop. You can learn a lot just by listening. Especially when they act like I am not there.

I learned they are meeting eight-seven delegates from all parts of the city-state. They were planning to decide on a new candidate from their group to run for the office of Leader of Gotham. After I ate, I had to leave them to change, I didn't have much time since we were expected to be downstairs at 1000 hours.

We made it to the auditorium with time to spare. After my delegation had signed in, I took their seats. That part of my job was finished. Now I had to join the other security details to make sure no danger came to the delegates. A young woman directed me to the man I wanted to see and then returned to her work. I walked towards the chief of security Thomas Wang.

Thomas Wang wasn't a tall man; he didn't need to be. I was surprised to find out he was in his mid-seventies. People rarely lived that long in the Wastelands, but I would never guess by looking at him. Outside his white hair, he had no signs of aging. He moved with a grace that many younger people could not do.

When he spoke, I could see why he was placed in charge. He knew his business. He made sure each entrance was secured. With a dozen guards placed in the auditorium. He ensured that an escape route was established and well-guarded if necessary. Now it was my turn to get my assignment.

Calmly, I introduced myself, "Duncan Walker reporting as requested."

Wang looked at me, sizing me up. I didn't mind. He stated, "You're the famous Duncan Walker. I heard of you."

Embarrassed, I replied, "You know how rumors spread."

"I do," he said, looking away at the stage. "I have a job for you. Come with me." I followed him behind the stage. We then walked to the outside rotunda. He turned to me and gave me my instructions, "Frazier says you can handle this job. If we had unwanted visitors, they would do the most damage through here. You are to make sure that doesn't happen."

"It won't happen."

"It better not," he stated coldly. "Are you connected?"

Showing him my communicator, I replied, "Yes."

"Good." He replied, "The event ends at seventeen hundred hours. I'll see you then."

After saying that, he left me. That left me no choice but to take my post. There I stayed for the next two days. Watching for introducers. Outside the hourly inspection by Wang. I remained alone. I found myself hoping that a person would try to break in through the boredom.

A young steward named Sandra offered a brief distraction from the tedious assignment. She was a short, pretty woman with a small, round face with blue eyes, and curly, light brown hair that she tied behind her. She wore a blue uniform that had a name tag that revealed her name. In fairness, I told her my name. A gesture that she appreciated. Her job was to bring drinks around the attendees of the rally. I just asked for some water when she made her rounds.

We spent our time telling each other about our lives. She lived in Union with her mother and daughter. They are barely getting by living in Red level. I told her about my life with Gabrielle and Cassandra in Gotham Prime.

"What level?" she asked me, curious.

Embarrassed, I muttered, "Blue Level."

My embarrassment had amused her. When I revealed that I was from the Wastelands, she was surprised by my demeanor. "You're not like other Outlanders," she told me. Living in Red level, she had lived with many 'Outlanders' as she called people like me. I took it as a compliment.

On the third day, I delivered my charges to their seats. Then reported to Wang. After briefing us on today's itinerary, he introduced me to my new associate, Peyton Wilson. A short man with a slight frame, he couldn't be more than twenty. He had a pistol that he concealed under his black jacket. Wang explained that his contractor had a credible threat, supplying a dozen extra guards. He told us both to be vigilant.

Standing at our post, we watched all who came by. Just before noon, we had some visitors arrive. They looked like normal tourists who were lost. I told Peyton to keep an eye on them. Not wanting to take any chances. Other than that, we rarely communicated. A few minutes later, Sandy came to make her rounds. She pushed a cart full of water and other snacks. She passed Peyton without making any eye contact, heading directly toward me. She stopped and coldly handed me a bottle of water. She was strangely aloof from the previous two days. Today she came later than usual. I did find her coldness quite odd, but I thought she had her reasons, so I ignored it. She just gave me my usual bottle of water.

As I was about to open the bottle. A look of fear came over her. She silently shook her head, telling me not to open it. Her eyes then looked over at the tourist down the hall. Immediately, I glanced over my left shoulder and saw they were joined by four other men. A more pressing problem, my partner, Peyton, was drawing his weapon and pointing it at me. I was in trouble.

Another thing I learned in the Wastelands is never go down without a fight. With the only weapon I had available, the water bottle, I turned and threw it at his face. It immediately stunned him as he hit him on the bridge of his nose. He staggered back. That hesitation gave me time to draw my pistol. I surmise that he didn't shoot me in the back because he didn't want to draw attention to himself. Fortunately for me, I had no limitations. I shot him dead. From both sides, people who I assume were his friends joined the fight. I grabbed Sandy, and we hid behind some crates. This is not an ideal position for us because we're in a crossfire.

"I couldn't go through with it. I'm sorry!" she stated. "They threaten my family."

I understood. Right now, we need to get out of this problem. Two security officers rushed in from the auditorium. One was killed instantly, and the second managed to take cover and give us some relief. On my communicator, I could hear, Wang and other men screaming for information. Gate seven has been attacked as well.

When I heard silence, I quickly responded, "We have two men down. Shots are being fired."

He inquired, "How many assailants?"

"Seven." I saw my friend shoot another gunman, so I needed to amend, "Now there are six."

He told us, "We had some moles in our midst. I will get you help. Just hold your ground."

Like we had any other choice. Three other men came in from the auditorium to help us. Moving in their positions more cautiously. Now, with five of us, we manage to force the attackers to give ground. Wang led some of his men along the rotunda, outflanking the assailants. A second group, led by Silas, attacked from the opposite end. Cutting off their retreat.

Wang called for them to surrender. An offer that they refused. If they can't escape, they will die where they stand. Some would call them brave. For me, I would call them fools. When the last one was killed. Wang came up to me for a report. Silas had joined him.

Glancing over at the dead body of Wilson, he asked, "Who shot him?"

"I did," I reported. "He was one of them."

Silas added, "Somehow, I knew you would be in the middle of it." I couldn't argue with that.

On a private line, he checked my story with his man, who was looking over security footage. Satisfied, he looked at me. "Your shot alerted the rest of us. Good job."

"Thank you, sir."

He walked away from me and talked to the event Chairman. My attention immediately turned to Sandy. Silas joined me as we went to check on her. I had left her over where we had huddled during the firefight. Walking over to her, my heart stopped when I saw her slouching over. I knew she was dead. Moving closer, I saw a burn mark on her temple. She didn't suffer.

Why did she do it? Save my life. If she had let Wilson knock me out, she probably would be alive right now. What did I do to deserve her saving my life? Did I do anything so special? Granted,

I did feel a connection with her. Another time, we could have been closer. We can never know.

A group of Watchmen passed by me with two men in white coats with a gurney. I watched as the lead Watchman gave the signal for the two whitecoats to place her on the gurney.

"Be gentle with her," I stated.

Ignoring me, they did their job. They gently placed her on the gurney and took her away. I watched as an inspector arrived to ask me questions.

"Name."

"Duncan Walker."

"Was she a friend?"

"I only knew her for a couple of days."

"What is she to you?"

"She saved my life."

"I see," he replied. "You can go. We are closing this event so you can return to your delegates."

I did as I was told. I joined my three charges and led them to our suite. Being more cautious, I made sure there were no more surprises. Wang being cautious himself brought me two more of his men to help with security. When I was satisfied, I returned to the hallway, and all three of us escorted them in. They walked into their respective rooms. Safe in their rooms, I turned to the two men and thanked them for their help. I dismiss them. Escorting them out of the suite. I turned and headed to my room. I was tired.

Lying down on my bed, I found myself staring at the roof. Every time I closed my eyes, I saw Sandra's lifeless body. Why did her death bother me so much? I had seen death before. But she was different. I had taken the time to get to know her. Her life and her dreams. Her daughter is alone in the world. I decided what I had to do.

After getting up, I headed to talk to Fletcher and Koch. I explained what I needed to do. They understood and gave me a short leave to do what I needed to do. I thanked them and immediately left. Heading down to the lobby.

An hour had passed before I managed to return to the suite.

When I entered, I was surprised to see all three of my clients getting ready. This three-day excursion of delegates is ending their day at a Cager's match. Union versus Capital, to be precise. A special car will be gathering all the delegates and the security guards in a private suite. Wang and twenty hand-picked men are there right now to secure the suite. Watchmen have been dispatched to guard the stadium. I was surprised.

I had thought that the delegates were planning to stay in until it was time to leave. That will be the safe thing to do. I made that opinion quite clear.

"Duncan, nobody ever became Chancellor by playing it safe," Fletcher stated confidently.

With that kind of logic, I knew I had to just go along with this night out. But believing that Gabby had probably heard about the attack earlier, she might be worrying. I asked, "When are we leaving?"

"In twenty minutes."

"Can I make a call?"

"Go ahead."

I entered my room and made the call. Gabby answered, seeing I was all right, she gave a sigh of relief for a moment. When that moment was over, her mood changed. "Just tell me one thing. Are you involved with what happened down there?"

"Yes," I replied. It wasn't going to do any good lying to her, she would be expecting that. However, I decided on a different strategy: "How did your doctor's visit go?"

"Don't change the subject," she said, annoyed with me. "What had happened? And why are you always at the center of these things?"

I really couldn't answer that. It is never my intention to be in the middle of these things, as she called it. To be truthful, I have tried to avoid something like this. A smile came over my face as I looked at Gabby, trying to hide hers. I just answered, "It's my job."

"Are you still coming home tomorrow?"

"That's the plan."

"I'll see you then. We have some changes back home. Love you."

She switched off the monitor before I could tell her the same. I will tell her when I see her.

With that done. I gathered my weapons and joined the others.

I came out just in time. A knock on the door startled us. Pulling out my pistol, I told the others to get back. Not wanting to take any chances with their lives. They understood and did as I requested. I stepped towards the door. In a loud voice, I asked firmly, "Who is it?"

From the other side of the door, I heard an answer, "Detail six. Ready to take you down to the car."

I stated, "Have your papers ready." Immediately, I opened the door. There were four men and one woman in front of me. I didn't recognize any of them. Holding out my pistol, they responded with their papers. Satisfied, I returned my pistol to its holster. I let the three delegates follow the escort out of our room. I was last, making sure the door was locked behind me. I had the key in my pocket.

There is a total of fifteen delegates on this floor alone. We stopped at each suite. The security guard in each room followed the same protocol as I did. Each bodyguard, once satisfied, allowed his delegates to join our group. After we visited the fifth suite, we proceeded to the lifts. Taking two transports, we headed down to the lobby. At the lobby, we took a final headcount. With everyone accounted for, we headed to the tube, and our private transport was waiting for us. I should say cars, four to be exact. Surrounding it stood six more of Wang's men. They gave us the go-ahead to enter the airship. With all of us securely in our seats, the shuttle moved. Hovering over Union District.

Union Stadium is thirty minutes away. Gotham was larger. But this stadium was nice, too. After the shuttle stopped. We were immediately greeted by six Watchmen. They were all determined not to take any chances. The six men patiently waited for all of us to depart our transport. All of us gathered at the entrance. The Watchmen proceeded to lead us through a secure pathway to our suite. As I looked around Wang had his men, Watchman details assigned to him, and stadium security posted along the entire route. As we headed high up on top of the stadium.

Union owners graciously gave us two adjoining suites. It could easily handle our entire entourage. Besides that, we had a buffet and a full bar on the tab of the host. I'm not sure who exactly that is, but he is rich. Once we settled in Wang appeared with his two top lieutenants. He came in to acquire the men that he had sent earlier to bring us here. Those who remained, like me, were employed by the respective delegates. When his men left the suite, he dismissed his two lieutenants.

Alone Wang made sure he could be heard by all. "My men will be posted all around to make sure you won't be bothered." Looking around for a moment, he continued, "The Watchmen and Union security have other duties. I must request your safety; you will all stay here. You will have everything you need to enjoy the game. We will see you at its conclusion." Wang now had one more thing to request, "I need to speak with your security."

Twenty of us surrounded him. During the attack earlier today, we lost three agents dead and one wounded. Wang had his men replace them for the afternoon. Now he has given us our instructions, as we are the last line of defense.

"If there is a breach. We have created an escape route from the suites to the shuttle below. It will be up to you to make sure they make it out alive."

A group responded, "Yes, sir."

With a burst of admiration, he stated, "Good luck."

We all disperse. I remained because I wanted to talk to him for a moment. He was annoyed with my request at first. But when I explained further, a sense of pride came over him, and he stated, "I would like to work with you again."

"It will be a pleasure," I replied with the same admiration for him. We shook hands. I watched him walk out of the suite. Strangely, I didn't think he liked me when we first met.

I checked the two escape routes he had mentioned. Just for a precaution. Both doors lead to an express shaft. Both were guarded by Wang's men. I remembered one who came to my aid earlier today, and he remembered me as well. We exchanged recognition.

From behind me, I heard the fans cheering. That meant I had to get to my post. He understood.

Back in the suite, I gathered myself a plate of something to eat and returned to my seat. Both teams were already on the field. At the center of the field, the lead official called the opposing teams' captains to join her. Capital team had on their road uniforms, gold jerseys, and red pants. Union had purple jerseys and orange pants on their home. A strange choice of color schemes, but it works somehow. Union won the toss and chose to take possession. It will be their only victory for the remainder of the night.

The game started well enough as they made it to the neutral zone, only to have a player being stopped. Capital responded with a quick kick into a goal. The next possession started well enough, working their way into scoring position only to have their Leader throw an interception in the scoring zone. At the end of the first quarter, Capital had three Union nothing.

As the first quarter ended, I noticed a few things. A few months ago, when I saw my first Cager match, I mentioned that all this was an elaborate plot to distract the masses. Highlanders don't share the same enthusiasm as the masses. During the entire first quarter, not one of the delegates paid any attention to the action of the field. Preferring to stand in the back and talk in the back.

Not that they are missing anything. Capital spent the second quarter scoring two successive drives. Union had no answers as Capital ended the half with twelve points, and Union has yet to score. A report from Wang gave us all the clear. That allowed me to get something else to eat and enjoy the rest of the match.

Capital started well enough, driving to the goal line, but that ended when their leader made his first mistake. He gave the ball away in the endzone, giving Union their first score of the game. When the third period ended, their fans had some hope that, somehow, they could get back into the game. That was not to be. In the fourth quarter, Capital started with three successful goal kicks and ended the final period with two successful scoring drives. If it wasn't for two interceptions in the goal, the score would have been much worse. In the end, the final score was Capital 27, Union 3.

Looking down at the fans below, I saw many disappointed souls leaving the stadium.

"How was the game?" I heard somebody asking me a question, and it startled me. Immediately, I turned, and it was Koch.

"Great if you're a Capital fan, not so much if you're with Union." I answered, "Union isn't very good."

"Union had some injuries."

"I see." That made sense to me. Union has looked out of since a bit. Curious, and I wanted to know about the gathering with the other delegates. "How was the game for you?"

"Very productive" he smiled, "you're looking at the Reform candidate for the office of Chancellor."

"Congratulation" I stated, "you have my vote." Not that I will vote or not. I never thought much about it. I just learned that's what you're supposed to say to a candidate. But as I said before, I kind of like Koch and Fletcher.

Wang arrived with his contingent. He is determined to make sure nothing else happens to the delegates. In an orderly way, we left the suite and headed to our transport.

I do have to say something about politics. After two and a half days of deliberations, they had accomplished nothing. After just three hours in a crowded suite in a Cager match, they managed to reach an agreement. I wonder how much more work Highlanders of Purple Level manage to get done during Cager games.

––––––––––

I had officially finished my assignment a few minutes before noon. All three of my clients complimented me for my service when they released me. A contingent of Watchmen will see to their returning to their homes. As I was heading home, I honestly felt quite proud of myself. That I was finally finding my place in this city. At first, I felt I was under Gabrielle's shadow. Not a person but something that belonged to her. She had never made me feel that way.

As I walked down the street towards our home, I noticed there was more traffic than usual. Forcing me to slow my pace down a bit. I was in a rush to get home and find out how she was. When

I left, she was going to the doctor. I wanted to know how she did. For the last four days, I had been worrying about her, along with Cassandra. She had been through a lot, and I wanted to know how she was getting along. At first, I tried to ignore the rumbling from my stomach because I wanted to get home. But then my nose picked up the fragrance of a sausage stand. I decided to have one. I ordered it with sausage and pepper, and the old man handed it to me. Paying him, I proceeded to put pickled cabbage and mustard on it. I forget what the pickled cabbage is called, but I like it.

Eating it as I walked. I managed to finish it as I walked up to the door. With my keys, I opened the door and walked in. Throwing the wrapper in the trash, I called out, When I heard no response, I surmised I was alone. The girls were probably doing a seminar with Caitlyn.

I quickly entered the bedroom and put my bag on a table. After that, I disarmed myself, putting my weapons in my drawer. When I opened it, I was surprised to find that Gabby had put her makeup in my drawer. We will have to talk about this when she gets home. I can't leave them lying around, and she knows that. Heading for the kitchen, I wanted a drink of water. I returned to the bedroom to lie down on the bed. Looking forward to sleeping in my bed for the first time in a week. Not wanting to bother Gabrielle while she was ill, and before that, Cassandra didn't want to be alone, so she took my place beside Gabby. Sitting down, I took off my shoes and socks and lay down on my back, staring at the roof. It was funny, I didn't realize how tired I was at that moment. I closed my eyes, and I fell asleep.

I don't know how long I slept. All I knew was I had a perfectly lovely dream. That ended abruptly. I felt a violent push on my shoulder along with a high-pitched scream, "You don't belong here!"

Waking up abruptly. I had no memory of the dream, that was bad enough. But as I opened my eyes, I saw a woman who looked about sixty, with crazy eyes. She allowed me to sit up at the edge of the bed. With her arms crossed she tried very hard to give the appearance of towering over me, but it was a futile gesture. Now I was awake I took a moment to get a good look at this stranger in my bedroom.

Looking her over from her feet upward. She wore simple black shoes that women chose to wear for comfort rather than looks. Her outfit was a light grey one-piece uniform that managed to cover her entire body. Not that there was much to see. She wore no jewelry on her fingers, around her neck, or ears. With no make-up on, she looked, as I said before, in her sixties. Her hair was a mixture of white and blonde that seemed to be all over the place. From the look of her face, I surmised that she didn't care about one bit of my description of her.

"Who the hell are you?" I asked her, believing that it was a fair question.

She replied with great confidence in her right to be there in this room, "I'm Regina Fontaine. Gabrielle Blue and Cassandra Towne's housekeeper."

When did Cassandra choose her last name? I wondered for a moment. Realizing who was behind this as a formality, I asked her, "Caitlyn hired you."

"Yes, she did" she replied, now it was her turn to get some answers. "Now who the hell you are?"

With the same confidence, I replied, "Duncan Walker, I live here." Her demeanor did not change. "I share this bed with Gabrielle."

She was still not impressed. Getting annoyed, I decided to challenge her a bit, "Somebody must have told you."

Taking a step back. She stood in front of the door. Uncrossing her arms, she admitted, "Yes, I did. I'm sorry I wasn't home to greet you. We had to make some changes while you were gone. Come with me."

Curious, I did as she requested. She immediately led me to the room I had slept in before I left on my assignment. As I started to look around, she started to explain, "I'm sure you will be comfortable here. It is the doctor's order. Her immune system had been compromised. I'm sure you understand."

I did. Looking in my closet, I found all my clothes neatly put away, but I still needed to ask, "Is this permanent?"

She politely replied, "That is up to the doctor."

While looking in my drawers, I asked her, "What are your duties?"

With an insincere smile, she replied, "I'll cook, clean, and help the two young women in their duties."

"What about me?" I asked her, not knowing what answer I would receive.

"I'll take care of you, too." That was her answer. Not sure what she meant by it exactly.

"I see" I replied, reminding myself that I was still fatigued, I requested, "Now if you excuse me, I had a rough four days, I like to continue with my nap."

Changing her tone a bit she stated eagerly, "We heard about it. The girls were concerned. The stories I heard about you must be true."

"They are." Sitting down on my new bed, "Now if you'll excuse me." Getting my polite hint, she started to leave, but not before she mentioned, "I have dinner to prepare, and I have to make Gabrielle's bed again."

I didn't care that much. It was, after all, an honest mistake. With my conscience clear this time, I just closed my eyes again and fell back to sleep. I'll figure out the enigma of Regina Fontaine later.

As I slept on my back, I felt a second tug at my shoulder. I opened my eyes, expecting the worst. I was pleasantly surprised. This time, it was Gabrielle looking down at me.

"I must be dreaming."

She lowered herself and put her lips on mine. I had no desire to do anything but kiss her. When she pulled away, she proceeded with a right to my temple. I reacted.

She stated angrily, "You promised me you would stay out of danger."

I reminded her as I sat up at the edge of the bed, "That is my job!"

She responded, "I'm sick of that excuse."

Reaching out for her, I managed to put my arms around her

waist, pulling her close to me. It was my turn to kiss her. Pulling away slowly, I asked, "Am I forgiven?"

"Not yet," she stated, as she lowered her lip towards mine.

When she had finished. I told her, "I missed you." I saw a tear on her cheek, that reminded me of something more important, "What did the doctor say?"

Either to put me at ease by reassuring me that it was nothing or it was nothing at all, she casually stated, "It was nothing. She said it was something to do with my immunity. An infection of some kind. She gave me some tonic to take. I was as good as new. She gave me two more dosages if the symptoms come back, and they haven't."

"Then why am I in here?" It is a fair question, don't you think?

"That is Caitlyn's idea. She thinks you're the cause of the infection." Realizing that she was going to amend her statement, she attempted to justify Caitlyn's decision. "We both signed a contract. She believes that you're constantly exposed going out there."

"Cassandra was exposed out there, why not her?" I asked, a little irritated by what I was hearing.

Gabrielle responded with logic in a way I couldn't argue, "I was showing symptoms before we came across her." Damn, she was right.

"Aren't you afraid you might catch something now?"

"I'll take my chances." In saying that, she kissed me again. This time, I leaned back, allowing her to fall on top of me. I started kissing her ear as she began to open the buttons of my shirt. All was going as planned, but for one thing.

A knock on the door forced us to stop what we were doing. That was followed by somebody clearing their throat. We both looked at the door and saw Regina standing there. She was not embarrassed.

She stated in a passive tone, "I'm sorry to interrupt," she wasn't, "but you must get ready for tonight. Cassandra is already. You can't be late, after being out of action for so long." It wasn't that long compared when the last time we were intimate together.

She watched as Gabrielle, who is rarely clumsy, got back to her feet and started to walk out. When she passed her, she looked at her, ashamed, as she left my room. Then she turned her disapproving gaze on me. Sitting up on the edge of my bed, I rebuttoned my shirt. When I finished, I exited my room to see Cassandra. We exchanged a glance as I passed her. She looked at me like she had won a battle.

Cassandra was sitting down in the living room. With her head turned to me, I walked up behind her, placing my hand on her shoulder. She turned to me and smiled. She looked up at me and smiled. I gave her my hand, she took it and stood up. The difference was amazing in less than a week. Her dark brown hair was set like a crown. Caitlyn picked a one-piece gown with a neckline that came down in a V, the sky blue matched her blue eyes. Most importantly, she looked alive. Far from the despair, I first met her that night at Star Casino.

She held me in her arms. She stated, "We were worried about you." She continued with her head on my chest, "Gabby waited next to the monitor until she knew you were all right."

I playfully asked, "What about you?"

Looking up at me, she stated, "I knew you were okay." She was right; we both knew we had unfinished business together. We needed to wait for Inspector Wells.

Changing the subject, I asked her, "What is going on tonight?"

She stepped out of my arms and was about to answer when Regina chimed in, "They are guests of the Patricians. They are introducing their new candidate, Vincent Herbert."

I didn't know much about Vincent Herbert, but I did know his father is the sitting Chancellor of Gotham. I heard from the Reformers that he is retiring. Directing this question to Cassandra, I asked, "Is it just you and Gabrielle?"

"No, Selene, Savannah, and Elizabeth are coming too."

Regina added, "And your escort will be here in twenty minutes. I must finish with Gabrielle." We watched her walk back to Gabby's room.

"She means well."

Ten minutes later, she returned and introduced Gabrielle to us. Her dress was black, in the style of Cassandra's dress. Her red hair was made up like Cassandra's as well. As she walked towards us, I proclaimed, "You two look beautiful."

Regina proudly added her opinion, "Herbert and his friends will be insane not to propose to you on the spot."

Gabrielle glanced over at me with apprehension. I just gave her a reassuring smile. The look on her face gave me all the assurance I needed.

A knock on the door distracted us. Regina immediately opened the door. She recognized the three men and let them in. Proudly, she told them, "Ladies, your escort is here."

I had seen all three in passing over the past few months. I didn't know much about them since we never had a chance to mingle. People in our line of work rarely do. But Regina knew them and made damn sure the girls knew about it. As for myself, I was satisfied with the knowledge that I had never needed any help in protecting the girls. Regina chattered away as she led the party out the door. With her shutting the door. She suddenly realized that we were left alone together in the apartment.

"I have your dinner ready in the kitchen," she stated. "If you'll excuse me, I'm going to bed." She passed by me and into her room. Feeling hungry, I headed for the kitchen. Where I immediately saw a large plate with a cover over it that had my name on it, to avoid any confusion, I guess. One thing I say for her is she is organized.

Gathering a knife and fork from a drawer. I sat down and lifted the dome, revealing my dinner. I wasn't sure what it was, but it did taste good. That is one thing in her favor, she is a good cook. Finishing my dinner, I found a glass to get something to drink. As I opened the refrigerator, I chose cranberry juice. Pouring myself a glass, I immediately returned the bottle to the refrigerator. I sat down and began to drink some cranberry juice.

Sitting there, I was reminded of the first time I had cranberry juice. It was the first time I was in Grand Junction. Aurora introduced me to it, among other things. I wondered how she was doing in Shenandoah. Her life now is far different from her life at Grand Junction. Back then, she had power in a decaying kingdom, and now she has a home, a husband, and a child. I never thought she would be content with such a mundane life. I guess you never really know someone. As I finished my glass, I thought it was best to stop thinking about

Aurora, she is married now. I placed the dirty dishes in the washer and headed to my room. I had some reading to catch up on.

I read for three hours in bed. I fell asleep ten minutes before midnight. Two hours later, Gabby and Cassandra discovered that old habits die hard. Despite their best efforts, I was awakened by their muffled giggling. I guess they had a good time. I just lay there and listened to their constant amusement at one of the honored guests they had met. A constant bore who thought he was an intellectual, as they described him. Then I realized it was one of Klein's sons; I'm not sure which. Not that it mattered. Frankly, I believed their father had cloned them from someone. Not wanting to risk it with nature. Finally, their voices were muffled as they entered their rooms respectfully. There I lay in bed for another hour trying to go back to sleep.

I woke up at 900 hours. I chose to start the day with a shower. Fifteen minutes later, I felt refreshed. I ate a quick breakfast before I headed out for a run. Carlos in Southpoint had warned me not to become complacent about living in the city. You can find yourself in a habit you can't break, he often told me. I didn't understand what he had meant until we made the move to Gotham. For a person who was forced to survive in the Wastelands, this lavish lifestyle can be intoxicating. That means an individual must keep active just for the sole purpose of keeping sane.

In the first hour, I ran an established course that I had already mapped out. I created this route a month ago. I made it a priority to follow the course at least once a week. Today was my last chance to keep that commitment. As I finished that first course, I immediately checked my watch. Please, I began preparing for the second run when I found an area that I had never been to and explored it. I finished the five miles in less than an hour. That will give me more time to explore.

I made my way to the point, the area overlooking the sea. I had already explored Grey Level a couple of weeks ago, so I chose Yellow Level this morning. Yellow Point, as it is called, is about one square mile with seven separate levels. As I walked around each level, I mapped out each neighborhood, making sure where security cameras were and how to avoid them, if necessary. You will never know when you will need to. When I finished my workout, I headed home.

I found that Cassandra and Gabrielle were finally awake. They were busy trying on their clothes for tonight. One look at them, and I knew what they were doing tonight. Attending a Cager match between Gotham and Queens. Bryce Allen is making his debut for Gotham tonight. That means Naomi will be joining us. I must admit Caitlyn chose their outfits well this time. Each one still had to wear Gotham's team colors. But they are more flattering and tailored.

Seeing me, Cassandra was excited. "Guess what we are doing tonight?"

"Heading to Queens to watch the game." I simply replied.

Disappointed, Cassandra asked, "How did you know?"

Not wanting to give away any of my secrets. I just smiled at her and changed the subject. "Who is coming with us?" I assumed when she mentioned we, she meant I was coming with them to act as an escort.

Now it was Gabrielle's turn to answer, "Naomi, Savannah, and Elizabeth."

A smaller group. Caitlyn must have a reason for it. Again, I decided to change the subject. "So, who were you making fun of last night?"

Cassandra looked over to Gabrielle, astonished, unfazed. Gabrielle simply responded, "Good, I thought you were losing your touch."

"Eric Kleist, he thinks he is charming," Cassandra added.

Knowing the answer, I felt that she wanted me to ask it anyway, "Is he?" She shook her head now. The two of them then looked over at each other and burst out laughing. He must have put on quite a performance last night. Truthfully, I couldn't help but feel sorry for him. I just excused myself and headed for my room to get dressed for the day. The girls did the same.

––––––––––

We made it to the stadium in Queens ten minutes before the challenge. Taking our seats, the two teams were in their positions, waiting for the challenge. Queens were in their home green jerseys and white pants, while Gotham had on their away red jerseys and blue pants. I looked around at the other guests of the owners, I discovered that Klein and his two sons were here with us. Of all in attendance, the most exciting one was easily Naomi. Her fiancé was standing in front of his new team's goal, wearing the number thirteen. I gave her a wink, and she responded with a smile of pure joy.

The game started. Gotham's gamble had paid off, and they won possession at midfield. Moving forward quickly, the Queens players had to rush back to defend their goal. But to no avail, Gotham was poised to score; only a great play by their Keeper saved his teammates and earned a point for his efforts. That proved to be the only score of the game after one period.

As the second period started, many in our party left their seats for something to eat or to mingle with the owner's guests, following Caitlyn's directive. Only Naomi and I remained to watch the entire second period. Queens scored quickly, kicking the ball through the goal. Giving them a three-nothing lead. Things went from bad to worse when Gotham failed to get the ball out of the scoring area, conceding two more points and possession of the ball. A second kick gave Queens a seven-nothing lead. Many more fans around us in the stands became discouraged, not wanting to see another disappointment.

Those who are stuck with their team witness something amazing. In the four possessions proceeding, Gotham scored each time. The result at the end of the first half was a twelve to seven score. Niomi proved to be the most exciting. Her fiancé had played well, keeping Queens away from the goal line. Wearing a very short red dress she jumped up and hugged me.

"You better join the others, "I whispered, "to keep up appearances." She nodded in agreement and walked up the stairs. Looking around to see where the others are. Checking each one, I was satisfied they were enjoying themselves. Looking around for Savannah, I couldn't find her. Growing concerned, I was about to head up when I looked over to my left and I saw her sitting on my left. Relieved I sat down.

"You're quiet," I snapped at her.

Amused, she simply replied, "That is my talent." Looking over at Cassandra, she stated, "That was a nice find you made."

Looking at Cassandra happy, was a welcoming site for me, considering what she had been through. But I was surprised about Caitlyn, wondering what her motives were. "I was surprised Caitlyn took her in. She doesn't seem the type."

Astonished, Savannah looked at me like I should have known this. "She is one of us."

"How do you know?"

With a dismissive tone, she answered, "I don't know. We just do."

I interjected, "But Gabby didn't know."

"She spent most of her life apart from us. She probably heard the signals but didn't know what it had meant," she explained calmly. She added, "Maybe that is why she had joined your party in the first place."

There are still questions I don't understand. If Mitchel is a Krieg and all Kriegs are blues, why didn't he give her to Caitlyn? I didn't get a chance to ask her that question. Savannah looked over at the scoreboard.

Nervously, she muttered, "Do you think Gotham is going to win?"

"It is quite possible."

She began to look anxious, like she was dreading something terrible that would happen. "I hope not." Looking to the floor, she confessed why we are here, "We are the team's reward if they win. An incentive."

I'm not surprised. I didn't want Gotham to win now. As the second half began, Savannah's worst fears were realized. Queens never scored again. Gotham quickly turned the match into a rout. They closed the game with thirteen unanswered points. The final score was Gotham 25 to Queens 7.

A steward brought us down to the players' lounge. I made it only as far as the door. I was sent home alone.

5 PAYBACK

INSPECTOR WELLS FINALLY CALLED US IN FOR A BRIEFING. WHEN Cassandra and I arrived, he immediately apologized for taking so long to get back to us. He blamed it on the reservations his superiors had about using two civilians. Their doubts had ended when Wang spoke up for us. With their support, the mission will go forward.

He started by letting us know that we had eight days to find the smugglers and lead them into a trap. Cassandra assured him that she could remember where they had left and find the ring leaders. As for myself, I had no doubt she could; Gabrielle has the same ability herself. Satisfied, Wells gave us each a transmitter that would lead his men to which wharf the boat would dock so they could apprehend them. We both put it in a secure spot and turned it on. Wells wanted to know if we needed anything ourselves. I requested a pistol for Cassandra. He agreed and handed her one much like mine. Finally, he gave us our exit and entry passes. It will be for nine days starting tomorrow. We promised that we would be ready to leave in the morning. Now satisfied, he sent us on our way.

Before we made it home, we made one stop together. On Yellow level, I found a small shop that sold weapons. It is one of a hundred along the walkways that connect Yellow Level. Inside, I brought Cassandra to a display case of daggers. She will need a second weapon, something she can conceal and use if her pistol has been compromised. I advised her to try each one, checking its balance and how it feels in her hand. She finally settled on a one-minded mind. We are about to pay when she finds something else. A small blade that she can conceal in a piece of jewelry made from a cheap material, something a bandit would not want. We bought that too.

Once at home, we began to pack for tomorrow. Caitlyn proved to be very accommodating for us to go on with our mission. Alone in my room, I gathered what I needed to take with me. It had been a long time since I had lived outside the city. But I began to remember the essentials. A lantern for light was the first thing I placed in my bag. Followed by a change of clothes. A thermal shirt for warmth. Finally, a book to read; after all, I must be a little civilized. Once I finished, I closed it and put it on a table so I could grab it. I then gathered my weapons. First, I made sure my pistol was fully charged. Next, I did the same with my stinger. When I finished charging my stinger, I placed it on the table with my daggers and pistol for tomorrow morning.

Looking up, I noticed Gabrielle standing at the doorway. She had a sad smile. I asked her, "How long were you standing there?"

Stepping out of the doorway. I could see her better; her hair was down, covering her shoulders. Caitlyn had given her the day off, and that made her choose a simple blue dress with a white flower print on a one-piece suit that fit her loosely. She turned and shut and locked the door. She turned and answered my question. In a light tone, she jested, "When you put your underwear in the bag."

I could tell she was reluctant for me to go. She wanted to go with us. But Caitlyn would never let all three of us do something so dangerous. Cassandra needed to go, and Caitlyn knew that, and I was expendable. It was clear she was nervous for us. Selfishly I was flattered, she was so concerned. Sometimes a man needs to be reassured.

It was my turn to reassure her. "We will be gone for eight days. We will be back before you know it."

Deep down, she knew it needed to be done. Cassandra and the others were our friends. They needed to be avenged. She tried to give me a brave face, but she couldn't hide her reservations. She moved closer to me.

"Come back safe." She kissed me hard on my lips. She held me in her arms so tightly that she was afraid to let me go; I would disappear right in front of her forever. When she pulled back, she gave me a gentle smile. She was content. "Punish them good." She kissed me again. A little less intense but with the same passion.

Pulling away, I asked her, "What about being infected?"

"I don't care. "She kissed me one last time. Maneuvering over to my bed, we proceeded to spend the night. Occasionally, we heard a knock on the door. Followed by Regina's voice asking to be let in. We just ignored her attempts to stop us. Sharing a sense of amusement by Regina. Finally, she gave up, and we fell asleep in each other's embrace.

When dawn broke, I was up. Taking my clothes with me, I went to take a shower. When I was finished, I found Gabby sitting up in bed, holding the blanket over her breasts. I walked up to her and kissed her good morning. She smiled.

"Let's have breakfast."

She nodded yes, and I left her to change. In the kitchen, Cassandra was already dressed and ready to go. Regina was cooking breakfast. She wasn't happy with us. Cassandra just sat there quietly as she drank her orange juice. I headed for the refrigerator to get myself some orange juice. I looked over at Regina and stated, "How did you sleep last night?" She said nothing. I just returned to the table and joined Cassandra.

"What did you do?"

Before I could answer. Cassandra happened to look over at my bedroom and watched Gabrielle leave the room with the same clothes she had worn last night. Cassandra looked over at me and knew what had happened. And she approved.

The only person who wasn't happy was Regina. She slammed two plates of food in front of each other respectfully and walked away. Fully dressed, Gabrielle joined us, and she had the same treatment. A plate of food was in front of her. Unfazed, Gabby just thanked Regina.

In a tense tone she said, "If you excuse me, I have some work to do."

Gabrielle replied, "Go ahead."

Regina retreated to her room. Leaving the three of us to finish our breakfast.

Cassandra stated as she finished the last morsel of her breakfast, "Poor girl, I hope she doesn't take it too hard."

Gabrielle replied, "She'll get over it." She glanced over at me. Cassandra quickly understood the hint. She quickly excused herself and entered the room alone. Gabby said, "Thank you for last night."

I had finished eating, taking her hand, I replied, "I'll miss you."

"I wish I could go with you."

"I know," I replied, stroking her hand, but we both knew that Caitlyn would never permit it.

"I'm going with you two as far as I can."

"I was hoping you would," I replied. "You better get ready."

I headed back to my room to gather my things. Taking my bag off the table, I put it on my bed. Gabby made it for me. I then returned to the table and placed each of my weapons on my person. I then put on a jacket to protect myself from the elements outside. Checking my watch, it was time to go. But first, I needed to look in my mirror. Just to calm the nerves. Now, I am ready.

Outside, Cassandra was wearing a blue jumpsuit and a black denim jacket that covered her weapons. She chose to wear a pair of boots that covered just below her knees. Her hair was disheveled, and she wore no makeup. Giving her the appearance of being out there for years. As for me, I hadn't shaved since the bay before the Gotham Cager match, so I had some good growth on my face.

We were both ready to go. We just had to wait for one thing, Gabrielle. To keep ourselves busy we cleared the plates from the table and put them in the washer. When we finished, we looked around, still no Gabrielle.

"How much money do you have?" I asked her.

Cassandra looked in her wallet. Taking out her chip, she looked at it and said, "A thousand credits. And you?"

"Five thousand." Reaching in my pocket, I took out five gold coins. Each one is worth around 1,500 credits a piece. I handed them to her, "This will go farther out there. Keep them in a safe place."

She placed them in a secret pocket on the inside of her jacket. I added, "We'd better visit a bank and get some more hard money." She agreed with me. Credit chips don't go far out there.

Still no Gabrielle. Cassandra volunteered to see what was going on. Five minutes later, they came out together. What was said between them was none of my business. Together, the three of us headed out.

We needed to get to Grey Section in Northpoint. It was no surprise that we took a shuttle north. Before that, we stopped at a bank and grabbed some hard money. After entering a public shuttle a few blocks from the bank, we were on our way. Heading through York, we sat together watching the district fly by us. To our surprise, there were open parts along the roof that allowed the sun to shine through. It proved to be a beautiful day outside. Being a public shuttle, we made a few extra stops, and each time, a new set of people entered, replacing the few who were excited. Many are wearing the same clothes. The blue and grey of their Cagers team. It was clear they were playing Northpoint today. I don't know much about Northpoint. I have a feeling we will learn much more about them soon.

As we entered Northpoint, fans of their team entered the shuttle, it was clear they didn't like York fans very much. They sat on one side of the car while York sat on the other, proudly wearing their black and white. Then there we were, sitting between them, trying to hide our amusement while they sang their team songs and hurled insults at each other. After two additional stops, we came to the stop for the rival fans. That succeeded in emptying the shuttle. With no new passengers entering the car, we had it to ourselves.

Quietly, the shuttle began to move again. We passed the stadium, overlooking the fans moving around and looking for their seats. Strangely, I kind of wished we were going to the game instead. With the attitude of the two groups of fans, I had a feeling this game would be fun to watch. But it was not to be.

Puzzled, Cassandra asked, "What was wrong with them?"

I replied, "They don't like each other."

"But why the hell not?"

Gabrielle interjected, "I have no idea."

All three of us just began laughing for a moment. They didn't notice but I quickly became sullener. I did. Each district of Gotham was a separate community for hundreds of years. When Gotham expanded, they overtook the neighboring communities. How that had happened is anybody's guess, but it was far from peaceful. This rivalry between teams is all that is left. I guess it is better than violence between them.

After an hour, we made it to the end of the line. All three of us were excited to board the shuttle. At the station, we watched the shuttle turn around for the trip back. The platform had a large window overlooking the wilderness bordering the other side of the wall. We prepared to part ways.

Gabby, while still apprehensive, tried to maintain a brave face, and gave Cassandra a loving embrace. Much like two sisters. When they parted, Cassandra picked up her bag and walked over to the lift. Gabrielle walked over to me. Despite her smile, I noticed she was fighting a losing battle to hold back her tears.

I reassured her, "We will be back in eight days."

"I know you must go. We made a promise." She kissed me goodbye. With all her feelings she kissed me, and finally, she pulled away from me, "Just be careful."

"I always am," I jested.

She began to laugh. I watched her laughing while smiling. She gave me a quick kiss goodbye and walked off to the southern line. Picking up my bag, I joined Cassandra. We headed down the lift. As we exited the lift, we entered Grey Section. A simple sign placed strategically in front of us revealed where we needed to go. To the right, it said. Heading down the corridor, we both saw the exit gate manned by one small Watchman. That is where we needed to go.

A few steps from the gate The Watchman noticed us. He probably doesn't get many people leaving the city. His glare became puzzled for a moment. Concerned, I looked over to my right and noticed Cassandra was no longer beside me. She had stopped in her tracks, visibly scared to go any further. I walked over to her. She couldn't look me in the eye. She just stared at the gateway.

Softly, I stated, "It's okay, take as much time as you need."

A minute later she looked up at me and nodded. She gave me her hard, support. To reassure her I placed her arm around mine and we walked to the Gateway together. Stopping only to show the Watchman our passes.

The Watchman took his job very seriously. He made sure that there was nothing wrong with our passes. He was a short man with a large belly, a person of age, living his entire life in Gotham. That is impossible outside Gotham. His hair is completely white, betraying his age of nearly seventy. It is clear to me that he didn't want to be here. This was his last job before retirement, and he didn't want to retire. But with each question he asked, he had this position because his superiors wanted to put them out to pasture, the ancients would say. After fifteen minutes, he was satisfied. He let us go through and leave Gotham.

Before he opened the gate, he gave us one warning, "Remember, you only have eight days. If you are delayed, you can only get back to the city through Southpoint. And there is no guarantee they will accept your request."

Cassandra responded, "We understand."

The gate opened, and we left the city of Gotham. It was strange to feel the wind on my face. It is far different than the circulating air that passes through the city. In the city it is never too hot or too cold, always just right. The cool breeze made the hot summer sun barrable as we followed the remains of a road to where we needed to go. A small village near a river.

———

By nightfall, we made it to that small village. After walking all day, it was nice to relax at a tavern for a late-night dinner. After we secured a room. The food proved to be far simpler than what we're used to in Gotham. Just a simple meat stew, that we dared not ask what kind of meat, and some cornbread. We washed down our food with a home-brewed ale. It wasn't much, but it was good. And it was nice to have something warm in our stomachs. When we finished, I paid the host with a copper coin, and we headed upstairs to sleep.

As we opened the door to our room, an immediate sense of awkwardness came over us. Our room was small, with one large bed in the middle of the room taking up most of the space. There was a bathroom down the hall. That was not an option. Not wanting to seek temptation, I turned to Cassandra and offered, "I'll sleep on the floor; you take the bed."

Cassandra graciously offered, "It is large enough for both of us. I trust you."

"I don't."

She gave me a mischievous smile. As she threw her luggage on the bed. At least the bed was real. She handed me a pillow and a couple of extra blankets and I managed to make myself a little makeshift bed for myself. I placed my pistol underneath my pillow in case of an emergency.

Seeing me do that, Cassandra curiously asked, "Why are you doing that?"

"For an emergency," I answered, "you should do that too."

Concerned, Cassandra stated, trying to convince herself, "This place is civilized. They won't hurt us."

I looked right at her. I didn't want to remind her of this fact, but if we are to survive, she must remember one rule: don't trust anybody. "Cassandra, the last time you were here, nobody came to your aid. We must assume they are in it."

Cassandra paused for a moment. As she contemplated what I had told her. A sense of resolve came over her. As she placed her pistol under her pillow. I made sure the door to our room was locked. I placed the key next to Cassandra. She turned out the light after I settled into my little spot on the floor. There we went to sleep.

I couldn't sleep. My time sleeping on a bed had softened me.

Checking my watch, I discovered it was midnight. I decided I needed to take a walk outside. Quietly, I walked over to pick up the keys and headed out. Glancing over to Cassandra, she was sleeping peacefully. Was it fair to her? I couldn't be honest with the answer. She volunteered, which is something I can reassure myself. But is it fair?

I just shut the door and headed outside. It was a pleasant night as I walked down to the harbor. It was empty. What light there had come from a small crescent moon in the black sky, except for two lights on two respective poles that illuminated the water below it? I walked over to the two lights. This is where the boats dock to smuggle people into Gotham. Frankly, I didn't care that they did it. I am all for people who are faced with the choice of staying in the Wastelands or living in Gotham, only the fool will not choose the latter. If they just didn't murder them. Worse for them, they murdered friends of mine. Who knows how many more people have committed this atrocity, too? They must be stopped.

At that moment, I looked over at the silhouette of Gotham. The lights of the city illuminated the outline of the buildings. Northpoint looked beautiful in the night sky. But I can't help feeling it looked different to me in some way. I knew Northpoint was different from Southpoint, where we first arrived. Back then, when I first saw Southpoint illuminated that summer night over a year ago. I was excited. A ten-year journey had finally ended. Many times, I had only hoped to keep going to find Sanctuary. Right at this moment, it feels like an enigma, a mystery that I will never be able to solve. For the first time, I realized it didn't feel like home to me. When I see Gabrielle again, I will be home.

I stayed there for an hour. Then I returned to the room. Opening the door, I quietly entered the room a tried to sleep again. This time with success. As I managed to sleep until morning.

I awoke, hearing Cassandra's voice invading my dream. I had no recollection of the dream. Just the pretty voice of Cassandra. As I opened my eyes, I saw her smiling at me. Sitting up, I looked at her as if she had already changed into her regular clothes.

"How long have you been up?" I asked her.

She replied, "About an hour." Sitting on the corner of her made bed, she added, "How did you sleep?"

"Not bad. And you?"

"Believe it or not, this bed is quite comfortable," she stated. "Are you hungry?"

"Give me five minutes."

She did as I requested. She left me alone to change into something else. As promised, five minutes later, I joined her downstairs. We sat down at the same table we had dinner at last night. Breakfast proved to be nothing extraordinary. A simple mixture of corn, oats, and honey mixed in with warm goat milk, judging from the small pen outside. Cereal, they called it. It wasn't much, but it was filling. As we ate, I noticed an older man looking our way. A portly man with long grey hair and a beard to match. His clothes looked like he had slept in them for the past three days. Still, the strangest thing about him is that those clothes were too big for him. He was talking to the lady who had given us our room and dinner last evening. Cassandra noticed their curiosity about us.

With a strange shot of courtesy, they waited until we had finished before making their way to join us. Sitting down in the two extra chairs at our table. We were about to be interrogated.

The crone-like landlady introduced her friend, "This is my brother Gabe. We run this place together. He was indisposed last night."

As he opened his mouth to introduce himself, his breath revealed why he was indisposed, a homebrewed concoction that can make you tipsy just smelling his breath. As I tried not to do that, he stated roughly, "How long are you staying here?"

Cassandra answered, "Until our business is done."

Her sister, in a high-pitched voice, added, "What is your business?"

"Or do you not want to tell us? "Her brother stated, thinking the worst.

"Nothing like that," I stated. "We are looking to book a package to Gotham."

The Crone injected, "There are less dangerous ways for citizens to return home."

Cassandra said calmly, "What makes you think we are citizens?"

Gabe and his sister gave a high-pitched laugh. We joined in for the sheer irony of the situation. Both Cassandra and I lived in the Wastelands longer than in Gotham. Cassandra added, "Our visa had expired."

"And we like to return quietly," I added.

Gabe looked at his sister. As he nodded in agreement, he stated, "We know of someone who can help you get home in one piece."

His sister added, "He will be here at noon."

We thanked them for their help. Heading back to our room, long enough to gather anything of value. I'm still not sure if we can fully trust our innkeeper friends. They may make enough with passing travelers not to risk doing anything dishonest. Then again, they may not. For right now, we are not taking any chances. When we managed to gather everything of value, we hid the rest of our stuff under the bed. As we left our room, I locked the door and handed her the key.

Downstairs Cassandra headed to ask the old woman one last question. From the door leading outside I watched their exchange. To my surprise, the innkeeper had been concerned for her. But she gave her the information.

Walking over to me, she happily relayed the information, "Gagnon."

He proved to be a person of interest. For now, we wanted to return to the harbor. Walking outside with the sun shining down on us felt like a real summer day. Gotham was always outside our home. I must be honest; I liked it better here. Around us, the few homes looked like they were remaining standing on their own determination. Nothing is more solid. Unlike the village, I could see the harbor was very well-preserved and clean. Two small boats had already docked. Bringing in goods from the city to be sold here. That is how they made their living.

A larger boat joined the other two. Two young crewmen jumped on the dock to secure the boat. An older man left the will and joined them. A young woman came from the hold with a ledger sheet. All four of the crew members worked together to empty their boat with cargo from their hold to a warehouse that holds everything that comes in. When they finished, a man and a woman had joined them. Walking closer, the ship's crew revealed exactly what they had brought from Gotham. When they had finished, the crew left the couple behind.

At that time, a fourth ship appeared from the south, and the process repeated itself. Three hours had passed, and five more boats of different sizes entered the harbor. When they unloaded their cargo and placed their crates in the warehouse. It was noon now, and we returned to the Inn to see this Gagnon.

As we walked into the inn, the landlady greeted us with a glance at a table. As we walked up to the table, we saw the large man and the young woman eating their lunch. We walked up to the table. Not looking up at us, Gagnon asked, "Something I can help you with?"

Standing behind an empty chair, I stated, "We have some business to discuss with you."

Annoyed, he replied, "I don't like talking business while eating lunch." Before I had any chance to protest. Cassandra entered his sight line. With a perverse smile, his mood changed for the better. "Please sit down." We did as he asked. Sitting down, he immediately introduced the young woman, "This is Donna."

Cassandra stated, "This is Duncan. I am Cassandra."

Now it was Donna's turn to be annoyed. She was threatened by Cassandra. But whatever protest she garnered she kept silent. Amused by his assistant indignation he stated, "Now my dear what business do you wish to talk about."

I let Cassandra handle that. She replied, "We want passage to the city. The Landlady told us you are the one to see."

Donna finally interjected, "Why don't you just go to Southpoint?"

Cassandra responded without missing a beat, "We like to enter the city quietly. We had made some enemies who are watching the Processing Center."

Donna wasn't completely satisfied with Cassandra's answer. On the other hand, Gagnon seemed satisfied with her answer. As he stated, "It will cost some money."

"We have it," I said proudly.

Gagnon looked over at me. Clean-shaven with very short blonde hair that was neatly cut. I guess he is a few years older than I. He was a powerfully built, large man, with strong hands that looked battered from years of work. His clothes were purchased from Gotham. Probably from goods that were stored in the warehouse. Payment from his service, I imagine. Looking over at Donna, I found her to be a pretty young woman, I estimate about the same age as Cassandra. She is tall and thin with short blonde hair and dark brown eyes. I am curious about what they are to each other.

"Then why do you need us?" Gagnon asked.

With the same confidence, I stated, "We have heard that some of these captains are more trustworthy than others. We want to find the right one."

Donna interjected, "How do you know that?"

I paused for a moment before I answered that one. Cassandra jumped in with a response, "It happened to me two years ago." Good girl. Putting a little bit of truth in a lie will go a long way. She had their interest, she continued. "There were five of us traveling together. We were promised a quick way into the city. Just a reasonable fee, that was all. Instead, they managed to steal everything we owned. When we had no more things to give them. We gave them something more. Three of us made it in. But we were sold like cattle."

Donna had changed her attitude towards Cassandra. Her expression changed from a potential threat to sympathy. Looking over at Gagnon, he had a look of admiration for Cassandra. But there was one more question to ask, "Why did you leave?"

Without flinching, she said, "The man who bought me was an important man in Tidewater." With a friendly glance at me, she continued, "He didn't like the fact that a young man stole me from him." Both of our new friends looked over at me, impressed with my actions. I don't believe either of them thought they could do something so noble. They would be right. Cassandra finished her story, "For the past month, his agents have chased us across Gotham. We thought if we escaped the city and waited until my keeper found other prizes. So now we want to get smuggled in. And I will have a surprise for anybody who tries that again."

Casually, but with deliberate action, she revealed her pistol. Donna nodded at her, showing that she understood. With that newly found empathy, she looked up at Gagnon. He understood and stated, "The crews will be together at the tavern down the street. We can help you find a good one."

"Thank you," I replied, "our apologies for interrupting your lunch."

We left them. After ordering something at the bar for our lunch we headed to our room. Twenty minutes later it was delivered. We ate together in the room. Once we finished, we agreed it would be better if we took turns watching the harbor to see if more ships would come in, until nineteen hundred hours when we will join Gagnon and Donna at the tavern.

During the afternoon, four additional boats docked in the harbor. Cassandra had noticed three boats while I observed one. After a modest dinner downstairs, we prepared for our night out. We took turns dressing in our room. Cassandra went first, changing into a sleeveless black dress that reached her knees. She wore her hair down, making her cream skin shine brightly under the week's hall lights. Confidently, she turned around, revealing how well she wore the dress. Finished like she already knew my answer, she asked, "How do you like it?"

Gently, I placed my hands on her shoulders and gave her the answer she had expected, "You look great." It wasn't a lie; she did look amazing. Unfortunately, it was my turn to change. "I'll be ten minutes." Entering the room, I shut the door behind me. I proceeded to put on a clean white shirt. I adjusted my stinger to be noticed on my hip. I joined Cassandra outside in the hallway.

"Ready to go?" she asked.

I was, but I wanted to be sure she was ready to do this. "I just want you to know you don't have to come."

Appreciative of my concern, she kissed me on my cheek, "I have to go, and you know it." She then added, "Duncan, I'm all right."

"Just let me know when you have enough."

"Yes, sir."

We left together. The tavern was the third house on the right from the inn. We were walking on a mixture of dirt and gravel. Remains of some kind of road that connected the various buildings of this village. The tavern proved to be the third-largest structure in town, smaller than the warehouse and inn. Unlike the smaller structures, it was well-kept in appearance from the outside. We went in. I opened the door for Cassandra, and we entered a crowded and loud establishment that strangely became eerily silent. Since the patrons' attention was focused on us. Their curiosity didn't end there as they watched us walk to the bar. That ended when we ordered our drinks from a very young bartender. The young girl returned with our glasses of red wine, and I gave her a copper. She placed it in a cup and said, "That will cover six more drinks between you."

Settling in at the bar, we waited for something to happen. It didn't take long. Donna joined us. I offered to get her a drink, and she stated, "A bourbon."

Relaying the request to the bartender, she quickly returned with the glass, and then she stated, "Five."

Donna drank haft of it with one sip. She then stated, "The lot here is reliable. They can get you in without any problems. Some will be reluctant at first but if the price is good, they can be persuaded. Unless they can get a better deal."

Cassandra asked, "What kind of deal?"

"Anything really" she answered, "better cargo or they may make enough on this haul they can afford to take some time off." She finished her glass of bourbon and put it on the bar. "Well don't be afraid to look around. If you need help, we'll be here for a little while longer." Then she left us.

That left us to look over every person in the room. In all, I estimated a little more than two scores of sailors. Calmly, I drank my wine as Cassandra inspected each man and woman. I am counting on her ability, and she can never forget a face. As I watched her take her time, her facial expression never changed. Finally, she had a look of disappointment that had come over her.

"They're not here," she confessed.

I wasn't surprised. It was foolish to expect to be this lucky and have them come today. Tomorrow will be the third day of our trip, and more boats will arrive. For right now we can get some information by asking for some answers from the sailors who are here tonight.

I turned to the bartender and asked for two more glasses of wine. She promptly returned to us with our order and smiled, "Three."

We separated, heading to opposite sides of the room. We spent a couple of hours mingling, trying to get information. I wasn't having much luck. Most of the crewmen were suspicious of people asking too many questions. When I mentioned that I was looking for a passage into Gotham. Everyone I talked to stated openly that smuggling people is illegal and that they will not do it. Checking my watch, I saw it was 2100 hours. I thought it was a good time to check to see how Cassandra was doing. I ordered another glass of wine from the bartender. Before she tried reminding me about my tab, I handed her another copper coin.

"That is yours."

She smiled and thanked me. I walked away from the bar and found my way to where Cassandra was holding court. I was not being sarcastic. She sat comfortably in a chair surrounded by seven young men hanging on her every word. Each one was hypnotized by her. With great subtlety, she would ask a question we needed to know, and without hesitation, she would get three different answers. Each one would be useful to us. If, on occasion, a man would get too friendly, with the same subtle motion, she would neutralize the threat by using a little move that Gabrielle had taught her. Four men were rubbing their hands in pain. I just stood there, drinking my wine and watching her show. Finally, when I finished my wine, I gave her a signal. Seeing it, she immediately made her apologies to her audience that she had to leave. Under the protest of her admirers.

"I will be back tomorrow," she proclaimed to her admirers.

The crowd separated down the middle, allowing her to leave. She gracefully walked towards me. We then walked out of the tavern. Once outside, she began to tell me what she had learned.

With excitement, she stated, "Most of the ships that do the regular runs are honest men and women trying to make a living. And they prefer it if you use the term ship. A boat is condescending."

"Point taking."

With the same enthusiasm, she continued, "The one we want doesn't make regular runs. They are especially for a nighttime run. Their boats are larger than my friends."

Interrupted her, "You mean ships?" I said in jest. Her sudden look of hate immediately made me realize my error, I muttered, "I'm sorry."

In a more serious tone, she went on, "There is one for us to look out for. It comes down from an area north of here. It is run by a man named Ken and his crew of four men: Brenden, Castro, Fontaine, and Lebrun. They have their place to dock a mile north of here. They told me that for the most part, they keep to themselves. Having some kind of contract with a group of gatherers."

"I think we should check that out in the morning."

"Agreed."

I opened the door for her at the Inn. She smiled and walked in. Together, we walked upstairs. Then we took turns getting ready for bed. Nothing had changed. I made my little place on the floor, and she slept in the bed.

After breakfast, we followed the harbor up north. Looking to see if the boat had docked here. It hadn't. Cassandra instantly remembered the area. She stated two boats were hired to take us in. Holding back her tears from events from a year ago. She pointed over to the opposite side of the river.

"That is where Mitchel and his friends brought us to. We never had a chance to see the village. There we waited for the boats to bring us to town."

I looked over and saw a little wharf. Cassandra dropped to her knees as her knees buckled from the memory. Sitting next to her, I tried to reassure her that it would never happen again. "We don't need to be here right now. Let's head back."

Silently, she agreed, and I helped her to her feet. We started to head back into the village when a voice cried out from behind, "Hello!" We turned around, startled by the unexpected voice. A man on a red horse stood idle. I calmly placed my hand on my pistol. He noticed it and said, "I mean you know harm, friend."

What concerned me the most was how the hell he had gotten so close to us without me knowing it. I must be losing my edge. A year ago, that would never have happened. Dismounting his horse, he walked up closer to us with his right hand holding the bridle of the horse. He continued, still in a friendly tone, "I heard this is the place I can get a passage into the city."

I replied, "It will take money."

Without hesitation, he confidently proclaims, "I have my horse."

Seeing the handsome man with his horse brought Cassandra into the present. She walked over to the horse and started to pet it. "What is her name?" she asked.

"His name is Apollo," he answered. Watching her gently stroke the horse's neck, he added, "He likes you." She responded with a shy smile, "My name is Robert."

"I'm Cassandra, and my friend here is Duncan."

His attention never wavered from Cassandra. I chose to take this time to size up this traveler. Keeping my distance, I looked over Robert. He stood up to my eyes with hair that was a shade lighter than my own. His face was long and thin with hazel eyes. He was thin and athletic and not yet thirty, I would guess. On his back of his horse, he had a canteen of water and a bedroll that had two small daggers on either end. At his side, he had a pistol with a rifle securely fastened on his horse. But it was the weapon that he secured on his back that immediately convinced me we could trust him. A sword. The three other men I had known carried a similar sword. I had put my life in their hands. Robert is the only one younger than me, however.

I joined them. "There is an inn in the village, I'm sure they have room. Are you going back for lunch? You're welcome to join us."

Cassandra happily agreed with my offer.

Robert said, "How can I refuse? Would you like to ride him?"

"Please."

He helped her up on Apollo. He joined her by climbing behind her. I decided to stay behind, thinking that there was most definitely a crowd. How should I proceed with handling this budding romance? I am happy that she has someone to make her forget what happened to her. Gabrielle and I could only do so much, but she will always be a third wheel in the apartment. Maybe I shouldn't trust this man, I keep telling myself. Just because Walker, Paul, and Austen were all honorable men. Better men than me, I had often reminded myself. That is a high standard for Robert to live up to. I am hoping he can and will not disappoint Cassandra. There is another reason I hope this relationship lasts: it will interfere with Caitlyn's plans. One more thing to keep her up at night.

Enough for that; now I had to get back to the task at hand. I walked north, following the river. About half a mile away, I found an old, rusted bridge that connected both banks of the river. Crossing over the bridge, I wanted to see what condition the trail crossing. It was a narrow piece of dirt road, about half the width of other bridges I had seen in my travels. A zephyr couldn't get through this one.

Seeing it was almost noon, I decided to head back. Following the river into the village. I found that three more boats had arrived. Donna is busy working alone, making sure every piece has been said for the sale of goods. People have been coming into the village in the hope of getting in for that market. People were touring the warehouse of goods. I joined Donna. She looked up at me and smiled.

I asked, "How is it going?"

She replied, "We are doing better than last month." A couple of people exited the warehouse we saw them walk away, she then turned to me and added, "When the locals bring in their goods, we will be able to build a second warehouse."

"How about the residences?" It was a bit of a joke.

Not amused, she replied, "That's up to them."

Something she had said made me ask, "You said this is monthly. Where do these boats go?"

"Home," she stated. She walked off, leaving me behind to watch other people enter the warehouse. I chose to head for the inn.

Cassandra and Robert were already seated. They had decided not to wait for me, as they had already served their food, not that they were eating it. They were too busy staring into each other's eyes and holding hands. Now I knew how Cassandra must have felt when she was with Gabby and me during dinner.

Awkwardly I sat down not trying to subtly get their attention. At first, it didn't work. It wasn't to the young waitress came over to ask me what I wanted for lunch that they noticed I was there. I simply ordered a ham and cheese sandwich and some water. The young girl smiled and left.

Cassandra asked me, "Did anyone arrive?"

I replied, "No."

Robert explained, "Cassandra told me why you two came here." Worried, I gave her a look. Unfazed, Robert added, "You had some problems in Southpoint."

Relieved, I said, "Yes."

"Cassandra told me you managed to get into the city down there. Cassandra tried to enter up here. Why didn't you stop her?"

Before I had a chance to answer, Cassandra interjected, "he tried to warn us. None of us listened. We trusted Mitchel and Natalie."

"Why didn't you trust this Mitchel and Natalie?"

"He was a Krieg," I answered him.

His lack of response made it clear that Robert knew who Krieg was. He would also know if Mitchell and the strangers were all Krieg. They will resort to more familiar tactics and seize everybody by force. Krieg gangs are well-armed and prefer to resort to violence over trickery to get what they want. Especially if they knew that the Watchmen inside Southpoint would not lift a finger to stop the carnage. Since it will mean fewer immigrants to process.

Robert simply stated, "An intelligent Krieg is a dangerous man."

I nodded my head in agreement. My sandwich arrived with my

water and a pickle. Starving, I took a bite of the pickle. The other two started to do the same. When we finished, Cassandra volunteered to show Robert to his room. I offered to pay the bill.

They walked up together, hand in hand. When the waitress returned for the dishes, I asked her for a lager. She nodded and walked away, returning the dishes to the kitchen. Taking out my little leather purse, I took out a silver, believing the silver would hold us to the end of the week. I placed it prominently on the table. When the girl returned with my drink. I handed her the silver, and she gave me a receipt that had the credit.

After she left. I started to drink the lager. It wasn't bad. Stronger than some I had found inside Gotham. I just stayed at the bar until dinner. Now more than ever, I was missing Gabrielle.

On Day 4, the local population gathered, bringing their goods to trade with what the captains had brought from the city. They had carried their goods any way they could. Whether on their backs or an animal. Lucky ones had a cart and some animal to pull it, less lucky people either pulled or pushed their carts themselves. A handful of fortunate people had some kind of motorized vehicles to carry goods to their neighbors. You could hear one of them coming a mile away. Gagnon announced that the sale would start in mid-afternoon. I offered to keep time for him.

Robert had joined us, looking to see if the barge had arrived. Robert decided to wait before he could sell his horse. Cassandra wasn't happy about the prospect of him selling Apollo. I joked with her that she liked the horse better than Robert. She laughed with us but didn't deny my accusation. However, she did understand that Apollo couldn't live in Gotham.

She rushed ahead of us, laughing at the beautiful day around us. Then she stopped in her tracks, frozen. Concerned, we joined her. As I looked at her face, all the joy she had had left her expression. It was replaced with hate. I quickly looked over to see what she had seen. Immediately, I understood what had happened. Across the river, as she had told me yesterday. Mitchel's friends had arrived with their new quarry. I counted about sixty poor souls guarded by a dozen men and two women, all armed. The poor souls looked malnourished and exhausted from their ordeal. Their clothes were in tatters, barely protecting them from the summer sun. I'm sure under close observation, they would have been abused by their tormentors.

Cassandra muttered, "We have to help them."

"We will, I promise," I tried to assure her. I then added, "Do you recognize any of them?"

"I do," she said, weeping.

Robert stated, "Let's go home."

We headed back to the inn. I put Cassandra to bed and joined Robert in his room down the hall. As I entered his room, he was gathering his weapons."

"Are you ready?"

"To do what?"

Outrage, he exclaimed, "To free the poor souls."

"We can't," I desperately responded. Surprised by my response, I felt I had to do something stupid again. I started, "I don't know why I should do this. I just have to say that the three other men who had that same sword. I will trust with my life."

Robert's demeanor had changed. He asked, "Who were they?"

"Austen, Walker, and Paul"

"You're that Duncan." He smiled at me, I couldn't understand how he would know about me, but he said, "You have quite of reputation."

I was left speechless. My thoughts were about how did they contacted each other. Not to mention what the hell they had said about me. The fact that I was surprised amused him. He mercifully changed the subject, "What is your plan."

I opened the door and glanced out of the hallway to see if anybody was listening. Once I was satisfied, I closed the door and walked over to where he was standing, so I could keep my voice in a low tone, "We are hired by the Watchmen. We are going to take passage on the smuggler's boat and lead them into a trap."

Cassandra had told him what had happened to her last year.

He understood the loss of our friends. He stated, "You're going to need some help."

"I appreciate it," I replied. "Now I had to ask him something. What had been said about me?" I had to know. He graciously complied with my request. "You helped Paul take down the Prophet and were his lieutenant at Cibola." Well, I don't know about lieutenant, but I was at his side. "Walker wanted you to be his successor." I was flattered. He had chosen me over men he had worked with for over twenty years. But it was this task we must focus on.

At thirteen hundred hours, we left for the harbor. Before we left, I checked on Cassandra. She was ready to come down and do her part. Despite my hesitation, she assured me that she had recovered. She gathered her weapons, and we walked down together. Robert was already there, looking over at the crowd of people.

Cassandra joined him while I had business with Gagnon and Donna. Both were standing in front of the warehouse. Trying to keep a crowd out of the structure. Gagnon looked over at me, hoping that it was time. Checking my watch, I found it was a little after thirteen hundred hours, casually I gave him the signal. Relieved, he immediately opened the doors behind him, the market was open. The crowd rushed in.

As for me, I rejoined my friends. We sat on the pier watching the selling frenzy from afar. I looked over to check on Cassandra as she looked over at two men. She had recognized them from across the bank. They had joined the selling frenzy, trying to buy goods. Probably using whatever they have stolen from the poor souls they have in chains right now. Hate had returned to her as she wanted to confront them. With purpose, she rose to her feet. She couldn't control it as she walked over to them. Immediately, Robert and I rushed after her, trying to keep her from doing something stupid. We tried to restrain her, but she was too determined. If she had to, she would go through us. Two other members of their gang joined them. A man in his forties and a young woman about Cassandra's build. All were armed, but Cassandra didn't care. I realized I had no choice but to take drastic action. I placed my stinger setting on stun and placed it at the base of her neck. She slumped into Robert's arms, unconscious. He picked her up over his shoulder.

"I'll take her to her room." He started and proceeded to walk away from me, returning to the inn. To the amusement of her enemies. Who were oblivious to how much danger they were in. As for myself, I decided to take this as an opportunity. Calmly I walked up to them. The oldest man looked up and saw me. Giving me a very unwelcoming glare he started, "You have business with us?"

He was a tall, strongly built man with a round face that was completely covered by white hair. I would guess he was about in his late fifties. His eyes were a hard greenish-brown that showed that he had survived this long by his determination. His three companions were all old enough to be his children. The girl is the youngest and in her late twenties. The other two men were well in their thirties. They did resemble the older man.

Unfazed by his apparent hospitality, I simply commented, "My friends and I are looking to get into Gotham. We were told you're the man to see."

His attitude didn't change; he just snarled, "It will take money."

"I have money," I replied, not showing any intimidation.

"Let's see it," he demanded.

He must have thought I was some kind of fool. Other times, I would be offended. But I have a job to do, and I simply stated, "I was told never pay the ferryman until he gets me to the other side."

The old man remained silent. His two sons began to maneuver around my flanks, waiting for the word to jump me. His daughter stepped back behind him; she would have given me the fatal blow after her family overpowered me. What they didn't know is that I had my stinger in my right hand hidden under my jacket, and it was set at full strength. I will give them a good fight.

The old man called off his sons. Placing his hand under his chin he thought over our situation. He finally asked, "How many?"

"Three."

With a wave of his hand, he directed his daughter to sheath her weapon. He changed his tone, revealing we had a deal. "Come tomorrow, up north. We will talk there."

They walked off. I headed back to the village. I needed to see how Cassandra was.

As I entered the room. I saw Cassandra on her bed lying on her back, just staring at the ceiling. She was awake. Aware that I had entered the room, she did not attempt to acknowledge me; she seemed oblivious to my presence. I sat down on the bed next to her. She remained focused on that spot on the ceiling.

Ashamed, she stated, "I'm sorry." A tear came down her cheek as she did her best to hold back her tears. "I thought I could handle it."

"You have nothing to be ashamed of," I stated softly, gently stroking her hair. I told her about meeting the smugglers tomorrow, I reminded her, "I need you to stay focused. Just remember, we are leading them into a trap."

She understood. "I will."

"I have no doubt," I stated, placing my arm around her shoulder. She leaned into me and kissed me. To my shame, I tried to stop her. When she pulled away, I said, "I'm sorry."

She replied, "I just wanted to know what it is like."

I had to leave. I just needed to be somewhere else. I walked around the town alone. Outside, I watched as the first day of the market had died down. Some of the boats had cast off as they headed down the river and dropped their goods in Gotham. Other participants headed to the tavern to spend what they had earned during the day. I had felt no need to join them. Walking north, I found the dock where Cassandra had previously mentioned that the human traffickers worked. Not wanting to be seen, I kept my distance as I watched the crew of the two boats meet with their coconspirators.

Cassandra had not mentioned the second boat. Perhaps it wasn't needed during that run, or it had already left for home before she made it with the other prisoners. The boat was about half the size of the larger one. With patches of rust along its rear and side. Remains of white paint covered the hull, not covered by rust. It looked sturdy enough; that is more than I can say for her sister. The larger boat looked in the worst shape since Cassandra had described it to us.

With sections of rotted holes along its hull just above the water line. That made her seaworthy.

I counted three men who handled the smaller boat while seven manned the large one. Glancing over on the other side of the river, the poor souls were eating from meager rations. Seven guards kept them under control. With darkness settling in, I thought it was a good time to get back. But something stopped me from going.

An argument between the older gentleman I had dealt with previously and two other men, probably the two captains of the boat. I was too far away to hear what they were saying. But something had come up that they didn't agree with. I wonder if it was about their six paying passengers. Whatever disagreements they had were finally resolved. The older man directed his gang to help load supplies on the smaller boat.

Carefully, I walked back to town. It was getting darker fast as I followed the river down to the village. Tomorrow didn't seem as dangerous as it did a few hours ago. I believed I had some understanding of how this band of criminals makes their living. That will give us an advantage.

The gang lives up north. For some reason, their village must have nothing of value except for two boats. Perhaps they couldn't make enough of a living. They decided to prey on unsuspecting people who were enticed by a quick way to enter Gotham. Only to find they are at the mercy of a gang of scavengers. Gangs will roam the regions outside Gotham, gathering people with a promise of entry. Once the people are isolated, they are chained together and robbed by the gangs in exchange for living. With what they steal, they buy goods for their village and send them north on a smaller boat. The larger boat will be sent south into Gotham with their human cargo. Selling them for what illicit desires their clients have. They then head back north for home. They will wait for a few months and start again.

Tomorrow we will be taking a dangerous risk. We must be ready.

I entered the inn. Tending the bar was the old woman, whom I remembered calling a crone earlier. When she saw me, she invited me to join her. Feeling hungry, I accepted her invitation. I ordered a bowl of stew and a glass of wine. She told me that my friends had already eaten. At least I hadn't ruined that chance for Cassandra. The innkeeper gave me a large glass of red wine. And assured me the stew is on the way.

Slowly I drank my wine, looking around the inn was almost empty. I gather that most of the people are at the tavern spending their hard-earned money. Not that anybody minded. That is how the tavern made their living. Here at the inn travelers had a roof over their heads and had something warm to eat. When the crowds leave, they will survive on the locals, until the next gathering.

The innkeeper brought over my stew and placed it in front of me. She hesitated to give me the spoon. Holding it up in front of me, I found her hesitation very odd, until she explained, "I heard you planning to take passage with those river pirates."

I wasn't sure exactly what a river pirate was, but somehow, I had a good idea who she was referring to. "We need to get back into the city," I casually confirmed her suspicion.

"The other captains can take you in just as easily" Her concern surprised me. It made me realize they had known what was happening up there. But for some reason that had done nothing.

"None of them wants to take the risk."

She insisted, "A few of them owe us a favor. We can put in a good word for you."

I had to ask, "If you know what they are doing up there, why don't you stop them?"

To stall, she quietly refilled my glass. When she had finished that, she had poured some wine on herself. She then proceeded to drink it in one gulp. She placed the glass on the bar when she had finished. She finally handed me my spoon. Now she was ready to answer. "This village was never large. But it was larger than it is now. They used to come down whenever they wanted. Looting and pillaging anywhere they desired. Taking away whomever they desired. Killing anybody who tried to stop them. Many people moved away to try to escape these damn pirates. About five years ago, they found a more profitable venture. It didn't matter how they had learned it, but they discovered that for the right price, certain people in

Gotham would pay a lot for certain people. Who doesn't exist in the eyes of the city? The pirates made a deal with us. They will trade with us. Patronize our establishment. And leave us alone. All we must do is let them do their business. We accepted."

"Why don't you get the captains to help you?"

"It wasn't their fight," she replied, frustrated by the situation they are living in. "Besides, what you see is a tenth of their numbers."

"I see," I muttered in understanding their problem, but I couldn't tell her the truth. What we are planning to do. It isn't that I couldn't afford to trust her. If I told her and the pirates to take their revenge on the town. They might take out their vengeance on the town anyway. I don't know. I just definitely stated, "All I can say is we have to."

"I'll get you another drink." She walked away, taking my glass, and a moment later she returned with a full glass of red wine. I thanked her. She walked away quietly.

As for myself, I just finished my dinner. The stew came with a generous cut of cornbread that proved to be the highlight of my dinner. When I finished, I left a copper piece and headed upstairs. Entering my room, I found it empty. The bed still had the mark where Cassandra had used it earlier. Other than that, the room was untouched. I didn't worry about her figuring that she was with Robert in his room. She needed to find some comfort that I couldn't give her. I just placed myself on the bed and fell asleep.

———

Looking out of the window, I lay on my bed and watched the sun rise before me. Light from the sun illuminated the green fields that went on forever. Several kinds of animals were busy grazing on the lush grass. But I had something to do that would be less tranquil.

I got up and prepared for my trip home. Determined to make it home alive, I made sure my weapons were ready if needed. Calmly, I placed each one on my person, keeping them out of plain sight. I then quickly changed my clothes. Now ready, I proceeded to walk down to Robert's room. I firmly knocked on the door. Cassandra opened the door wearing a long blue nightshirt that fell below her knees. When she looked at me, she was visibly embarrassed for a moment, then she had a playful smile came over her face. Giving a coloring that lit up her cream-colored skin. I wasn't surprised that I had found her here. I was just glad to see that color of life return to her.

"You two better get ready. I'll meet you downstairs."

Robert had joined us at the door. He was just wearing some pants, nothing else. I knew where his shirt was. He stated, "Give us ten minutes we will be ready." I nodded and headed downstairs.

I ordered some porridge with honey for breakfast and three sausage links. I'm not sure what exactly the meat was. Out here, it is best not to ask too many questions. I ate my food quickly. It did taste good. But I was in a hurry.

As I finished the last morsel of porridge, Robert and Cassandra came down and joined me. The young woman who had worn many hats during our stay took their order. They both ordered eggs and the mystery meat sausage. I decided not to wait for them.

After standing up, I stated, "I'm going on ahead. I'll meet you there."

Grabbing my arm with hers, she frantically said, "No, Duncan, please wait for us."

I gently took her hand away and assured her, "I'll be all right, our friends are waiting outside." She had concern for me on her face. I calmly added, "I won't do anything dangerous."

She mentions sardonically, "That's not what Gabby says."

I just smiled at her. Having her still care about me after my selfishness yesterday afternoon. It gave me a sense of relief.

Heading outdoors. It proved to be a nice summer day. But from the southwest, storm clouds were gathering along the horizon. That was something to worry about later today, I had thought. As I headed to the harbor, I found many boats had already left. Their hauls are already full, heading south to sell to whoever their buyers are. I wish them luck as long as they are not hurting anybody in their endeavor to make a living. Strangely, Gagnon and Donna were nowhere to be found. I walked to the warehouse and discovered that it was about half full. From a distance, I heard the distant rumblings of thunder. Taking a glance at the dark clouds forming along the horizon, I estimated it was maybe two hours away. I waited for a moment, looking at the river for Cassandra and Robert. Before I headed north to the pirates. When I return home, I will try to find out what a pirate is; it sounds interesting.

Finally, Cassandra and Robert arrived together as we watched the remaining boats loading their goods. Hoping to avoid the coming storm. Many merchants had chosen to leave. Something was wrong.

"Where is everybody?" Robert asked. He sensed that something was wrong.

"Not sure," I replied, looking around. Trying not to scare Cassandra.

We started to head north, following the river to where the large boat was docked. While walking, that feeling became stronger. Now I knew something was wrong. It was too quiet, like prey becoming silent when a predator came near. Only the occasional thunder cracking in the distance broke up the silence.

When the boat came in sight. I froze in my tracks. Instinctively, I grabbed Cassandra, holding her tightly. She turned towards me before she could ask me why I demanded, "Stay here."

Taking out my spyglasses, I ran ahead to get a better look, hoping I was wrong. I found a place where I could observe them without being seen. Kneeling behind a stack of crates, I looked through my spyglass and focused across the river where they had held their captives. They weren't there. That is where I found one. Where there is one, there are others, an Overseers' ship.

This discovery made the oncoming storm not seem that important to me anymore. With great haste, I looked over the entire area for Enforcers. The Overseers are from Cibola! I had hoped that I would never see those bastards again. Now I found four ships surrounding the pirate's ship. Frantically looked over to check each one of the intruders. I found ten Enforcers and two Overseers; each one was busy checking the captives. They haven't changed since the last time I saw them. Immediately, I thought of Cassandra. Like Gabrielle, she was what they were looking for, a certain type of person who could save their worthless existence from destruction. They are the reason why we came to Gotham.

Robert joined me. I handed him my telescope. It didn't take him long to see what I had. I looked back at Cassandra and said, "Take her out of here and hide."

Robert immediately looked back at Cassandra and said, "She is one." I nodded my head. Now we knew why the harbor was deserted. He looked back at me and asked, "What are you going to do?"

"I'm going to talk to them," I replied. We need to know if there are more ships. He ran back and joined Cassandra, taking her away. I am taking a lot for granted with him, but somehow, I trust him.

I turned and headed back to watch the Overseers. Hoping that I had never met them before. I managed to look over each one of the Enforcers, but none of them looked familiar to me. I scanned the area for the Overseers. Previously, I had counted at least two. Finally, I found a tall, stout young man, about in his late twenties, with dark skin and hair like night. When I managed to find the second Overseer, I had an idea. It will mean I have to revive some old habits.

With my spyglass, I focused on a pretty young woman, about the same age as Cassandra. She had a petite frame with short brown hair. This must be her first mission outside of Cibola. She showed amazing restraint in dealing with the pirates. She had allowed her men to test the captives. I felt this was a good time to introduce myself.

Walking toward them in a casual stride, like I have anything to hide. I am ignorant of their search. And most importantly, I had never been to Cibola before. Let alone being part of an invading army that rescued three of their most prized possessions. Now I must make them believe those lies.

Her partner had noticed me first. He ordered one of his Enforcers to intercept me. Slowly, I raised my hands, revealing that I had no weapon other than what I had under my jacket. Then I remembered my damn stinger. That is a weapon of the Enforcers. It will be hard to explain that away.

"Hello!" I started innocently, "I mean you no harm."

Nervously, I waited to be searched. The Enforcer waited for a comrade to cover me while he checked me for weapons. I confessed, "I have a pistol in my belt." I don't know if that will satisfy them. I revealed the pistol at my hip. The Enforcer immediately grabbed it out of its holster. "That leaves my daggers."

A second Enforcer finally arrived and was not satisfied by my confession. He covered me while his partner moved closer to search for me. I couldn't let that happen, but I am not in a good position to resist.

"I'm not a fool." That is all I got out.

The female Overseer gave me a reprieve, "Stand down."

She walked up and placed herself between her men and me. With no fear, she looked me over. In her right hand, she had a stinger of her own. She held it hovering over my face, she stated calmly, "We are all friends here."

"My lifetime ambition."

She returned her stinger to her belt. "What are you doing here?"

Dropping my arms slowly, mistakenly thinking I had her permission, I quickly discovered her two Enforcer friends didn't agree with me. They held their rifles in firing positions. I rushed with a response, "My arms are tired." She ordered her men to stand down. Relieved, I answered her question, "I have business with that gentleman there." I pointed at the old man from yesterday. He was talking to the Overseer and a representative from the belt.

She summoned the old man to come forward. A third Enforcer escorted him to join us. When he stopped next to her, he looked me over with disdain. She asked him, "Do you know this man?"

He spoke grimly but thankfully for me, truthfully, "He wanted passage with us."

Satisfied, she turned to me and stated, "We will be gone tomorrow. You can do your business then."

"Fair enough," I replied calmly, "Can I have my pistol?" She instructed the Enforcer to hand it to me. Reluctantly, he obeyed. I still had one more request: "Would you like to have dinner?"

Surprised, she responded hesitantly, "I don't know. I have work to do."

"I'll be over at the Inn at eighteen hundred if you get hungry."

She smiled shyly, "I'll think about it. My name is Julia."

"Duncan," I replied, taking her hand, I kissed it gently. "Until then."

I walked away. This is business, that is what I repeated in my head repeatedly as I walked back. For nearly ten years, I learned the best way to deal with people from Cibola is to help them in their quest. That will earn you some privileges living among them. That allows a person to learn their weaknesses, and that will give me an edge. I found the best way to do that is to charm a woman. Julia will be next.

At the appropriate time in the dining area, I sat at a table that seated two people, waiting for Julia to arrive for dinner. She hadn't arrived yet. Not that I minded that much. To be honest, I didn't know what would be happening this evening. I knew I needed information on how long they would be here. She did say they would be gone tomorrow, but that plan could change very quickly. Constantly, as I sat there, I reassured myself of the importance of doing whatever I had to do to get that information, to keep Cassandra and the others safe from them. Nearly two years ago, I found out what Cibola had planned for her and others like her. It is a far worse fate than the life she had endured in Gotham.

Relief came over me as I became convinced she wasn't coming. I singled out the young helper whose job was a waitress tonight to take my order. That is when I saw her at the door. Immediately, I singled her out, and she walked towards me. She made quite a sight as she walked through the dining area, wearing a tightly fitted metallic grey suit. Overseers don't believe in giving their people a change of clothes. Her hair was elegantly set, revealing her beige-colored neck. It must have taken her an hour to set it like this. As she stopped before the chair, standing up, I rushed over and pulled out the chair for her. Nervously, she sat down, turning her head towards me, and she smiled, trying to hide her apprehension. I returned to my seat, and the young waitress arrived to take our order.

She asked the young waitress, "What's good here?"

The girl hesitated, not knowing how to answer that question. Amused, I decided to help her, "Their cornbread is very good." That gave her time to think about an honest answer.

"We have meatballs in mushroom gravy covered over potatoes," she proclaimed confidently. Julia ordered her recommendation along with mine. I did the same with a bottle of wine for us to share. Happily, she walked away.

"How did your search go?"

"We didn't find anyone," she answered happily. "We can't be here too long. Gotham doesn't like us this close to their airspace. One of my pilots noticed the caravan and thought it was worth the risk."

That was very obliging of her. Not ten minutes into dinner, she had reassured me that they would be gone tomorrow at dawn. Part of me thought we could eat and go our separate ways. As I looked into her amber-colored eyes, I found that I couldn't.

I reassured her, "Well, I'm in no position to tell anybody."

She smiled at my little joke and asked, "Why are you going into Gotham?"

"I'm trying to get back to someone."

"Your wife?"

"Not exactly."

When our food came, we continued to ask each other questions while we ate. I was right; this was her first mission outside of Cibola. She revealed that recovery had been very slow. Many leaders had been considering new approaches with their neighbors. Her excitement in telling me this news made me believe that she is in favor of this new strategy. I found Julia to be refreshingly different from her people. Much like my friend Hillary. Just a little naive. I hope she will never change.

With excitement, she then confessed something shocking: "We have made contact with Atlantis." I didn't know the relevance of her statement, but she smiled and explained, "That is the home of the Blues."

As for myself, I had wondered where Gabrielle had come from. Then I made an error of judgment, "I hope you treat them better than the ones you had already found."

That was a stupid mistake. The young waitress arrives in time to get our empty plates. She offered dessert and recommended strawberry rhubarb pie. With her success in recommending our dinner, we ordered her pies. I had hoped the distraction would make her overlook my mistake. Anxiously, I waited for her to inquire further about what I had revealed to her.

"I was thinking you could help us," she stated nervously.

Relief! But then I had a new problem: how could I politely refuse her kind offer? Because she was sincere in my offer. It was impossible. Too much blood had been spilled. I needed to turn down her offer, "I'm sorry, I can't." Looking away from her, I gave her an explanation: "Your people destroyed my village."

Ashamed, she looked away from me and muttered, "I'm sorry."

We ate our dessert in silence. Neither of us dared to say anything further at that point. It was foolish. But when we finished, I paid the bill, and we left our table. I walked her to the door. She turned to me and said, "I think it is too late for me to head back to camp." In an attempt to flirt with me, she softly reached out for my right forearm with her left hand. Looking into my eyes, she waited for my answer.

"My friend isn't using his room. We can find room."

We walked upstairs to my room. I let her into my room. Within the frame of the door, she turned to me and confessed, "It is expected of me."

I didn't say anything when she entered. After I entered the room myself, I turned to close the door. Make sure it is unlocked. I stated, "You can sleep here if you want."

As I turned towards her, I received the shock of my life. Standing a few steps away from me, I found Julia completely naked. She walked up to me and kissed me with all her might. I felt her body on me. Holding her in my arms, I could feel her apprehension. This was expected of her, as she had told me. Gently, I pushed her away, looking at her.

"You don't have to do this," I told her. "You can stay the night. Tomorrow after breakfast, I'll walk you back to your ships and kiss you goodbye. They won't know the difference."

I wiped a tear from her cheek. She leaned into me and kissed me again. Damn! she he was making this hard. When she finished, she hugged me and whispered in my ear, "Thank you." Holding me tighter, she stated, "Forgive us. We are desperate."

I stated softly, "I forgive you." She pulled away from me. I stated, "I'll see you in the morning."

I left her there. I locked the door as I left her room. Robert's room was fortunately unlocked. So I slept there alone. Thinking of Julia, I was sincere in forgiving her for what her people had done.

Early the next morning, I kept my promise. After a quick breakfast. I walked her to her men. In full view of her men and the river pirates, I kissed her goodbye. She left and entered her ship, followed by her men. Other crews entered their ships, and I watched her squadron rise into the area. They moved gracefully through the air. As the storm from the horizon, the previous morning had chosen a different path. It was a pretty day as I looked around me. Having Julia around managed to distract me from noticing the world around me.

As I watched her leave, a terrible sound filled the air. It came from behind me. Very quickly, that sound revealed itself to us all. One of the airships disappeared from the guy. I looked behind me. It came from Gotham. The city was firing upon the Enforcers for invading their airspace. A second shot from the city crosses the sky. It missed the three remaining ships. My eyes remained on Julia's ship as I hoped she would escape. After a few minutes, Gotham had not fired a third shot. Maybe they made their point, I had hoped. But it was not to be. The second ship disappeared from the sky. Julia's ship began to make evasive maneuvers. A fourth shot flew by her. A few seconds later, her ship disappeared from the horizon. She had escaped. I could breathe now.

A tap on my shoulder brought me back to earth. I looked over to my right and found the old man whom I had talked to earlier. He was joined by a younger man. The old man introduced him, "This is Fontaine, the master of our ship."

I held out my hand, but he didn't take it. Fontaine was a tall, thin man with a face like a horse and thinning light brown hair. He chose not to speak more, like he couldn't be bothered to make the effort. His clothes needed to be washed with him in them. The old man turned to me and announced, "We will be leaving after dusk if you want to come with us. How many are you?"

"We'll be ready," I proclaimed. I answered his question, "There are three of us, two men and one woman."

That had piqued Fontaine's interest. In a near whisper, he revealed another interest, "What about payment?"

"How much do you want?"

"How much do you have?"

"I don't trust you that much," I replied, waiting for a response from the master of the ship.

With a rare smile, it was the old man who made the offer, "A thousand per person."

"Done," I proclaimed. We shook on it. "I'll give you half when we leave and half when we get into Gotham." Before I left, I had one more question to ask. To the old man, I inquired, "What is your name, sir?"

"Kenneth Dyer."

Satisfied, I left them there.

I walked into my room. To my relief, I found Cassandra sitting on the foot of her bed, waiting for me. I was in trouble.

"Did you have a nice time last night?" she asked me. Not waiting for an answer, she continued, "Sleeping outside wasn't that bad if we had a fire. But that would bring attention to us, so we didn't have a fire."

"How did you know?"

"The staff have very loose lips," she answered. "Besides, you don't smell like flowers."

"I needed information. I slept in Robert's room."

Cassandra's demeanor changed; she decided that I had suffered enough. With a playful smile, she stated, "I know."

"We'd better get ready."

I told her what had happened this morning. We needed to get our stuff together and meet with Robert. When we finished packing, I gathered our two transmitters and handed them to one. We understood the plan Wells had laid out for us. When we leave the pier and head south, I'll activate my transmitter. That will alert Wells that we are on our way. Once we are in sight of the dock, she will activate hers.

"Then hopefully, Wells will keep his word."

"What if he doesn't?"

"We'll worry about that later."

We left our room. Heading downstairs, we paid our bill. Giving the old Inn Keeper two silvers. Robert joined us, and we left together.

We headed to the harbor to prepare ourselves for the tasks ahead of us. As we looked over the empty harbor, we found the other boats had already left to bring their goods into the city. I hope they make it. They were never my target. My vendetta was with the River Pirates. Walking towards the warehouse, we found it mostly empty of goods. Inside the warehouse, we found Gagnon and Donna counting their profits for the past few days. Two young men were helping in checking their supplies for the next month. They were satisfied with what money they had made. When they saw us staring at them. They immediately hid their treasure. Standing up, they walked over to wish us a good trip.

"Did you do well?" Robert asked them.

Gagnon smiled proudly. "We did. Now we can build a second warehouse."

"Don't forget about the harbor," Donna added.

Cassandra said, "We can help." She handed them some of her money.

They joined us north. We were behind them as they looked over the prisoners. They manage to save three men and four women, all young, about twenty. The seven individuals were released, and they left with the Harbor Master and his assistant.

Now it was our turn. I secured six gold coins, and we headed to greet the Master of the Boat. Cassandra hesitated. Frozen in place, she couldn't move forward. I had Robert go along. I turned to Cassandra and laid out our situation. "You must do this. We've gone too far to back out now. I'll be right by your side." But she had recognized Fontaine. He captained the boat a year ago.

She looked into my eyes and nodded. Her brave attempt to smile convinced me she was ready. To give her strength, I held out my arm. She promptly put her arm through it. Together, we walked towards the den of vipers. Determined to finish our mission.

His job was done; Ken Dyer had left with a few of his friends. That left Fontaine a dozen men and the young woman named Aliaca to bring their human cargo in. Fontaine's second, a small parasite, stopped Robert with an ancient-style gun. It's loud, but it kills. We joined Robert. Behind Fontaine and his second, a man named Castro was our fellow passenger, waiting to discover their fate. Casto was a beast of a man with blond hair who stood guard with seven other men. He was my age and my height, but he was fat.

"No need for that, we're all friends here," I said calmly, but just in case, I reached for my pistol and stinger. In a friendly manner. Robert did the same.

Believing he had the advantage; he ignored our precautions. In his monotone voice, Fontaine coldly stated, "Do you have the money?"

"One moment," I reached into my pocket and took out the six gold coins. Placing it into Fontaine's hand. He called over Aliaca. Handing it to her, she counted each coin. Once she was satisfied that they were genuine. Fontaine ordered his rodent friend with a shotgun to lower his weapon.

"Welcome aboard," he said in what was supposed to be a friendly manner.

"Thank you," replied Robert, releasing his weapons. Cassandra remembered each person standing in front of her. But she handled her hatred with grace.

Now, with their attention turned to their cargo. I counted fifty poor souls. All sitting on the grass with what clothes they are wearing are in tatters. They had given the pirates all they owned just to get home, refusing to go on the boat. We watched as Fontaine chose who would be allowed to join them and who would be put out of their misery.

Forcing all fifty prisoners to their feet. He proceeded to look over each person carefully. A young woman or man who was pleasing to look at was taken away and escorted onto the boat. If any person resisted, they would feel the fury of the beastly second officer and his cudgel. He had counted out eighteen young women and six young men. Fontaine proceeded to people who had a useful trade or a strong back. Cassandra had explained that some of their buyers needed workers who could do dangerous jobs and would do their jobs for little money, and if something happened to a worker, nobody would care. Fontaine chose ten men and two women. That left sixteen poor souls who had better find something valuable to barter, or they would not see another sunrise. Harry and Deb manage to barter for their passage, only to be betrayed by the pirates at the dock. After they had transferred their entire wealth to the pirates. Five people managed to prove they had something or someone in Gotham who would make it worth their effort. One man manages to barter an entire family of five to join him. That left six people who had no prospects. Castro and the second officer, Brenden, gathered them to be executed; their bodies were thrown into the river.

Cassandra couldn't stand it any longer; she exclaimed, "You can't!"

The first officer pulled out his shotgun and aimed it at her. Undaunted, Cassandra ran towards the prisoners. Brenden was a younger man with dark short hair and stubble on his face, trying to look handsome, I guess, but it didn't work. Fontaine walked over to us and stated clearly, "I suggest you take her inside."

"We can pay for their passage," I interjected. "We have money in the city."

Fontaine gave us a rare smile. "Then we have a deal." He turned to his men and ordered, "Take them aboard."

His men obeyed. Fontaine followed, leaving us alone. Ashamed, Cassandra looked over at me. "I'm sorry."

"For what?"

Robert took her on the boat. After making sure I was alone, I hesitated long enough to board the boat. I activated my transmitter. I then joined the others. Our trap was to be set.

6   THE TRAP

O N THE DECK, WE WATCHED THE NINE-PERSON CREW PREPARE
the boat to cast off. Once free from the dock, the engine
started to move us downriver. In the darkness, I checked my watch;
the light it gave off revealed five minutes after twenty-one hundred
hours. Fontaine had mentioned it would take four hours to travel
to our destination. As we traveled on the river, a strange silence
surrounded us. Like we're in between worlds. As it became later,
the air became cooler, giving me a feeling of death. Everybody on
this boat was heading for their own kind of reckoning.

An hour into our journey, we first caught sight of Northpoint.
Its light brightens up the river. On the opposite side stood a great
forest bordering the river. Making a clear contrast between nature
and the world of man. For now, thankfully, the crew kept to themselves. Busy sailing the ship and guarding their captives. One thing
they made clear to us was that the other passengers were off-limits.
Twenty minutes earlier, Cassandra and Robert had tried to bring
down some food but were turned away. She surrendered the cornbread to one of the guards. She could only hope that the prisoners
managed to get some of it.

At the beginning of the second hour, we started to enter. This time, on the opposite side, is the District of Westminster. Westminster was larger than York in size but not in population, so York was brighter in the night sky. As both Districts drowned out the stars. Only the crescent moon was left to illuminate the river. We remained in the area designated by Fontaine on a little rise along the stern. Out of their way. Still, the silence is what stood out to me; they were planning something, but they knew we were armed. Robert felt it, too. If Cassandra did, I don't know, but she was holding on.

The boat had to slow down. As a lookout along the bow saw some debris in the river. Two crewmen carrying three long poles rush to join the lookout to make sure the debris does not harm the hull. Twenty minutes later, the pilot increased speed. Gotham was in our sight. The boat gently veered to our right as it prepared to enter the dock. We are half an hour away from the end of the journey.

I turned to Cassandra and said, "It is time." She looked at me and understood it was up to her now. "I can do it if you want."

"I'll do it," she stated and left us alone.

Five minutes later, we heard a splash in the water. Both of us became concerned. We scattered to look for Cassandra. Cries of man overboard disturb the dead silence. As members of the crew began looking overboard. Fearing the worst, we were about to offer our help, fearing the missing person could be Cassandra. As we turned towards the steps down to the main deck. What we saw stopped us in our tracks.

Standing in front of us, petrified with fear, stood Cassandra. She had in her right hand a bloody dagger; the same one I had helped her buy. Her eyes were wide open as if in a state of shock. But not from fear, more like she was surprised by what she had done. Carefully, we both walked up to her. At first, she didn't see us. It was not until we were right next to her that she acknowledged our presence. Slowly, she looked at Robert. She proceeded to look into my eyes. Her mouth opened, and she confessed, "He remembered me." We paid no attention to the crew in their attempt to locate what will be their missing crewmen. She continued trying to make sense of what had happened to her, "I knew what he had done. He tried again."

She paused as her memory came back to her. Robert began to listen to the pirates fetching the body from the river. Turning her head forward and staring into space, she stated, "I stabbed him... Now he will never hurt anybody again."

"Cassandra, give me the dagger," I ordered her. She obeyed, not looking at the weapon. Once in my hand, I wiped the blood off the dagger and handed it back to her. She returned it to its scabbard.

Remembering why she had left us, she murmured, "he didn't see me."

I grabbed her gently and sat her down. Looking at her, I said, "Cassandra, I need you to focus."

She looked into my eyes as tears came over her. Cassandra looked at me, and she said, "I'll be all right." She closed her eyes, and she was ready.

I hugged her. She stood up, and we were joined by Robert. "They found the body. We are going to have trouble."

"Get ready. I'll talk to them."

Fontaine, followed by the beast and parasite, came towards me. I made sure they didn't get any closer to Cassandra.

"One of my men is dead."

"He attacked my friend."

The three men weren't surprised by my excuse. Not bothering to call Cassandra a liar. For they knew it to be true. They just didn't give a damn.

"We want her."

"You can't have her."

Fontaine looked behind me and saw both Cassandra and Robert with their pistols out. Ready to shoot any one of them who wished me harm. Fontaine gave a smile. He murmured, "We'll see."

He ordered his men back. I watched them retreat across the deck. I knew they were going to be back. I pulled out my pistol and joined my friends. We spent the time we had fortifying our position, finding whatever we could find in the hope of giving us a chance to get out of this with our lives. Luckily for us, a searchlight from Gotham distracted them. Those must be their friends from the city. Reinforcements in their attempt at revenge.

When Fontaine was ready, he gathered his well-armed men to attack. From what I observed, he left behind one man to pilot the ship, one to man the engines, and two to guard the prisoners. That left him eight of his crew to back him up.

They attacked in force. Separating themselves into three groups of three, they methodically maneuvered themselves as close as they dared. They used their antiquated tactics to ensure we didn't have a clear shot. Once safely in their position, they decided to wait for something. Finally, Fontaine signaled the pilot, Alicia, and she shut down the lights on the boat. In near darkness, they charged us. It was a brilliant move; they knew where we were, but we would not be able to see them until it was too late. And that is what happened. Two things they didn't figure on: Cassandra was a blue and Robert had a couple of torches that gave us enough light to see them coming. Cassandra managed to wound one pirate. Two others were quickly killed. The six who survived retreated. Placing themselves around us. A few minutes later, the lights were turned on, and the pilot steered the boat to dock on Gotham.

Their friends on shore will be well-armed. From the dock, they could easily flank us. Fontaine knew that. All that was left for us was to hope the Watchmen were there waiting for us to dock. A few meters away, two lights appeared on the shore. I could see four shadows. They were standing along the dock. As we moved closer, I could make out that they were armed. When Fontaine turned off the lights, that must have warned them of trouble.

With Robert watching the pirates. I took Cassandra aside. I placed all our money and cards in a small pouch, using a piece of iron on the boat as a weight. I told Cassandra to do the same. When we were ready, I handed the pouch to Cassandra.

"When we dock, I want you to throw this in the river. Unless I tell you different."

"Why?"

"Just trust me," I told her. She agreed to do it. I turned to our small barricade and called out, "Fontaine!"

"What do you want?" I heard from the shadows.

"I want to make a deal."

"There is nothing to deal with." He stated confidently, walking closer toward us in the light, "We are going to kill you and take what you have."

"Then you will have nothing. Because Cassandra is going to throw our money overboard when we land."

"You're bluffing."

"I never bluff!" I proclaimed defiantly. It is true, I will have Cassandra throw it in the river. I would prefer not to do it, to be completely honest, but I don't like to lose.

Fontaine took time to ponder the situation before him. Finally, he asked, "What do you want?"

"We are willing to forget this misunderstanding if you will." I am not being honest, but I'd like to get out of this in one piece.

Fontaine delayed his answer for a moment. Finally, he inquired, "I am willing to go back to our original deal."

I would be a fool to trust him. But we have no choice. I agreed to his terms. "You free the prisoners down in the hold. We will wait here. When the time comes, we'll transfer the funds."

"That is fair." He called his men back. I joined Robert to observe their compliance. Most of his men didn't like our terms. But they did what they were told. It's a little too easy for my liking. Cassandra joined us with the pouch in her hand. "If they attack, throw that in the river."

"You don't trust them?" she asked.

"Not at all," I answered her. We needed to find a solution that didn't require Wells and his men to come to our rescue. Right now, we must wait and hope for the best.

There, we watched what was left of the crew doing their job. They are efficient, I give them that, doing the same task over a hundred times at least. Securing the boat on the wharf requires a lot of work. If they go in too fast, they can damage the boat, the wharf, or even both. If the boat comes in at the wrong angle, that could cause problems. That required the crew to focus on their task ahead of them and not on us. Silently, each one did their job. As for us, the city dock began to take shape. Along with it, we could see silhouettes of ten men with rifles. Three others were selected to help land the boat. On the port side, three crewmen threw ropes at their counterparts, who easily caught the ropes and tied them to the dock. The engine was shut off, allowing the boat to be docked at the edge of the wharf. Immediately, the three shoremen placed a loading ramp on the deck.

With his rifle, the monstrous second mate placed himself between us and the hold. The three shoremen joined the remaining crewmen in gathering the prisoners from the hold. Two additional men from the shore joined the second mate. Both were normal-sized men but were dwarfed by the creature. Looking towards my right, I noticed four armed men placing themselves in a position to flank us. Looking over at Cassandra, she instinctively knew what I wanted her to do. Quietly, she crawled, left our little fort, and got right next to the water as she could.

Castro began barking orders to the captives as they were rushed out of the hold. Their screams enhanced the tension in the air. We waited to discover our fate. Once on dry land, the captives were placed in the floodlights. The other shoremen joined the pirates, making sure none of them tried to escape. In ten minutes, the captives were secured. Allowing Fontaine to deal with us.

Fontaine joined Brenden with three other armed men. On the bridge, the female Alicia held a rifle on us. Where the fuck is Wells? I asked myself. I looked over at Robert, hoping he had an idea. He didn't. I looked at my watch and saw it was almost two hundred hours, three hours until dawn. Maybe Fontaine and his men will be more reasonable then.

Three vehicles arrived in the parking area overlooking the wharf. Great, more trouble for us. However, it wasn't the trouble I had thought it would be. They had no interest in helping the Pirates. They just wanted their merchandise. Castro gathered their prisoners for inspection. We watched helplessly as the buyers personally inspected each subject. Once satisfied, he had his men place their property in their vehicles. He then went on to the next person and did the same thing again.

When he came a young woman's turn. Her half-naked, thin body appeared clearly in the light. She couldn't be older than sixteen. With blonde hair that hadn't been washed in a long time. Her near-skeleton frame revealed that she hadn't eaten for a long time. She had been through a lot and could take it no longer. Moving into the light, I saw the man doing the buying. He was a tall man with dark brown hair and a large build. His clean-shaven face revealed that he did have perverse pleasure in his work. It was clear he was old enough to be the girl's father. That didn't stop him from getting closer to her.

With all her might, the young woman pushed the buyer to the ground with a scream of pure horror. A moment of surprise gave her enough time to escape. She ran towards the city and to safety. Castro, unfortunately, was too good at his job. He easily chased the girl down. Viciously, he knocked the girl to the ground with the butt of his rifle. He was about to make an example out of her, as he proceeded to beat her with the butt of his rifle. Ignoring her pleas of mercy. She held her arm up for protection. His motion was enough in the darkness to have a target. I aimed my pistol carefully and fired. Castro slumped over her, covering her body. He won't be hurting anybody anymore.

As you might have guessed, that started the fight. Fontaine and his men open fire. Their weapons were antiques made during the time of legends. That gave us an advantage. Something we were determined to exploit. Fontaine soon had another problem. His buyer friend had no intention of joining a fight. He had his men gather all the captives he could put into his vehicles and prepare to leave. Leaving his second to deal with us, he was going to help his men on shore. From the bridge, the pilot was slowly bearing down on our position. One of us had to deal with her. Robert volunteered to do the job, giving him cover so he could make a clear shot. Robert lowered his pistol and fired two shots. Both bolts of energy hit her body, and she slumped to the floor. She died instantly. Without her, the pirates had to give ground. That gave us a much-needed rest to recharge our pistols. Robert watched Brenden and his men while I checked on Cassandra.

Two shots came from where Cassandra was. Foolishly, I jumped up and ran over to where I could see her. I found she had shot the engineer dead. She looked up at me with a sense of relief. Before I could respond, a rifleman on shore had her in his sights. I fired widely and killed him. A second came into sight, and Robert killed him. Holding out my hand, she immediately grabbed it, and I pulled her up. I was relieved to find she still had the pouch with our money in it. It didn't matter anymore because the time for further negotiations had passed.

For now, we just wait. Onshore, Fontaine managed to take control of the situation on land. The chief Buyer was allowed to leave with one transport. The occupants in the two transports that remained gathered their weapons and joined the fight against us. Leaving four of his men to watch the remaining prisoners. He had his new reinforcements join his second mate on the boat. As for himself, he took his remaining men and tried to flank us again.

To all three of us, the outlook seemed clear. We are going to die. I wanted to say I'm sorry to both. But I couldn't find the words. We just watched as, with extra firepower, the pirates and their friends moved at will, surrounding us.

Sirens came from the city. Along with powerful floodlights that illuminated everything around us. It is clear to all of us that; is the Watchmen. Wells had kept his promise. In five minutes, they had secured the entire area. Fontaine wisely had his people surrender.

A contingent of ten Watchmen entered the boat and took the pirate away in chains. A fitting punishment for them. Five additional Watchmen entered the hold to see if anybody was hiding. Finally, three Watchmen came over to detain us. With our hands up, we were escorted out of the wharf right up to Wells, who was waiting for us. He stood there with a smug look on him. That I found annoying.

I had to ask, "Where the hell were you?"

In an arrogant tone, he stated, "Gotham is a large city. We have hundreds of responsibilities all over Gotham."

I will never know why they hesitated. Currently, I don't care. They made it, and that is all I need to know. I just made a request, "Can we talk to you tomorrow? We are tired."

"I don't see any reason." He said with a sense of compassion for what we had gone through, he added, "I'll see you at fifteen hundred hours."

"We'll be there," Cassandra stated.

We left him. Cassandra and I looked for Robert. He was gone. Disappeared into thin air, we both thought. Not that it was surprising, after all, he was being smuggled in. As for us, we still needed our citizen passes when a lone Watchman challenged us. But our ordeal was finally over.

We made it home twenty minutes later. By this time, Gotham is beginning to wake up around us. Here we are trying to get home and rest. When we arrived at our door, Cassandra turned to me. Holding my arm, she wanted me to wait. I turned to her. She reached up and kissed me on my lips. Pulling back slowly she whispered, "Just wanted to say thanks."

I opened the door. And we both went to bed.

7   OLIVIA

AFTER A FEW DAYS, INSPECTOR WELLS HAD SENT FOR US. IN A message, he proudly said our reward for the capture of Fontaine and his men had been approved. "All you have to do is come down to headquarters and get it," he had assured us.

The next morning, we headed down together. I needed some time outside the apartment. I had no assignments since I made it home. I informed Caitlyn and my other usual clients when I made it home. Still, there was no response. I guess I am one of hundreds of operatives working in Gotham, but I thought someone would have inquired about my services. To make matters worse, Gabrielle had barely spoken to me, a word a day to be exact. When I tried to ask her why, she just shrugged it off silently and headed into her room. Leaving me to find my answers from other people. Regina, to be exact.

Regina explained in a condescending tone, "Gabrielle had been infected again. It will be best to stay away from vermin." I quickly understood I was the vermin she was speaking about. In a feeble attempt to ease my ego, "You're the only person in her life, not a Blue."

Feeling a deeper tension at home, I just left it at that. Now I am walking to my only friend I had left in Cassandra.

As for Cassandra, it was quite the opposite. Robert had managed to elude the Watchmen that night. Later, his associates managed to get him papers. Cassandra had wanted to get together and introduce Robert to Gabrielle. Only to have Gabby balk at the idea. Walking together, I had a feeling that Cassandra knew what was happening between Gabby and me, but couldn't tell me. For right now. I choose to focus on the last person in our group, Olivia.

Wells greeted us at the door. It is a strange change of procedure. Not that I expected anything permanent in our working arrangement. The moment he saw us; he rushed over to keep us from getting too far into the department. I had the distinct feeling he didn't want us there, or at the very least, he wanted to keep us away from someone. In his right hand were two credit chips.

"I'm glad you made it so quickly," he stated earnestly. "Here is your fee. Minus the money you wanted to be sent to that address at Union." He carefully placed a credit chip in each of our hands. Immediately, I put the chip in my pocket.

Cassandra stated, "Thank you." She put her chip away.

"You two did a good job," he reassured us.

Curious, I asked him, "What will happen to the River Pirates?"

Wells hesitated in giving his answer. Now, I was beginning to understand what was happening. Somehow, our actions had caused some kind of backlash. We had upset some very powerful people. A sense of accomplishment came over me. He finally answered, "They won't be doing this again anytime soon."

His response surprised Cassandra, she stated, "Aren't they going to be punished?"

"We have sunk their ship," he stated, "it will take some time for their gang to get another ship."

With growing frustration, Cassandra interrupted, "What about the crew?"

"They were expelled. We have them on record."

Sharing Cassandra's rage, I added, "They are free to do it again."

Wells made no reply. He knew she was right. Now, they are

going to learn to be more careful in the future. He admitted something to us, "You best be careful. Some powerful people are not happy with your actions." I could think of a few. He added, "They will want revenge."

"We'll be careful," I told him.

Thinking that I wasn't taking him seriously, he emphatically added, "He will kill you or worse."

"What was worse than being killed?" I wondered out loud.

"Trust me, in Gotham, there is."

Cassandra wanted to know about other people, so she inquired, "What about the poor souls who were brought in?"

Lowering his head in shame, he simply replied, "They were immediately expelled."

"They had sacrificed so much," she stated.

In a vain attempt to defend the undefendable, he sullenly admitted, "That is our policy. My hands are tied."

With nothing more to be said, we left. Politely saying our goodbyes. Walking home, we both felt depressed. Cassandra had her reasons. For myself, I didn't feel we had accomplished anything. Risking our lives for nothing. In a few months, they will be returning to their business of smuggling people into the city, robbing them blind in the process. Worst, we exposed some prominent people who protect the smugglers. As for me, I am done with it. This is Wells' problem, not mine.

Outside our apartment, I said goodbye to Cassandra. Telling her I had an errand to run. To be polite, she didn't inquire any further. When she opened the door and went in, I walked away. Heading down to the parking area. In truth, I had a stop to make. First, I had to head to the bank. I knew there was a branch along the way to my destination. Traveling three levels down, I made it right when it opened. Handing the mature woman my new credit chip. She promptly put the chip in her system, and the balance came on her screen. An expression of admiration came over her as she was impressed by my balance. She wondered how somebody like me could make so much. If she only knew.

"What would you like to do today, Mister Walker?" she said

in cold professionalism. In my head, I had estimated my expenses for the past few hours. I wanted to be fair but not too dangerous. Between Cassandra and me, we shared a bounty of a hundred thousand credits. That made it fifty thousand apiece. Twenty thousand credits, I had directed Wells to send it to Sandra's family. To ease my conscience, you can say. I had to make a decision that was fair to me.

Finally, I requested, "I'll take five thousand in hard credits." She promptly followed my request. As she was counting out, I made my second request: "I would like to transfer the balance to this person. I handed her the request form that had the name on it. It was Deb and Harry's daughter. It wasn't everything they had lost, but it was something.

The teller handed me an official request form to sign. Something I promptly did. She handed me five thousand hard credits. Four gold credits are worth a thousand each. One platinum is worth five hundred credits, four silvers worth a hundred each, and five coppers worth twenty. You can have a great night at the casino with that, I thought to myself. Not that I would.

"Will that be all, Mister Walker?" She asked, just to be thorough.

I replied, "Nothing else, thank you." With a smile, she handed over my credit chip. I quickly walked out of the bank. Taking the lift down to another level.

Twenty minutes later, I found myself in front of their daughter's apartment. I'm not sure what to do next. Should I just slip it under the door? To spare them further anguish. I did go so far as to look at the bottom of the door to see if my idea was feasible. It wasn't. It didn't fit. After a minute, I decided I couldn't be so careless with this much money, so I rang the doorbell.

In a moment, the husband answered the door. He didn't recognize me at first.

"Can I help you?"

"I'm Duncan Walker. We met a month ago. I was with your in-laws out there."

He knew what I had meant. Out of instinct, his eyes looked through me, trying to see what I wanted. I could hear from behind him his wife inquiring who was at the door. He answered her, "Duncan Walker, your parents' friend."

She immediately stopped what she was doing and ran to the door. With great interest, she wanted to hear what I had to say.

In a contrite tone, I said, "We managed to stop the gang that murdered your parents. They will be out of action for a while." That made her happy for a moment. But when she stopped to look at me, she knew I had more to say, so I continued, "They were exiled."

She knew what that meant. She stated, "They will be free to start again."

"They must have prominent friends," added the husband.

He was right, but I had to give her a sense of closure. "But they have no boat. It will take them time to find a new one." I don't think that helped them at all. As Ester began to sob.

Her husband grew hostile in his tone. "Anything else?"

I handed him the credit chip. Their money was lost. But I managed to take this from them. It is about twenty thousand credits."

After saying that, I walked away. I heard him close the door behind me. I debated walking back there and handing him the hard credits in my pocket. On the boat, Cassandra managed to secure everything we had given Fontaine. In addition to other money, they had gathered. It was divided among the three of us. That meant I didn't lose money in this venture. I don't know why I didn't give them more credit. It would have been something. I just needed to go home.

———————

At home, to make me feel worse, I managed to see Regina. She had a talent for reminding me about how much Gabrielle could do better than me. Not that I could disagree with her. Gabby deserved better. Worst I believe is that she has finally convinced Gabby about what we all know.

I tried not talking to her. But she insisted on talking to me. I politely listened to her while my eyes scanned the room for clues about what the girls were doing. On the table, I saw two packages, both were open. With my focus returning to Regina, I realized she was eagerly telling me what the girls were preparing for tonight and who was escorting them out.

Koch was taking Gabrielle out. While another Highlander called Justin King was taken out by Cassandra. I had never met him before. Heard about him. He is running under the Labor Party for Chancellor. I couldn't help but think this would be an interesting ride over. Regina mentioned this is the final event before the election. All the girls will have escorts.

Cassandra was the first to come out with a sapphire dress; whoever had designed the dress had decided not to cover her arms, but everything else. As she turned around, I quickly discovered the designer had forgotten to cover her entire back. Her hair was tied up, exposing her cream-colored neck. In contrast, Gabrielle came out of her room with her curly red hair down below her shoulder blades. Her dress was as red as a rose. It had a low neckline but covered her arms. With a smile, she gave me a pleasant acknowledgment. I couldn't help but hate this world. I was losing her, too.

Meekly, I excused myself and started for my room. As I passed by Gabrielle, she placed her hand on my shoulder, causing it to go numb. She stated, "Caitlyn wants to see you tonight, in her office."

"When?"

She replied, "Eighteen hundred hours." I looked over at Cassandra as she tried to get my attention. A look of concern came over her. Silly girl, I had wanted to tell her that Caitlyn was always plotting against me. But the best way to foil a trap is to sometimes walk right into it. That is exactly what I plan to do.

"I'll be there."

For a moment, Gabrielle looked concerned for my safety. Like she didn't want me to go either. In the end, she had grown to understand that I would go no matter what she may think. Before I had a chance to reassure her that I would be careful. Regina stepped in and separated.

She proclaimed, "You two better get out of those dresses and rest up. It will be late at night. Remember to be ready at nineteen hundred thirty. Naomi, Elizabeth, and Savannah will be joining us.

Remember, it is a happy time. Selene is getting married." Not one to waste time, she gently shoved them back to their respective rooms.

"When did that happen?" I asked.

Gabrielle turned to me and said playfully, "Well, if you stayed home more instead of roaming around the countryside, you would know these things."

I couldn't argue with that. But there are things I knew that she didn't. Regina continued in her campaign to have Gabrielle get back into her room and be safe from me. With her attention focused on Gabrielle, Cassandra had taken this opportunity to tell me something important: "Don't go alone. I'll ask Robert to go with you."

I placed my hand on her cheek to reassure her that I would do what she asked. I didn't mind; Robert was a good man to have around. Finished with Gabrielle, Regina turned her focus upon Cassandra and guided her to her room. Closing the door behind her. Regina turned around and gave me a dirty look. I decided the best thing was to go out for a run.

After my run, I showered and headed up to meet Caitlyn. Taking the lift, I had just realized that this would be my first visit to her office. Not that I minded either way; I just thought it was strange. Thinking further, I hadn't seen her since our visit to the casino when we found Cassandra. It was funny; I hadn't thought of that. I never missed her. When the lift stopped at her level, I walked out. Heading down the passageway. About midway there, I noticed Robert and two others waiting for me. As I walked closer, I remembered his two friends. They were both members of a group that called themselves Disrupters, which disturbed the event Kleist was holding at his casino.

When I joined them, Robert introduced the man and woman. Her name was Jill Cassidy, about twenty-three, I would guess. A cute girl, she was short with long brown hair. She wore baggy pants and a simple blouse. I thought if she wanted to put the work in, she could be pretty. Her friend was dressed just as simply. He was about the same age, maybe a year older. His black hair was longer than what other citizens had, but not too much longer; he didn't want to stand out. His height and weight were average, making him very unremarkable. After two sentences, I discovered his main ambition in life is to be a martyr to a great cause. If only he knew what that great endeavor was. His name was Lucian Gorstich.

The four of us walked the rest of the way together. After a few minutes, it became clear to me that they were not impressed with Caitlyn and her mission. Lucian called it conquest by mating. He used more choice words. He went on calling her charges no better than a bunch of whores. I politely turned around and reminded them that I was fond of each girl, and two were my friends. Embarrassed, Jill immediately apologized for his comments. Lucian wasn't as contrite, but he remained silent, correctly believing I had killed people for less reason.

We stopped together outside Caitlyn's door. I turned to Robert and the others and said," I'll be all right."

Robert said they would wait half an hour if I didn't come out, and they would come in after me. I thanked them and went inside.

As soon as I walked into her reception area, I suddenly realized how much of an enigma Caitlyn is to me. Her office was huge. Twice as large as our flat, with two dozen people running around doing whatever their task demanded. I headed for the front desk, which had both her secretary, Sonja, and a security guard stationed behind it. Neither was ready to acknowledge me, so I stood there looking around the front office. I noticed two steps away, two more security guards taking their positions to act as a deterrent for visitors who wanted to cause trouble in the office. She wore a simple black skirt and blue blouse; her hair was like when I first met her at Southpoint. Thinking about Robert and the others, five minutes had already gone by. I spoke up.

Without looking up at me, she asked for my name. I did as she requested. That made her look up. She directed her attendant to take me to see Caitlyn. With a refreshing sense of courtesy, Sonja asked me to follow her. I gladly did as she asked, ignoring the two at the desk. We walked down a long hallway to a door at its end. She knocked on the door and opened it, giving me a friendly smile as I entered the office.

Caitlyn was sitting behind her desk, waiting for me. With a more sinister smile than her assistant, she rose from her desk. Sitting casually at the edge of her desk with her arms folded in frustration, she asked, "Duncan, why do you hate me?"

That was a rhetorical question. I never had that much to hate her. To be honest, I didn't like her, but I never thought about it. I calmly answered, "I never hated you."

"Really, that is strange," she started with, then she gave me her examples, "That business with Wynn."

"You wanted Cassandra away from them."

"You killed his representative five days ago."

Now I remember. He was the pig who harassed the young girl that night. For me, I cared more for the well-being of that young girl.

Standing up, Caitlyn walked over to me. As she walked closer, I began to get nervous. Caitlyn wore a fashionable black dress, not as elegant as the dresses she picked for her wards. But flattering nonetheless. She is attractive like the others, but the same age as me. Standing close to me, she answered me. "He was hoping to get a replacement.

"The girl was old enough to be his daughter."

"True," she said, revealing a rare sense of empathy. "Don't worry, I'll fix it." She placed her arms around me and added, "How about those three Disrupter friends outside my office?"

Surprised, I asked her, "How did you know?"

Amused, Caitlyn freed me and walked away. Taking a control pad on her desk, she pointed at the walls around her. A hundred moving pictures surrounded us. One was in my flat. Now I knew her secret. I don't know if I can ever use it.

"What do you want, Caitlyn?" I was growing impatient with her small talk.

Amused with my impertinence, she stated calmly, "Koch wants you to escort him on his campaign for the next two weeks. He is covering Gotham and the surrounding areas. He will pay you the reasonable rate."

"Why now?" I asked her, it was a fair question.

"There have been rumors of another attempt on his life. He

trusts you." She said calmly. Stepping forward, she looked into my eyes. "If you do this, I have some friends, and I'll find this Olivia you have been looking for."

"I'll do it," I stated. I had no choice, and she knew it.

Walking behind her desk, she smugly sat down in her chair and stated, "Good, you start tomorrow."

Before I left, I requested to give half my fee to Sandy's family. Caitlyn eagerly agreed. Walking out, I joined Robert and his friends. When I told them what she wanted, Robert did not comment, he understood it was my job. Jill made no reply. Lucian quickly made his opinion known. Not that it surprised me. Finally, I had had enough, I decided to give him some friendly advice, "You know, I have only had known you for barely an hour. And I discovered you don't like anything. Why don't you ally with the Reformers and make changes that way?"

Lucian quickly replied, "They are all crooks."

"Then the Labor."

He made no reply. It forced him to ponder his position in Gotham for a moment, probably for the first time. Jill was amused that I managed to silence Lucian. Gladly, he remained silent for the rest of the way home. I needed to make it home in time. I needed to warn Naomi and Cassandra to be careful. At the lift, I said goodbye to my escort and entered it alone.

As I arrived at my level. I stepped aside to allow an old couple to step inside before I exited. Walking at a quick pace, I managed to make it home. Opening the door, I found, to my relief, that nobody had left yet. I assumed that Caitlyn was sitting at her desk watching us right now. I had to be careful.

To keep Caitlyn guessing, I made sure to talk to Koch first. I told him I'd see him tomorrow. He was pleased that I was joining his team. Regina moved towards the door. She reminded them that they would be late. I volunteered to escort them to the lift. One by one, we walked by Regina. I chose to be the last one out. As I passed her, I gave her a dirty look. The nine of us walked down to the lift. As we waited, I took Naomi and Cassandra aside.

I told them, "Be careful who you let into your home. Somebody will know."

They both understood what I meant. When the lift arrived, all eight of them entered. I wanted to join them, thinking they needed some protection. Koch assured me that a contingent of Watchmen would be waiting for them. The door shut, and I headed for home.

———————

Two weeks of never-ending campaign stops finally ended. Nothing of note had happened. Other than Koch giving the same speech with a few variations a thousand times. For a little variation, I did manage to hear his two opponents, Herbert of the Patricians and Reyne of the Labor Party, give their speeches. All three were pretty much the same: I have your best interest at heart, a vote for me will be the smartest thing you can do, a vote for them will be a disaster, and most importantly, I am your friend. After the first day of this foolish banter, I found myself hoping that something would happen, just to save me from boredom. That was not to be.

However, I did learn a few things on the campaign trail. Each level had its hopes and desires. Red level wants the best of everything: wages, housing, and living conditions. Yellow Level wants control of prices and wages. Green Level wants investment in food and power supply. Grey Level wants stronger laws and control of their borders. Brown level wants low taxes and wages, and control over supplies. Blue level wants to be purple. Finally, Purples just wants everybody to stay in their place. Of all the factions, the Purples fear the Reds.

One evening after a long trip to the district of Island, during dinner, I revealed my findings to Koch. He didn't deny it. Hoping that he would explain it to me, I asked, "Why."

Koch immediately ordered two more pints of beer. Believing that I would understand it better, the drunker I get. When the server returned with his order. He started, "On paper, we are considered a democracy. There is one drawback to that form of government, and that is majority rule." I did remember something about democracy while I was in school. I never thought I would see it in action.

"The problem is the Highlanders want to stay in power. But they control about three percent of the population. Blue makes up six percent, and we don't always agree. Now ask yourself how they can maintain power?"

I thought about his question for a moment. Then the answer came to me, "You keep the other sections in competition with each other."

"Very good," he stated, "now between the two levels, the Reds and Yellows control nearly sixty percent of the population. The Grey, Green, and Brown sections control the remaining thirty-one percent of the population. Because of their status, those three levels are willing to join the Highlanders to maintain their position. Now, the Highlanders have one other advantage: they control the wealth. And they use that money to convince the Reds to hate the Yellows and vice versa.

"That makes the election a sham."

"Not necessarily," he explained. "For the first time in a hundred years, the Patricians are in danger of losing power. The outgoing Chancellor is very unpopular. Herbert, who leads the Labor Party, has gained strong support within the Reds and Yellows. Then, here come the Reformers, who have gathered strong support from the Greens and Browns."

"Why did you tell me all this?" I asked him.

"You already figured it out," he replied, but he wasn't finished, "and I respect you. Usually, people from the Wastelands are ignorant savages. But you are intelligent. Where they struggle while living here, you have flourished." I think that was a compliment. But he had one more confession to make: "With Fletcher, you saw how far they would go to stop that."

He didn't have to say anything else. Agents hired by the Highlanders were behind the attacks on Fletcher and the raid in Union a few months ago. That is why they hired private security firms for protection. Most of the Watchmen are Greys, and they are loyal to Patricians. Koch and the others didn't trust them. Now, it is too close to the election to resort to violence, so they hope.

We left the restaurant together. As I escorted him home, I began to ponder my very quick lesson on politics. In the end, I have a new disdain for politics. While we were walking together, something began to nag at me. Why did he tell me all this? When we entered the lift, I felt it was a good time to ask. I turned to him and asked, "Why did you tell me this?"

"Because you would figure it out eventually" is all he said.

When we arrived at his level, I escorted him home. Outside his door were two Watchmen serving as sentries. The two guards stared straight ahead, oblivious of their charge returning home. Koch did the same. Before I entered, I glanced at each man. They didn't return my acknowledgment. I understood. I made myself comfortable on his couch. My assignment will end in the morning.

One thing I must admit about Caitlyn is that she keeps her promises. Now, as part of our agreement, it was time to see if she would continue her one noble trait. It was early morning when I headed for her office. Koch will be all right. He will have a contingent of six watchmen who will spend twenty-four hours a day. I assume that the other two candidates will have the same protection. That means I will not have any more assignments for a while. Not that I minded, don't get me wrong, the pay was good, but it was quite dangerous. Wasteland was never this dangerous. And I'm only half joking.

I walked into her office. Unlike the last time I was here, I was alone. It was too early for her staff to report for work. Knowing she was expecting me; I walked towards her office. Knocking on the door, I waited for her to answer. When I heard her voice, I opened it and casually walked in. Standing in front of her desk, she walked towards me. She wore a black dress that she must have worn for forty-eight hours straight. Her reason was her business. Right now, I just care about what she has learned. I didn't like it, but she was my best option.

Walking towards me, I noticed that she had no shoes on. Looking at the wall, I noticed all but one of the screens was shut off.

This must be her break from ruling her little empire. She gave me a pleasant smile when she said, "You did a good job."

"It was quiet this time."

She stepped closer trying to see how I would respond. The fact I didn't flinch impressed her. Looking up at me she asked, "Have you had any breakfast?"

"No."

"Would you like some?" She walked over to her desk. I followed her, wanting only to get my information.

"I want to know about Olivia."

Sitting down she replied, "A shame." She took some paper from her drawer and placed it on her desk. "There you go. Contact Katrina Kleist, she was taken by you." I read the report it made clear how Mitchel had exploited Olivia and other young women. As I looked deeper into the details I found no mention of Natalie. "Another person who is taking by you is Wynn. But not in a good way."

"That doesn't surprise me."

Her tone changed when she said, "Just be careful."

"I will. Thanks." I walked out and headed home.

As I made it back to my level, a strange thought came over me. It was so bizarre that I didn't realize it twenty minutes ago. The reality of the situation was alien to me. For a moment, I had thought that Caitlyn was sincerely concerned for me. This was another side of her I had never expected to see. Purely out of instinct, I thanked her for her concern. But it didn't register. When you have a woman figured out, she gives you a new wrinkle. Not that it will change anything between us. Especially when she is winning.

I entered the apartment. Cassandra was waiting for me to sit on the sofa with her. Regina was cooking in the kitchen. Smelling the pleasing odor from whatever she was cooking, I suddenly realized I was hungry. Gabrielle must have heard me because she quickly joined us. Sitting together, I revealed to them what Caitlyn had found out: "Mitchel has created a service for Highlanders. It is called slumming."

"What is that?" asked Gabrielle.

Before I answered her, I looked over at Cassandra. Her expression made it clear she had heard of it before. I replied, "When the Highlanders want companionship for some night. But they want a free hand to do what they wish. They take a girl or a boy that nobody will miss."

Gabrielle took a seat next to Cassandra and hugged her. She couldn't do that to Olivia. When they had finished, I told them the rest, "Mitchel will give her back to us. For a price."

Afraid, Cassandra asked, "What is the price?"

"He wants me?"

Cassandra screamed out, "You can't do it!"

Regina ran out, wondering what had happened. Gabrielle managed to quickly calm her down. She got rid of her by mentioning that something was burning. Regina ran back into the kitchen. That sight gave us all some small amusement. I wasn't finished.

"That is our better option," I stated. "Our other choice is that Wynn wants you back."

Gabrielle immediately shut that option down. Not that I ever would consider it. Cassandra then stated the obvious, "It's a trap."

"Why does Mitchel care?" asked Gabrielle.

"Our little adventure with Fontaine and his pirates had cost him plenty," I answered her. I then added, "Sometimes the best way to foil a trap is to spring it." Looking at their faces, it was clear they didn't believe me. I can't blame them, I don't believe it myself. We just have no other option. I stated, "I have a plan."

Cassandra stated with authority, "You're not going alone. I'll ask Robert."

"I was hoping you would."

With rare confusion, Gabrielle inquired, "Who is Robert?"

With a mischievous smile, Cassandra admitted, "A friend of mine."

I looked up overhead for a moment. Caitlyn had hidden that damn camera very well. Maybe she wasn't listening. Subtly, I stated, "I was hoping you would."

'When are you leaving?" asked Gabrielle.

"I am meeting with Katrina Kleist in a couple of hours."

"Be careful," Gabrielle said first, and it was repeated by Cassandra.

"I will," I reassured them. Thinking back to Caitlyn, I realized something: she was no fool; it was clear to her that her inquiries would lead me to a trap. Some strange impulse in her wanted to warn me. A strange thing since she had wanted me out of the pitcher since we first met.

Katrina Kleist's office is a whole floor below her husband's. A reminder of who is in charge of this petty kingdom. Not that she cared. She was free to do the assignments she was entrusted with as she saw fit. I found her to be a valuable officer in this company. She provides a sense of empathy and charm to people who wish to do business with her husband. I had discovered that the first time I had met her.

The casino still didn't impress me. I found it noisy and crowded with fools looking for a quick fortune. That made me rush through the ground level to the central tower. Inside the lift, I pushed her floor number, and I headed up. The other two times I had met her were security details for the other two factions vying with Koch for the Chancellor's chair. In either event, I had somehow managed not to meet anybody important. My assignment was to guard the entry and make sure there were no interruptions like what had happened during the Reformer's gathering. Considering that nobody disrupted the event, I did my job. Katrina was very pleased with me because her husband's temper tantrum had damaged his position with the Reformers. She didn't want him to repeat his mistake with the other two factions.

With the door opening, I brought myself back to the mission at hand. Stepping out of the lift, I stepped onto the floor. I suddenly found myself surrounded by a score of assistants rushing around six offices doing their jobs. Katrina runs an efficient ship, I have discovered; each person has a particular job to do that he or she is responsible for. Each person will report to her when their task is finished. My only problem is walking through the main hallway, dodging four of her assistants along the way to her office. Somehow, I managed to do that.

Entering her outer office, I found it strangely tranquil in contrast to the chaos outside. Her secretary, a young woman no older than Cassandra, manned the desk. Seeing me, she told me I could go in. I thanked the young woman and did as I was told.

Opening the door, I found Katrina sitting at a side table, nibbling at a sandwich she had made herself. I noticed a loaf of bread and fixings spread out on the table. Seeing me, she immediately swallowed what was in her mouth and stood up.

She explained, "The calm before the storm, so I eat."

"No need to explain."

She offered me a chair. When I sat down, she did the same. Looking at me, she had a grey business-type dress on. Her hair was styled to be out of her way. She had shoes that were supposed to make her look taller. I couldn't find any other reason for them. She had forgotten that she had glasses on. When she realized this, she immediately took them off and held them in her right hand. She didn't need to; wearing her glasses enhanced her elegance.

She gave me a welcoming smile and said, "You went through Mitchel's proposal. What have you decided?"

"I'll give myself up." There is no other option.

A look of admiration came over her. "You know it is a trap."

"I do." I replied, "Why are you in this?"

"Privately, I don't like Wynn," she replied," Publicly, he is a good friend of mine."

I knew what that meant. Her husband doesn't want to embarrass Wynn. But I had an idea that she could help me without helping me. I asked, "If there is an altercation that endangers your guest, what will you do?"

Kristina knew what I was implying. She asked, "When would you want me to make the call for the Watchmen?"

"I say a half hour."

"Consider it done."

She then gave me the location where they were waiting for me. Her people had told her about how many men Wynn and Mitchel had gathered. She believed they had ten thugs with them. I thanked her for her information, reassuring her that it would help me. She had offered to have a security detail ready to help. Not wanting to get her in trouble with her husband, I politely refused.

After I finished, I left for the casino.

If you're thinking I'm being foolishly heroic, you would be wrong. I did get some help. As I exited the lift to the main floor, I signaled Jenna, who was waiting for me. She relayed my message to Robert and nine other Disrupters. It was not surprising to me that Lucian wasn't with them. He made it clear he was a pacifist. Whatever that is.

We moved separately to our meeting point. Robert had joined me as we walked to a storeroom behind the large structures. It wasn't much of a building. As we entered together, we found it was nearly empty. Joining us inside, Jenna immediately found the controls for the lights. That brought Mitchel, Wynn, and Olivia into the open. A thug stepped out of the darkness and joined them. Wynn singled his thug to step forward and block our path.

He said, "That's far enough." Placing his hand on my shoulder, he said, "Weapons."

"We all have weapons. And we're not giving them up." I told him, looking him square in his eyes. The thug looked behind him. Mitchel told him not to press the situation. He did what he was told. This gave me a good look at Olivia. Like Cassandra, a few months ago, she looked dead inside. Her porcelain skin had traces of bruising near her lips and eyes. Covered with makeup to hide any lasting damage. Her eyes remained down, daring not to look up or smile. She had on a low-cut white dress that ended above her thighs. Her blonde hair was still cut short. Her skin was deathly pale.

"Olivia, it will be over soon." I tried to reassure her.

Mitchel was amused by my vain attempt to comfort her. Staring at me with a sinister smile, while keeping his hand firmly on her shoulders, he stated confidently, "That's right, old friend, there is no need for violence." Keeping that damn smile, he turned to Olivia and continued with that same confident tone, "Olivia honey why don't you show Duncan here that you're glad to see him."

Carefully raising her eyes, she whispered, "How do you want me?"

Looking at me, he told her, "By kissing him."

He pushed her towards me. She staggered into my arms. To steady herself, she placed her arms around my waist. Placing my hands on her arms, I gently steadied her. With dead eyes, she looked up at me. She then proceeded to kiss me as she was told to do. There was nothing behind it, no joy or passion. I wanted to keep her and have Jenna take her somewhere safe. But any sudden movement would get us all killed. I had to let Mitchel play his hand first.

"I think that's enough, Olivia. We have business to work out."

As ordered, she pulled away from me. She took a moment and looked at me, and a tear ran down her cheek. With a determined act of defiance, she gave me another quick kiss. After that, she returned to her place beside Mitchel.

Now it was Wynn's turn to gloat. "Where is the lovely Cassandra?"

"She is safe," I told him. "I'm afraid you have to deal with me."

He stated confidently, "Maybe after we finish with you. I'll take her and her friend."

I knew who he met, Gabrielle. That wasn't going to happen. To back his statement, he called on his men to join him. All his men moved into the light. In response, Robert called his people in. From behind us, Wynn and Mitchel's confidence had disappeared. Now it was a problem. Jenna and Robert stepped away from me. Jill led three disrupters and flanked their right.

As for Mitchel, he had no desire to fight it out. With a firm hold on Olivia, he looked at Wynn and stated, "This is your problem now." Looking towards me, he stated, "If you're still alive, come and find us." He then dragged Olivia and disappeared into the darkness. Wynn wasn't sure what to do next. Should he stay and lead his men to try to kill us, or should he leave like Mitchel and let his henchmen handle it? Knowing that there is a good chance that his men might choose to desert rather than fight. It is unfortunate for him that he never had a chance to make that choice. I am willing to bet he wished to choose to leave.

It was the henchman who remained at his side who started the fight. He proved he had no patience to wait any longer. Reaching for his pistol, he never managed to get it out. Robert proved to be a little bit quicker and shot him with one shot. Wynn panicked as his remaining men opened fire at us. He looked around frantically and searched for a safe place to hide. When Jenna, the other Disrupters, and I joined, Robert didn't calm him down. Two of his men fell around him. He held out his hands to say he was a noncombatant. The fight ends when the Watchmen begin to arrive. Katrina had come through. Wynn's men immediately surrendered, dropping their weapons. Robert directed his people to do the same.

Robert turned to me, "Go. We will take it from here."

I quickly ran after them. Taking time to give Wynn a look of disgust, I passed him. He had his head between his hands. I turned my back towards him and headed into the darkness. From behind, I heard one last shot. As I turned, I saw Wynn on the floor, dead with a pistol in his hand; he was shot in the back. I looked at Jill as she dropped her pistol. It was clear that Wynn had that gun to shoot me. I thanked her. Jenna was the last to surrender to the Watchmen. I made it out to a cargo lift.

The lift was there waiting for me, daring me to enter. Not having much of a choice, I entered the shuttle and felt a sudden jerk as it rose through its shaft. A dim light kept the lift from being pitch black. With a second sudden jerk, the lift stopped. I watched the door open to the outside. Night had fallen when I walked out onto the roof of the fourth tower of the casino. The night was cool as I walked away from the lift. Looking around, I realized I was no longer under the influence of the city. It wasn't a surprise. With my adrenaline flowing through my body, I barely felt the cool air. I managed to maneuver around a few small structures that dotted the roof. Walking towards the opposite edge of the roof. There, waiting for me, were Mitchel and Olivia.

Olivia had her mouth gagged. She was trembling as her wrists were bound together by metal restraints. Her dress gave her little protection from the elements. In contrast, Mitchel kept his sadistic smile. He was enjoying this little game. His arm had locked around hers as I walked closer to them.

"I knew you would make it," he proclaimed as I walked closer to them. Concerned, he added, "That's far enough."

I understood I had to talk to him. If I can get close enough, I might be able to get her away from him. It was a long shot, but I had to try. I calmly stated, "We are all friends here."

He explained, "You have caused a lot of trouble to some friends of mine. They want you to be punished."

"But using Olivia like this." I took a step forward in a vain attempt to reason with him. "You can easily replace her." He remained silent as I cautiously tried to get closer.

He looked over at Olivia and dragged her forward. He wanted to make his point, "I put a lot of work into her. When I first got her, she was malnourished. It had taken me three months to get her into shape." She closed her eyes as he caressed her breast.

"Just let her go. We can pay double what you want."

"I want quite a lot." He realized I was getting too close. He immediately grabbed her bonds and threw her to the edge of the building. She tried to scream in vain, as tears came down her cheeks. "You are killing her." He told me.

I froze in place. I threw my hands out to stop him. "No!" I screamed.

That made him pull her to safety. He began to reconsider his position. "You know, like Natalie, I think Olivia has run her course."

"Then let me have her. They say the Kreig has no soul." That was a mistake. He knew I had discovered his identity months ago.

He looked over at Olivia, he was studying her, she looked at him, still helpless in this game we were playing. While his attention was on her, I carefully took a few more steps. I was close enough to grab her if I needed to.

"Still, she has been properly trained." He caressed her face gently. She tried to struggle. That had amused him, he pulled the gag off her mouth. She was too frightened to speak. He continued," My clients had raved about her ability to kiss." Placing his hand on the back of her neck, he pulled her violently towards him and kissed her hard on the lips.

Her eyes revealed the outrage of his actions. When he pulled away from her, he was pleased with himself. With a sudden burst of anger, she struck him across his face with all her might. Her bonds had bloodied his mouth. She screamed, "Bastard!"

But her act of defiance was to be her last. He casually pushed her off the edge of the building. Her expression of shock was on her face as she tried somehow to catch herself. Mitchel walked away as I rushed over to catch her. I was too late. With one desperate lunge, I tried to catch her, but she was just out of my reach. I watched her as she fell into the night sky, out of sight.

"There won't be any trace of her when she lands." He stated in a mocking tone. He walked away laughing.

Hearing that, I couldn't help myself. Out in the Wasteland, I had two rules that came to mind. Never take things personally. The second rule is never to give in to rage. Right now, I don't care about stupid rules. Rage came through me, and I welcomed it. Rage was my friend, and this was personal.

The bastard, as he walked away, had turned his back towards me. That is a mistake I intend to make him pay for. I wanted to kill him with my bare hands. With all my might, I punched him in the kidney. He staggered forward, and I punched him again. Turning towards me, I quickly punched him in the stomach, which knocked the wind out of them. With another hard punch, I struck him in the chin. Unfortunately, that was the last punch I managed to land. For he responded with a brutal barrage of strikes against me. I was barely standing when he began to push me towards the edge of the building. He intended for me to join Olivia. Coming to my senses, I pushed back, forcing him to fall back. On the ground, I shoved my elbow into his side. I followed with my left elbow and did the same. I should have drawn my stinger, but I wanted to kill him with my bare hands. I lunged at his throat, but he managed to regain his composure. I don't remember anything after that. I was knocked out cold.

8 RECOVERY

I AWOKE IN A STRANGE BED IN THE MIDDLE OF A SPARSELY FUR-
nished room. When I finally became aware of my surroundings,
I noticed that certain things had happened to me. My torso was
wrapped tightly by a thin piece of fabric. That managed to restrict
my movement greatly. Not that it was a bad thing, but when I
tried to move, I felt a sudden, powerful burst of excruciating pain.
I decided to sit still. When the pain in my ribs had subsided, my
head began to throb. Lying on my back, I tried to go back to sleep.
When that didn't work, I brought up my hands to massage my
temples, hoping that it would somehow help ease the pain. That
is when I noticed my head was wrapped with the same fabric that
was on my torso. It didn't work. That is when I noticed my wrist
was connected to a device that monitored my heart and other vital
statistics. Now I had an idea of where I was: in a hospital.

While wincing in pain, I looked over my bed, looking for something that would get the attention of a nurse or, better, a doctor.
Hoping they out of mercy will give me something out of mercy for
this pain. I managed to find it on my service table. With both hands,
I pressed the button and collapsed on my back. Being in pain alters

an individual's perception, it turns a minute into an hour. But two nurses finally entered the room.

The older nurse, about fifty, took the lead. Walking towards me, she said, in a tone that was strangely indifferent and concerned at the same time, "How are you doing, Mister Walker?" It was almost second nature, like she had been saying it for so long.

Staying completely still, I replied, "Do you have something for this pain?"

She immediately directed the younger nurse to gather some medication. The younger nurse, barely twenty, did what she was directed. I watched her leave the room. While we waited, the older nurse checked my vital signs. Satisfied, she explained, "Miss Hopper is getting you some water, a protein bar, and some crackers. We need you to eat those first before you drink the water. It will help your stomach."

That is when I realized I was starving. Enduring this pain had somehow distracted me from that fact. Right now, I have so many questions that need answers. I started with the obvious one, "How long was I unconscious?"

"Four days. We were worried about you for a while."

Now, the next question is, "How did I get here?"

"A rescue brought you in. You had a concussion and six broken ribs. Not to mention your left hand was broken. That must have been some fight."

"I don't remember."

"That's not surprising," she stated. The doctor thinks your memory loss is temporary. She will join you later."

The younger nurse entered the room with what she had been directed. She placed it on my service table. I ate the crackers first, wasting no time; after four days, anything would have tasted delicious. Next, I had the power bar. It was called food, but only in the most liberal description. It was a mixture of ingredients that somehow managed to fool my stomach but not my taste buds. The younger nurse, called Kimberly, smiled as she gave me three white pills and some bottled water. Looking at her, I put the pills in my mouth and drank the entire bottle. When I finished, I gave Kimberly the bottle.

Kimberly told me, "Your doctor has been notified that you are awake. She will be in here in ten minutes." I nodded my head as I began to feel the pain go away. She added, "Just relax."

She signaled Kimberly and left the room. Before Kimberly left, she gave me a reassuring smile and said, "I'll order some real food for you. It will be here shortly."

I thanked her. She was a lovely girl with dark brown eyes that matched her dark brown hair. Her skin was a gentle shade of cream. Out of instinct, I had found myself flirting with her; old habits die hard, as I tried to get her to do extra favors for me during my stay. After a moment, she realized she was neglecting her duties. She meekly excused herself and hurried out of my room. Leaving me alone in this bed.

What kind of person am I? I lay on my back, looking at the white roof. As my pain gradually subsided, it allowed me to wonder how I had gotten here. As hard as I tried, I couldn't remember anything in the past month. I have been asleep for four days. How did I get here? I knew it was because I was in a fight. But what are the details, again? I couldn't remember. Just flashes of images that I feel I should know, but for the life of me, I couldn't. I closed my eyes slowly to relax and tried to recollect just one image in my head.

From the darkness, an image did come to me. It was of a beautiful young woman standing in front of me. Her fiery red hair was long and straight and fell to the small of her back. It matched her ruddy complexion. She was tall and thin as she gracefully moved closer to me. I could look into her green eyes, and I knew she could see into my soul. Her smile reassured me that she liked what she saw. Every time I tried to say her name, I couldn't. No matter how much I tried, I couldn't say her name. To reassure me, she placed her finger on my mouth. She leaned towards me to kiss me.

A knock on my door forced me to open my eyes. Before I had time to respond, a young woman in a white jacket entered. Somehow, I knew she looked familiar. Another mystery for me to solve. With a familiar smile, she walked up to me. Her long, curly black hair parted on opposite sides of her face, revealing a pale complexion. She could be no older than twenty-seven. As she checked my vitals, she asked me, "How are you feeling, Duncan?"

"I'm hanging in there."

"It's been a long time," she said, checking my eyes. Her familiarity turned to concern, and she immediately changed the subject. How is your head?"

"It is a little sore."

"How is Gabrielle?"

I didn't know who that was. Thinking she could tell me, I asked, "Who?"

"I was afraid of that." With a small flashlight, she shined it into my eyes. Despite it being a little thing, I couldn't help but divert my eyes. She asked me, "What is your last memory?"

It took me a minute to understand the question. I tried to think about what my last memory was. Not able to focus on anything specific, I stated what I did know." My name is Duncan. I had been living for the past few years in the Wastelands, hoping to find Sanctuary." I looked around and asked, "Is this it?"

Concerned, the doctor answered, "Well, that is a matter of opinion." She took off the bandage on my head. I could feel her touching a bump on my head. "Does that hurt?"

"When you touch it!"

"Do you know who I am?"

"I'm sorry, I don't."

"I am Doctor Samantha Adams. We met in Shenandoah a year ago. Caitlyn helped me get into the city a few weeks ahead of you."

Damn if I couldn't remember. I just looked at her with a lost look. She gently stroked my cheek, giving me some reassurance. She then inquired, "What does Blue Light mean to you?"

That I knew. I answered, "Those are the people whom the Overseers are looking for. I don't know why." That is all I dared to tell her. I'm not proud of my part in their search. Something came to mind, and I asked, "Who is Gabrielle?"

"She is a Blue, that you found," she answered coldly. Then she told me, "You have short-term amnesia. It should come back on its own."

"And what if it doesn't?"

"We have a few things to try," she said calmly. "I'll let you eat and try to get some rest."

"I will."

"Nice to see you again." After saying that she walked out of the room. I didn't respond. I just lay back in my bed and calmly waited for my food.

For the next two days and nights, I tried to retain my memories. Sometimes, they came while I was sitting up in my bed. A certain gesture or movement brought a vision to the forefront. Something I should remember. At night, it was a far different experience; images of violence and danger came to me in nightmares, and many times, I would wake up screaming. The nightmares were so bad that I became afraid to close my eyes for fear of what I would witness. Only the effect of my drugs would allow me to return to sleep.

On the third day, Samantha mentioned the bandages around my torso could finally come off. With Kimberly helping her. She methodically cut off each strip of bandage while Kimberly gathered them from the floor and disposed of them. After twenty minutes, Samantha was finished. She wanted me to move carefully, with no sudden movements, just to see how the ribs had healed. Slowly, I moved my waist first to the left and then to the right. She watched me do as she instructed. Satisfied, she asked me to lie back. I did as she had requested. Her hands fell around the bump that was on my temple. She had rebandaged the area to protect it from me fidgeting with that bump.

"That is coming along fine," she said.

"What about my memory?" I asked her.

She looked me straight in the eye, "I wish I could tell you." She then thought of something. "I'm going to try something. A friend of yours keeps wanting to see you. I'm going to let her in if you want to."

"Is it Gabrielle?"

"No."

That made me more curious. "Please send her in."

"Good, I'll check on you tonight."

She and Kimberly left the room. I chose this opportunity to exercise my legs. I had been stuck in this bed for almost a week. Slowly, I tried to throw my right leg over the edge of my bed, followed by my left with a similar effort. With both legs dangling a few inches over the ground, I waited for the time to be right before I pushed myself up on my feet. I'm not sure what will happen next. Placing my hands at my sides, palms down, I readied myself for what would happen next. Taking a deep breath, I closed my eyes and pushed myself up. Neither of my legs collapses under the sudden burden of my weight. With my hands, I reached out for my table to steady myself as I regained my balance. When that happened, I stood upright. That is when I decided it was time to take my first step.

I must have looked silly. As my muscles had to relearn how to take a step. At first, I'm sure I looked like I was waddling rather than walking. Then my muscles remembered, and I opened the door that led to a sterile white hallway. Before I walked out of my room, I hesitated for a moment. Then I remembered that nobody told me that I couldn't attempt this little endeavor. In truth, they wanted me to get on my feet as soon as possible. I'm just going down the hallway and back. Nothing too strenuous.

That is what I did. Heading down the hallway, I knew immediately where my destination would be. A set of four large windows gave me a commanding view of blue skies. Looking out the windows, I immediately knew where the hospital was: Grey Section. The windows faced the east, and as I looked down over the river, I could see Queens District. I decided to head back as I began to feel a little tired after my brief excursion. That is when my ribs began to hurt, forcing me to take a slower pace. When I made it to my room, I returned to my bed and tried to relax. Hoping a nurse will come soon with painkillers.

Unfortunately for me, Kimberly went home for the day. Her replacement had told me she had the day off tomorrow. A couple of years older than Kimberly, Amber had straight black hair with traces of light brown hair along her temples. Her skin was light brown, and her eyes were like black coals. Taller than Kimberly with the same build, I found her attractive. She proved to be immune to my charms. She gave me a confident smile, held up her left hand, and announced that she was married.

She asked me, "Is there something you need?"

"Some painkillers, please."

"That's why you shouldn't go walking around without help."

That surprised me. I didn't see anybody around. I stated, "How did you know?"

She replied, "It's my job to know." With a smile, she patted me on the shoulder and reassured me, "I will get you some after dinner. It should be here in a few minutes."

I thanked her, and she left.

As she promised my dinner came after she left. Five minutes later she returned with the pills. As instructed, I took them both and relaxed. Letting my food digest. Amber felt my chin and stated, "I think you need a shave."

Amber returned with shaving equipment and a little bucket full of hot water. She asked me if I felt better. I was glad that the pills did their job. She offered to shave me. I graciously accepted the offer. After ten minutes, she had finished shaving my face. She handed me a mirror. I complimented her on her job. Emptying the bucket of dirty water in the bathroom. She gathered everything and headed out. Remember, if I need anything, just ring. But don't do it too much.

Now, I lay down and tried to sleep.

After another night of terrible nightmares. Tonight was far worse than the previous nights. Each nightmare had ended with somebody that I didn't remember dying at my hands. After my fourth victim, I woke up screaming. Looking around, I checked the time on my watch. It said: 0418. Not wanting to irritate my ribs again, I chose to lie down on my back. Looking at the roof, I couldn't help but wonder, what kind of monster am I? I heard a knock on the door.

Sitting up, I said, "Yes." The door slowly opened, and a young woman walked in slowly.

Seeing her, I remembered what the doctor said about somebody familiar possibly bring back my memory. I remembered her, it was Cassandra. Tears formed in my eyes as I saw her. As the memories of the past four years had returned to me. Cassandra ran to me and hugged me. All that time I whispered, "I'm sorry."

She responded gently, "It's not your fault."

It was Olivia whom I had seen in my nightmares. Her falling to her death was repeated in all my nightmares. To comfort me, she placed her head on my shoulder. Her eyes looked up at me as she remembered her friend Olivia.

"There were twenty of us when we left our homes. Something had infected the water. We never found out what. We just knew we had to find a safe place. There were tales of a city east of us, so we walked. Taking all that we could carry, we started our journey. After the first week, seven of our friends had died. The slow poison had taken its toll on their bodies. But we couldn't stop, not even burying them. We just took what we could and continued. Then came the Stalkers who preyed on us. Too cowardly to attack us, they waited to take us as they preyed on stragglers. Until we made it to a small village."

She stopped for a moment. Pausing to gather herself to tell their story. Neither of them had ever told us this story before. For all the time together outside in that damn line waiting to be allowed in Gotham. Choosing to keep it to themselves. She glanced over to nothing, and she continued, "At first, we thought we were all safe. The Stalkers wouldn't dare attack a village this large. The people proved to be perfect hosts. We decided to stay and wait out the Stalkers. We were fools. Over the course of three days, other bands of Stalkers gathered and surrounded the town. They did not attempt to hide it. Early the next day, our host broke into our quarters and seized us. We were left there tied together, all but our friend Justin. He managed to escape. At dawn, we were awake and untied except for our wrists, which were tied behind us. In a single file, they silently marched outside the town. When I close my eyes, I can still see those posts. Quietly, they tied each one of us to a post. Then, a town elder signaled the Stalkers to come and take their offerings. There we waited to be offerings to the Stalkers. They didn't come right away. They were being careful. We watched them finally come out from their hiding spots, moving closer to us. Two came to Jadian first. She tried to break free of her bonds. But she couldn't. They began to stroke her long black hair. I tried to help her, but I couldn't."

She held up her wrist in front of me to prove that she did what she had said. I could see traces of scaring. Thinking back, I remembered she had been wearing gloves. Gently I took her wrist and kissed each one. That allowed her to go on.

"A female Stalker came up on Devlin. Devlin is Olivia's older brother. She wasted no time in freeing Devlin from his post. Devlin tried to defend himself. Attacking the two male Stalkers. He was knocked out and carried back into Wasteland. Jadian finally suffered the same fate. Her bonds were cut, and she was carried off on a Stalker's back. It was like some strange ritual. The rest of us waited for the others to come for us all that time we struggled vainly to free ourselves. After what seemed to be an hour, a couple of older Stalkers, a man, and a woman came to inspect Jordan. He was a friend of Justin's. They cut his bonds and took him away. After they ran out of sight. Six more came for the rest of us: Shannon, Olivia, and I. That is when I heard something behind me. I glanced over my shoulder. It was Justin. With a knife, he cut my bonds. Giving me the knife, he told me to free the others. He took out a hatchet and machete and headed forward to intercept the Stalkers. While he tried to fight off the Stalkers, I freed Shannon and Olivia. As I looked at Justin, he had killed three Stalkers before others killed him. He had bought us time with his life."

She stopped again as she lifted her head. Choosing to sit at the chair. I had heard of this practice. Sometimes a settlement will send out sacrifices to roaming bands of savages. Thankfully I had personally never seen the practice. I'm not sure what I would have done if faced this problem.

Cassandra was ready to finish her story, "For a week we stayed together. Doing our best to avoid any contact with anybody else. When we did, we stole what we needed. For we're done asking for help. Now we were taking what we needed. Finally, we made it to the line. Shannon had disappeared. We never knew what had happened to her. One morning, we woke up and she was gone. The next day, we met you and Gabrielle. And you help restore our hopes."

That ended her story. Now, she is the last of her people. Someday, she may discover that some of her friends survived their ordeal like I did almost two years ago. But for now, she must live with her guilt of surviving when many didn't. She sat down in the chair.

I tried to comfort her as she wept in the chair. She put her arms around me and held me tight. Placing her head on my shoulder. She then pulled herself away and looked at me. Looking into her blue eyes, I saw something strange in her stare: curiosity. She leaned into me and kissed my lips. I didn't stop her. Then the thought of Gabrielle and I pushed me away. Undeterred, she tried to kiss me again. This time, I stopped her and kissed her on her forehead. She understood.

Samantha came in for a visit. As I greeted her, she knew that her plan had worked. My smile gave her confidence that no more examination was needed. I had only known her for a short time. She had arrived at Shenandoah with her father and a few others. Her father was a doctor, and she served as his apprentice. She came to Gotham hoping to finish her training, then she was to return. What she had found in the city was suffering. Believing she could make a difference working here, she decided to stay. For now, she reassured me.

I told her that I understood. That made her happy. I can only imagine what she had gone through, if she was doing the right thing. I am not one to judge. The best we can hope to do is the best we can.

Now that my memory has returned. It was time to heal me physically. She patiently checked my ribs as Cassandra watched anxiously. When she finished, she revealed her diagnosis to me. "Tomorrow morning, I want you to get some X-rays. If that comes out good, you can get out of here in three days."

I was glad to hear that. I needed to find out where the hell Gabrielle was. Cassandra had not been talking. She had her own problems that she had to deal with rather than speaking for her. She promised to see me tomorrow.

Finally, after four sleepless nights I slept peacefully. Now I had discovered who I was, I had no doubts of what kind of person I was.

At seven hundred hours the next morning, I was woken up by two different nurses who silently placed me on a gurney and pushed me into a lift, heading two floors down, they pushed me down a hallway and into an X-ray room. Four orderlies placed me on a table. Now, secure on the table, I was left in the room alone. I looked over to the control room. Inside stood the tech person, who politely gave me directions. Once he was satisfied, he proceeded to take his required images. When he finished, the four orderlies brought in the gurney and placed me on it. The two nurses then brought me back to my room.

After a quick breakfast, Samantha arrived with her findings. Her pleasant manner gave me a slight hint that I was getting out of here very soon. And I was not wrong. Three days she had promised me. After some minor exercises to get my muscles working again. The first session will start an hour after lunch, she directed. I understood. She then left me alone.

One thing I learned lying down on a hospital bed is that it can get tedious very quickly. A couple of days ago, I was under the influence of painkillers, so sleep was a good option for me. Now with the medication gone from my body, I'm not tired. I'm just stuck in this bed, with nothing to read. If I decided to go on a walk, I could only go as far as my floor without somebody accompanying me. I knew every inch of the floor. As a last resort, I turned on the view screen. That didn't help either. I couldn't find anything interesting to watch. I decided to leave it on the Sports service, hoping to get the results of the matches I had missed.

Laying back on my pillow I just listened patiently for the results. Looking at the sky, an image on the screen caught my attention. Turning my head to get a better look I saw something that made me very concerned.

Gotham had won its match with Eastpoint, 37 to 25. The hero of the game was their recently acquired Keeper, Bryce Allen. Next to him, for all to see, stood proudly Naomi. You couldn't have missed her with his arm around her waist. After finishing his interview, he immediately turned to her and kissed her passionately, which made it worse.

'Foolish girl,' I couldn't help but think. I had told her to be careful. Caitlyn will not like this affair. I guess when you're young, you don't think about these things.

Seeing a figure in the doorway forced me to reach for the controls. I promptly turned off the view screen, hoping she, whoever she was, didn't see it. I could tell it was a woman, but I wasn't sure which one it was. It didn't matter that I had made a promise to Naomi to keep her engagement secret. Slowly, the young lady came into my room. I could see it was Savannah. I turned off the viewscreen.

Standing next to my bed. I was happy to see her. Next to Gabrielle and Cassandra, she was my favorite. Over the months I found her to be a kind and intelligent young woman.

'Have a seat."

Sitting in the chair beside me she stated, "Thank you." Taking a moment to relax she added calmly, "Cassandra couldn't make it, so she sent me. You know work."

"I understand, Cailyn."

She smiled as if to agree with a common problem that we all have. Not sure what to say next I decided to give her aid, "Where is Gabby?"

Turning towards me with a surprised look, she stated, "She has been away for two weeks now."

"Doing what?"

"Some entertainer forgot his name," she stated. She was coy with her answer. To reassure me, she added earnestly, "It's not what you think. She is singing."

"I see," I stated, amused. I decided to torment her a little bit, "So Caitlyn has given up with politicians, I see."

She was oblivious to my attempt at humor, she blurted out, "Not really, they made their choices."

Curious, I asked her, "Who are they?"

She replied, "Elizabeth is marrying Herbert."

"And Koch?"

With a triumphant smile, she proclaims, "I am."

"Congratulations."

"Thank you."

We just sat there silently. Awkwardly looking at each other, trying to think of something to say. I was happy for her to marry Koch. I did like him. I knew that Caitlyn had wanted Gabrielle to land Koch, but the two had other plans. Savannah sat there trying to think of something to say.

"Does Gabby know what happened to me?" I asked her.

"I don't know," Savannah answered plainly. "Caitlyn knows if she decides to tell, she is anyone's guest."

Nothing else needed to be said. Savannah had been honest with me about Caitlyn's agenda with me. Whether she knew it or not, she had kept me informed to counter Caitlyn's moves against me.

We started to talk about other things for the rest of her visit. She stayed until my lunch came. Kimberly told her that after lunch I was going to physical therapy. Savannah understood, and she kissed me goodbye. Kimberly didn't like that very much. As for me, I just ate my ham and cheese sandwich, orange juice, and an apple. I wasn't that hungry.

As promised, I was released from the hospital two days later. Kim had brought me my clothes and valuables. She waited outside as I changed into my newly cleaned clothes. When I finished dressing, I opened the door, and she came in with a wheelchair. I sat down, and she drove me down to the main entrance. Cassandra was waiting for me down in the main lobby. She helped Kim get me to my feet. I turned to Kim and thanked her for everything the other nurses had done for me. She nodded her head, gave me a melancholy smile, and walked inside.

Cassandra and I walked to a lift and headed down six levels. After that, we had to take three different tubes to make it home. Three times is what I had asked her about Gabby, and three times she refused to answer. That made me think something had happened to her. A few doors from home, I decided to ask one more time. Perhaps they thought I was going to find out anyway. She told me that she hadn't come back from her trip yet.

In a vain attempt to make me feel better, she added, "Regina went with her." Her smile left her face when she saw it didn't work.

Both Savannah and Cassandra had been evasive in their answers about Gabrielle. I had had enough of it, so I asked them a direct question, "What is it you're not telling me?"

Cassandra knew she had to answer. Looking down at the ground, she replied, "She knows about Sandra."

"How did she find out?"

"Caitlyn found out about your payments to her. She told Regina while they were on tour. I don't know what lies Regina has been telling her, but they seem to be working. When I told her what had happened to you and Olivia, she didn't care."

Damn it, I should have told her about Sandra and what had transpired at the Reformers meeting a few months ago. Perhaps I didn't because I didn't know how she would react. Afraid she would be against my conscience payment. While it was true that the money I had sent her family was what I had earned. It was my burden, not hers. Before Caitlyn returned to our lives, I would have told her about Sandra without hesitation, but now, I had to admit to myself that we had drifted apart. The sad part is that I still love her.

"When did she find out?"

"Just after you had left to bring Olivia home" she answered, looking up at me she added, "I tried to tell her what had happened. But I'm afraid that didn't help much. The knowledge that I had known before her, made her even more angry."

"When did she leave?"

Early the next morning. When we didn't hear from you, she was completely apathetic about what had happened to you."

She opened the door. Heading directly into her room we didn't see much of each other until dinner. We decided to go to a neighborhood bistro down the corner. Nothing fancy but after a week of hospital food anything would taste good to me. After dinner we had a notice from Caitlyn, she wanted us to report for a briefing, tomorrow morning at 800 hundred hours.

9   KIDNAPPED

AS INSTRUCTED, WE MADE IT TO OUR MEETING WITH CAITLYN. Arriving promptly at eight hundred hours. Walking into Caitlyn's headquarters, we were escorted into Caitlyn's private office. Inside, we found Isabella and Naomi waiting along with Caitlyn. Isabella was wearing a one-piece blue jumpsuit. She stood there silently. Caitlyn had her long blonde hair up as she walked confidently up to Cassandra, taking her from my side to join her other girls. With her other two girls, she patiently inspected her three wards, as she called them. Naomi had her black hair up in a crown. That allowed her to wear a white blouse and pants that she wore tightly. Caitlyn silently took a step away from her. Finished with her inspection, she was satisfied. She graciously allowed them to sit. I decided to see if Caitlyn measures up to her standards. She had a modest black dress that left her arms bare and much of her legs. Her shoes made her look taller.

As Caitlyn walked back behind her desk. Niomi gave me a quick flirting smile. I didn't respond. Honestly, I still couldn't believe her actions on the news feed a couple of days ago, what was she thinking. Her attitude made me believe that Caitlyn doesn't like sports. But she is playing with fire.

Caitlyn used her intercom to summon people from another room to come in. Curious, I looked over to the door. When it opened, I saw Kayla walking in first. She had a striking blue dress, and like Caitlyn, she had matching blue shoes that made her look taller. Her hair was neatly tied in the back. But it was the second woman who made my heart sink. It was Gabrielle. She was as beautiful as ever. Her long red hair had a fresh perm. She had on a low-cut blue dress that fell above her knees; it was new. I wanted to walk over to her and kiss her hello, telling her I had missed her. Her cold stare made me freeze, not daring to speak with her.

Cassandra had seen her cold stare and wanted to jump up and intervene on my behalf. Caitlyn had stopped her. She had seen her reaction, and a sense of satisfaction came over her. She had won.

Taking all five of the chairs that surrounded Caitlyn at her desk. I was left to stand for the meeting. I decided to look at her view screens, which were all on as Caitlyn started her special meeting. "As you may know, we have lost three of our sisters."

"Sisters?" That was a strange term to use. I don't believe that any are related by blood. The only one whom I would personally call my sister is Cassandra. Caitlyn continued, "We will welcome three new members to our little family." The women did not react to the news. Unfazed, Caitlyn said, "We will be meeting them today in a few minutes. To celebrate, we are going to visit the Capital and watch the most important Cagers match of the season. Gotham will be facing an undefeated Capital. We will be joined by new clients. That I'm sure you will be happy with." She looked over at me and stated, "You will be coming as a chaperone, Duncan."

The screen behind me caught my eye. It overlooked the entrance. Four serious-looking men forced themselves inside. They quickly overpowered the receptionist before she had time to sound the alarm. Pulling out their weapons, they secured the entire front office. As three other men entered the office, I quickly looked around for the alarm. Caitlyn proved to be distracted. I noticed that the emergency button sat on her right. Not wasting time, I reached over to her desk and pressed the alarm.

Angrily, she exclaimed, "What the hell are you doing?"

Pointing at the screens, I replied, "Do you know these guys?"

She looked up and saw that three of her men were immediately shot by the intruders. "Shit," she whispered; she opened a drawer in her desk. Taking out a pistol, she rose to her feet and ordered, "Duncan, you're with me. You girls stay here. I'll get people to get you to safety."

Not wanting to argue, I followed her into the hallway. The assailants were fortunate not to have left the reception. Undaunted by the alarm screaming over their heads, they began to head down the hallway.

As we entered the hallway, we. Caitlyn gathered a handful of her men to join her in a counterattack. We followed her down the long corridor, ready to engage the attackers. Her reaction betrayed the fact that she knew she had sent them and why. But she will be very unlikely to share that information. Not that I expected anything at this time. From a distance, we heard shots being fired quickly, getting closer to us. One of her assistants, a woman about her age, joined us with three more of her guards. She ordered her to take two men and guard the girls in her office and lock the door from the inside. A woman with short black hair understood and picked two others to join her. Nine of us continued to face the attackers. Turning the corner, we found a good defensive position to wait for our enemy. But Caitlyn wasn't one waiting for anything. She pressed on, with her men following her, as did I.

My heart was racing, as we walked further down the hallway. Each step brought us closer to the battle, but in the same way, a step forward pushed them back. At this moment, the distance between her suite and the front office had increased in distance.

I quickly got my wish. As we turned another corner, we came upon the battle. In front of us were two lone security guards holding their ground against six attackers. Around them were the bodies of their dead comrade killed by a security guard. Three dead security guards littered the floor. Unfazed by the losses of her men, Caitlyn charged into the fray. I joined her. With the others right behind us. In her exuberance, Caitlyn had left herself exposed to one assailant and had a clear chance of ending this fight with one clear shot.

Seeing her danger, I immediately pushed her into some crates to protect her. The attacker's shot hit the heart of the guard who had the misfortune to be right after us. Now it was my turn to fire, and the attacker slumped to the floor. Now, there were six of them.

Now, with greater numbers, we opened fire. The attackers, realizing their position was hopeless, chose to retreat. That wasn't good enough for Caitlyn. She wanted to send her unnamed enemies a clear message of revenge. Raising her pistol, she ordered her men forward. Not one to be left behind, I joined them.

The four remaining attackers made a desperate retreat outside to safety. Hoping that a contingent of Watchmen will arrive and they can surrender to them. Right now, I believe that would be their only hope. As they made it to the lobby, four other guards managed to cut off their retreat. Caitlyn fired and killed another attacker. I looked at her, and she was enjoying this fight. Her eyes were wide with delight. The assailants wanted to surrender. But she was in a killing frenzy.

Four Watchmen burst into the lobby. In seeing their saviors, the men threw down their weapons. Caitlyn either didn't see the Watchmen or didn't care. With my stinger, I disarmed her by placing it under her ribs. With her hand becoming numb, she dropped her gun. I did the same. Her men did the same.

An hour later, the Watchmen were still busy gathering evidence. To the annoyance of Caitlyn. It was enjoyable, watching her charms fail; the Inspector had no intention of giving her what she wanted. Her refusal to inform on who was behind this attack. Her coyness was frustrating the Inspector. When he realized he wasn't getting anywhere with her, he turned to her people. Taking each one into a private room to be interrogated. Finally, it was my turn. A Watchman escorted me to a private room.

The Inspector sat on one end of a table. He politely directed me to take the seat on the opposite end. A woman dressed in the same attire as the Inspector sat beside him. He introduced himself as "Inspector Charles Fazel, this is Inspector Sergeant Helen Collins. We want to talk to you about what happened here this morning."

"Very well," I replied. Fazel was an older man with white hair and a chiseled face, his eyes were a cold blue. His suit was brown with a grey shirt. Despite his small stature, he was an imposing man. Most likely because of his position. His sergeant, Helen Collins, had light brown skin and black hair, which made her amber eyes seem brighter. She wore a blue suit with a white blouse. I guess she was in her early thirties and was about the same height as Inspector Fazel but of a smaller build. And she was pretty if you're wondering.

He said, "You can start by giving me your name."

"Duncan Walker."

Fazel's eyes lit up with recognition. He looked over at his partner, who did not share his information. He stated, "You worked with Inspector Wells in helping break up that human trafficking ring a few months back."

"I am."

"He spoke highly of you."

"That is good to hear."

Sergeant Collins asked, "What do you know about the raid?"

"Less than you two," I answered. Looking at her I had to tell them, "I know she had to leave Gotham to hide out for a while. Some power struggle."

"I see," she stated.

Frazel continued, "How long ago?"

"About a year and a half ago," I replied.

Frazel assured me, "We'll check into it."

Collins wasn't satisfied. "What is your relationship with this woman?"

"I am close to one of her wards. I am part of her entourage."

Helen escorted me out. As we walked out together, Caitlyn ran over to me. Collins began to order her men to leave. She turned to give Caitlyn a cold stare, calmly waiting for the Inspector to walk out. When he did, she walked over to him. I overheard her telling him, "The four assailants are under guard at headquarters. I sent the men away."

"Very good," he said, looking over at us he added, "still one more thing to do."

Stepping ahead of Collins, Inspector Frazel came up to us.

Coldly, he stated, "We are wrapping up for now. If you have any information, please let us know."

"I will," she responded, still trying to give off her seductive charm.

Frazel wasn't impressed. He let Collins continue, "When we interrogate your four friends, we will have more questions for you."

"I will be here," she said simply.

Frazel turned to me and with a friendly manner stated, "If you need anything from us, don't be afraid to ask."

"I won't thank you."

The two left. She turned to me and asked," What did you do?'

I replied in a smug tone to annoy her, "They heard of me." For the first time since I had known her, she was speechless. Looking around, I suddenly noticed that we were alone.

Knowing what I was about to say, she calmly interrupted," I had the men take them to a secure location. My new clients will be meeting them there. That's what I want to talk to you about."

"We are alone?"

"Pretty much. I'll join you in my office."

I had to know something. I asked her, "With all your people, why am I the only one here?"

Looking into my eyes, she decided in a rare occurrence to tell the truth, "Because Duncan Walker, you're the only one I trust."

That satisfied me. I did as she requested. I turned around and headed down the hallway. Then I heard something behind me. A slight struggle or something. Curiously, I turned around and saw nobody. Thinking it was nothing, I started to head on my way. When I saw a strange image in the mirror on my left. Two people with their backs toward me were struggling to leave the office. Between them, I saw why they were struggling; they were carrying Caitlyn with them. Pulling my pistol and stinger, I headed out to stop them. With cold resolve, I raised my pistol, and I ordered them, "Let her go!"

Both women turned their attention to me, raising their weapons. In full restraints, Caitlyn was being held by Sonja, while the other stepped away and raised her pistol. Her assistant tried to find some cover. It made sense. If the raid failed, Caitlyn would drop her guard, making it easier for them to strike.

Keeping my eye on both, I pointed my gun at Sonja, who was not holding Caitlyn, believing she would be an immediate threat. I stated, "I won't ask again." Stepping closer to them for a better shot. Believing Sonja's assistant was about to shoot me, I quickly fired. She fell to the ground instantly. She was dead. Wasting no time, I turned to Sonja, who had Caitlyn. She desperately tried to keep herself under control as she tried to break free from her captor. I stated, taking another step closer, "You don't have to die."

Sonja then turned her gun towards Caitlyn's head. She stated, "I'm walking out of here with her." Feeling the cold point of the pistol ends Caitlyn's struggle. For the first time, I could see fear in her eyes. She didn't like not being in control. Her life could end in a moment, and she wouldn't be able to do anything to prevent it. Her mouth was gagged; she couldn't speak. But her eyes were begging me to help her.

Taking another step, the young woman made a new threat." I'll kill her right now. I get paid the same way."

Seeing Caitlyn so vulnerable, I had no other choice. I lowered my pistol. Feeling she had won, she celebrated her victory by striking Caitlyn on her head. It stunned her. Making it easy to move outside the office.

I waited for a few seconds before I went after them. Not wanting to panic the assailant into doing something we all would regret. Granted, Caitlyn would get the worst of it. I walked carefully out of the office into the public walkway. The sudden shock of pedestrians had taken her mind off me. She constantly jerked Caitlyn to each passing bystander, making sure that none of them would get the idea of being a hero. I didn't think she had anything to be concerned with, everybody was trying to keep their distance, too scared to get involved. But she was just as scared as they were. Coming up from below us, hovering in the air a few feet behind her, was a strange-looking pod. It was clear to all that was how they were going to escape. A door opened from its metallic exterior, revealing two men inside. One of the men leaned out, calling for her to bring Caitlyn to him. She immediately turned around and ran to join him.

That is when she made her mistake. I had one chance to stop her. I placed my stinger in my right hand, turning it to full strength. Running to get some momentum, I threw my stinger at Caitlyn's former employee. I thought that would be a safe assumption. The stinger hit her at the base of her neck. The sudden burst of energy stunned her. Forcing her body to become limp. She fell to the ground, releasing Caitlyn. Caitlyn, still in her restraints, fell to the ground next to her.

Her friend in the metallic pod pulled his weapon. No time was wasted; I fired my pistol with my left hand. It wasn't accurate, but it was effective. That and the Watchmen prowlers arriving. The pilot believed it would be prudent to run. The pod turned and disappeared within the cityscape.

I secured the young woman's pistol. Turning to Caitlyn. With my knife, I freed her from her restraints. I gently picked her up. She placed her head on my lap. With tears in her eyes, she hugged me. She then pulled herself away. With her hand behind my neck, she pulled herself up to kiss me. This time, I didn't fight her. This was something different; this time, she was sincere. When her lips touched mine, I held her gently. This is how she chose to thank me, and I didn't mind at all.

She pulled away, I whispered to her, "You will tell me what the hell this all was about."

With her usual smile, she answered, "In time." She kissed me again. We stayed like that until the Watchmen returned. Right now, I felt pity for Caitlyn, she was vulnerable.

———

For the record, she never told me what was going on that day. In the end, she could never bring herself to tell me the truth. This time, she couldn't bring herself to lie to me either. That was something, I guess. When we gathered the next day to head down to Capital, she was her same old self.

She chose not to join us on our trip. Nor did she share that I had saved her life that day. I didn't mind. Cassandra, through Inspector Wells, had found out and relayed the information to the others. Neither did I mind her not joining us either. Thought of sharing uncomfortable glances wouldn't help either of us. We agreed that it would be better if we returned to our familiar roles as adversaries. One thing she did know was she owed me a favor, and she didn't like that. Then, I had another personal reason for not wanting Caitlyn to join us. I wanted to repair the rift between Gabrielle and me.

Fortunately for me, Regina didn't join us. That gave me a fair shot with her. Since she entered our lives, she had done her best to bring me down in the eyes of Gabrielle. In stark contrast, Cassandra did her best to build me up. She is here with us. My hopes were high on this trip.

We all shared one private car on the tube. There were nine of us in the car. Caitlyn's three new wards joined Gabrielle, Cassandra, Naomi, Isabela, Kayla, and me.

At first, I sat alone, choosing to read a bit before taking a nap. Cassandra had other ideas. She joined me, sitting across from me. Casually, she told me the new girls were told not to talk to me. Not that I cared, and I told her so. Telling her that the original eight gave me enough trouble. She gave me a sardonic smile. When she noticed that I was glancing at Gabrielle, she excused herself. I just looked out of the window, watching the early morning sky. Just as I chose to close my eyes, Naomi sat with me.

"I have a surprise for you," she said.

I looked at her disapprovingly because it was clear that she was excited. I inquired, "Did Caitlyn talk with you?"

"No, why?"

"You kissed Allen during a news feed for all to see," I told her directly.

Seeing my concern, she just casually brushed it aside. "That? I explained it to her. She knew it was part of the job."

"Well, be careful. If Caitlyn knows the extent of your relationship, she will be furious."

"I can handle her," she said, brushing off my concern. She then added, "Don't you want to hear the good news?"

"Not now, "I replied, believing it could wait.

She left me angrily, walking back to her seat. Barely a minute later, it was Kayla who joined me. I was surprised about that; she had never wanted anything to do with me in the past. At least she didn't wait too long to speak to me.

She opened with, "You had an exciting month."

I wouldn't call it that. It is more stressful if I choose a word to describe it. I simply said, "I kept myself busy."

"What do you know about Capital's star player?" she asked me.

"I know he is a wingman. Pretty good one." I told her.

Leaning back deep into the seat, she looked out the window. She said defiantly, "I don't know why I'm seeing him, and Gabrielle gets our star player, Reese. It's not fair."

I knew why. Like Naomi with Allen earlier in the season, the owners want him on theirs, and Kayla is going to help them get it. At least that is what I told her, "Gotham wants Martel to play for them. You're there to make that possible."

Outrage came over her. She couldn't believe she would be part of something so vulgar. Now it was her turn to walk away in a huff. Slightly amused, I watched her leave and sat down. Now that was finished, I decided to take a break. I closed my eyes and relaxed.

It wasn't too late. Despite my eyes being closed, I felt that some-body had joined me. Not wanting to open my eyes at first, I tried to ignore the mysterious stranger. Finally, my curiosity got the better of me, and I opened my eyes, to my delight, it was Gabby watching me. Sitting up I gave her a welcoming smile. She didn't respond.

With a serious tone, she said, "Thank you for what you did for Caitlyn." She said it in a very formal tone. She needed to get that out before we said anything else between us.

With a low amount of modesty, I replied, "I just did my job."

She gave me a rare smile. Her manner became more familiar, she stated softly, "I think it's time you should find another job."

"I agree," I simply replied. After all, she was right: this job is getting dangerous. I looked over at her, and I felt I had to tell her something about Sandra. I explained, "She saved my life and died for it. She had a mother and a daughter who would have nothing. I had to do something. I never used your money."

Getting up, she sat next to me. She assured me, "I know now." She placed her head on my shoulder, and we stayed there for the rest of the trip. I looked over, and Cassandra smiled at me. She said, "I didn't know you were in the hospital. Regina never told me." I just stroked her hair as she placed it on my shoulder.

We pulled into Capital Central Station at 1215. We waited an additional five minutes before a private car arrived to take us to our hotel. As we gathered in, we soon discovered it was an airship. As we flew around the many levels of Capital, we soon flew over Capital Gardens and landed in a hangar on top of the hotel.

The match didn't start until nineteen hundred hours, giving us a few hours before leaving for the arena. Having a room to myself gave me the privacy I needed to think about what I would be doing next with my life. I still love Gabrielle; that much is certain, and I want to be with her. But where? Gotham isn't for me, and I'm pretty sure it is not for her. On the trip down, she seemed tired to me. Not physically, but mentally, worn down by the daily means of her life. Her once constant smile is now forced. But how could I tell her? It was my idea to come here. Believing that we will be safe in Gotham. She joined me on my journey to find sanctuary because she trusted me. How could I tell her I had made a mistake? What would happen if I had guessed wrong, that she loved it here, and everything I had noticed was an illusion I hoped to see to justify my desires? But this is a problem for another time.

Promptly at 1645, we were expected to gather at the hangar. Like in previous games, the menagerie was overdressed. All were dressed in blue except for Kayla, who wore an elegant gold dress. When the door opened, each girl entered. Naomi chose to be last. Before she entered herself, she turned to me and said, "We look ridiculous."

I didn't disagree. I just followed her inside. We then headed directly to the arena. It was a little smaller than Gotham. But it was filled with people who wanted their daily ration of bread and circus. And I was one of them.

Like we did before, we had a suite of our own. We were joined by four other guests of Gotham's owners. Some local politicians and their sons or something. Not that they wanted to spend any time with me. It is clear to me that their attention was on the new girls. Isabella was left to be the chaperone. Gabrielle and Kayla are excused since they had intimate evening plans after the game. Kayla seemed not to care as she mingled with our suitemates. Gabrielle sat down next to me as we waited for the start of the game. Gabrielle looked over at Naomi. She was alone, sulking in her chair. Naomi had actively ignored the suitors.

"What is wrong with Naomi?" Gabby asked me, concerned.

"She has other plans," I answered, looking over at Naomi.

"What are they?"

"Not my secret to tell," I replied.

I turned my attention to the field. Both teams had taken their positions. Capital had on their red jerseys and gold pants. This forced Gotham to wear their third option, white jerseys and red pants. Gotham doesn't like wearing their white jerseys that much. That is what Gabby just told me.

That slight, no matter how small it is, motivated them to strike first. Allen and his defenders managed to keep Capital off the board. In the second period, Capital scored twice, moving down the field easily. Giving them a lead. Gotham wasn't done; they scored twice themselves, retaking the lead during the half. I looked over at Naomi, as she was pleased at the exploits of Allen. It was his play that scored the go-ahead points.

Halftime was over, the third quarter started with both teams scoring with their first possessions. At the end of the third quarter, the score was tied: 17-17. The fourth quarter was much the same. Both teams exchanged scores, keeping it a tie until almost the end of the game.

The final score was Capital 27, Gotham 26. What had happened was Gotham had taken a one-point lead with a minute left. Allen led his defenders on the field, their job was to hold the razor-thin lead. Capital played their game, moving slowly down the field trying to find a hole in Gotham's defenses. With thirty seconds left,

Gotham had succeeded in keeping the Capital from crossing mid-field. That is when Capital decided to gamble.

Their Leader took the ball and punted it deep into Gotham's territory. Allen fielded the punt cleanly. Unfortunately for him, it was too deep, and he had to run it out. That is when tragedy happened. One of his guards had missed his block. With all his strength, the Capital player had hit Allen hard around his neck. A second player hit him low almost simultaneously. Allen fell hard on the turf. Capital won the game on a safety. Allen didn't get up.

Naomi gave a loud shriek. That forced us to look over at her. She was terrified. Rushing to her feet, she ran to the door in a heretical state. Struggling to open the door. When she discovered it was locked, she frantically banged on the door, ignoring the pain. Screaming for Bryce.

I rushed over to her, hoping to calm her down. Pulling her away from the door. She looked at me franticly, and pleaded, "He needs me."

"I'll get you down."

I rang the bell. An attendant came to the door. I explained to her that Naomi was Allen's fiancée and needed to be with him. The young woman promised to help us. As we waited, Naomi revealed, "We are going to have a baby. What will happen to us now?"

Everybody had heard that. As the attendant returned, she asked us to come with her. She led us down to the players' infirmary. Before we entered, Naomi collapsed in my arms. As I picked her up, she regained her strength. I allowed her to lean on me as we entered. We walked into the infirmary together.

Inside, a Security Guard stepped in the path of our guide. She immediately explained to him who Niomi was. He looked at her for a moment. Then he looked at me. I recognized him from previous times in the secure areas for players. He shared that recollection with me. Lowering his hand, he stepped aside to let us pass. She shyly looked at him to thank him. He nodded his head.

What is considered triage is not used that much. It is used only for emergencies. Unfortunately for Allen, it was needed tonight. Our escort had taken us as far as she could. I thanked her for her help, and she left. We walked further inside a makeshift waiting room, overlooking where Allen was being worked on. A doctor and three nurses treated him. Their job was to stabilize him before traveling to a hospital so he could be operated on. Tubes of various sizes had connected his body with a variety of machines. Each one had a particular task to save the young man's life. Naomi, seeing this display, walked closer to the window. She gasped at the sight, placing her hand over her mouth to keep herself from screaming in despair. Her knees became wobbly as she began to swoon. Two of Allen's teammates kept her from falling. Guiding her to a chair. A third player grabbed her a cup of water. Taking a little sip, she regained her composure, thanking her friends for their help. I needed to give her some space, taking a seat away from her. During the next hour, every one of Allen's teammates came up to her and gave her their respects. They offered their help to the young couple. She graciously thanked each one. When the last player showed their respect. The last player to do it was the player who had missed the block that caused his injury. He knelt to apologize for his actions. In an act of compassion, she hugged him. They were both in tears.

Next, it was the coaches' turn to offer support. Lastly, the team manager offered his support. No matter what happened tomorrow, they managed to distract Naomi for a while.

As I glanced into the treatment area. I saw the doctor and his staff do all they could do. A lead nurse signaled for two orderlies with a gurney to come over. It took four of them to place him on that gurney. The doctor came into the room. Niomi stood up first. The entire team stood next to her; all were still in their uniforms. Refusing to change until they know he will be all right.

The doctor started, "He is stable now. We will be taking him to Read Memorial here. we will be operated immediately."

"What happened?" asked the Manager. He was almost fifty, with grey temples. From his build, you immediately could tell he was a former player who turned to coaching.

The doctor, who didn't look older than thirty, had to answer the question, "He has suffered two breaks along his spinal cord. That was why we had to stabilize him for the trip. They have a good chance to refuse the severed parts of the spinal cord. After that, he has a good chance to recover." But the manager wanted to know something else, and the doctor knew it. "With luck, he could regain most of his abilities. It will take some time."

"Doctor, can I go with him?" asked Naomi. "I can hold his hand."

For a moment, the doctor looked like he was about to refuse. Until he realized he was about to contend with twenty-nine angry Cagers. He said yes. She joined him.

"I'll see you at the hospital," I yelled at her.

She turned back and nodded.

It was 315 when he finally got out of surgery. Allen had been in surgery for almost four hours. Niomi and I sat together in the waiting room. During that time, we were joined by Cassandra and Isabella. An hour later, at midnight, Gabrielle joined us. Her date didn't feel much like having company, she told us.

There we sat until the sun rose into the sky. That is when Kayla finally joined us. Unlike the rest of us, she enjoyed her night. As we waited, Cassandra suggested, "Why don't we get some breakfast?"

Gabrielle agreed, "That will be a good idea."

Naomi, who had been in a state where she could not sleep out of worry nor was she fully awake just out of exhaustion for the past twelve hours muttered, "I'm not hungry. You can go."

Isabella joined her and said, "You need your strength."

Naomi didn't hear her. Looking at Naomi, I interjected, "You four go ahead. I'll stay here with her."

They did as I asked. I sat next to her and said, "You're not going to help anyone in this condition."

Still in a daze, she looked up at me, and with a determination I didn't expect, she said plainly, "I'm not moving until I know what we're up against. I looked at her with newfound admiration. She had a resolve that I didn't think she possessed.

I kissed her forehead and told her, "He is a lucky man."

She smiled. Knowing what she had signed on for.

An older doctor entered the waiting room. She was well past

fifty but in good shape. Her blonde hair was in a bun. Upon seeing her, Naomi immediately jumped up. She asked, "How is he?"

"He is doing well. We wanted to make sure there were no complications with the repairs to his spinal cord. He is resting in his room."

"Please, I need to be with him."

The doctor smiled, "Go ahead. But you should know that he will have a long road ahead. He might never play again."

"That's not important. I'm not going to leave him. He needs me."

A nurse had taken her to his room. The doctor turned to me and said, "She is quite a young woman."

"I'm proud of her myself," I replied.

The doctor excused herself and had to see other parents. Leaving me alone in the waiting room. Before she left, she told me his room number. I thanked her and headed to join the others for breakfast.

At noon, we were expected home. But Naomi had no intention to leave. She was determined to stay with him. Caitlyn had been alerted by Kayla about what had happened. She wasn't happy. Naomi didn't care. Kayla volunteered to stay with her for a couple of days, saying she had some free time. Caitlyn reluctantly agreed to that.

At the hotel, we gathered our things and headed home. During the journey, Cassandra and Gabrielle sat with me on the way home. Both were concerned about Naomi and what she would face. Gabrielle wanted to know some things. She was going to get some answers. And I was the one to give them to her.

"How long did you know?"

"That she was pregnant? Just now." I told her.

"How about the rest?"

"A few months."

"And you didn't think to tell me!" She exclaimed, outraged that I had kept it from her.

"I had promised her," I replied, amused by her attitude.

Gabrielle understood. But she needed to know one more thing. "Did you tell Cassandra?"

"It never came up," I replied.

That satisfied her. Her tone had changed to a friendlier demeanor. She stated, "How is it every day you surprise me?"

"It keeps you from getting bored," I answered her.

She leaned over to me and gave me a passionate kiss. She then sat next to me. Putting her head on my shoulder and closing her eyes, she remained there for the rest of the trip. At its end, my arm was asleep. Not that I had minded. I just let her sleep, stroking her long red hair gently. Wondering what she was dreaming about. She had a contented smile that I didn't want to disturb. We have been through a lot for the past week. It was nice to have some peace for a change.

Thinking back on what had happened next, I should have known sooner that Caitlyn knew about Naomi and Bryce. She had tolerated it for reasons she had no intention to share. For almost a week, Cailyn had kept me occupied with jobs that kept me away from home. She had planned to keep me busy for another whole week before I caught on.

It was between jobs when I realized that I hadn't heard from Naomi about how Allen was. I called Capital Hospital. A very helpful lady on the other end mentioned his family had taken him to a private hospital. She assured me that he would get the best of care there. I asked her for the address, and she gave it to me. It was when I asked about Naomi that she was a little evasive. Saying she had no recollection of a young woman named Naomi. She did mention that a young woman named Kayla had been around for a while, but she had to get home. Something was up.

I met Cassandra at a small café. She waited for a few minutes. I ordered some iced tea, and when it was ready, I joined Cassandra. We had a few minutes together before we were expected at her appointment. Her eyes betrayed the fact that she was exhausted. Caitlyn had been running her around town the same as I. She had welcomed this minor respite. Unfortunately, I had to ruin it.

I asked her, "Have you heard from Kayla recently?"

"She was still with Naomi," she replied curiously, like she knew I was going to tell her something to contradict what she was certain about.

"Allen had been moved to a private hospital. Two days ago. Kayla was with him until the day before he left."

With apprehension, she asked, "What about Naomi?"

"She disappeared," I told her. Somehow, she already knew the answer. She was disappointed with Kayla.

"Kayla told Caitlyn everything. " She said, enraged.

I was surprised by her accusation. It was a logical deduction that Kayla had done what Cassandra accused her of doing. It made the most sense. But it was her tone that surprised me. When she looked away from me, I realized she knew something.

She calmly made her confession, "You must understand. I'm only telling you this now because I'm sure. Since I had joined Caitlyn's little menagerie, the other girls told me to watch out for her.

"Gabby too."

"Not that I remember." She answered me coldly. There was something she wasn't going to tell me; it wasn't important right now. Finding out what had happened to Naomi is important. She asked bluntly, "What do we do now?"

I answered plainly, "I'll talk to Wells and Humphrey and see what they can do to help. I have a feeling they like to expose Caitlyn."

Cassandra volunteered, "I'll track down Kayla."

We agreed, but first, we had this assignment to do. Cassandra is to mediate a merger between two firms arguing over something petty. I asked her if she had ever had any experience in this field. To my surprise, she said no. She explained that her job is to keep the two opposing sides civil with each other. Her client wants to make sure that the two representatives remain at the negotiating table and find a solution. Having both a beautiful and intelligent woman will help in that cause and get a favorable result for all parties. For that, Cassandra was perfectly suited.

We chose tube seven and headed north for seven stops. Getting off, we made it to a lift and headed to level thirty. That took us to just below Purple Level. Getting out of the lift, we felt a sudden chill. Realizing that her royal blue strapless dress was not suited for this kind of temperature. I gave her my jacket. She appreciated my gesture as we walked down the pathway to an office space. I opened the door for her. An attendant met us in the lobby. Cassandra gave the young man her name. He nodded and led her to a conference room out back. I sat down in the lobby and waited for her.

My assignment was simple: I was to escort Cassandra to this conference and wait for her until it was over, no matter how long it took. What Caitlyn didn't count on was that she didn't say anything about a capable replacement to bring her home. One that Cassandra will be happy with. It seems I had my replacement already picked out. A man that I had no doubt Cassandra would approve of. That escort is Robert.

An hour later Robert had arrived. I immediately thanked him for coming down and helping us like this. He was eager to help find our missing friend. Leaving him, I headed to Watchmen headquarters. After I discreetly recovered my jacket from Cassandra. She would prefer Robert to be the gentleman.

Traveling in Gotham, I learned one thing. There is no such thing as a straight line. You could start at the same place and take a different path each day for a year. Not that you want to, but in some places for no reason, a detour will be set up, forcing you to change your route. That is what I had to do today. Adding an extra twenty minutes to get to Grey Section. Four lifts were being repaired along my journey. The fifth tube managed to take me to the desired level, but I had to take a V Tube to make it to the proper H Tube. That had left me half a block away, so I walked the rest of the distance.

Inside the office, I checked in with the desk sergeant. He was an old man too young to retire but too old to serve in the field. It was clear to me that he wanted to be out there, and he hated to be put out to pasture like this. Fortunately for the service, he was a dedicated man determined to do his duty no matter where it may be. After giving him my name, I asked to see Inspector Fazel. I made sure to mention that I had information on Caitlyn. Not that it meant something to the sergeant, but to Fazel, it would mean a lot. My hunch worked, and I was allowed in.

Not wanting to use another machine. I chose to use the stairs, and after climbing six floors. I made it to the Department of Special Branch. That is where I had met Wells earlier. Something was up with Caitlyn, who is far darker than I had first thought.

When I entered the office, I was greeted by Detective Sergeant Collins. Seeing her was a pleasant surprise. With a curious smile and professional demeanor, she led me to an interrogation room. Inside were Inspectors Wells and Fazel, waiting for me as they sat on one side of a rectangular table. I took a seat on the opposite side of the table. Frazel took a seat on my right. Once she was settled Well decided to start this exchange.

Wells stated politely, "What can we do for you?"

"It is what I can do for you" I answered, "You wanted help getting something on Caitlyn Wylde."

That got all three interested. I proceeded to tell them the story about Naomi Smith and Bryce Allen. Being Gotham fans, they were aware of Allen's injury. Neither was surprised that Naomi was missing. I had to know what Caitlyn was doing. I had my ideas, but that is all I had.

"What is Caitlyn doing?" I asked them directly.

All three paused for a moment. Trading glances with each other. They are silently deciding how much they can trust me. After what felt like an hour, both inspectors finally made their decision and nodded to Frazel. It was her task to tell me about Caitlyn.

"Caitlyn Wylde is a Partisan." She said there was another word I didn't understand, I silently debated whether I should humble myself and ask what partisan meant or if I should remain silent and hopefully figure it out when Collins would elaborate on the meaning. I chose the latter. "A power struggle between various factions for control of Star Casino, between your friend Wynn and Kleist, and another faction led by a man called Beaumont. Caitlyn managed to seduce a member of Beaumont's inner circle. Together, they managed to steal a large amount of money from Beaumont. Forcing him to be bought out by his partners. When Caitlyn returned, she gave her friends what she had stolen in exchange for some favors."

It was strange, I couldn't remember her friend's name either. I never even thought about him until now. But I still needed to know more. "What favors?"

"To help her and her operatives seize control of Gotham from within." She answered.

"How are they planning to do that?" I asked her.

"By gaining access to the Highlanders," she replied.

It all began to make sense. But there was a flaw in her plan. She was moving too slowly. If Watchmen are already aware of this, she can be neutralized. Frazel was aware of my skepticism and added, "She has friends along their ranks already. We will need hard evidence to move against her."

"Then that attack on her, Beaumont was behind it."

Humphrey chimed in, "He is our only ally in this investigation. Your interference gave us some trouble."

Now I understand why I was granted this interview. Whoever this Beaumont was he must have had tremendous influence in Gotham. Whatever his motives are he is the enemy of Caitlyn. I do not want Cassandra and especially Gabby involved in her mad scheme. That means whatever they want I am more than willing to help.

"What do you need?"

It was Wells's turn to speak. "We must find Naomi. When we do, you must get her out before we make our move. That will keep you in her good graces."

We spent an hour going over every detail of their plan. Making sure there will be no mistakes. If there are any Special Branch that could be dissolved. I chose to have Robert and Cassandra help me with this. I didn't want Gabby anywhere near this plan. When all four of us were satisfied, I was dismissed. I headed back to rendezvous with Cassandra and Robert. I told them what we had planned. To my surprise, both eagerly volunteered. Robert offered some of his Disrupters to give us aid. I agreed.

We made it home an hour later. Robert knew he couldn't be seen in our flat since Caitlyn would be watching. Once inside, we made no mention of it, besides Caitlyn's constant watch. There was still Regina to contend with. At dinner, Regina mentioned happily that Gabrielle would be home tomorrow. That made us feel better, but she couldn't know what we were planning.

The speed at which The Watchmen had discovered where Naomi was being held. It led me to believe that they had already known. That they were prepared to leave her to her fate until I had arrived didn't give me much confidence in their true motives. But I needed their help. In a coded message they sent me her whereabouts. I knew it well it was where Gabrielle had gone that made her sick.

Cassandra and I gathered what we needed. We managed to lock Regina in a closet before we left, knowing she would become aware that something was going on. Today, Caitlyn had assignments for us. We had no intention of doing it. It was a distraction we had no intention of doing. We left with Regina screaming, demanding that we open the door.

Outside our flat, we met Robert. After we told him the address, he relayed it to his friends, who would meet us there.

We met five Disrupters: Jenna, Lucian, Jill, Liam, and Nigel, the latter two of whom I had seen during our fight with Wynn. They came to visit me while I was at the hospital, where I learned their names. I was surprised by Lucian. He didn't look like a fighter. A fifth Disrupter named Emma stepped forward after doing a reconnaissance of the place.

"It is a special clinic for discreet procedures," she had mentioned.

"How are we going to handle it?" asked Liam.

"We'll walk right in," I said, "we are all on the same side." But our pistols will be ready. In case some unwanted visitors decide to arrive.

We walked in together. An attendant rose from her desk to obstruct our path. Before she had a chance to speak, I told her, "We don't have much time. The Watchmen are planning to raid this clinic. I need to get Caitlyn's ward to safety."

The woman stated, hesitantly, "I have to talk to the doctor."

"I'll go with you." I insisted. Turning toward Robert, I ordered, "Take your positions. Let me know if you see anything." Playing the part, I told her, "If you have security, I suggest you summon them."

She agreed and called security agents. While she was busy giving them instructions, I made my way to the back room. Cassandra was close behind me. We found the place almost empty. Not sure we're Niomi is being held. We separated and checked each room. I found nothing. At this time, the attendant had chased after us, and Cassandra turned to deal with her. Freeing me to continue with my search. Somehow, Cassandra had satisfied her, as she headed back to her desk. I waited for her.

"What did you say to her?"

"I suggested to her that she should destroy anything that could be incriminating."

I gave her a quick smile to show my admiration. In front of us was one final room. She had to be in there. Slowly, I opened the door, allowing Cassandra to enter first. She stopped in her tracks. Walking in, I made it to her side. I was frozen by what I had witnessed.

Lying on a slab naked, we found Naomi bound to it. Her eyes were open, making me hesitant for a moment. I wondered if she was alive. Seeing her stomach breathing gave me a sense of relief. Wires were implanted in various parts of her body. Naomi was comatose as she seemed to be oblivious to what was happening to her. We needed to get her out of there.

I walked closer. I could see her skin was pale as snow. Her grey eyes were just staring at the roof. The redness around her eyes showed me that she had been crying; worse, she still wanted to cry, but her tears ran dry. Standing over her, a young man in his late twenties finally noticed me standing over Naomi. Out of pity, I stroked her forehead gently just to let her know I was there. That made the Technician angry. He walked over to me.

"Don't do that," he protested.

Not that he succeeded in his attempt to intimidate me, a truth that the short technician was aware of. But I had a job to do. I said," I need you to get her ready to be moved."

With a whiny voice, he protested, "We can't. She isn't finished with her treatment."

Curiosity had gotten the better of me, I asked, "What are you doing?"

With a smug expression, he stated, "Two things. The first is to break her rebelliousness. She was too willful for our client's taste. Then we must erase her memory. We had to terminate her pregnancy. Our client thought it best that she didn't remember being pregnant.'

I looked at her. She was overjoyed with the thought of having a baby. To take everything from her is beyond contempt. But I had a job to do. I turned to Cassandra and said, "Find her something to wear." She headed to the next room. Before the Technician could mount a protest, I told him, "I have my orders." Looking down at Naomi, I asked him, "Will removing her cause any damage?"

"No," he reluctantly admitted. He then added, "The problem she is resisting. I might have to increase the voltage." Thinking it was safe, he put his hand on her thigh. She made no reaction. I had had enough revolution for both of us. Before I could protest, he stated, "Our other termination was much easier. A pretty redhead had three terminations. She never knew."

I knew who he meant. Gabrielle her three strange infections, she was pregnant. My hand reached for my pistol. With clear malice, I pulled it out of my holster and calmly raised it at the technician. All I could think about was killing this little man. Only Cassandra's return managed to stop me. The technician, realizing his peril, immediately freed her from the machine. Cassandra gave me fresh clothes and freed her from her bonds. She helped her sit up. I handed her the white shirt. Cassandra put her over Naomi's shoulder. Holding a needle, the Technician came over to Naomi. I stopped him with my pistol.

He looked at me timidly. "This will help her."

I looked over at Cassandra, and she assured me, "Let him do it."

Dropping my pistol, he proceeded to give her the shot. Quickly,

Naomi began to regain her senses. Cassandra handed her some pants. She put them on. As planned, the alarm had sounded. Robert was going to hit the alarm after thirty minutes. Putting my pistol away. I stepped towards Naomi and picked her up in my arms. Cassandra led us out of the treatment room.

The technician had no desire to protest. He ran off. Together, we took Naomii to the lobby. We rejoined Robert and his Disrupters. Together, we left and headed away. As we walked away, the Watchmen rushed in to finish our ruse.

By the time we made it to a tube, Naomi began to regain her strength. She was able to walk into the shuttle herself. She sat down on a seat alone, looking out the window in personal thought. Cassandra and I went on alone, leaving Robert and his friends to make final preparations for Niomi. One thing was for certain: Caitlyn was not going to have control of her again. Robert and his contacts promised to make it happen. For the present time, we need to repair her.

When we had to change tubes, Naomi was able to walk to the next tube on her own. Her faraway expression hadn't changed. Her mind was on autopilot, just doing enough to get by. In the tube, a slight hint appeared in her eye. Looking around, she realized she was in a different place. Her eyes still had a sense of sadness. In a voice barely over a whisper, she asked, "What day is it?"

Cassandra answered, "Thursday."

Naomi's eyes widened with the sudden realization of what she had endured. "I had lost four days." She closed her eyes in a vain attempt to produce tears. She asked, "Kayla, why?"

After she said that, she became silent. All we could do was watch her.

Samantha had been told about Naomi earlier in the day. When we arrived, she was ready for us. Her orderlies gently took her to a treatment room. Calmly, she told us to sit and wait. We sat down and waited. An hour later, she came out to give us a report.

"Physically, she's fine." She started with, then she told us the bad news, "Mentally, she is damaged. Whatever she went through these past four days. I want her to stay here for at least one day. After her system flushes out toxins."

Cassandra asked, "Can we see her?"

"She is resting right now. Perhaps later."

We eventually were allowed to see her. She was able to converse with us without any hesitation. But she never smiled. I believe she won't smile for a long time. Somehow, she knew that her baby was taken from her, and that gave her a silent rage underneath her calm demeanor. I do not want to be in Caitlyn or Kayla if they ever come across her path again. When I told her about the detectives wanting to talk to her, she jumped at the chance. Her help will give her some measure of revenge. I can't say I blame her.

Frazel and Collins talked to her later that night. For over an hour, they had talked to her alone. When it was done, the Watchmen had enough to execute a warrant. For now, Caitlyn is out of business. Will it be enough for her friends to abandon her? We will all have to see. For now, I had to make sure Niomi got into safety. That meant Cassandra had to go. But she can't go home.

"You need to go with Robert for a while." I told her, before she could say a word in protest, I added, "Neither of us can know where she will be hiding. I'm going to take her so far."

She lowered her head in agreement. She knew I was right. If Caitlyn retains her influence, she will get whatever information she wants. Cassandra looked at me and asked, "What's next?"

"I'm going to get Gabrielle, and we are going home," I stated to her. She knew what I had meant, she had heard us both talk about Shenandoah many times. I then added an invitation, "You can come too."

Smiled at my invitation and replied, "Maybe."

In saying that, she stood up and walked out. After she left, I walked into the room where Naomi was sleeping quietly. There I sat in the chair next to her in constant vigil. Making her a silent bow that nobody will ever hurt her again as long as I am around. That was a bow I was determined to keep.

Early the next morning Samantha had her discharge. Yesterday Cassandra managed to get her some clean clothes. It was a simple white denim jumpsuit with fresh underwear and practical shoes. They were far from stylish but were comfortable. I think she liked them.

From the hospital, we traveled to a landing area that had a pod waiting for us. Two men came to greet us. Their faces were covered with dark visors. They were in all-black uniforms with helmets and boots. The taller pilot addressed me, "Robert sends his regards."

His partner added, "This is our passenger."

"She is," I replied.

The taller man said, "We'd better go."

Naomii then hesitated and made a request, "Can we have some time?"

The tall pilot stated, "Take all the time you need."

Naomi turned to me. Without a word, she gave me a full embrace. There she stayed as I held her. She looked up at me with tears in her eyes. I was never so glad to see her cry. She stated, "Thank you for caring."

"Part of the service," I replied. I wasn't finished; I had to tell her something else. Holding her shoulders, I said, "You came a long way."

She pulled me down and gave me a passionate kiss, goodbye. For that all it was. She then silently walked over to the pod and walked in.

I left.

———

My trip back home was full of anticipation. Gotham wasn't what I had thought it was going to be. It was far from being a safe haven. Strangely, I had dreamed of sanctuary for over ten years. No, the real sanctuary was Shenandoah all along. We both knew it. We left there believing that it was best for them, believing that someday hunters would come looking for Gabrielle, or worse, Enforcers would return with their airships. Willing to risk the wrath of Gotham coming so close to their territory. It has been nearly two years since we left. They must have given up by now. Now we were free to go home.

Thinking about returning home and seeing our friends again gave me a strong sense of delight. Feeling I was sure that Gabrielle would share. When I told her what her infections were, she would agree with me. Caitlyn lost.

When I made it home, I found the door was locked. I used my key, but it didn't work. Using the bell to get the attention of Gabby, I heard someone come to the door. To my disappointment, it was Regina who answered the door. She had no intention of letting me in. I didn't care, I stormed past her. Standing in the living room was Gabrielle.

I gave her a loving embrace. She stood there frozen. I was too set in my plans to notice. Stepping away, I said, "Let's pack." I hurried to my room. And grabbed my bag. Putting in the clothes I wanted to keep. It didn't take me long to fill it. I went to check on Gabrielle. She was still in the living room; she hadn't moved from that spot. I urged her, "Come on, you're wasting time." Regina joined us at this time and stood beside her.

"Where are we going?"

"Home."

"We are home," she said defiantly.

I stated, "This isn't home."

"I like it here. Caitlyn was good to us. And you betrayed her."

That surprised me. I walked up to her and said, "She is using you."

Gabrielle walked towards me. In a tone I had never heard before, she proclaimed, "Like you used me. The first chance you had, you turned me over to the Overseers."

I stepped back, ashamed. What she had said was true. But I did come back for her. I felt somebody standing behind me. Curious, I looked behind me and saw Caitlyn standing behind me. With her there were three henchmen.

"I think you're done here, Duncan." She had lost everything but had time to gloat.

"Why don't you get out? I'm done listening to you." Gabrielle angrily supported Caitlyn.

I knew I had lost. This was the battle I had wanted to win the most. I just left, not caring where I was going.

After I left the flat. I don't remember very well.

PART 6
UNDERGROUND

1   BLACK SECTION

I AWOKE IN THE DARKNESS THAT NEVER ENDS. I'M NOT SAYING THAT the world stopped spinning, nor did the sun stop rising in the east and setting in the west. Nothing that drastic, I assure you; just the plain, simple fact is that sunlight rarely reaches down here. How long I was unconscious down here is anybody's guess. My first memory was a musky stench that had awoke me. That was the best way I could describe it. It never left you. The best you can do is to get used to it. It is part of living down here in Black Section.

Sitting there in the darkness, I discovered my head hurt. Gently, I rubbed my temple to ease the pain. That didn't work as I had hoped. Sitting with my back on a brick wall, I rested my head on the rough surface. That had helped relieve the pain. That is when I decided to check my surroundings. Looking around, I began to make out figures along the backdrop of the darkness. I began to understand where I ended up. More importantly, I knew who had sent me here and why.

Officially, this place is called Black Sector. It has other names, such as Underground and Obelisk. The Obelisk is the most telling for me; it is a dark dungeon where people go to die. That is what

Caitlyn has in store for me. She thinks she has beaten me. I am going to make sure she is grossly mistaken.

At this moment, I had to see what I had on me. I had no money on me—just the clothes on my back. To my surprise, I still had my dagger and stinger. A thank you from Caitlyn for saving her life. She wasn't that bad. Looking in my pockets, I found my compass. Then I placed my hand in my back pocket. There was something in it. Something thin was wedged inside. Whoever had checked my pockets didn't think it was important. I pulled it out, and relief came over me.

They couldn't have been more wrong. Standing up, I immediately looked for some little source of light. Taking a few steps, I found a source of light; it wasn't strong, but it sufficed. It was a picture of Gabby and me on the day we went on a cruise. She was looking at me, sitting comfortably on my lap, her hands around my neck. To keep her from falling, I held her around her waist. I was looking up at her, our eyes had met that day. As I wondered how the hell I was so lucky to have her with me. What she had felt that day, I can only guess. That love she had for me had soured. What happens isn't important to me right now. All I knew was I must get back to her somehow. I had been selfish, only thinking about what I wanted from her. I wish to redeem myself in her eyes. Whatever happens after that, whether she takes me back or not, it doesn't matter; if she is happy, that is important to me. But that is a long way away.

For the present, I must find a way to survive. That means finding food and shelter. After that problem, I will find a way to escape. Both Carlos and Silas had told me that it was impossible. Once you come down here, you stay here until they let you out. For Carlos, it was allowing himself to be mutilated for money to buy his way out. Silas never told me how he was freed. The people of Gotham are confident that once you are placed down here, you will be dead and buried. One thing I learned from my dealings with the Overseers of Cibola is that confidence breeds complacency. Seven times, I escaped their force fields that tried to keep a population under their control. The last time, I had helped over a hundred escape along with Gabrielle and me.

I carefully returned the picture to my pocket. Walking into the main passageway, my empty stomach reminded me it was time to eat. I found it to be a little brighter from that alley. Straight lines of artificial lighting went straight down the path on a roof that was barely twenty meters over our heads. As I traveled along with a crowded mass of humanity, I found it difficult to move quickly. As I carefully maneuvered my way through other people. Many had a better idea of where they were going. Checking my compass, I found I was heading north. Lacking any better ideas, I decided to remain on this path. As I walked, I kept my hands close to my pockets. Sometimes, I had to slap away someone else's hands trying to take away what I had left for valuables.

Along the edges of the pathway sat various kinds of people. Sometimes, entire families lived in makeshift homes that barely kept them safe. Desperately, they tried to barter their goods with whatever they had to offer a passerby. Sometimes, it could be just a primal urge for sex. I just focused on what was in front of me.

Gradually, I realized this parade was heading uphill. I couldn't see too far in front of me. I just followed the crowd. As they looked at the faces of my fellow travelers, they seemed dead to me. Just going through the motions of surviving. Having no sense of joy or sorrow, living down here. At the summit of this rise, I found a new passageway. I saw a sign that intrigued me. It said, '1 First Charity, twenty meters.' I decided to see what it was all about.

As I turned right, I found this passageway a little narrower than the main passageway I was on. It is too narrow for people to camp on its sides. I found this passage to move at a quicker pace. In a short time, I came upon a rotunda. In the center of the circle was a large encampment with twenty people inside, helping twice as many people with various things. I walked inside to see if they could help me. After all, I hadn't anything else to lose. Then again, I remembered, I still had my life.

That thought didn't stop me. I found myself walking in. Once inside, I found this group to be highly organized. That made me feel secure in their intentions. A malevolent group would never be so neat or orderly. In the Wastelands, I found that people who prey upon other people had given up on the concept of civilization. The law was nonexistent except for the law of the strongest.

Many of the tables were full of clothes. Surrounded by people wearing rags were looking over the cast-offs from people up above. Other tables had little trinkets like blankets or pillows. For people to use to make life a little easier down here. Then there were a few tables that had packages of food and water. That is where I needed to go. Looking over the first table, I found it was covered by hundreds of boxes loaded with protein bars. Each box contained a separate flavor. I didn't bother to count how many because I was too hungry to care. From a box, I managed to take out three bars. Placing two in my pocket, I unwrapped one and started to eat it. My hunger helped me endure the taste of it. I just finished it and put the wrapper in my pocket.

Moving to another table, I found it covered by energy bars. Never having one before, I decided to try it. Taking a red bar, I quickly unwrapped it. I found it tasted better than the protein bar, but that isn't saying much. After eating the energy bar, I put two more in my pocket for later. I immediately stepped over to a third table, this one had bottles of water and energy drinks sealed in bottles. Other bottles had something fermented, but I never found what it was. But it was helpful.

As I reached for a water bottle, I found I was being watched. A tall, sturdy man with fiery, long red hair and an equally long beard. Had his piercing, cold blue eyes fixed on me. Not daring to open the water bottle, I just stood there, wondering what to do next. Casually, I looked over to my right to see if I could escape. Another man stood there, much smaller and younger than his red-mane friend. He made no secret that he was there to keep me inside their compound. My last hope was to make a run for it, using the only potential escape route I had left. I looked to my left and found another man standing there. He was a sturdy man with short black hair and dark brown skin. I would guess he is about forty.

Now surrounded, I had noticed that neither of the three was

coming to challenge me. They were here to contain me for somebody else. I gave each man a good look over. None of them were
armed; that was an advantage I could use. Calmly, I opened the
bottle and began to drink it, holding it with my left hand. With my
right hand, I revealed my stinger, making sure each of my captors
knew I was armed. Believing that I had made my point, I finished
the drink. Defiantly I place it on the table. I placed my hand on my
stinger.

"You do not need your weapons. We mean you no harm." I
heard from behind me. I turned around and saw a tall, average-built
man well past sixty. He had a full beard and long curly hair that
was completely white. His clothes were neatly tailored. At his side
were two young people; one was a young girl in her early twenties
with light brown hair. On his left side was a young man about the
same age as the young woman. His hair was darker but just as long.
With a small gesture, his men joined him. He said, "My friends
wanted to know what your intentions are?"

"I was hungry. I didn't see prices," I stated calmly.

The leader replied, "We do accept money. But we are willing
to trade."

"I didn't know."

Amused, he smiled, "How long have you been down here?"

It must have been obvious. I answered, "I woke up an hour ago.
I have been wondering ever since." That satisfied him. I decided
that it was a good time to ask him, "How can I make this right?"

The old man asked me, "What do you have to trade?"

I humbly confessed, "I have nothing but my weapons."

He smiled like he wasn't surprised by my statement. He asked,
"What did you do up there?"

"A courier in Southpoint. Security in Gotham," I answered him.

"The way I see it, you have two choices," he stated calmly. "You
can work for us doing security, or you can trade your clothes. We
will give you a fair exchange."

"I'll trade you my clothes," I decided.

"My granddaughter Alda will help you."

"Who are you?" I asked him.

"Call me Sheppard," he replied proudly, "And this is part of the flock." He looked around and gathered some more of his people. I had a feeling of regret for asking him. "I already introduced Aida. On my right is my grandson, Lionel." He looked over at the bulky older man, "Here is my good right arm, Bell." I nodded my head, and he silently responded. Sheppard looked over at the younger man, "Here is my chief scrounger, Ethan."

"Hi," he said.

Finally, he looked over at the giant with the red mane, "My chief of security, Kristof." With his introduction, the giant walked up to me and hit me squarely on my back. It was his way to say hello. I just nodded my head. Sheppard turned to his granddaughter and said, "You better see to him."

She stated, "Come with me." Without any hesitation, she led me to each table. Quietly, she looked over each table, picking out something that fit; with amazing focus, she checked out every piece of clothing. Something she did very well. In no time, she had picked out a navy blue denim jacket that she handed to me. On the second table, she found a black shirt. As for pants, that proved to be difficult. After going through all the contents of four separate tables, she proved to be more determined than ever. As I watched her, I noticed she glanced up at me. Not for any other reason, just wanting to make sure I was still there. A few times, she gave me a shy smile. When she saw me looking at her, she immediately looked down and continued her task.

Something had caught her eye. A simple pair of black denim jeans. Not bothering to ask for permission, she held the pants up to my waist. Looking down, I found it was long enough. She advised me, "You better try this on."

"Right here?"

Amused, she replied, "Modesty doesn't exist down here."

Looking around, I said, "I guess not." I gestured to her to turn around. Something she did reluctantly. I took off my shoes first. I could feel centuries of dirt on the soles of my bare feet. It didn't feel good. As quickly as possible, I exchanged pants. I handed her my old pants. Taking off my old shirt, I handed it to her. This time, she looked over and took a quick forbidden glance at me, topless. I didn't mind. Putting the shirt and jacket on. I then returned my shoes to my feet. Now I was ready for her inspection. "How do I look?"

She turned around and inspected me from head to toe, taking her time. She was pleased with the result of her task. "You look like you belong."

"I guess I do," I replied. The clothes felt different from what I had on before. More natural is the best way I can describe it.

"You will find it is a lot simpler down here." She began to fold my old clothes. "We better get back to Grandfather."

With her leading the way, it didn't take long to find her grandfather. He was going over plans with two of his associates. Then she came up to him and whispered into his ear. Turning around, he looked at me and smiled, "We can give you a week's rations, including what you had in your pockets." He showed me the energy and protein bars I had put in my old pants pocket. "Or you can stay here for a while and try us out." Looking over at his granddaughter, he added, "Aida would like you to stay."

Aida looked away, embarrassed. Before I answered, he stated, "We will give you a safe place to stay. In return, do some tasks for us."

Suspicious of what my task would be, I immediately stated, "I'm tired of killing."

"Kill," he stated, outraged by the prospect, "We don't kill here."

Looking around, I wondered if this man was for real. Everybody kills. I looked at him skeptically at his statement. But I was also intrigued. To discover if he is sincere. Maybe it's worth my time to find out and risk disappointment. Bell joined us as I was making up my mind. She was a good ten years older than I. She wanted to know what my intentions were. I had taken chances before in acquiring food, water, and shelter. This time was different, I was placing my faith in the word of another man. I decided, "I'll stay." I felt that it was worth a chance to find out if any of this was real.

Bell immediately came up to me and shook my hand, "You won't be sorry."

But I had to make it clear, "Remember, it is a trial."

"Any time you wish to leave, you can," Sheppard assured me.

Bell led me to my living space; it was in a large room above the rotunda. Aida was already there with a pillow and a blanket. With a welcoming smile, she handed them to me. I thanked them both, and they left me to my new home, such as it is.

2 GANGS

HAD COUNTED EACH DAY I HAD BEEN IN THE UNDERGROUND. IN my quarters, I had managed to find a piece of paper and a small pencil. Just before I went to sleep, I made a mark on that piece of paper. Then, when I woke up, I counted each mark. This morning, when I counted, I found I had been down here for twenty-two days. For breakfast, I had an energy bar and a bottle of water. After breakfast, I headed down for work.

Living down here, I did notice a few things that people above seem to take for granted. The most important thing is the changing of the seasons. The crisp air of autumn is coming. Down here, there are no weather controls to shield us from the excessive heat of summer or the cold of winter. Winter will be coming fast, and we need to prepare.

In many ways, I found that the Underground is much like the Wastelands. To survive, you need to find the three essentials: food, water, and shelter. There are many ways you can get them. As for me, I found somebody who had possession of the three essentials and made myself invaluable to the owners. Sometimes it was on intimate terms. I was willing to do whatever it took to accomplish that task, but more importantly, I wanted to know when it was a good time to leave. Living down here, there is one more essential: gangs. People who are alone seldom last too long. Dark areas are filled with the remains of lonely people who are now forgotten. For now, I have a gang.

The rotunda was already full of people looking for goods to trade. Sheppard was busy delegating the day's assignments to the others. When he saw me. He quickly finished with the others, so I waited for my turn. Working for him had proven to be a pleasant surprise. He had managed to get me a ration card that would get me food and medicine if I needed it. My job was to provide security for the people while in the rotunda. Along with going out to scrounge for unused goods that we can salvage for our charity. Sometimes we can find enough metal to trade with people up above. That is how he manages to support his little enterprise. It isn't from bartering. Many times, he will just give things away. He calls it trading to give people living down here some of their self-esteem.

When he had finally finished with the others, he turned to me. He said in all seriousness, "I'm glad you finally joined us, Duncan." I had been around him enough to tell when he was joking and when he was serious. I paid him no mind. "I need you to take Lionel and Ethan to line 7."

"I'm ready to leave now."

"Just be careful. They have their own rules down there."

"I will."

Satisfied, he moved on. I looked for Lionel and Ethan, they were waiting for me at the western edge of the rotunda. Both men were armed with small swords. Ready, we left for Line 7.

The central region of Black Level had three separate rotundas. Each one serves as some kind of center of community. Our rotunda was in the center of Gotham. An old map had told us that. Looking at the map together, we decided that our best way was to head to the northern Rotunda and take the western line to Line 7. It will take us about an hour.

Lionel wasn't happy about using the northern rotunda. He confessed that his grandfather had dealings with them in the past. The gang that runs it has been wanting to expand its influence. Why? Lionel told me he didn't know; I would have to ask their leader.

Ethan had known about a little-used side route that headed directly into the rotunda. Once inside, we can easily go through without being detected. We followed the route that Ethan had laid out for us. I can see why it wasn't widely used; it was very small and easily missed by people who didn't know it existed. For the past twenty days, I have primarily worked with Ethan. Between the two of us, we covered most of Gotham. During that time, we began to communicate with each other. I found his strange language not much different from the common tongue. His people just developed a different language. To save you from any confusion, I will use the common tongue.

When we made it to the rotunda, I found it to be strangely less crowded than our rotunda. I didn't want to stay around to find out why it was that way. We made it out of the northern rotunda and headed east. With fewer people maneuvering around, we maintain a good pace. Making it to Line 7 faster than we had earlier estimated.

Standing at the entrance, we investigated the abyss that was the old passageway, I found it didn't look inviting. But we had to go through it. Instinctively, I took out my torch from my backpack and raised it to illuminate the pathway, only to be stopped by Ethan. He looked at me and said, "Best not to announce that we are here." I looked over at Lionel, and he agreed with Ethan. Believing they knew something they didn't want to tell me. I returned my torch to my backpack.

Together we walked into the darkness. Now one thing I have learned about being in total darkness is that your other senses immediately compensate for sight. Every sound becomes magnified. The slightest touch will distract you. A smell becomes more prevalent within this dark world. Then when your eyes adjust to the darkness you become self-aware of what you're traveling in.

We found ourselves heading downhill. It started at a slight angle. Then it became steeper as we walked deeper. Finally, the tunnel leveled off, and we were able to move constantly again. In front of me, I heard a constant drip of water. Like several faucets dripping in a precise order. Hitting the stone ground. Walking underneath the drips. A few landed on me. Curious, I tasted the unmistakable salt water. I figured out we were under the water that separated Gotham from Queens. For now, this tunnel is withstanding the weight of all that water.

Another thing is that the tunnel has become wider. In front of me, I could still see the silhouette of my companions. I had a strange fear that I was not alone. But then I had a worse feeling come upon me, that something was watching us inside the darkness. I wasn't sure who or what it was, but I began to believe there was something. Then I began to see the shadows. A human figure moving in the darkness, allowing my eyes to see the movement. Not wanting to take a chance, I pulled out my stinger. My friends must have seen them because they pulled out their weapons. We began to walk into a triangle, with Ethan and I taking the base positions in the back and Lionel in front of us. We made sure that each of us was in constant sight. Still, we remained silent as we walked, trying to be careful as we stepped.

We began to head uphill. It was not as steep as when we began moving through the tunnel, but still noticeable. Our friends were still following us. Then we saw the light at the end of the tunnel. It was a larger entrance than on the west side. Somebody must have had a reason for this construction. Outside Tunnel 7, we returned our weapons to their sheaths.

We headed down an artificially lit pathway. Unlike Gotham, Queens' Black level was far from crowded. The pathways were much wider, with a higher ceiling. Like in Gotham, people are camping out along the edges. The edges were three levels high, connected by ladders. Serving as sentinels were armed men, making sure nobody would infringe on their territory.

Lionel knew where we were going. He led us to a stone stairwell that headed up. We headed upstairs to a processing center. It was an exit, a way to leave Black section. I found myself thinking about dashing the gate. Employees from Grey Section were too busy with other people trying to leave or enter the underground. As I moved closer to the gate, I made my decision not to try it. It was too well guarded. I counted twenty Watchmen keeping their eye on what was going on. Along the roof were security cameras watching us with unseen eyes. Remember what happened outside the city walls and what lethal traps they used to keep control of the masses. If this is to work, I will need a diversion.

Ethan came over and tapped me on the shoulder, "We are supposed to go this way." I said nothing; I just followed him to join Lionel, who was waiting for us. Together, we headed into another large room. Twenty Watchmen were stationed as people waited in lines for their rations. Their job was to make sure nobody caused trouble while they were there.

Lionel looked at me and requested, "I need your ration card."

Taking it from my pocket I handed him my card. He looked over Ethan who had given him two more. When it was our turn Lionel handed over our ration cards. When the older woman asked what Lionel wanted. Lionel responded, "Vitamin bars."

The woman understood the demand. She handed over a dozen boxes. Lionel grabbed them and handed them over to us. Ethan immediately placed them in his bag. He handed me the two boxes that he couldn't fit.in his. After putting the two boxes in my backpack, Lionel handed me six more boxes. He placed six boxes in his bag. We left the line.

"What is with these vitamin bars?" I asked, surprised we came all this way for something we could get at Gotham processing center.

Lionel answered, "We needed to get these. Each shipment to the processing centers is strictly rationed. Regardless of population. If we don't get this, we will have an outbreak on our hands."

Ethan added, "Aida and Bell headed down in Gotham. We sent other groups to Dukes and York. Hopefully, that will be enough to hold us for the month." He then handed me a vitamin bar. I opened it and took a small bite. It tasted better than a protein bar, but that's not saying much.

"We'd better go," Lionel added.

Before we headed home. We first stopped at a marketplace. Lionel bartered with the shopkeeper for a dozen illuminating sticks. They agreed on a price and shook hands. He handed him some aluminum and our business was done. They will help us on our journey through the tunnel. That is what he told us.

Before we left, I noticed someone was watching us. I looked over, I saw who it was. Peeking out of a tent, I thought I saw Isabella. How did she get down here? I had to be sure. Heading for the tent I saw it was her.

Isabella, I had barely known. I was assigned to her individually only once. If she had recognized me, it didn't stop her from cowering at the farthest point of the tent, huddling in fear. Her face was pressed against her knees. Daring not to look up at me dreading her fate. Carefully I walked into the tent lowering to my knees. She was trembling with fear when I came up to her. I could hear her weeping.

"Isabella, it's me, Duncan," I tried to assure her.

With a tearful voice, she stated, "Duncan?" She looked up at me.

She was a ghostly shell of herself. Malnourished, her skin was pale white. She pushed her matted hair off her face as she turned towards me. She had on soiled pink underwear that made it clear to me that she had endured living here. As I tried to stand her up on her feet. She relied on me to give her balance for a moment. When she was able to stand on her own, that is when I saw the greatest indignity she had suffered. Her foot was chained to a post. The sudden reminder of her captivity made her collapse to the floor in despair. Returning to my knees, I pulled out my stinger and set it on high. I placed it directly on the lock of the chain. A burst of energy from my weapon pulverized the metal; she was free. She lunged at me, placing her arms around my neck in gratitude. We walked out of her cell together.

As we walked together people turned towards us curiously. Isabella held on to me tightly. Nervous that somebody will see us and tell her captors. Secretly I was hoping for that, I very much wanted to meet her captors. To give them my regards you could say.

Before we rejoined Lionel and Ethan. We stopped over at the market to get her something to wear. It wasn't much. Just a black shirt that was perfect on me, but when she put it on, it covered her to her thighs. Next, we found some shoes for her to wear on her bare feet. The bastards didn't think she needed any. Guessing that she was hungry, I handed her a power bar and an energy bar. I had guessed right. She just devoured both bars too quickly to taste them. With five small brownish coins, I paid the clerk.

We rejoined Lionel and Ethan. I immediately introduced Isabella to them. They were both polite with our new member. All of us left for home.

At Tunnel 7, we prepared to enter the darkness. We pulled out our weapons, anticipating that we would be attacked by whatever lives there. All three of us knew that was a great opportunity. Lionel entered the abyss first, and Ethan walked in next as he disappeared into the darkness. Next, it was Isabella's, and then it was my turn. She nervously had her arms around my waist, too scared to let go. But she knew her former captors would never follow us through the tunnel. To assure her, I placed my left arm around her waist, and we entered together.

Up in front, Lionel counted out a hundred meters in his head and stopped to throw a light stick, illuminating the tunnel around us. That will neutralize the dwellers' advantage, who use the darkness to pounce on their prey, hiding their presence until it is too late. Another benefit is that we can move at a quicker pace. We made sure we remained in the blue light.

Everything was going according to plan until Lionel held up the last stick. We knew what that meant, it was the last one. As hard as he could, he threw it ahead of him. Shadow figures scurried away from the blue light. Not wanting to waste any time, we moved forward. As we ran, that is when I saw it. A faint light in the distance. It was too faint to shine in the darkness, it needed the blue light from the torches. If Isabella hadn't been with me, I would have checked it out. But I didn't want to endanger her. We walked together. Lionel had guessed the length of tunnel 7 wrong. We had managed to cover about two-thirds of the tunnel. Now, we had to circumvent the remaining tunnel in the darkness. Once they realize we have no more sticks, they will surely strike.

Moving into the darkness, we all noticed the shadows gathering around us. The sticks helped us to be able to detect our friends in the darkness. They were waiting to be sure that we were vulnerable. That time came in one quick moment as they rushed us. I moved Isabella behind me as I waited for the impending attack. But we had one more surprise. That came from Ethan. He had brought two firesticks and didn't tell either of us. With the result, we weren't going to make a protest.

He quickly threw each firestick within the ranks of our attackers. A series of endless explosions forced the shadows to return to their home in the darkness. Unfortunately, the two attackers didn't get scared too easily. The first attacker came at me with a homemade stick with metal spikes on it. His attack was sloppy, and he allowed himself to miss me and hit the ground instead. I used my stinger to hit him in his ribs. He slumped down and turned to face his friend. Only to find Ethan had taken care of him. Not wanting to wait around for the shadows to regain their courage. We made a mad dash for the exit. Once outside, we were safe. We returned home.

At the rotunda, Sheppard was there waiting for us. Lionel immediately handed him all three of our bags with vitamin bars. He placed it on a table with the other food. His attention quickly turned to Isabella.

"And who are you?" he asked her.

Looking down at the ground, she whispered, "Isabella."

"What do you do, child?"

"Whatever you wish."

He signaled for Aida to come over. He told her, "Those days are over, child. But first, you can look up." Carefully, she lifted her head and looked at Sheppard in his eyes, not sure what her fate was to be. He explained to her, "Aida will help you get settled."

Aida walked up to her and took her by the hand. They headed off together. Somehow, Sheppard knew I was behind our new member. Without hesitation, I told her all I knew about her. Who was she up there in the real world? How she suddenly disappeared from the menagerie she was a member of. I was surprised to find that he was aware of this practice of the menagerie. How could he have known about living down here? Then I told him where I had found her. How she was chained in a tent. How timid she was when I first approached her. He immediately looked over to my companions for confirmation. They both backed my story. His focus returned to me with a concerned look. I finished my report with, "My job was to keep an eye on them."

He looked at me for a moment. I think I surprised him. But there was something that made him hesitate in accepting what I had done. He finally told me, "She is welcome to stay. Hopefully, her captors won't want her back."

I exclaimed, "Nobody is going to take her away." Ethan made the same promise.

Sheppard had one thing more to tell us, "That is all well in good. Considering she is a property of one of the Lords of Queens." Thad immediately surprised me. He wasn't there. How could he make that assumption? He quickly explained, "Metal is rare down here. So, he must have means. He had no guards around her. Because nobody will dare to do what you did."

I boasted, "That was his mistake."

Sheppard just shook his head. He was about to give me another spiritual lecture about the dangers of pride or something when Aida returned with Illyana. With pride, she presented her latest creation of picking out a new member's wardrobe. She had outdone herself. Isabella had taken a bath, which made her feel more alive. She had a long grey sweater that covered her body down to her knees. She had black slacks that covered the rest. Her feet were covered with small shoes that covered her ankles. For pure decoration, she had on a white belt that was wrapped around her waist. Most importantly, a smile had returned to her face. Sheppard dismissed us.

It was a week before she felt comfortable enough to tell her story. It was late at night, and I was on guard duty. Making sure that idle hands try to help themselves with our merchandise. That was Sheppard's job description, not mine. For myself, I found it strange that he would willingly give it away. Why was he so concerned about theft? He explained that he only gives what they need. To make sure they have enough for everybody. An individual who steals in the night will take it all for themselves. He can't allow. It made sense.

Nighttime in the Underground is much like daytime. The area is dimly lit by artificial light sources. I sat on a perch overlooking the entire rotunda. As I watched over the quiet rotunda. I had only three hours of sleep before my shift started. I had just finished my second energy drink and was about to open the third can when I sensed someone walking towards me. Quickly glancing to my right, I saw that it was Isabella walking up to me. Without asking for permission, she sat down next to me. She placed her head on my shoulder. We sat there together, looking at the silent space below.

Isabella had found her place in our gang very seamlessly. She chose to help Ethan and me in our scrounging duties. On a personal note, I noticed Ethan had taken an interest in her. She has been slow to return his interest. Ethan understood her reluctance as he had confessed to me. But I was happy for her.

"Why do you go out alone?" Her question broke the silence.

"I'm looking for a way out," I replied. I made no secret of my intentions.

"It is impossible. I knew of three who tried, each one returned to us dead. A warning for the rest of us," she stated, "I don't want that to happen to you."

I placed my hand around her waist, looked at her, and replied, "I have spent my life getting out of places far more difficult." Yes, I was embellishing a little, but there was some truth to it.

"Why do you want to leave?"

"Gabrielle is up there."

She looked away from me for a moment. There were many other reasons I could have given her. Deep down, she knew that was my only reason. She then said, "Caitlyn has her. She won't let her go." Looking up at me, she hesitated for a moment. I knew she had something to tell me. In a low voice, she confessed, "Kayla and I were sent up to Purple Section for a party. She had sent a two-person escort with us. When we arrived at the host's flat, they immediately left. They were giving directions to return at one hundred hours. That should have been a warning, but we were too excited to think about the four handsome young men who were there waiting. They immediately offered us food and drink and thanked us for coming to their annual slumming party. None of us knew what they meant by that. Very quickly, we found out. They planned to do whatever they wished with us as long as we were not too damaged. That was Caitlyn's only request."

She stopped there. Ashamed of that night that wasn't her fault, she needed to tell her story to me. Just to let me know who exactly Caitlyn was. When she was ready, she continued, "When it was over, I wanted to report those bastards. I told the others to come with me. Kayla said she was with me. Alone, I headed to report the crime to the Watchmen. I never made it. Kayla had betrayed me. She had been working with Caitlyn in setting up these parties. Three of Caitlyn's operatives overpowered me and brought me to her. She gave me a choice to let her take care of everything, or she would release me from my contract. I chose the latter. She then sold me to the man who owned that tent. That is what you're up against."

"I know."

She looked into my eyes and immediately knew it was in vain to convince me of my endeavor. She lowered her head on my shoulder and started to cry. I kissed her on the top of her forehead to give her some comfort. Together, we just sat there. Isabella was another person whom I failed. I just didn't know.

I heard something moving below us. We were not alone. I looked around, trying to find where the sounds were coming from. Finally, I saw the shadows in the distance. I looked at Isabella and told her, "Stay here and stay out of the light."

She wiggled back into the darkness. I quietly walked over to the noise. Following my advice to Isabella, I stayed in the shadows myself. Pulling out my stinger, I was ready for anything. Every time I do something like this, I always get apprehensive. Right now, it was a different reason. I had a feeling this was a diversion. If my goal were to recapture Isabella, this would be the way I would do it. But how would they know she would be there with me? That would be an unnecessary risk of being spotted. That reassured me that Isabella was not the target. Just in case I needed to handle this quickly.

Fortunately for me, they were too busy scurrying around boxes to notice me. Walking down some steps, I noticed there were three of them. Once I was on the same level, I cried out, "You can walk out of here with nothing or stay here permanently."

That startled them. All three rose to their feet. Noticing I was between them and the exit. They pulled out their weapons. Two rushed me at once, and with my stinger, they slumped to the ground. Leaving the third. As the figure walked into the light, she held out her knife. That knife looked familiar to me. I looked over at the figure's face. I moved closer to her. The assailant held up their knife. I froze and cried out, "Paloma?"

"Duncan?" she muttered. She looked at me like she had seen a ghost. For a moment, she wasn't sure if I was a benevolent spirit or an avenging one.

"You don't need that dagger with me," I assured her.

She lowered her knife. With her other hand, she pulled off her hood that covered her long black hair. She had been through a lot since the last time I saw her. She wore those burdens on her face. Yet she had survived them, making it here. Without warning, she had lunged at me, not for violence but to greet an old friend. Her arms were wrapped around her waist. She began to weep. Finally, she whispered, "I've done terrible things."

"We all have done terrible things."

She confessed, "You don't understand. I couldn't get revenge on everyone. But I did on her."

"On whom?"

"Natalie," she cried, "we met down here, and I put this knife in her back."

I kissed her on her head. Who am I to judge her? She had lost her family and friends getting to Gotham. She had found a new family in line with us. Then she was lied to and forced to watch her new family be destroyed before her eyes. Down here, she has another family. That she will protect with her life.

"Join us." I encourage her. "We have plenty of room." Looking behind me I saw Isabella and Kristoph standing there. Neither was very happy. Isabella looked jealous and Kristoph didn't like being awake so late. I just stated, "Isn't that right."

Kristoph stated, "That is Sheppard's call." His demeanor had changed, and he asked, "Who is this?"

I turned to Paloma, presented her with two of my other companions, and stated, "This is Paloma."

Now, his office of chief of security presented himself and asked, "Who are those two?"

He referred to the two companions of Paloma, still unconscious. That was going to be a problem. Palloma answered for me, "They are with me."

Ethan and Bell brought eight other men to support Kristoph. Kristoph without looking at them ordered, "Place them into the den. Keep them under guard." Without a word, the ten men passed us and headed for the two accomplices. A young man named Dylan who brought up the rear, stopped and looked at Paloma. She was too concerned with her friends to notice her admirer. He joined the others and carried them to a side room behind Kristoph and Isabella.

Knowing she had no right to ask, she hesitated to inquire about them. So, I asked her, "What about Paloma?"

"I'll take her," Isabella said. She took Paloma by the hand and dragged her away, leaving me, Kristof, standing there at each other.

"Get back to your post, " he told me. Quietly, I returned to my perch. Alone, I just kept watch, overlooking the quiet rotunda. Sitting there, I tried to keep myself awake by thinking about Paloma and Natalie. How could things become so insane? Somehow, I have failed everybody I have come across.

3   THE FORGOTTEN

AFTER A WEEK, I STILL HAVEN'T GONE BACK TO TUNNEL 7. I KNEW it would be dangerous to go there alone. In my free time, I managed to cover much of Gotham. Without any luck, I might add—the people up above to great pains in their attempt to keep us down here. Still, I am determined to find that way out.

As for Isabella, she has found a kindred spirit in Paloma. Both have suffered greatly since they arrived in Gotham. Living here with Sheppard, they have found some form of normalcy. Sheppard had allowed Paloma and her companions to join us. Paloma had accepted his offer; her companions did not. That was their choice. It is foolish of me to continue trying to steal it rather than share it with the rest of us.

I have just finished my daily chores for Sheppard. There is a section along the southernmost point of Gotham. I wanted to leave quickly, so I will return in a few hours. Without telling anyone, I headed out of the rotunda. Moving through the crowd, I headed south. After a month of traveling along the passageways, I have managed to move at a greater pace than before. It helps to have a clear destination in mind.

It seems that more people are arriving here every day. Making it insanely crowded. Soon, people will have no room to move down here. Not that the people up there cared. They want that to happen, they plan to drive the inhabitants to mass murder. Fewer people to support is what they theorize. Now, I can't prove that theory. But it is the best one I could come across. Then I thought of something: someone must have brought me down. I doubt that they volunteered to stay down here; that meant they must have had a way out. That led me to make a quick detour. I came up to the familiar alley.

The alley hadn't changed much. Nobody had claimed it as there's yet. I found that to be strange. As a precaution, I pulled out my stinger. With no light source of its own, I had to use a flashlight, but it did little help. I did manage to find the place I woke up in over a month ago. Moving my light around, I tried to find any other way into the alley other than the way I had come. Eventually, I found it; around a corner was a small hallway. Without hesitation, I walked down the path. I could barely fit through the narrow passageway. It would have been difficult to carry me through this way, but right now, it is my best lead. I had to know if I was right about this. Then the passageway ended. Now I understand why this small alley wasn't large enough to support any settlement. I looked around to see if there was any other way to continue. I couldn't find one, so I decided to head back.

That is when I felt a hand on my shoulder. Startled, I turned around and saw Kristoph standing in front of me. I was amused to find that he had more difficulty maneuvering down this alleyway than I did.

Not wasting time, he said, "Sheppard wants to talk to you."

"I'll see him when I'm finished," I replied. I hadn't done what I came here for.

"You're finished now," he exclaimed, making sure I understood this wasn't a request.

I had no desire to argue with Kristoph and disobey Sheppard. I just muttered, "Lead the way."

Without saying a word, Kristoph turned around and led me out of this passageway.

At the Rotunda, I headed to my little camp. Choosing to wait for Sheppard here. Everybody kept their distance from me. That didn't give me confidence that this conversation would go well for me. Looking back over the past month, I tried to figure out what I had done wrong, but nothing came to mind. I had never neglected my duties. My attempts to find my way to escape have been on my own time.

When he finally arrived, he was accompanied by Bell. Sheppard casually sat down next to me. Bell remained standing in the background.

"Thank you for coming." He stated.

"Kristoph didn't give me much of a choice."

"I have to talk to him about that" he assured me, looking over at Bell who nodded in agreement, then he turned to me and returned to what he had wanted to talk to me, "Well I wanted to ask you about your future with us."

"Go ahead," I stated, not sure where this was going.

"We had hoped you would make your stay permanent," said Sheppard sincerely. Aida had joined us. I greeted her with a welcoming smile. Sheppard had seen it, but he didn't show concern.

I simply responded, "I like you all very much. But I can't join you."

Aida interrupted, "Why?"

It was a clear reason. During my travels through the Wastelands, I came across many like the Sheppard. The latest was the Prophet. But there were others, from Archangels to Saints, the Faithful to Zealots, all were the same, and spread the same lies to create their own kingdoms from the ashes of an ancient civilization. I have heard of others that I had the good fortune not to come across. They murdered anybody who stood in their way. One group wants to finish what the four horsemen had started; they are called Doomsday. Fortunately for me, I only saw the remains of where they had been.

Aida wanted an answer. She doesn't have her grandfather's patience. Before she could show her displeasure with me, I replied, "I have met too many of your kind before."

Sheppard wasn't surprised by my answer. Nor was he offended. However, Aida was offended. She was about to make her feelings known, and Shepperd interjected, "I've thought we had proven that we are not like those fanatics."

I stated, "I have other reasons."

Again, Sheppard wasn't surprised. He stated with full confidence, "You haven't given up the world above us. Your friends Isabella and Paloma proved that. But why?" I didn't say anything. Reaching into my pocket, I pulled out my picture of Gabrielle and me and handed it to Sheppard. He looked at it. Impressed by it, he handed it to Aida. She looked at it, then she handed it to Bell.

"Duncan, she is lovely," said Aida, clearly her tone had changed.

"Her name is Gabrielle. I must get back to her."

Sheppard inquired, "For what reason?"

I replied, "I love her. She needs to know."

He asked me, "And if she doesn't love you in return?"

"Then I'll tell her goodbye and wish her happiness," I said, revealing to him what I had already promised myself.

Sheppard gave me a look of satisfaction. He finally understands me. He said, "You're finding a way to escape."

"That is impossible," said Bell emphatically.

I heard that before. My experiences taught me something different. I said, confidently, "There is always a way out. No prison is escape-proof."

Sheppard admired my tenacity, but he had to make his concerns known, "If I can't discourage you in this endeavor. I must ask you not to go out alone anymore. Bell can go with you." Bell returned my picture. I returned to my pocket.

I asked, "Why?"

"Others might want to join you," he said, "But you will do it if I forbid you to go. This way, I can make sure you will be safe."

"Thank you."

Sheppard and Bell left me alone. Aida stayed behind and sat down next to me. She asked me, "When you first came here, you told my grandfather that you would fight to defend us, but not for us. What did you mean?"

"I joined the army of the Prophet a few years ago. We were trying to free some captives. He used to pay his soldiers. In exchange for food, shelter, and companionship, they will help him spread his message of death."

With apprehension, she then asked me, "What happened?"

I explained, "A lieutenant in his army. He was abusing a woman. I claimed her as my mate, saying she was pregnant. We fought in single combat, and I won."

"Was she pregnant?"

With a mischievous smile, I replied, "I lied."

A smile came over her face. To show her approval, she leaned over and kissed me on my cheek. She then left me alone. I just ate some food and kept my distance from the other people. Taking out the picture of Gabrielle, I studied it for a while, wondering if she was happy up there.

Over the next month, Bell and I managed to cover the entire district. Sometimes, Paloma joined us on a few occasions. Aida had made her feel at home, working her magic on Paloma. It was during the last trip that the three of us had managed to find an old map inside some building that used to be a tavern or inn. It was placed proudly on the wall for all to see. For some reason, people here didn't realize the significance of this map. We needed to take it home with us.

The map was encased in a smooth surface that was fastened to the wall. Bell, using his device, managed to free it from the wall. He handed it to me. Together, we left the old tavern and made it to the passageway. It was getting late, so we met Kristoph and Ethan, whom Sheppard had dispatched to check on us. Together, we headed south through the northern rotunda. It never fails; over the past month, we have traveled through the northern rotunda nearly a hundred times, and never were we noticed by the people who lived here. This time, we did. It didn't help that we had something of theirs with us.

Flynn was the leader of the Northern Rotunda. He was a short, handsome man with long black hair and cream-colored skin that he somehow kept clean shaving. Which made him look even younger.

The few times we had met before, he was well-spoken. That hid his violent side, which he never hesitated to use on other poor souls. He wore loose clothing but was most proud of his hat, which he had never taken off.

With a charming demeanor, Flynn greeted us, "Good day to you can I help you." He was surrounded by four large men that he controlled with the sheer force of his own will.

Kristoph answered in a slow, clear tone, "No, we are on our way home."

Flynn looked over at me who was holding the map, "Your friend here has something that belongs to us."

"That's funny, I didn't think anybody had any claim on it. The people who put it there are long dead." I replied calmly.

Kristoph, still trying to keep the peace, stated, "What do you want for it?"

Flynn thought for a moment, he said, "That will be a difficult thing to estimate."

He didn't know what I had in my possession. All he knew was that it was from the ruins of that old tavern. That made it valuable to him. I decided to start the negotiation, "I can give you a week's worth of rations."

Flynn looked at his men, and with a confident expression, he said, "Well, that is a good start. I will accept a full month of rations."

"We can always put it back," Kristoph said. "Bell, bring it back." Bell nodded in agreement. I was hoping that the two men were bluffing. Flynn wasn't about to lose his potential bargaining chip. Kristoph then added, "Our friend Duncan is looking for a way to escape."

This made Flynn hesitate for a moment. He was ready to reassess his situation. He gives us his final proposal: "I will let you have it on the condition that if you find a way out, you will share it with us."

"Why do you think we are looking to escape?" Kristoph asked.

"I'm not an idiot." Flynn was preparing his men for a fight.

"Deal!" I said that I managed to calm him down.

Before Flynn could finalize the deal, he had to ask me, "Can you find a way out? Others had failed."

They all looked at me. Each of them wanted me to answer that question for their own reasons. It was clear to me that they all wanted to believe I could do it. All I could say to them was the same as what I had done for the past ten years of finding a way to escape from the Overseers. I finally said, "I can do it."

"You better" stated Flynn. He signaled his men, and they left us to continue our journey. All of us were relieved. As we walked down the pathway nobody was talking. We just headed for home.

I don't remember how far we managed to get. Kristoph and Bell were leading us. Ethan and Paloma were with me, bringing up the rear.

A scream came from Paloma. Before I could turn my head to see what had happened to her. A figure had lunged at the map. Instinctively, I held on tightly to the map, refusing to let it go. Ethan rushed to help Paloma, who had an assailant holding a rusty knife at her throat. Both Kristoph and Bell came to aid Ethan in trying to help Paloma. The man holding Paloma did a good job distracting Ethan and the others. His mistake proved to be not paying close attention to Paloma. Acting calmly, she slowly reached for her dagger. Holding the blade down, she plunged it into her attacker's ribs. The man slumped down, freeing Paloma. She pulled out her dagger. Kristoph took my attacker by placing his hand on the top of his neck and the base of his spine. In one move, he threw the poor soul into a wall. Kristoph then followed that move by pushing the man's head into the wall. The man just fell and didn't get up. It was then that a third man struck. With his knife, he slashed Bell in his back. Ethan struck the attacker with his sword. He had done his damage and run off.

Paloma immediately ran over to help Bell. She tore off the sleeve from her left arm and used it as a makeshift bandage. When she finished, she looked at the rest of us. "We need to get him to a doctor."

Kristoph placed his hands under his wounded friend's back and proclaimed, "The clinic is not that far. Let's go."

Together Ethan and Kristoph picked the man up. With Paloma

keeping pressure on the wound. I had to help them. I didn't hesitate, I dropped the map and joined Ethan. The four of us rushed through a side spur that led to a medical clinic the government had established to help the forgotten.

For emergency cases like ours. We were allowed to come in quickly. Placing him onto a gurney we stepped aside for the nurses to come in to help Bell. A doctor came in to treat him. Looking over I saw the doctor rush in. It was a pleasant surprise when I saw it was Samantha. Her attention was focused solely on her patience, she didn't see me. A nurse pushed us out to wait for news on our friend.

We sat together in a small parlor; we were off to the side. Sitting there, we watched the chaos unfold before our eyes. Hundreds of people were standing in line with various degrees of illness, waiting to be treated. The majority were given a quick check of symptoms and were diagnosed. A nurse will give out some medicine and send them on their way. One mother had brought their children to be checked out. As I watched the nurses go over their symptoms. She discovered that they were severely malnourished. Her actions were simple: she gave them what food she had on her. I walked over to give her my ration card. Surprised, she thanked me and led her kids away. I returned to join the others. Kristoph gave me a rare smile that I could barely see through his thick beard. I knew he was smiling because his eyes lit up. When I sat down, he immediately sat next to me.

With his eyes looking into the chaos that is the clinic, he stated, "I can't figure you out. When we first met, I thought you were selfish, manipulative, and arrogant, a typical elite from up there. And I'm usually a good judge of character." He then looked at me and finished his thought, "But you're not selfish."

That was a compliment if you were wondering. I just replied, "I'm full of surprises."

Turning his attention back to the clinic, he asked, "Was that map really that vital?"

"It would have made it easier" I replied, looking towards the clinic waiting anxiously for Samatha to arrive with news, I added, "Nothing is worth Bell's life."

He nodded his head in agreement. He then said, "Those children may not belong to that woman. She might use them to get hand-outs. Did you ever think of that?"

Still looking away from him, I answered, "Not really." There is simply too much suffering in this world. If I have a chance to relieve someone's burden, I'm going to take it.

He then looked over at me and stated, "You're all right." I didn't respond, there was nothing else that needed to be said between us. We just sat quietly, waiting for news about Bell, hoping that it would be good.

After an hour, a nurse came out to talk to us. I remembered her from one of the three nurses who had helped Samantha work on Bell. When we saw her, all four of us stood up to meet her. Her demeanor didn't give us much hope. In a serious, professional tone, she announced, "Your friend will be all right. We managed to stop the bleeding. He will need to rest here for a couple of days. After that, he needs to be on light duty."

We all gave a collective sigh of relief when we heard her. Kristoph asked, "Can we see him?"

She answered, "Let him rest." Her demeanor had changed to that of being tired. She then continued, "The doctor will be here shortly." After saying that, she turned and headed back into the chaos that was her job.

Kristoph turned to us and stated, "You three don't need to wait any longer. Go home and tell Sheppard what had happened here."

"I like to stay for a while."

"You don't need to."

"The doctor is an old friend."

Kristoph looked at me for a moment, he said, "You know a lot of people."

"I get around," I replied.

He laughed. There was no doubt about that. Everybody in the clinic heard him. Paloma and Ethan left us alone. We just sat down again and waited for Samantha to come. Another hour had passed before Samantha was able to come to see us. When she entered the makeshift waiting room, she looked tired. As soon as she entered the room, she noticed me, and a smile came over her tired face. Walking up to us we rose to our feet to greet her.

She started with, "Your friend is lucky you had someone with medical training, or he would have bled to death." Her expression changed when she added, "We made up a room for him. I would like to keep him here for three days. Just to watch him."

Kristoph asked, "May I stay with him?"

"We don't have any place for you to stay," she stated.

"I can sleep here," he stated emphatically. "I can help out here."

Samantha relented, "All right. He is awake now, if you still want to see him." Looking over at me, she added, "Just one of you."

Kristoph left and headed into the back room. Samantha turned her attention towards me. "Somehow I knew you would end up here," she said plainly.

I replied, "I'm surprised to see you here."

"I work here three months out of the year," she stated with surprising enthusiasm. "I love it down here. Down here, I am needed."

"I'm happy for you," I told her. I then asked her, "When do you go back?"

"In two weeks."

"I'd like to give you a message to Cassandra."

She was surprised, she expected me to say, Gabrielle. I had no desire to explain to her why it wasn't. She decided to leave well enough alone. "Not a problem."

I thanked her and said goodbye. I needed to retrieve that map, and it was getting late.

It didn't take that long for me to get back on track with where I had dropped it. Our two dead friends were still there. Both men had been stripped naked. Everything of value had been scavenged by passersby. Soon, their very bodies will be taken away. They could be used for various reasons. I will just leave it at that. One thing I couldn't find is that map. Somebody had taken it, probably the surviving attacker or some of his friends. I had an idea of who was behind this attack. I took a moment to check my weapons. I headed to the northern rotunda and confronted Flynn.

If I had stopped to think about it, I should have headed home and gotten some help. The truth is, I was mad. Bell was seriously injured, and Paloma could have suffered a worse fate. This time, I wanted to personally give them payback. I don't know how I am going to do it.

When the lights flicker, it means night has fallen above, the power grid must adjust for the demands of Gotham's needs during the night. Down here, people begin to head home for the night. That meant fewer people were at Flynn's Rotunda. That made it easier for me to find him. He was with a young woman who was often by his side. I wasn't sure what she was to him. Walking up to them, I did not attempt to hide the fact that I was there. Seeing me, he turned towards me, and with his lady friend in tow, he walked up to meet me.

With a strangely sincere smile, he greeted me, "Our savior."

"How so?" she asked, looking me over. I did the same for her. The first thing I noticed was that she was armed with an impressive machete. I had the belief she knew how to use it. Her hair was red much like Gabrielle although cut short. That was the only similar feature between the two women. She is a few years older and shorter than Gabrielle. Her skin was deathly pale and looked malnourished. She is still attractive.

Flynn introduced me, "Ari, this is Duncan, the Pathfinder. He says he can find a way out of Black Sector."

Damn it, he had that same sincere smile on him, but I know he was mocking me. But I didn't care, he already had enough to answer for me. In a pleasant tone, I simply stated, "I just came from the Emergency clinic. One of my friends was injured when my map was stolen." Okay, I wasn't exactly accurate, but I got the point across.

When his smile disappeared from his face and he gave me some satisfaction, he said, "Who got hurt?"

"Bell" I replied, "he is going to be all right. But since our agreement is for us to make it home. And we were attacked in your territory our agreement is voided."

Flynn signaled his men to come over. Five men answered the call. Just in case, I placed my right hand on my stinger. Ari did the same with her dagger. Flynn made no moves to defend himself. In a sincere tone, he said, "I will get you your map tomorrow. These are my best men."

Taking my hand off the stinger, I said, "I'll leave you to it."

I decided to trust him and walked away. Heading home to report to Sheppard.

To put it plainly, Sheppard wasn't happy with me. Not for what had happened to Bell. Neither was staying so long after dusk. It was for the stupid act of confronting Flynn like I did. He told me that it was not only dangerous but reckless as well. His demeanor changed a bit when he reminded me that people were counting on me and that getting killed would not help anybody, especially me. As for me, I quietly listened to his lecture. Simply because he was right, I did act recklessly. When he finished, I humbly muttered, "You're right. I'm sorry." That satisfied him, and I walked to my little home.

That night, I didn't sleep that well. Winter has come. While living above, you would hardly notice it. Just something that happens to the earth outside Gotham, down here, you feel it. All I have to protect myself from the cold is a thin blanket. Ethan had told me he had seen entire families freeze to death during the night. He then explained that is why Lionel and he had gathered three dozen large metal cans for the past few days to prepare for the winter. To light fires in them to help keep us all warm. It does help a little, but I am still cold.

Paloma was watching me try to sleep, wrapped in a blanket of her own, she was struggling to fall asleep as well. Finally, while she was still wrapped in her blanket, she walked over to me. Without saying a word, she lay down, picked up my blanket, and placed herself underneath. Sitting up she had placed her blanket over us and laid down on her side facing me. Placing her arms around me, we managed to keep each other warm for the night somehow.

We stayed together until late morning; neither of us wanted to get up, preferring to stay together for a little longer, if possible. Unfortunately, it was not to be. Ethan and Isabella came over to wake us up. We were both annoyed. I looked up at our tormentors with one eye open.

I inquired. "What is it?"

"You have visitors," replied Isabella.

Ethan quickly added, "From Flynn."

I immediately got up. Paloma did the same. She proceeded to fold our blankets as I headed down to the rotunda with Ethan. Walking next to him I found he was strangely silent, like he was hiding something from me. My mind was on our visitors at the time, I didn't care about his secret.

Standing next to Sheppard were five men. The same men that Flynn had told me were his best men. The largest of them had in his possession my map. With a stern demeanor, he silently handed it to me. When I thanked him, it didn't change his attitude. We then stared at each other awkwardly, trying to decide what to do next. That is when his friend spoke up.

Being dwarfed by his friend by a good foot, he is the appointed spokesman for the group. He chose to speak slowly and precisely, and he started, "I am Trey." With his left hand, he placed it on the giant's shoulder. He looked at him, annoyed. "My serious friend here is Julius."

He held out his hand, I took it in friendship. His demeanor hadn't changed, with his long black hair and a strangely well-groomed beard. His clothes were practical and comfortable.

"He likes you," Trey confidently proclaims. I hoped he was telling me the truth. He wore his hard life on his face. His dark hair was long and straight. His mustache was as wild as his hair. Whereas Julius was about forty, I think Trey could easily be in his fifties. But he still looked like he could cut me in two. He turned his attention toward a man with an equally hard-looking face. He was only a few years older than I. He introduced him as "Jerome."

"Please to meet you," said Jerome with a sinister-looking smile.

"I'm sure," I replied.

Trey walked over to the most impressive of the five men. Standing next to Jerome was a man who stood an inch shorter than his friend. He had not an ounce of fat on him, only bone and muscle. It is a very incredible accomplishment living down here. He is a few years younger than Trey. I had come across people like him before, living peacefully up north. They were a strange contradiction of mistrusting outsiders, but at the same time, they were kind. I spent a winter with them. When it was time to leave, I had to promise never to return. A promise I had kept.

"My friend here is Wes." Said Trey. Like Julius, he steps forward quietly and holds out his hand, I accept his act of friendship. Looking at his eyes I could tell they were like a hawk trying to see what kind of a man I am.

Trey came to the last man of the group. He wasn't as tall as Julius but just as impressive. His demeanor was that of a killer. Not that he enjoyed it is more that it was a cost of living in this kind of world. In many ways, he and I are the same. Trey introduced him as, "Titus."

With a charming smile, he said, "Please to meet you." He had short blond hair and cold grey eyes, he then added, "We are here to help you find that escape."

"I have some work to do today. Tomorrow morning be here before dawn we will get started."

Looking at his friends, Titus said, "We will be here."

"I'll see you then."

They left together as the rest of us watched them. I just went to my loft and studied the map while eating breakfast. Isabella and Paloma sat with me, helping me remember what areas had been checked.

4   DELUGE

WHEN I FIRST MET MY FIVE COMPANIONS, I THOUGHT THEY were the last people I would want to meet walking alone in a dark alley. What I quickly learned was that I was dead wrong. In truth, they are the first people you want to come across; if you are with them, you can be assured that you will come to no harm. I regret my first thought.

We had spent the cold winter months covering much of Gotham and Queens. When Kristoph, Bell, and Ethan joined us, we split ourselves into two groups, which allowed us to enter Dukes. After each day making our rounds, I came home to Paloma. For the winter, we decided to pool our resources together to survive the winter months. I leave the judgment to others. Now that spring has arrived, we have made no further plans.

I said goodbye to the others just as we entered home. Flynn still expected his five best men to return home each night. Tomorrow, we agreed to try York. Ethan greeted me when I came inside the circle.

"How did it go today?"

"Still no luck."

"Where are you going tomorrow?"

"York. Want to come?"

"I'll be ready."

We headed up to our den together. I followed Ethan to his den, where we found Isabella waiting for him. Much like Paloma and I, they decided to pull together to endure the winter months, although they started well before winter. I was happy for them both, especially for Isabella, whom I had noticed frequently smiling. She immediately jumped into his arms, kissing him passionately when she saw him. I just stood there awkwardly watching them for a moment. I was reluctant to head home myself. Not sure what to do with Paloma. When I glanced over at our little place, she noticed me. I realized I couldn't delay it any longer. Quietly, I walked over to my little home and joined Paloma.

She walked up to me and hugged me. I smiled at her. Keeping her arms around my waist, she looked at me and said, "I have two power bars and energy drinks for dinner."

"Energy drinks?"

She stated proudly, "We just got some today." With her right hand, she guided me to our two blankets. She had done her best to make us more comfortable. Now I was going to say goodbye to her. But the truth is, I didn't want her to leave. I liked having her around me. All through the cold, I couldn't shake the feeling that I was betraying Gabrielle. Each night, I made myself believe she would somehow understand what we had to do to survive.

Taking my hand, she guided me to the ground. She then handed me my dinner. Together we ate. Eating with her made power bars taste good. We ate slowly as we silently watched the other enjoy our meager rations. When we finished, she asked, "Where to tomorrow?"

"York," I answered her, not sure how I was going to say what I needed to say. Finally, I just said calmly, "Winter is over."

She answered, "I know." When she lowered her head, she had anticipated what I was to say next. But she decided to let me know what she wanted, "I liked being with you. However, if you want this to go to, I will be fine with it. But before you decide, let me say this: I am here, and Gabrielle is up there."

She made a good argument, I confessed, "I don't want it to end either." But I needed to have an understanding with her, I don't intend to stay down here for the rest of my life. "What happens when we escape?"

"That is tomorrow, I'm focusing on today." In saying that, she leaned over to me and kissed me softly on my lips. We made our agreement, today we are together. What happens tomorrow is not our concern. I started to kiss her neck. I laid her on the ground, kissing her. We stopped briefly to place our covers over us for some privacy. She reached over and turned out the light. In the dark, we held each other lovingly.

Morning came quickly, as the flickering of the lights indicated. I had a lot to do in preparation for our expedition. I sat up and grabbed the map. Paloma and Isabella, both helped me keep track of where we had searched by coloring each quadrant with a blue marker. I looked over at Paloma, who was still asleep, her face down on a pillow she had said she found. Her long hair covered her naked back. I leaned down and kissed her shoulder, wanting to let her sleep.

Studying the map, I noticed something. Using a magnifying glass, I looked closer at what I thought I had seen. Battery Garden is directly underneath the Southern Rotunda. More importantly, there was an old maintenance shaft that had a direct route to the surface.

"How could I have missed this?" I exclaimed. Paloma awoke. Sitting up, she covered herself with the blanket. "Sorry."

She gave me a morning kiss on my cheek. I was too busy with my discovery to notice her. I finally stated, "I think we have a way out."

Disappointed, Paloma said sadly, "I see."

I turned to her and kissed her passionately. When I was finished, I reassured her, "That is for tomorrow." I then kissed her again. She smiled at me.

Ethan and Kristoph volunteered to go with us. At our briefing, I told them all that I had discovered. Assuring them that I was positive that it was there. Each one agreed to try Battery Garden. Numbering eight in total, we were hard to miss. Moving down the western passageway, with people yielding to us, we manage to keep a good pace.

The Southern Rotunda was the largest of the three. It was made up like the way Sheppard had constructed our place. We entered as one group, purposely making our presence known. Just in case other gangs wanted to give us trouble. For me, this was the first time I had ever been there. I didn't know much about who runs it. When I inquired about who runs this place, nobody wanted to say who they were. They just never had a kind word about the people who live here.

The most descriptive thing I got was from Kristoph, who said, "A bunch of troublemakers."

That didn't help me much. After encircling the entire rotunda twice, we decided to split up. I headed to the ladder. Thinking that was the way to go, I started to climb up. Reaching the sixth step, I heard a familiar voice below me. Looking down, I saw Jenna, Miles, and Carla staring at me. Three of Robert's disruptor friends. They helped Robert and me in our ill-fated attempt to rescue Olivia. Seeing them again brought back the image of Olivia falling to her death almost six months ago. For me, it could have been yesterday.

Other Disrupters joined them. Now I knew why my companions weren't impressed with them. This group has a severe image problem with the people they want to help. I don't think they care very much. I immediately climbed down. Jenna recognized me. She told the others it was all right; she would take responsibility for me.

I walked up to her. She tied her long, curly blonde hair behind her. Like everybody else living down here, she makes do with what the people up there decide to throw away. Jenna had on clothes that were at least three sizes too big for her, the faded brown shade didn't do her any favors either. Not wasting any time, she stated, "I thought you would end up down here."

Feeling the same about her, I replied, "I thought the same thing about you."

Amused, she said, "Why are you here?"

"I'm looking for a way out of here. I believe that it's up there." I pointed to the high roof. She looked up, unsure whether she was more surprised by a possible escape over their heads or my honesty in answering her question. I believed it was highly unlikely she would report what I was doing to the authorities. Besides Flynn, they could be valuable allies.

Her voice betrayed her excitement as she said, "Are you sure?"

"I have to look first," I told her.

"I'm coming with you. Stay here," she said, rushing away from me. Five minutes later, she returned with a pistol and a torch. "Let's go."

We climbed the ladder as far as we could go. Jenna was ahead of me. At the top, there was a small bump with a metal circle in its center. With her right hand, she tried to turn it, without success. The metal circle was too rusty to move after being unused for centuries.

"It won't budge," she said, frustrated with her struggles.

I took out my stinger and handed it to her." Hold it at its joint," I told her.

She did it. The rust was instantly pulverized. Temporarily putting my stinger in her belt. She twisted the metal circle. After four spins counterclockwise, she was able to open the bulb. With her right hand, she pulled down a second ladder. She stepped onto the lowest step on the ladder and headed into the darkness. I followed her.

Making it to the end, we headed for a passageway. Taking a flare, I lit it so we could find our way back when we needed it. I then held out my hand. She gave me my stinger back.

Standing in the light, I said, "We have three hours before that goes out." She nodded, understanding what I told her. Curiosity got the better of me, and I asked, "How did you get that pistol?"

With a smug expression, she said, "We are not without our means."

That was good enough for me. Taking out our torches, we headed down the pathway. It was entirely made of stone. Thousands of rectangular bricks are placed neatly together. There was very little disrepair of these bricks. We remained close together as we walked through the tunnel. Moving our torches around the walls, we tried to find any trace of a sign of a possible escape route.

After a few hundred paces, I looked behind me and saw no trace of the blue light of the torch. Jenna looked at me, holding her torch in my face.

"Do you have another one?" she asked me.

I suggested, "Let's take a few more steps first."

In my head, I counted out twenty paces. Reaching into my pocket, I took out another flashpoint and placed it on the ground. In the blue light, she turned to me.

"I have one more," I told her.

"Then we'd better hurry," she said to me.

As we walked, I needed to ask her how she got down here. Still looking ahead, she stated, "It seems your friend Caitlyn still has some powerful friends. To make matters worse, Kleist didn't like it when we killed Wynn on the grounds of Star Casino. That led to mass arrest, and we were sent here."

"What about Robert?"

"He and Cassandra are safe, for now," she replied, trying to reassure me, believing it was my turn to explain that I had found myself down here. She said, "Now tell me your story."

Fair enough, I thought to myself. I said, "My fault. I was done with Caitlyn and had wanted to leave Gotham. I mistakenly believed that Gabrielle would want the same thing. She didn't. I didn't give her any choice."

With an understanding tone, she replied, "That gave Caitlyn what she needed." All I could do was shrug. She turned around and walked forward a few steps. When she thought of something, she turned around. "Is your friend Gabrielle Blue?"

Surprised, I answered, "Yes." It was a strange thing that I never went into detail about her. I knew I had spoken about her from time to time, I just had to ask, "Why?"

"She is Caitlyn's new partner." That didn't surprise me but when she added, "She is also an advisor to the new Chancellor." That surprised me. Not that she couldn't do it, but she and the other women were considered outsiders.

Curiosity had gotten the better of me, I had to ask, "Who won?"

"The Reformers"

Good for Koch; I liked him. More importantly, I was happy for Savannah, believing she could help her new husband.

I checked my watch by placing it next to my torch. I noticed we were wasting time. Jenna realized the same thing. We headed down the tunnel. As we walked further down, I noticed something strange as I placed my hand on some bricks. I found them to be wet. Not all, but more than a coincidence. Jenna looked over at me.

"This was part of the old aqueduct system, "she explained.

When we could not see the blue light of the second flashpoint. I activated the third flash point immediately. Again, we continued. Not sure what to do after we walk out of range of our final light source. Should we go on? Or should we stop? While we were walking, we found other tunnels. This system was a labyrinth in which a person who wasn't careful could be lost forever.

We arrived at the edge of the third blue light's range, Thankfully, we didn't have to make that decision. Jenna had found a set of ladders. Excited, we hurried them up. We found another barrier; this one was a heavy piece of metal. Working together, we managed to move it. For the first time in months, we had felt the rays of sunlight in our eyes. With our hands, we had to block it out. To give our eyes time to adjust. After a minute, our eyes became used to the natural light again. We rose from underneath the ground and saw a full spectrum of colors again. We were lucky that nobody had seen us.

Together, we just stood there looking around the small green patch in the middle of buildings made of cement and steel. Like Capital Garden, the people from the red and yellow districts were excluded from this oasis. Eight lifts lead people from Blue and Purple to enjoy it. As I looked around, I felt vindicated, I was right.

Stepping onto the green grass, I muttered proudly, "It couldn't be this easy."

Jenna joined me and politely tapped me on my shoulder. When I turned my head over to her, she gave me a smug grin and pointed to the south. I looked and saw what she had silently wanted to show me. Disappointed. It was easy to see what she had seen before me. Grey Section. We may have been able to get around security to enter Blue Section. But Grey is the center of government. It is the most secure area in the city. Even now, we may be observed by Watchmen. But this is only a new obstacle for me to overcome. It can be done.

We left the same way as we came in. Walking down the old tunnel, we made better time as we became familiar with the tunnel. Luckily for us all three blue lights were still illuminating. Jenna climbed down the ladder first, and I followed her taking the time to close the lid. Making sure I eliminated all traces of our little exploration.

Reaching the main floor, I found a crowd waiting for us. Anxious about what we had found, standing ahead of me was Kristoph.

"Did you find it?" he asked.

"We did." I started with the good news first. Not sure why I did it. Maybe it's more for my own ego to prove that I was right. Now I had to tell them the truth, I explained, "It is surrounded by Watchmen."

Each person had a look of disappointment on their face. All the work they did. To be so close and to come up short. Now I had to find a way to convince them we hadn't lost anything. I said, "If there is one, there are others."

We headed home together. I was quietly thinking of how we could get past the security system. Being so close to Watchmen headquarters could be a blessing. It forced me to think about how to remain up there once I made it. My status was terminated once I was thrown down in the Underground. Up there, I will have nothing. If I were to be caught, I would find myself down here again or worse. What we need are papers so I can move through the city levels. That gave me an idea.

Once I made it home. I immediately sat down, securing a pen and paper, and wrote a letter to Cassandra. I needed her help. The fact that Jenna had a pistol convinced me that Disrupters have connections up above. In case you are wondering why I didn't send the letter to Jenna and the other Disrupters. I don't trust them. I do trust Samantha. Besides, Jenna is no fool; she had thought of the same idea. I'm not going to be so naive as to trust her to mention anybody outside their group.

Early tomorrow morning, I will leave alone for the clinic. Samantha is about to finish her first deployment here. In a couple of days, she will be leaving for home. When I arrived at the clinic, I found a crowd of people had already gathered. A dozen receptionists have started to process each visitor. Each one decided who should be seen first. I had taken my place in line. An hour later, I asked to see her. Another twenty minutes passed until I was permitted to see her. She was already exhausted from the morning rush. I handed her the letter. She promised to deliver it as soon as she arrived home. I thanked her and headed home.

I then headed to Central Gardens to join the others. Believing it would be logical that a forgotten aqueduct existed, like in Battery Gardens. Last night, I looked at the map and discovered that part of Central Gardens is over Central Rotunda. Sheppard didn't like having us look around. For the first time, he refused my request in my search. Word of our discovery had spread far beyond our gang and Flynn's. Almost immediately, groups of people had gathered to inquire about this possible escape route since last night. Someone with an abundance of patience like Sheppard had worn thin. I sent the others to the northern part of the Garden. I was thinking about looking around on my own at the Rotunda.

As I arrived at the Rotunda, there was a commotion. I quickly headed over to see what was going on. Standing at the center of it all was Sheppard, trying to be a peacemaker. As I got closer, I saw Bell and Dylan restraining Paloma. At the top of her lungs, she was screaming obscenities at a group of visitors, she was promising to kill them. Moving closer, I quickly found who she had directed her venom toward. It was Fontaine, the leader of the river pirates. He was standing there, amused by Paloma's outburst. Not one to take any chances, I pulled out my stinger and held it to my side. I immediately understood why Paloma was acting the way she was. Fontaine and Brenden, and their surviving pirates had come to the rotunda. This was their fate. Right now, Paloma needs my help. I walked up to her and whispered in her ear. Her eyes were full of tears as she looked over at me. She calmed down. I looked over at Fontaine, and as I expected, he immediately recognized me.

"Is this your little whore?" he asked, not caring about an answer he added, "Keep a leash on her." That enraged her again. I placed my left hand firmly on her shoulder, and she calmed down.

In a rare display of anger, Sheppard exclaimed, "Get her out of here."

I had to drag her to our space. She was fighting me at every step we had taken together. I had never seen this side of her. Not that I could blame her; she had lost a lot since I had known her. Being powerless to stop the killing of her family and friends had taken a heavy toll on her. Now, with a chance of revenge, maybe the dead will rest easy. But she had to learn that vengeance requires patience.

At our den, I threw her to the ground. When she tried to get up. I managed to stop her. Pulling her knife, she held it in front of my face.

"Killing me won't help you."

Reason returned to her eyes as she lowered her dagger. Her rage had left her, and it was replaced by despair. I tried to comfort her by placing my arms around her. She pulled away in revulsion. I just allowed her to have a moment alone.

An hour later, Aida came up to see how Paloma was. Paloma refused to look up at her. She needed to punish everybody who denied her revenge.

"I want to understand," Aida said. "Please help me."

Paloma looked up at her. She then told her story of how she came to Gotham and was eventually cast down into the Underground. I had heard the story before from Cassandra's perspective. When she was finished, Aida was near tears. She embraced her.

"I'll explain it to my grandfather. You won't be forced to leave," she assured her.

That night we slept apart. What peace she had found with me over the winter was gone. She had returned to a person of rage when I first saw her that night. By morning, she was still withdrawn. When it was time for me to leave, she said nothing. I asked Isabella to keep an eye on her.

Later that day, I returned home after failing to find an alternative escape route. It is getting frustrating; it makes no sense that there were no aqueducts underneath Central Garden. But we had covered the entire area of the Garden and found nothing. That night, sitting alone in bed, I took out the map. I was alone. Paloma took her things and found another space near Isabelle and Ethan. Isabella had told me when I first arrived that Paloma neither ate nor spoke all day. She just lay down in a little ball. I decided to give her some space for now.

With what I had learned from reexamining Battery Garden. I tried to see what I had missed. That is when I noticed a third large park in Gotham. It is called Castle Garden right on the river. I had never known of its existence. I decided to take half the group there and the rest will head to York Gardens. Placing it down I looked over at Paloma. She was sleeping peacefully, for a change.

Now alone, I decided to walk around the Rotunda for a little while. Quietly, I headed down to the main level. People are still wondering about the encirclement, looking for something to trade. Others were heading to whatever home they had made down here. As for me, I was lost in thought. When I felt a hand on my shoulder, it brought me into the present. I looked over and saw Sheppard standing next to me. He had a pleasant smile, and he wanted to give me a lecture; I knew I had to listen.

"How is Paloma?"

"She is dead inside."

"Maybe you should stay with her."

"I have people counting on me," I stated, looking for the others. "Besides, she doesn't want me around."

Here comes the lecture: "Are you sure it is others you care about or what you want?" Damn it. I knew he would bring that up, he added, "She thinks you're going to abandon her at the first chance you will get."

"I never lied to her."

"She will be happier if you are content with staying down here with her."

I can't give up now. To stay in constant darkness. It wasn't an option I would settle for. Somehow, Sheppard understood what I was feeling. He said, "Maybe you both must learn to let go."

He might have something there, maybe we should let go of what we have lost. We are both running from ghosts. But there was something I needed to ask him, "Would you raise a child here?"

He hesitated for a moment to ponder my question. Children were born down here. Almost all had died in a few years. He admitted calmly, "Then maybe you should continue."

"When I come back, I'll talk with her again." I conceded.

"In that case, there is a place you should look at. I'll show you when you come back." Sheppard walked away.

When the others arrived, I told them about our new location. We agreed to split into two groups. Julius and I will go to Castle Gardens. Kristoph will lead the others to York Gardens. With that settled, we separated on our missions.

Julius and I had managed to find an easy path through an old, abandoned tunnel that everybody else but him had forgotten. With two lanterns we walked down the tunnel. We splashed through ankle-high water. That is why this tunnel was abandoned long ago, it was built too close to the water, making it impossible for people to live down here.

Julius was still an enigma. He rarely gave me a friendly word or smile. To my surprise, he chose to break the silence by singing. I was amazed at his talent. He was as good as Gabrielle. I thought they could be friends if they ever met. Taking my picture out, I had to take another look at her. I held it close to the light as I stopped for a moment. Julius had noticed that I had stopped for a moment. He walked back to see what I was doing.

"What do you have up there?" he asked me. I responded by handing him my picture. He took it and pulled it against his light. A look of understanding came over him. "She is pretty." He handed me my picture back.

"She is the reason I'm doing all this," I replied.

We continued. As we walked, he asked, "What had happened?"

"Our patron had other ideas for Gabrielle, and I was in the way."

Somehow, he understood. We made it underneath Castle Garden. Julius made it to an area he was familiar with. The water was at our knees when we made it to a ladder carved in stone. Julius looked around as he remembered something about this area.

"About thirty of us lived here when I first came here," he opened with, "Believe it or not, when you looked up there you could see the sky." Instinctively, I looked up and saw only darkness. He continued, "Only six of us didn't drown when they sent a deluge and forced us out. I haven't been back since."

Without saying a word, I started to climb. After I returned my lantern to my belt. Julius was right behind me. As we climbed, he told me how he found himself down here.

Julius was a Cager. A good one, he was annoyed that I had never heard of him. I explained I hadn't lived here that long, and that had satisfied him of my ignorance. He told me that he had played Center for Queens. With pride, he boasted that he led them to two championships. That was when he was at the height of his fame. His fall came when a younger player wanted his position. The young player had to settle for being his wingman. During the opening game, he and his wingman were making a play together; the play was simple, and they had done it perfectly a hundred times before. It was simple: their leader threw a pass to Julius, and his nameless winger would provide an escort. His teammate purposely missed his block. Allowing three opponents to tackle him. Julius didn't get up. While he was being treated by the medical staff, that bastard came over to gloat over his victory.

After finishing, I reached the top and felt a recently placed wooden lid with my right hand. The wood didn't feel rotten, so I grabbed my dagger with my right hand and searched for the lid's edges to find a latch. Once I found the latch, I replaced my dagger with my stinger and managed to pulverize the latch. After putting my stinger back in its sheath, I opened the wooden door and carefully pulled myself out of the shaft. As I stood up, I couldn't believe my eyes as I saw the sun shining through the window. Julius climbed out and joined me. A rare smile came to him.

We walked down a hallway and found some stairs. At the top of the stairs, Julius managed to jimmy the door open. He opened the door carefully, and as he did, we found our second escape route.

We walked out of a stone arch that sat off some ruins. Around us stood larger buildings that were built as some kind of vanity project of an ancient Highlander. After his death, he gave it to the people of Gotham to enjoy. Not knowing that most of the citizens would be denied access. Strange people, these ancients.

For an hour, we walked around the park. It was a nice change for us. We managed to find that the security was lighter here, making it possible for us to escape. We will need papers to get through security, but we could disappear. For now, we have accomplished our mission. We headed for home.

I left Julius at North Rotunda. He immediately reported to Flynn. Alone, I walked the remainder. My thoughts had turned to Paloma. What would I say to her? I had no answer to that question. I knew that I had to think of something. Many things stand between us right now. How can I convince her to let go when I refuse to? But I must try. I do care for her.

Moving through the crowd of people walking through, I was determined to get home as fast as I could. With the rotunda in sight, I felt some apprehension, It was time to confront Paloma. Somehow, I managed to enter the rotunda without being seen. Immediately I walked up the stairs and entered the hallway that is our home.

Isabella came up to greet me. I looked over at Paloma and found she hadn't moved. I told Illyana about the second escape route. She was pleased. Ethan and the others are still not home. I reassured her that they had a long journey. She understood and headed back to her den. I walked up to join Paloma.

I sat down in front of her. She refused to lift her head to acknowledge me, but she knew I was there. I stared at her momentarily, trying to think of something to say. Then I decided to try, "Paloma, "I said, her head looking at a spot on the floor, "Is there something interesting on the ground?"

Still, she didn't respond. Right now, I am getting annoyed. I exclaimed, "This must stop!" That didn't work, so I decided to try something different. In a softer tone, I said to her, "We agreed to be together. I want to help."

From her position, she murmured, "You don't care."

"That isn't true," I replied, happy I had finally gotten a response from her, granted it was a small one. It's a start. I told her, "You must have hated your family."

She looked up at me. Her eyes were red from crying. Anger returned to her eyes, and with venom, she said, "What do you mean?"

What did I mean? I needed to find an answer quickly. I replied, "If you loved them, you would honor them by surviving. Revenge only serves you." That was pretty good. It must have worked; her anger had subsided.

She told me, "I can't."

"You think you're the only person who has lost someone in this world." I moved closer to look her in her eyes. "I lost my home, family, and friends when Cibola attacked my village." For a moment, I needed to gather my thoughts. However, as the images of that day returned to me, I needed to make this point: "If I had gone after them, I would have been killed. I would have never learned that some of my people had survived."

"It's hard."

"I know."

She put her arms around my neck. Placing her head on my chest, I gently caressed her hair. After a moment, she looked up and smiled at me. "Let's go home."

We returned to our den. I helped her carry her stuff and put it away. Once she settled in, she immediately grabbed a power bar and wolfed it down before me. She explained, "I didn't eat for two days." I didn't need to say anything. I just handed her a vitamin bar. She ate that quickly as well.

Paloma had a look of concern. She looked like somebody had come to take me away. I immediately turned over my shoulder. It was Jenna. She had a folded piece of paper in her hand.

Coldly, Jenna handed me the paper. She said, "It's from Cassandra."

I quickly read it. A smile came over me.

Paloma asked, "What does she say?"

"She says hello," I told her, "They will help us."

Jenna stated, "We want to join you."

"Can you be here tomorrow?"

"We will be here." After saying that, she left us.

I looked over at Paloma, who looked sad about the news. I knew why she was depressed. She is afraid that if we return to the surface, I will return to Gabrielle. "There is no guarantee she will take me back," I reassured her.

From the rotunda, we heard Kristoph calling my name. I held out my hand for her to take. Reluctant at first, she finally grabbed it. We walked over to the entranceway. Below us was Kristoph bellowing to all that would hear that he had found a way out of here. A crowd of people began to gather around him for details. Not amused was Sheppard, along with Bell, Ethan, and Lionel, who arrived to silence him. They quickly ushered him away into a side apartment. Illyana joined us as we watched the crowd disperse in different directions. Determined to spread the news of escape all over the Underground.

Aida came up to see us. She was visibly not happy with me. It was clear that she held me responsible for Kristoph.

"My grandfather wants to see you now," she commanded.

I followed her to that side room. Inside his little office, Sheppard had gathered all his chief aids for this meeting. He stood in the center of the room, Kristoph sitting next to him. With both of his hands on his forehead, he realized what he had done. I was amused, although I did my best to hide it. Sheppard saw me and looked over at Kristoph.

"Give Duncan his report," Sheppard told him.

Removing his hand from his forehead and standing up, he said, "We found seven passages in York Gardens."

"Are you sure?"

"We all had used them," he said, looking at Ethan. "Tell him, Ethan."

Ethan supported him, "He is telling the truth."

"Did you tell Flynn?"

"His men did."

"We will be meeting with Disrupters tomorrow on how we go further," I told them.

Lionel added, "What about the others?"

Sheppard said, "Kristoph had been drinking heavily today. He was not making any sense." He looked over at me and then at Kristoph, "Do you understand?"

That was not a question. It was an order, and everybody in the room understood it. We all agreed.

―――――

Early tomorrow morning, Flynn and his entourage will arrive. Jenna and three other Disrupters arrived a few minutes later. None of her friends I had met before. Sheppard offered to serve as an arbitrator since it was clear to us all that he had no desire to leave the Underground.

In his makeshift private office that serves as his living quarters. In total, about a dozen of us crammed into this room. All were looking at me to give a report. Sheppard then looked at me and permitted me to start the meeting.

I eagerly reported, "We have found three escape routes. All three lead to a Garden."

"We will need papers to leave each Garden," Flynn stated, still seated, with his entourage. That means we will be right back here."

A murmur rose through all three factions. Only Sheppard remained silent. Flynn was right, but we had a solution. "We have friends up above that can help us get papers."

"We just need to know how many to smuggle down." Jenna had interrupted me, but I didn't mind.

Flynn asked, "How long will that take?"

"About a month?" Jenna answered, she added, "The faster you can get me the information. The faster I can pass it along."

That satisfied Flynn. He promised to get a number tomorrow. Jenna agreed to Flynn's promise. Taking responsibility for our group, Sheppard agreed to fulfill his part. With no other business before us, he adjourned the meeting.

We all left the office. I was about to do the same when Sheppard stopped me. As we remained alone, he wanted to ask me a favor, but didn't know how to say it. I had an idea of what he wanted. Although he made it clear that he desired to remain down here. His grandchildren should have a chance of living on the surface. He fears they will stay down here out of loyalty to him.

"Even if you have to tie up Aida, I want you to take her when you leave."

That surprised me. I had expected that he would ask if both Aida and Lionel would leave with us. My curiosity had arisen, and I was compelled to ask, "What about Lionel?"

He explained, "Lionel's talents serve him better down here. If he does want to leave with you, I won't stand in his way." I understood. I had expected both would want to stay behind him. "But I want you to promise me to take care of her."

"If I make it up there. I'm not planning to stay in Gotham." I told him. I wanted to make sure he understood that.

He said honestly, "Anywhere up there is better than down here."

"I will keep her safe," I promised him.

We walked out of his office together. Kristoph stood there waiting for us. He was concerned about something that he saw.

"Flynn is up to something, "he stated, looking over at a crowd of people who had left with Flynn and his people.

Sheppard stated, "We made an agreement with them."

I agreed with Sheppard and headed home.

I made it home in a few minutes. I found Paloma waiting for me in our den. Her body was lying on a new mattress she had discovered the previous week. Back then, she was quite proud of her discovery, but that seemed long ago. A lot has happened to us since then. She had refused to go with me to the meeting. It was clear that she had disdained our endeavor. Believing it will end our relationship. Somehow, I had to convince her I would never leave her down here.

"How did your meeting go?" She sniped at me. Her back was to me when I gently placed my hand on her shoulder to comfort her. She didn't flinch.

"It went well. We will be leaving in a month." I replied, "Aida will be joining us."

"I'm not going."

I turned her flat on her back, hovering over her, I said, "Listen to me. If you stay down here, I'm staying here with you."

She turned her head away from me. Her eyes teared up when she said, "Then you will hate me."

"Not true," I told her, "I need to know you will be all right. Whatever happens up there, I will never hold you to anything."

I lowered myself and kissed her. Today is the only thing that matters.

I sent Ethan and Isabella down to South Rotunda with our list of candidates for our escape. To my surprise, Bell had chosen to stay down with Sheppard. Like Lionel, he felt loyalty to Sheppard and his work in the Underground. I never expected Kristoph to abandon Sheppard either, I was proven right. In total, we made seven requests for papers in our escape. They both volunteered for this mission. I had chosen to remain with Paloma for the day. I didn't mind.

Together, we did our chores. We spent our time around the Rotunda helping visitors gather supplies. This was the first time for me. Most of the time, I was sent off to scrounge for discarded items.

I found the work boring. I anxiously kept glancing at my watch, waiting for our shift to end. Paloma was happy. That was worth being bored.

Aida arrived to give us a hand. She was upset. I knew why she had found out that she was going with us, no matter if she liked it or not. And she didn't.

"Let me make this very clear. I'll go with you, but I'll be walking out, not carried."

"Understood."

Now that we had an understanding, her mood had changed. She understood that her grandfather was thinking about what was best for her.

By noon, Ethan and Isabella had returned home. Their mission was now complete. They were joined by Titus and Jerome, who had delivered Flynn's list. Both men had survived in the Wastelands as hunters. They worked together hunting prey for anybody who would pay them. They had admitted to me that they worked for Cibola. They confessed to me that they had been hired by Overseers to find three fugitives: a man and two women. I didn't tell them that they had found one of them. Not that they cared. When Cibola was attacked, they lost interest. They arrived in Gotham for a job, and when it was over, they were cast down into Black Level.

Ethan was far different. He lived in the lands north of Cibola. He was cast down here for poaching. He fished in the waters that Cibola believed to be theirs. He was captured and sentenced. That was five years ago.

For each of them. Who am I to judge? With what I had done and how I came down here, I was no better than either.

"How did it go?" I asked.

"Flynn wants a hundred passes." Jerome stated, amused, "he plans to sell the others."

"As long as you get yours, I don't care."

"We will be with you when the time comes," Titus proclaimed.

"I'll see you guys tomorrow."

They left us. Ethan looked at me and asked, "What's tomorrow?"

"There are other ways to escape."

Sheppard joined us.

"Trouble?" he asked.

"It seems Flynn is planning a business venture."

"I'm not surprised." He said, amused at the obvious double-cross by Flynn. It wasn't out of character. If he and his gang can make out to the surface, he will be back down to the depths of Black Level. His organization is too small to flourish in Gotham. That was what Trey had told me during a search a couple of weeks ago. They were defeated in a power struggle against Caitlyn and her organization. She does have a talent for making enemies.

A loud mechanical sound was heard all over the underground. Sheppard immediately looked around. A look of dread came over his face. He knew what it meant. As I looked around there were many people who had concern on their faces.

"They can't be doing it again," muttered Sheppard.

Aida had joined her grandfather, and for the first time, I saw fear in her eyes.

People began to rush into the Rotunda in a panic. Kristoph and Bell tried to control the scared crowd. Lionel and three others came to help them. All this time, Sheppard stood frozen.

"What's going on?" I asked Sheppard.

He didn't respond. Ethan spoke for him, "Sometimes Gotham will flood the fringes of the Underground."

"Why?"

"Because they can," Ethan said bitterly.

"Those poor people," Isabella interjected.

Looking back at that moment, I didn't know what had come over me. If I stopped to think about it, I wouldn't have done what I did. All I knew was that I had to do something.

"Ethan, get some rope and torches!" I told him. I ran off to where the screams were coming from.

––––––––––

At first, I was running blindly. I'm not sure where I needed to go. It was when Bell and Kristoph caught up to me. They led me to where the zenith of the flooding was happening. We made it to the edge of the water. In the darkness, we could see people struggling through the water to safety. The lights had been shut out during the deluge. In near darkness, I walked inside the tunnel. The water was up to my knees when I saw the first of the poor souls. They were thankful to see my light. They passed me. As I headed onward alone. The water quickly came up to my waist as I saw a score of people who immediately came towards me. From a distance, I heard the screams of others trapped in the rising water.

"Ethan has come with others," he told me, "Isabella had gone to get your friends."

I nodded and continued into the cold water. Kristoph followed. Fortunately, the water remained at our waist for a few more meters.

Gradually, others managed to see us and came to us. Somehow, they knew we represented the path to safety. At this time, Bell had joined us. We decided to stay together and pressed on. As we walked, the water became deeper. We passed the bodies of poor souls who had quickly drowned in the rising water. With the water at my chest, we were risking our own lives if we pushed on. Already, my muscles began to go numb in the cold water. But I still heard the voices of people calling out in despair.

"If you can hear me, follow my voice," I exclaimed at a volume that I had never reached before. It had worked when people began to come to us. Bell and Kristoph did the same, and more people came to us. Soon, others joined us. I decided to take a few more steps, but that proved to be a mistake. I immediately went underwater. Only Kristoph kept me from becoming another victim, as he pulled me to my feet. With my hand, I removed the hair from my face. I tasted the water, and it was salty. Not that it mattered. With the voices dying down, we decided to head back.

We tried to follow the way we had come, the best we could. Bell led us as the water slowly fell to our knees. Then I heard some other cries for help. They came from another passageway. I didn't notice it before. I decided to risk it. Bell remained in the main passageway as Kristoph, and I followed the voices. With the water remaining at our knees, we could follow the tunnel even deeper into the maze. Both of us took turns calling out for the survivors. Finally, they responded to our calls.

Passing through a large archway, we saw a sorry sight. Two dozen people were trapped. Surrounded by bodies of people who had drowned, many were children. Those who remained alive were stuck on some foundation that gave them a brief respite from the rising water. It was clear that it was temporary. What made it worse was that the water around them couldn't be waded, and the current was too strong to swim against.

I had an idea. Immediately, I turned to Kristoph and said, "Get me some rope." He ran off.

I looked around for something to secure the rope. I found a ledge that was still above the water line. I stepped carefully on it to see if I could find an alternative route. Keeping my hands along the wall, I walked down it and found another passageway. With my torch lighting the way, I investigated the next room. I saw more people trapped in the same structure behind me. Four children were in a dire situation as they were treading water. I stood there contemplating my next move. If the others didn't get back here soon, I would have to risk swimming in the treacherous water alone. The room was full of others who tried and failed to escape the flood.

Then I felt something grab my ankle. Looking down, I saw a woman holding onto my ankle. I pulled her up to safety. I told her to go down the ledge, and she will be safe. She refused.

"Not without my children," she cried out. I glanced at the four children. My option had gone, and I had to try to swim through the current.

"Duncan!" Kristoph had returned with more help.

I told him, "We need to act fast. Bring the rope to me." Looking over the other victims, I knew I couldn't do both. "One of you will have to help them."

Wes volunteered to bring the rope to the other victims. He understood what I was thinking. He tied the rope around his waist. I saw Trey tie the rope securely on a post. Kristoph brought me the rope. While I tied it on my waist, I heard Wes's dive into the water. Kristoph secured the rope. I had dived into the dark water. With the young woman, Kristoph held the rope, making sure the current didn't carry me away. It wasn't easy, but I made it.

Calmly, I tied the rope and told the children what we were going to do. I had placed the children in front of me, and with our hands firmly on the rope, we waded through the current. Making it to the archway. Bell and Kristoph pulled each child out of the water. Ethan took them away to safety. Wes had already finished with his quarry. I listened to other voices in the darkness. All I heard was the rushing water. We headed back to safety.

———

When we made it to the Rotunda, Sheppard had set up a shelter for the displaced people. I was soaked through, so I headed home. Paloma was nowhere to be found. Nobody knew where she was. Aida arrived with some new clothes. She smiled as she turned around to give me privacy. When I finished, I told her she could turn around. Her eyes widened as she was instantly proud of herself for her taste in clothes.

"What happened to Paloma?" I asked.

Concerned, she said, "Her friends had come for her."

"Where are they?"

"York." She replied, "But we need help here." I understood. We had people who needed help.

7   ESCAPE

AFTER A WEEK, THE WATER STILL HADN'T SUBSIDED, FORCING the survivors to find refuge in safer areas. Rumors were spreading in the Underground that Gotham was planning to flood all of Black Section, killing everyone. It wasn't out of the realm of possibility, after all, who was living on the surface would care if thousands of people died in the depths of the city? Nobody. A belief that I shared with others.

The city wasn't helping matters. Recovery was up to us. The government gave us no help. To make things worse, they announced they were lowering all rations. More radical agitators began reminding us that we had all been forgotten. They called for us to rise in revolt and reminded them we were here. A thought that I couldn't support, we have no weapons to speak of, it would be a slaughter. However, to some, suicide would be better than living down here. I couldn't disagree with that. But something had to be done.

Underneath the growing tension down here was some hope. This flood was less devastating than previous disasters. Sheppard has become a hero; he was given credit for rescuing hundreds of people from drowning. The credit for his actions, he modestly denied. I disagreed. I was one of five different groups that he had sent to help those who were trapped. One he had led personally. All of them were better organized than mine. Flynn, ironically, had been given some credit as well, for the actions of his men, in contrast with Sheppard, whom he accepted with pleasure.

As for me, I had other matters to attend to. Paloma was still missing, and I was determined to find her. Seven times I had left for York alone, trying to find Paloma's old gang, but nobody was talking. It wasn't hard to figure out why; I was a stranger. I quickly knew that this would not be easy. On the eighth day, Ethan volunteered to join me. He had some knowledge of York. Along with some countrymen who lived there.

He led me to the northwestern corner of York. There stood two dozen makeshift tents, and two fire pits created for cooking and providing heat for the people. Ethan led me inside the small community. As we made our way to the center, the inhabitants made their way out of their tents. I counted about forty men, twenty women, and a dozen children. From the crowd, three men and one woman came to the forefront. All four smiled when they saw Ethan and greeted him. That gave me some relief.

The woman of the group came up to him, she stroked his chin, and smiled, "Still vain, I see, keeping that pretty face bare."

One of the other men cried out, "Without a mate, he is still not a man." The crowd laughed to show their agreement with his statement. I looked around and noticed all the men who were old enough had a beard. Feeling insecure, I felt my chin had some hair growth on it, maybe that was enough to satisfy them.

"Who is your pretty friend?" she asked, looking at me with contempt. That made it clear to me that they weren't impressed with me.

Ethan introduced me, "This is my friend Duncan Walker." I stepped forward to present myself to them. Ethan continued, "This is Rachel Pierce-Stark. Her husband, Caleb Stark." It was Caleb who had made the critique of his manhood and mine.

"Why so many names?" I muttered loud enough for them to hear.

"We follow the practice of our forefathers," Caleb explained to me.

This is going well, I thought to myself. I looked over at Ethan for help. He then introduced the other two men, "This is Seth Mullins and Miles Briggs." The two men nodded at me a greeting. I did the same. Thinking it will be better to keep my mouth shut. Ethan looked over at Rachel and asked her, "How about Sarah and Gideon?"

"They are well," she replied, "They are out forging. You remember you have no claim to her."

Ethan lowered his head and whispered, "I know."

"What brings you here?" asked Caleb.

"We are looking for a friend of ours. Her people came from here." Ethan went on to describe the gang and how they came across Paloma.

His four kinsmen huddled in discussion, finally Rachel stepped forward and answered, "The Hoodies."

"Cowards," Miles added. "They kill you as you sleep."

Seth finished with, "We lost four to them. Before we punished them."

"Where are they now?" I asked them.

All four of them looked at me with disdain. Ignoring me, Miles directed his answer to Ethan, "They are with the shadows."

With a step, I tried to assert myself in this conversation. Other men step forward to intimidate me. They succeeded. I didn't know what would happen next. What happened nobody could see. A young girl, about ten, came forward. She was tall and thin with long blond hair and blue eyes. She wore a simple dress made from fabric that was never intended to be used as clothing. But they had no other choice. With a rare friendly smile, she ran up and hugged me. Rachel grabbed the young girl.

"Leah, what are you doing?" She cried.

"Mother, this is the man I told you about. He saved me from the water last week," she answered. "I want to thank you." She didn't need to thank me. Her actions right now, paid me back three times. I was the one who needed to thank her.

Caleb walked forward, embraced me, and said to all who could hear, "You are welcome in my home."

Moved by his kind gesture, and promised him the same courtesy in my home. After that, things went well. They told me it was Tunnel 7 that the Hoodies had retreated to. Somehow, it was spared by the deluge. That will be the place I will go to tomorrow. On the way home, I had to ask what his second name was. He answered," Peck."

That morning, I was preparing my weapons for what reckoning I would face today. I had decided to borrow another dagger from a table. Aida saw me take it last night but said nothing. I couldn't eat breakfast. With my weapons ready, I gave myself a final check. Satisfied, I started to leave. Isabella sat there crying, she would not say a word to me. I bent down to reassure her that I was coming back to her. Fontaine and his gang didn't scare me; I had dealt with him before and found him quite dumb. That is what I told her. Isabella nodded, and I went on my way.

If she believed me, I didn't know. But I'm not a fool. Living in the Wastelands, I lived by a set of rules. Recently, I broke some of them. One rule I dare not break is: never to underestimate your opponent. I wasn't lying about Fontaine; he was quite stupid, but sometimes an idiot could get lucky. I had to make sure it wasn't today.

When I descended the stairs, I found four obstacles standing in my way. They were by the name of: Bell, Kristoph, Dylan, and Ethan.

"You are not going anywhere without us," Kristoph told me.

I replied, "This is my fight."

"We are either going with you or not at all," Ethan stated with a rare firmness I had never seen before.

"How could I say no?"

"All right, we'll go together. But let me go in first alone."

Ethan interjected, "You will be walking into a trap."

"I know," I replied confidently, "then you will spring ours."

"I see what you're getting at," Bell stated. He doesn't say much, but he listens very well.

We headed off together.

I walked down Tunnel 7 alone. The others had promised to give me a half-hour before they followed me. I was being watched; that much was clear. The same people who stalked and tried to attack us last year were still around. Still, shadows are moving at the fringes of sight. I paid them no mind. They were not the problem.

A figure came to me from the darkness. Standing right in front of me was a short person with their head completely covered by a tightly fitted hood. The way the figure wore their clothes, I couldn't tell whether the person was male or female.

"You're here for Paloma?" The hoodie asked. I nodded my head. The person smiled and said, "Come with me."

While the person led me further into the darkness. I dropped two small beacons, having a time delay so they will send out a signal in half hour for the others to follow. Heading down the hallway I immediately recognized the area where I had been the previous year. We followed the hallway to the source of the light. It illuminated a metal door that was closed.

Hoodie turned to me and said," She is in there."

"Open it."

Hoodie turned to open the door. While she did, I pulled out my new dagger and hid it behind my back. The door made a terrible screech as she pushed it open. So much for the element of surprise. With a sinister smile, Hoodie turned to me and led me into the room. She stopped after a few steps. There in the light was Paloma.

She was tied firmly to a chair. Ropes were tied around her ankles and knees. Her hands were fastened behind her, and more rope secured her to a chair underneath her breast. Her mouth was gagged, so she couldn't scream out. But she was still struggling to free herself.

Out of the corner of my eye, I saw Hoodie pull a knife of her own. She stated, "Here she is."

Before she could react, I sliced her neck with my dagger. Her face looked shocked that she would be dying soon. Taking out my stinger with my left hand, I walked into the light. Paloma's eyes teared up when she saw me. But she was shaking her head. I knew she was trying to warn me of the impending trap.

We didn't have much time. I quickly cut her bonds and freed her from the chair. While I freed her legs, she took off her gag.

After taking a moment to catch her breath, she said, "You can't be here; it's a trap."

Almost finished, I looked up and stated, "I know."

Looking over at the corpse of her former gang member, she stated, "I thought they were my friends." Her legs faltered when she rose from her chair after being confined for so long. She fell into my arms, and carefully I caught her, keeping her steady until she could regain her strength. I handed her the new knife. Wasting no time, we started to leave when a new set of lights came on. Stepping inside, the light Fontaine, along with twenty of his gang, surrounded us. His trap was set. In a vain attempt to protect Paloma, I shielded her by putting myself between Fontaine and her. Fontaine hesitated for a moment, like a predator who wants to torment his prey before killing him. I knew my part in this.

"You had cost me a lot," Fontaine stated. Moving his head, he addressed somebody else, "You three did a good job."

"Glad to help," replied somebody from behind. Paloma screamed as if something had stroked her hair. Turning, I saw Brenden with three Hoodies standing too close to us. How did they get this close? With my left arm, I guided Paloma away from them.

"Your friend there did a good job getting you here," Fontaine stated proudly. Just keep talking. "She thinks that I would remember her. I don't."

The leader of the Hoodies, who wore red, added, "She was like that."

"You were my friends," she told Red.

That's it, somebody, keep talking for a few more minutes.

Paloma looked at me and whispered, "Duncan, I'm sorry." I just smiled at her, trying to reassure her that we would get out of this somehow.

Fontaine stepped forward; he was holding a pistol. "I'm going to enjoy this."

I saw my chance. Adjusting my dagger so I would be ready to throw it if I needed to, I asked, "You're going to shoot me?" I gave him a mocking smile. "I saw your aim. You couldn't hit the deck of your boat if you were standing on it."

His men laughed. I had hit a nerve. Fontaine replied, "I'm going to enjoy them beating you down."

"You're going to need more men," I boasted.

"A lot more men." Fontaine immediately turned around to see who had said it. It was Kristoph. Our trap was sprung. Standing with him were eight others. Trey and Jerome had pistols of their own. Where did they get those guns? And why didn't anybody give me one?

Before Fontaine could react, I threw my dagger and disarmed him. He was going to be mine. I lunged at him, hitting him in the right arm with my stinger. He winced in pain. Not wanting to stop, I placed the stinger on his arm to give him some extra pain. Paloma's cries for help stopped me. Immediately, my attention turned towards her, and I saw that she was cornered by her three former friends. Rushing to her aid, together, we manage to drive them off. We then joined the others.

Although outnumbered, my friends and I were all far better fighters very quickly; those who could still run did, leaving their fallen comrades behind. Paloma rushed to me and embraced me. She thought it was over. Unfortunately, it wasn't. Fontaine had regained his pistol. With his left hand, he held it up, ready to kill us both. He never had a chance. His face suddenly contorted into a look of shock and pain. He fell face-first to the ground with a hatchet in his back. With no emotion, Wes simply retrieved his hatchet and returned it to his belt. Brenden had abandoned his friend.

"You are slipping, Duncan," he told me.

Before anybody else thought about it, I took his pistol. The others did the same, taking their bounty from a great victory.

We made love that night. A weight had lifted from her. It gave her a sense of relief that now she could move forward with her life. She had no hate in her heart. I told her the story about why Fontaine had wanted to kill me. She was happy that I had a hand in defeating the river pirates. But she was upset that Mitchel was still alive and had killed Olivia. I wasn't sure if it was right to tell her that. I felt she had a right to know how I had failed Olivia.

To quell the rising tide of tension in the Underground. Sheppard had agreed to host a conference of gang leaders to decide what would be an appropriate response. Although the waters had subsided. The outrage still lingered, even after two weeks.

Delegates from six districts arrived at the Central Rotunda. Paloma and Issabela counted each delegation as it arrived. The rest of us were busy taking the tables and merchandise away to make room for the large crowd. After the last delegate arrived, the two girls reported to Sheppard that there were 634.

He thanked the girls and headed up to the highest point of the Rotunda with his grandchildren at his side. At his right stood Flynn, and on his right stood Jenna, representing the Disrupters. On the other side of the upper level were the leaders of one gang in each section, in total thirteen delegates were overlooking the others. The room was full of people arguing about what they were going to do about this latest insult.

As for me, I had chosen it was best to stay out of it and watch. Paloma was sitting with me. Isabelle and Ethan chose to hide in their den. I had a good idea of why one of the gang leaders must have been her keeper. Keeping order became the job of Kristoph and Bell. They had a tough job ahead of them.

After twenty minutes of an endless chorus of arguing, Sheppard asked for silence. With Kristoph and his men policing the crowd, it gave Sheppard what he wanted.

"I understand your anger," he calmly addressed the crowd. "What we do must be thought out. We can't be rash." The crowd remained silent for a moment. Many of them knew that violence would play into Watchmen's hands.

From the floor, Rachel Stark shouted, "We must do something!' Others joined her in support.

Another woman stated, "They are murderers."

That brought the radicals out. They want war. Never mind, it will lead to their destruction. But I agreed with Rachel and the other woman that something had to be done. They can't get away with this. An idea came over me: escape. A mass escape will send a clear message to the people on the surface. But it can't be small, somehow, it must be in the thousands. Then I thought about Robert and Cassandra, who could help.

I stood up. "Escape!" Everybody in the crowd turned to me. Escaping the abyss is a dream for all of them. "We have friends up there. They can shut down the security systems, and we can rush out in masses."

A man, a little older than Sheppard with short white hair, said, "How long will this take?"

I looked at Jenna, hoping she would be my lifeline. Jenna gave me a dirty look, which made me worried. Finally, she said," We will need a month."

The people on the floor called for a vote. Sheppard agreed and called a vote. All agreed. A mass escape would be launched, causing chaos. It was then decided that the mass exodus would happen a month from today. A cheer came across the assembly. For the first time in a long time, they had hope. Kristoph and Bell led them to the exits.

Walking through the crowd, Jenna stormed over to Paloma and me. He exclaimed, "How many fucking papers do I have to make?" It wasn't a question. And she quickly showed that she wasn't done asking rhetorical questions, "Not to mention. How are we supposed to shut down the security system?"

Amused, I replied to her first question, "You're Disrupters; it should be second nature."

"We have never done anything like that before."

"Now is a good time to start," I said. Maybe they will take you seriously."

She revealed, "I'll contact the others. We have made extra passes."

"We can use them."

She walked off. Leaving Paloma alone with me. We all had work to do.

Over the next month, detailed plans were made. The attending gangs had chosen twenty leaders to join Sheppard in organizing the mass exodus. Every member of the newly formed committee agreed this undertaking couldn't be just a mass escape. No matter how many manage to get through security, the Watchmen would be able to regain control. It had to be something more. This must be a revolt.

Since this was my idea, Sheppard had me sit in on the meetings. I think it was because he was mad at me. Each time we met for a meeting, Sheppard pulled me aside and told me he didn't like my plan. I said nothing.

A week ago, I confessed to the other members that we had found several escape routes that led to York and Battery Green. The people were not impressed to be stuck in a public park, waiting for the Watchmen to force them back down to the Underground.

"That would be perfect," stated Dustin, a fellow Disrupter. I found him less annoying. "It would be a symbolic act." I had to admit that was a good idea.

Rachel added, "Can't we use something to break through the barriers?"

Everybody looked at Flynn. He answered, "We could make something."

That made the difference. All the members of the committee agreed that three days before the escape we would send people to gather at the garden to occupy them.

Exactly a week before, it was time to go. We had gathered to discuss our escape. Kristoph and Sheppard had asked to sit in.

Despite Flynn's objections, I allowed it. Jenna started to hand out the passes. She had a few extras. When she asked if she had missed anybody, Kristoph raised his hand. Surprised, she handed him his.

He looked at me and said, "Somebody has to watch your back."

I just smiled. But Flynn had pressing matters to address. "Just to be clear, we will be leaving before the others."

"That's the plan," I replied.

That satisfied him. Flynn makes no pretense that he doesn't care about his neighbors. When we dispersed, he came over to talk to me. Paloma joined us. She placed her arms around me. Ignoring her, Flynn said, "When we get up there, I could use you."

I looked at Paloma, but she said nothing. I turned towards Flynn and politely replied, "I can't."

Not one to give up, Flynn said, "Together we can do great things."

"There is only one thing I want up there," I told him. I looked over at Paloma and added, "I have reasons to stay here." She smiled at me and placed her head on my shoulder. Flynn walked away, confused. Amused, Paloma led me to our home.

Early the next morning, Lionel came to visit me. He had a message from Sheppard. He didn't know why, but Sheppard wanted to see me. I told him I would be right down. Paloma was still sleeping, so I quietly got dressed.

When I came in, Sheppard was sitting at his desk. He looked up at me and directed me to take a seat. I did. This was another lecture. It was a matter of time. Finally, he looked up.

"Tonight, I would like you to do security," he started.

"Sure," I said. It wasn't unreasonable for him to ask to stand guard; I hadn't stood guard for over a month.

He continued, "Are you helping the people or yourself?" That was a strange question. Then I thought about it for a moment. He then said, "No matter how it ends, people will die. But you will be free to live your life."

"I did want to help."

"I hope you do. Because we will be left to pick up the pieces." That was all he had to say to me. I quietly left him to his work. I passed Lionel and headed back to my den. Paloma was sitting up. I sat down and kissed her on the cheek. She smiled.

Sensing something was wrong, she asked me, "What did Sheppard want?"

"Nothing," I replied, "he just wanted me to do security tonight."

Her eyes lit up at the prospect of having the rotunda to ourselves. She asked, "Do you want company?"

"I have something to work out. I'll see you tomorrow," I replied, not wanting to disappoint her, but I did. We ate breakfast in silence. For the rest of the day, we remained separated.

That night, after saying goodnight to Poloma, I stood guard alone. She was still not happy. Taking my place on the perch where I could see everything, I started my vigil. There I sat in the darkness, thinking about my life. Who am I? I asked myself. Have I truly evolved from that selfish bastard who uses people for his own needs? And I'm being kind. Or have I truly redeemed myself?

Certainly, the past three years have made up for the previous ten years. Have I truly been selfless in my endeavors? I say yes. I have done enough. Whatever god Sheppard talks to has to be satisfied with me, if not to hell with them. I sat back confident in my conviction that Sheppard was wrong this morning to ask me if I was using these people to cover my own. I looked over at his den, thinking of storming in there and telling him he was wrong.

I turned on my torch and pulled out Gabby's picture. It is a strange thing. When I first came here, I pulled out her picture and looked at it easily four times a day. I spent hours studying every part of her face as I remember that day. Now, I barely look at it. The worst thing was that I noticed water damage. I had forgotten that it was still in my pocket during the deluge. Fortunately, the water damage remained on the edges. Gabrielle's image hadn't been touched.

Looking at her, I began to reconsider my previous conclusion: Memory and conscience can be dangerous allies. I remembered escaping from the Overseers with Gabrielle and Constance. A riot broke out while their neighbors rebelled against the Enforcers. Hundreds of people followed us to freedom. However, the majority were either killed or recaptured, and that wasn't my fault, I told myself; things just got out of hand. I then thought about the doctor. I used him to barter passage for us to Great Junction. Once there, I made a deal for passage east. When the Train People betrayed us. I fired at the Enforcers to provoke them into a fight with the clan. That allowed us to escape. The clan was about to turn us over to the Overseers, they deserved what they got. When I arrived at Cibola, I allied myself with a rebel army led by my sister-in-law, Jennifer, and my friend Paul to distract the overseers enough for us to escape. I never stopped to find out if they had won or had been defeated. I did find out Cibola still exists, but are they much better neighbors? Now I have done it again. For the first time in their history, the people of the underground are united. They have a newfound hope. You can argue whether I have been either directly or indirectly responsible for it, but this time, I will see it through. I can't ask the others to join me, but I will have to tell them my plans. I owe them that much.

That morning, I told Sheppard of my plans. He seemed to be pleased with my choice. He then looked up to the roof and pointed at a small ledge.

"After you rest, check up there," he said.

I did what he suggested. After I had rested, Paloma and I checked out that ledge. Holding out torches ahead of us, we walked through a tunnel. After a few yards, we found a large ladder. Paloma headed up first to another ledge. There, we saw three circles with lids on them. This time, I stepped up a small ladder and was able to open the cover. Lifting myself out onto the cement, I was in the middle of Central Gardens. Paloma followed me to the surface. Standing next to me, she looked around. She felt alive as she felt the sun on her skin for the first time in two years.

"That bastard knew!" I exclaimed, realizing that Sheppard had allowed me to search almost the entire Underground for an escape route. And he knew about this one.

Paloma thought that was funny. All she could do was laugh. I joined her. Thinking of the irony of it all. I led her onto the grass. We were alone as much as we'd ever been. With my hands on her shoulders, I looked at her for a moment. After looking at her in dim or no light for a long time, I wanted to see her in the light.

Feeling awkward, she looked at me and said, "Is there anything wrong?"

"You are beautiful," I told her. I pulled her close to me and kissed her for a long time.

"Do we have to go back?"

"No."

We lay on the soft grass, looking up at the sky, stopping to have lunch under the trees. After an hour we headed back home. I gave Sheppard a dirty look when we passed each other.

The next day, I told the others about the new escape route. After we decided on the date of our departure. That is when I revealed my decision to stay behind to help with the mass escape we had planned together. The others protested, refusing to leave me behind. I understood, but I was equally insistent on them leaving me. After much more debate, we agreed that Kristoph would stay with me and Ethan would leave with Paloma, Isabella, and Aida. Without his five best fighters, Flynn would have gone above and beyond in a different way. Jenna and her people will head out and help Robert sabotage the reactors.

6   RIOT

I WALKED PALOMA UP TO CENTRAL GARDENS ALONE. ETHAN LED THE others a few minutes after we had started. We spent our last moments together in a long embrace. She was crying. I knew she was getting the worst of this deal. The worst thing is that I was selfish, allowing her to get so close. From the first moment I saw Paloma, I felt an attraction for her. I could fight it then because I was in love with Gabrielle and wanted to make a life with her. I still do. Living down here with Paloma, I was happy. But I must know where I stand with Gabrielle. If she rejects me, I can move on and start a life with Paloma, but if she takes me back, I will hurt Paloma. That is something I never wanted to do.

When Ethan arrived with the others, she pulled away from me. We said our goodbyes. I then watched them enter one of the lifts and head straight for Blue Level. They successfully escaped. Before they left, we agreed to meet at an appointed place a week from today. I walked home alone.

The next morning, a crowd of people gathered at Central Rotunda. They all hoped that they would be able to join us in our little protest. We intend to occupy the four largest gardens in the area. Our movement started slowly. A small number of people made it through the forgotten tunnels. In time, we filled all four parks. Kristoph and I were the last to make it into Central Gardens. We did we had control of the entire park, and the Watchmen offered no resistance. Titus and Jerome joined us as we walked through the entire park. It was quite a sight to see. Children were playing in the sunlight that many had never felt before. Julius and Trey met us at the northern border of the garden. I looked up at the structures and saw crowds of people watching us.

After three days, we were surprised that things were going quite well. People from Blue Section had come down to give us food. Many visitors stopped to ask us why we were there. We made sure that every person who answered the question of the curious was someone who had lost a loved one during the deluge. Up above giant telecoms gave us images of the other parks, making us feel less alone.

I walked around inspecting each visitor. I was hoping that Gabrielle was one of them. I never found her. Did she even know about what we were doing here or was Caitlyn sheltering her?

Walking around alone in the park, I discovered I had a shadow. His name was Aidan, barely twenty with sandy brown hair, thin with a slight frame, he was a willing kid.

"What is it, Aidan?"

"Trouble," he replied, "They are harassing some of our people."

"Were."

He led me to a bridge that overlooked a small pond. On that bridge, three men were harassing two young women. Before I could react, Aidan took the initiative and attacked the three men. I pulled out my stinger and helped him. I have to say, the kid held his own against the three men. Distracting the three men enough to allow the women to escape. He was finally knocked down. That was when I slashed at two of the men with my stinger. They fell to the ground. The third attacker was able to defend himself. Aidan pulled out his weapon, a heavy club, and surrounded him.

Kristoph and Trey arrived to help us. His friends were still out of action, so he wisely decided to run for the lifts. Trey looked over the unconscious men. He found that each was armed with a pistol and a knife.

"Who wants a weapon?" Trey showed us the pistols.

I looked over at Aidan. "He earned it." Trey handed him a pistol and a dagger. He then kept the remaining weapons.

Kristoph discovered something more concerning: "They are Watchmen." He held up two badges. "We were being set up."

"What are we doing with these two bastards?" Trey asked.

There was no other option. I said, "Bring them to a lift. Let the others know we are being set up.

The others understood.

When the Watchmen regained consciousness, Trey and six volunteers escorted them to a lift. The rest of the day was quiet.

On the fourth day, things began to change. Early that morning during the newsfeed on the telecoms a series of images of people gathering around the processing centers. Thousands of our people were getting ready to escape. Then the telecoms went black. Through the windows, we saw hundreds of Watchmen gathered in riot gear.

It was clear they had been very patient with our little demonstration, now they wanted it to end. Kristoph looked at the small army waiting for their orders to come down.

"We are sitting ducks," he said.

I couldn't argue. I asked him, "What are they saying?"

"They want to fight." He said confidently.

Trey and Aidan joined us.

Trey reported, "People are getting scared."

Kristoph added, "We better get the children out of here."

"Agreed," said Trey.

"Get the others," I said. Somehow, I had become the leader. I didn't want it.

Julias was selected to lead the children to safety. We assured them it would be safer for the children with Sheppard. When the children were finished being evacuated. Julius brought back reinforcements. We would not be intimidated. An hour later, we began to arm ourselves. We did not attempt to hide it from the Watchmen who were still watching us, anxiously waiting for orders to attack.

Then, the telecoms were activated. A loud burst made us all look up. There, we saw their final warning.

DISBAND AND RETURN TO BLACK SECTION. ALL WHO REMAINED WILL BE SUBJECT TO ARREST FOR SEDITION. YOU HAVE TWELVE HOURS.

A timer then appeared to count down from twelve hours. Nobody was leaving. We just sat and prepared for the fight that was coming.

"When are the Disrupters to strike?" asked Titus.

I replied, "An hour after that turns to zero." I pointed at the telecom, it read six hours, twelve minutes, and twenty-two seconds.

"That will be too late for us," stated Trey.

"We will give them a good fight," Jerome readied his pistol. "Not with that," I said. The others looked at me, surprised at my protest. "If this is to work, we have to use that as a last resort." I added, "Don't worry, we will give them a good fight."

Kristoph was the one who asked the question the others wanted to ask about our strategy:" How do you see this going?"

I looked up at the Watchmen looking down at us. Then I answered, "When they come down, they will form their shield wall. We will meet them with one of our own."

Jerome said, "Those lances hurt."

Julius held up a large rubber circle. "That's what these are for."

I said, "We need to break their formation."

There is one thing I learned in dealing with Enforcers, Watchmen, and the soldiers of the Prophet: they are brave when they are in their formation. Break that formation, and it comes down to the courage of one lonely individual.

When we had finished all our preparations, we tried to sleep.

———————

That damn audio blast woke us all up! As I rose to my feet along with the others, we all looked up and saw the telecoms showing all zeros. Then it went black. It was the time of reckoning. Watchmen entered the lifts and descended to our level. Each lift held about a dozen Watchmen, with twenty lifts already providing a sizeable force to face us.

"Get everybody ready," I ordered the others, "Make sure they understand if they want to leave now is the time."

I began to do the same. Taking our makeshift weapons, we moved into place. A second contingent of Watchmen had joined their comrades. Spectators in red and yellow sections gathered for the coming battle. It was at this time that I saw the last person I ever thought I was going to see. Flynn.

He arrived with about thirty of his men. Not the one to explain how he managed to get here. Right now, I don't care. We had given up on his promise of explosives to open an escape route through the glass. But there it was in his hand. A disc that will be able to shatter the protective glass.

"Sorry it took so long, "he explained, "Good help is hard to find." His men had other things, pistols and stingers of our own. He directed his men to pass them out. He then finished with, "The Disrupters are ready to strike."

"That will divert the Watchmen's attention from us."

Now, we are ready to fight. The fourth and last contingent of Watchmen arrived to join their comrades. They gathered in the formation I saw in action nearly two years ago outside Gotham. The first line was armed with shields and stingers; behind them was a line of men armed with long spear-like stingers. They had successfully surrounded us, so there would be no escape for us, and our only option was to surrender. But we had our surprises.

Their officers gave them the order to advance. With our rubber shields and metal clubs, we charged them. A loud crash was the result of the two armies making contact. Initially, the Watchmen had the advantage with their spears making contact, but we learned to keep our distance. Our handmade weapons managed to hold their own. Seeing a stalemate, the officers ordered their spearmen to fall back and let their shield men do their work. A second line of shield men reinforced the first line. We still outnumbered them.

The Watchmen's experience proved to be the difference, as they began to force our lines to give way. But our determination allowed us to maintain our formation. That was when the Disrupters struck. Alarms sounded through the city, and the power went out across all sectors of Gotham. At every checkpoint, crowds rushed through the gate, overpowering the guards. The Watchmen facing us finally found themselves isolated. Now it was our time to strike.

We only had twenty flashpoints, so we had to make good use of them. As we disengaged the Watchmen, twenty men through the flash stick within the Watchmen's ranks. That created gaps in their ranks. Large enough for us to exploit. I led the charge, with my six lieutenants beside me. No longer in formation, the Watchmen's lines disintegrated. The Spearmen had no option but to support their comrades. Kristoph managed to disarm one spearman. He used that Watchmen's weapon against the others. The adrenaline of battle dulls his pain.

Flynn and his men activated their disc, shattering the glass that separated the people of Red Section from Central Gardens. A loud cheer from the people of Red Section welcomed us. We had done it, we were free.

Now, with our discipline relaxed, we rushed through the remaining Watchmen into Red Section.

We were now a mob. No longer working together, we rushed through the streets of Red Section. A handful of our people began to loot the very people we needed to help us. I have done my duty towards them. It was time for us to leave this mob. I gathered my six comrades, and we headed to safety, leaving the rioters to their fate. I never saw Flynn again. I could only hope that he and his men had managed to escape.

We only had a few minutes before Gotham's engineers repaired the power grid. With caution, we headed up to Yellow Sector. Now we could relax. We carefully hid our weapons underneath our clothes and walked to the closest lift. There, we just waited until the power returned. Overlooking Central Garden, we saw crowds of people returning to Black Section with their spoils from their looting. The fools had no idea what we had wanted to show the people of the surface that we were worthy to be treated as human beings. Now they will be facing retaliation from the government.

Then the power returned. The empty lift opened its doors, and we walked in. Inside we headed up to Blue Section and safety for us. The doors opened and we walked out. Standing there we watched the fate of our former comrades.

The rioters' destructive path was suddenly stopped by a new contingent of Watchmen. Each one was armed with a rifle. Then their officers gave them the order, and they marched and opened fire on the mob. They killed hundreds instantly. Feeds from every breakout were the same, our people were being slaughtered. A few of your friends who were armed with either a pistol or rifle managed to get a shot off. Killed a few Watchmen. That did no good as another Watchman replaced their fallen comrade. Other citizens joined us as we watched the massacre together. A few began to cheer at the carnage. I looked at the others and told them not to respond to the ignorant bastards. They weren't worth it.

Now it was time for me to leave and find Gabrielle. I left alone.

EPILOGUE

1   REUNION

I MADE IT UP TO OUR APARTMENT. ALL THE TIME, I SAW IMAGES OF the massacre on the news feed. Then I saw idiots talking endlessly about it and getting everything wrong about what had just happened. Sheppard was right after all.

At the door, I tried the code. It didn't work. I'm not surprised they changed it. With my stinger, I decided to use a different approach. Technically, I was a fugitive, so I had no time to waste. The door opened. I called out for her. She wasn't home. Neither was Regina. I found her itinerary for the day and left.

Walking out the door, I saw her; she had a long-sleeved white dress on, and her long red hair was treated with curls. Scared, I just looked at her, wondering what she would do next. When she smiled and ran towards me, I jumped a mile with excitement. We embraced her and I picked her up.

'I'm sorry,' we said to each other before we kissed.

"I knew it was you down there," she said to me. A look of admiration came over her.

I replied, "I would do anything to see you again." A bit thick but it was true.

When she pulled away, she said," Caitlyn killed them. Our

children. I didn't know." She began to cry as she tried to comprehend what Caitlyn had done to her. To comfort her, I held her
gently. Caitlyn had stolen a lot from her. All I could do was reassure her that it was all right. She placed her head on my chest as
she mourned for her loss. Like Naomi, if one of her wards had a
child, it would interfere with her plans. Therefore, she decided to
terminate the lives in their bodies. Now, for the first time, I could
say I hated someone.

"I should have told you," I said, "I don't know why."

Taking her head off my breast, she looked up at me with her
green eyes still red from crying, she asked quietly, "Can we put this
behind us?"

I then asked her what I should have done almost a year ago.
"What would you like to do?"

She smiled and answered, "Let's go home."

We kissed again. Then we gathered what we wanted to take and
joined the others. While we packed, my thoughts began to ask a
nagging question: Where is Caitlyn? Part of me was glad she wasn't
here, as she would know Gabrielle and I were planning to escape.
Caitlyn would want to stop us. I wanted her to try. I wanted to
finish this right now. Gabrielle noticed that my thoughts were somewhere else. Instinctively, she knew why, and she told me, "Caitlyn
is on the run. An old rival of hers wanted revenge."

I knew who that was. Flynn was doing me another favor. I am
not sure that he knew he was doing me a favor, but I did appreciate
it. When we were ready, I gave her one more kiss and we headed on
our way. Neither of us will miss this place. It belonged to Caitlyn.
Unknowingly, we did too.

Along the way, before we met the others who had escaped with
me. I told her what had happened to me down in the Underground.
I especially told her about Paloma. How we kept each other alive
during winter. I confessed to her that I developed feelings for the
young woman. But I never lied to her. I always told her that I had
to see you first before I could move on with her. To my surprise she
understood. I don't know why.

She then said, "I have done things I'm not proud of, I need to tell you."

"You don't have to," I reassured her. I took her hand and we walked away together.

At the rendezvous point, we met everybody. Being the last to arrive. Gabrielle immediately hugged Illyana first. Next, I introduced her to each of my new friends, everyone was taken by her. Only Paloma kept her distance. I wanted to go to her and bring her with the group, but Gabrielle stopped me. She wanted to talk to her, believing that she was best suited for the task ahead. I don't know what was said between them, but it ended with a long embrace then they joined the rest of us.

Robert and Cassandra joined us with our passes out of the city. He made all the preparations for us to be guided by Walker back to Shenandoah. We then said our goodbyes and left Robert and Cassandra, who chose to remain in Gotham.

It took us an entire day to make it to the rendezvous point. It was well past dusk before we made it to the clearing where we were expected to wait for Walker to guide us home. Wes made a fire for us to have a hot supper, courtesy of Robert. Ethan volunteered to cook. It was a stew of some kind. Far different from what we were used to in Gotham. Far better than the food bars we had living in the underground. Only Gabrielle seems to be disappointed by our dinner. Her opinion would have changed if she had eaten energy bars for a year. After dinner, we made ourselves ready for bed. The night air wasn't cold, but that didn't stop Gabrielle and me from sleeping together. It was when we noticed Paloma alone looking at the fire, Gabrielle decided she would prefer to sleep with her instead of me. I understood, but I didn't like it much. Julius volunteered to take the first watch, followed by Titus, and Kristoph would take the third. That is when we fell asleep.

A series of violent shoves on my shoulder woke me up. When I opened my eyes, I noticed it was dawn. Standing over me was Kristoph.

"We have visitors," he said, looking out at the forest.

Wanting to sleep a little longer, I reminded him, "We are expecting visitors."

Undeterred, he added, "We have to be careful."

I couldn't argue with that. I grabbed my weapons, "Wake the others."

Within a minute, we managed to get the others up. As we heard someone coming closer, we waited for our visitors to enter our camp. Relief came over me when I recognized the two men. It was Walker and his friend Grant. The two men hadn't changed much in the two years we had been away.

When Walker saw me, a tired smile came over him. He finally will be able to retire, he immediately thought. Gabrielle ran up to him and hugged him. He was happy to see her. She then did the same to Grant. Then it was my turn, I shook both friends' hands. We then escorted them to meet with our new friends. After that was over, we broke camp. Choosing to eat breakfast along the journey. We ate protein bars. Gabrielle didn't enjoy it very much.

We made it to Shenandoah three days later. During each night, we told Walker and Grant about our adventures in Gotham. Neither man was surprised by what we told them about Sanctuary. He knew it wasn't what we had hoped. But he wanted us to discover that by ourselves. Before we left on the final morning of our journey, Walker had left us for a moment. When he returned, he remained silent on why he had left us.

Arriving in the town of Shenandoah, it had grown a little since we left. Walking to the common, Constance arrived to meet us. She had one small child in her arms and was expecting another one. Constance handed her daughter to her foster sister, She said, "Her name is Danielle." Gabrielle cried and handed the baby away. Constance was shocked by her reaction. I told Constance what had happened to Gabrielle. Constance gave Danielle to her father and walked over to comfort her friend. What was said between them was personal. All I know is what I had seen; when they finished, they had a long embrace. Then they returned to us.

That evening we had dinner in the town hall. Many of our old friends came to meet our friends from Shenandoah. Constance and

Walker's wife, Laura, provided a bountiful table for about twenty people. Living in the underground made us all eat more than we should have. Everything I ate tasted better than anything I had in Gotham, and I immediately mentioned that to our host. Constance smiled. When dinner was finished, Austen and his bandmates got up to prepare to play some music. They succeeded in enticing Gabby to sing with them, for old times' sake. We watched as she sang two songs with her old bandmates. Each one had known her far longer than I did. After the second song, she called up Julius. The couple proceeded to sing four more songs.

Looking around, I noticed everybody was listening to Gabby and Julius, but one person was watching the concert. The only person who wasn't listening was Paloma. Her head was down in solace. I realized that she hadn't eaten much. Somehow, I had to reassure her that things would get better. I sat down next to her. Although she didn't look up, she knew I was there.

She asked me, "One last act of pity?"

"It was never pity, Paloma," I told her. Gently, I placed my hand on her shoulder and requested, "Please look up at me." Slowly, she did what I asked her. With her brown eyes, she looked at me sadly; her eyes had no more tears left to cry. She looked over at Gabby; in contrast, she was as happy as a person could be. I looked at her too, as I couldn't believe my luck. "You know you have the better of the deal. "

"How so?" she asked me.

"Gabby will be stuck with me," I said in total truth, "Look around, there are dozens of young men who will provide for you far better than I. Ask Gabby, I will let you down."

Finally, a smile came over her. She told me with a strange confidence, "You never did."

"You haven't known me that long. Several people would have different opinions." There were some things I did while living in the Wastelands that I wasn't proud of. But what I did was in trying to survive. Some survived and did far worse than I. And some who survived did it far better. In the end, I ask the people who like to judge, what would you do in my position?

"You're not so bad," she reassured me, "What my family did to survive out here would make you cringe."

We didn't want to go any further. She looked over at Ethan and Illyana happily dancing together. Keeping her eyes on them, she stated, "They are planning to get married." She smiled and turned to me, "What about you?"

"Be patient," I told her.

Aida came over to us. She had been dancing with a series of young men. One especially was Walker's oldest son, Taylor. "Paloma, there is someone who wants to meet you." Aida didn't take no for an answer. She immediately took Paloma's hands and brought her to the dance floor. Leaving me alone.

Paloma was right. I should propose to Gabrielle. We always intended to get married, but something always kept us from getting in our way. Mainly, it was Caitlyn. I realized I didn't have any more distractions.

I walked over to the band's stage. Gabby saw me while she was singing her final song. She smiled as I watched her. Nervously, I stood there waiting for her to finish. It is funny that I was more nervous now than at any time before. When she finally finished her last song, she jumped down into my arms laughing.

"I'm thirsty," she confessed, "Let's get something to drink."

She started to head for the bar, but I stopped her. "I have something to ask you first." Julius volunteered to get her a drink. Taking her hands into mind, I knelt. Somehow, she knew it was coming. "Gabrielle Blue, would you do me the honor of being my wife?"

Without hesitation, she answered, "Duncan Walker, yes, I will be your wife."

Rising to my feet, I held her in my arms. We kissed each other with renewed passion. Around us, people cheered in approval. When we parted, we swarmed over us. Julius was the first to congratulate me. After he put down his two cups of lemonade.

2   WEDDING

THAT WAS A MISTAKE. DON'T GET ME WRONG. I STILL WANTED TO marry Gabrielle. But now the whole damn town is involved. We agreed that the wedding will take place in two weeks. In the meantime, I will stay at Walker's house, while Gabrielle will live with Constance, until the wedding, they assured me. The worst part is that we can't even say hello to each other. Telling us it would be bad luck for us. A foolish thought, but they insisted.

Walker made sure I was busy during the following three weeks. He had to show me each rendezvous point where I would bring new people to safety in Shenandoah. He made a point to me that I would always appear to have to be confident that I could lead them to safety. If there was a problem, I would have to figure out a solution alone. On longer journeys, we were accompanied by Kristoph, Ethan, Jerome, Titus, Julius, and Dan came with us. Wes told us he was planning to stay for the wedding but wanted to return to his home. He had been gone for a long time. From the town, two old friends joined us, Ivan and Josh volunteered. Both arrived with Gabrielle and me when we first came here over two years ago.

After going out for ten days, mostly on horseback, we returned home. Inside my room, Laura was preparing the suit I had brought from Gotham. Now I know why Gabrielle insisted that I should bring it. She was anticipating this moment.

"There, it's nice and clean for your big day," she said as she hung it safely.

"Thank you," I said, "How is Gabrielle?"

"She has never been happier," she replied, "Her gown is almost ready."

I knew that it was the same gown that Constance had on. It was a pretty gown. A local tradition is that each couple that gets married has their choice of three gowns. After the wedding, the bride must preserve it for the next wedding. It was then that I understood what was happening here. A wedding is no simple task between two people or families. It was for the entire community. A brief distraction from the endless days of hard work required to earn a living in this small haven of green against the bleakness of what is only a few miles away.

"Any chance I could see her?" I asked.

She smiled, "Duncan, you will see her tomorrow." In saying that, she started to leave, but before she left, she had one more thing to say, "You better get to sleep."

I did as she requested.

At dawn, a group made it their mission to ensure everybody in Shenandoah was up and ready to go. We all gathered at a small piece of land a mile outside the town. Dotted across the land were piles of lumber and other building materials.

On the first day, I managed to get a brief glimpse of Gabrielle. We had a very brief exchange of acknowledgement. But we all had work to do. Laura and Constance pushed her to the makeshift kitchen. I began to build the foundation of what is to be our new house. It was hard work building a house; we worked for twelve hours, only breaking for lunch and dinner. By the end of the third day, we had built a lovely two-story house. When we parted ways, I headed home with Walker, frustrated.

That night, I decided, the hell with tradition. I was determined to go out and visit Gabrielle. What was the worst they could do? We are both of age. It was no secret that we had been intimate for the previous two years. Patiently, I waited for the lights in the house to be turned off, believing they all would be asleep. When the lights were turned off, I did the same.

For some reason, I was nervous. I couldn't figure out why. This is nothing new for me. This is something for me to work on later. Quietly, I climbed out of the window. Sitting on the windowsill, I reached over a ladder that was fastened onto the house. Quickly, I climbed down to the ground. I was free.

I ran towards Constance's house. Mark had already built his house before he had met Constance. When I got in view of the house, I noticed that a light was on in her room. Not wanting to waste any time, I made it underneath the window. She had left it open because of the warm night air. It was there that I came across an unforeseen obstacle. It came as a hard blow to my chin. On the grass, I looked up to see who had hit me. Standing over me was Kristoph. But he was not alone. Behind him stood Dan, Titus, Julius, Jerome, and Wes. It was clear that I would have to go through all six of them to get to Gabby.

"What the hell are you doing here?" I asked them.

Dan was to speak for them: "We are protecting her honor."

I stood up. Gabrielle was watching from the window. As I walked closer to the ladder, Kristoph flattened me a second time.

Dan continued, "This time you are going to follow the rules."

I relented, "I guess I have no other choice." Kristoph helped me up I had to ask, "How long were you standing vigil?"

"Every night," Dan replied, he added with more certainty, "And we will be here tomorrow night too."

Kristoph then added, "You're being selfish. Let her have her wedding."

Defeated, I walked home, climbed up, and entered my room. I went to bed.

On the fourth day, Gabrielle led a painting crew as she wanted light blue paint. On the fifth day, we had a new house to live in, along with furniture. It was lovely. Together, we thanked our friends and neighbors for their hard work and generosity.

Tomorrow was our dress rehearsal. The next day was the wedding.

We couldn't ask for a better wedding day. I was standing at the altar with my seven chosen men to stand with me. Ethan had the ring; it was something borrowed. Another strange custom. A town elder will do the service. There we waited for the music to start. When it did, my knees buckled for a moment. Kristoph managed to catch me and allowed me to regain my balance. Walker served as giving the bride away. He walked Gabrielle in her wedding dress and a blue veil that covered her face. Another superstition. Trailing Gabby were her ladies in waiting, with Constance leading the way, Aida, Paloma, Isabela, Constance's two sisters-in-laws, Rachel and Heather finally Stephanie, another old friend who came with us when we first came to our new home. I was told that the groom couldn't have a larger party than the bride; it was bad luck. Why do people get married? I thought for a brief moment. Until Gabby had Walker kiss her good luck, and she stood next to me.

The elder said the words. I placed a ring on her finger. She did the same and placed one on my finger. Then the Elder pronounced us man and wife. I gently opened her veil, revealing her pretty smile. Not one willing to wait for permission, I immediately kissed her. Around us, our guests cheered. Behind me, I heard whimpering from my best men.

We sat together at a long table, beside us sat our respective entourage. People we barely knew came up to us and offered their congratulations and wished us luck in our future lives together. We politely thanked them, and they returned to their table. During dinner, we had a brief rest from well-wishers. After dinner, it started again, until the last had paid their respects. All that was left were the Elders. They had a table together with their mates on our right. They just sat there talking to each other. Occasionally, they looked over at us; they were talking about us, that much was clear. When they stopped talking, they looked over at us together one last time. Whatever they were talking about, we were about to find out.

The nine elders surrounded us. There were six men and three

women. The elder who officiated at our wedding was elected speaker. "We have a question for you?"

"Go ahead," I replied.

"It is for your wife," he said in a serious tone. "Can we talk alone?"

"We can talk here," Gabby stated.

The Elder then started, "We have a favor to ask you." Gabby was intrigued by his statement. He continued, "Naturally, you are welcome to sing as long as you wish. But we have been waiting for somebody like you."

"I'm intrigued."

"You can remember everything you can read," he stated.

"Yes."

"We want you to serve as a storyteller. A librarian will be your title." He told her he felt he needed to explain further, "We need to preserve our stories. People must remember what was done here. Our struggles and triumphs."

A woman who was here when we first came to Shenandoah was growing impatient; she needed to give her opinion. "We also want people to come and tell you their story. You will record it and keep it for perpetuity. Then you will tell the stories to our young people. So we will never forget what had happened to us all."

Constance, hearing their conversation, volunteered, "I'll help."

Gabby made her decision: "When do you want me to start?"

The Elders were pleased with her acceptance. They walked away satisfied.

With a smile, she turned towards me and demanded, "You will be my first subject."

I knew better not to argue. Or waste any time pretending to be modest, I just kissed her.

We celebrated until dusk. Finally, under the light of candles, we were escorted to our new home to consummate the marriage.

Now we were alone in our bedroom. Standing together in front of our new bed, I kissed her. She pulled away from me, annoyed. She said, "I was hoping you would come and visit me one night. I was waiting for you, but you never came. Why?"

"You had six chaperones. Who was protecting your honor," I replied. She knew who I was talking about.

She said, "That never stopped you before."

"They believed the wedding was for you. Right now, is for me." I told her.

"Well, I certainly set them straight about that."

I kissed her again. Placing my hands at the top of her dress, I began to unfasten her buttons. Hesitantly, she pulled away from me for a moment. There she made her only demand for me, "Wherever you go or whatever you do, no matter how dangerous it is. I want you to promise me one thing."

"What's that?"

"Come home to me."

"I will."

I then kissed her. What happens next is private.

"And all the times he had left me. No matter what dangers he had faced. And what adventures we faced together. He never broke his promise, he always returned home to me."

After saying that, she began to weep, sadly. She stood up and walked home. Her great-granddaughter Danielle walked home with her. I was asked to join them. Inside her house, Dannielle brought her upstairs to bed. While they were upstairs, I entered the living room. There I saw a photograph on a desk. Danielle is being trained to be her successor. She looked much like her great-grandmother, and more importantly, she had her ability. It was old and had damage along the edges.

Danielle approached me from behind and whispered in my ear, "They were a handsome couple."

"It is hard to believe this was real," I told her.

She kissed me on the cheek. Gabrielle's story was nearly done. Ours has just begun.

ABOUT THE AUTHOR

ALFRED KHOLI IS AN ACTOR, WRITER, AND director. Three of his short plays, *Time Menders*, *We Actors 4*, and *Woodstock Inn* were produced in Providence, Rhode Island. He lives in Attleboro Massachusetts with his two cats Roger and Sam, along with his dog Shelby. *Spectrum City* is his second novel.

www.ingramcontent.com/pod-product-compliance
Lightning Source LLC
Chambersburg PA
CBHW050028030726
47506CB00001B/171